Dear Reader:

The novels you've enjoyed over the past years by such authors as Kathleen Woodiwiss, Rosemary Rogers, Johanna Lindsey, Laurie McBain, and Shirlee Busbee are accountable to one thing above all others: Avon has never tried to force authors into any particular mold. Rather, Avon is a publisher that encourages individual talent and is always on the lookout for writers who will deliver *real* books, not packaged formulas.

In 1982, we started a program to help readers pick out authors of exceptional promise. Called "The Avon Romance," the books were distinguished by a ribbon motif in the upper left-hand corner of the cover. Although the titles were by new authors, they were quickly discovered and became known as "the ribbon books."

Now "The Avon Romance" is a regular feature on the Avon list. Each month, you will find historical novels with many different settings, each one by an author who is special. You will not find predictable characters, predictable plots, and predictable endings. The only predictable thing about "The Avon Romance" will be the superior quality that Avon has always delivered in the field of romance!

Sincerely,

Walter Mead

WALTER MEADE
President & Publisher

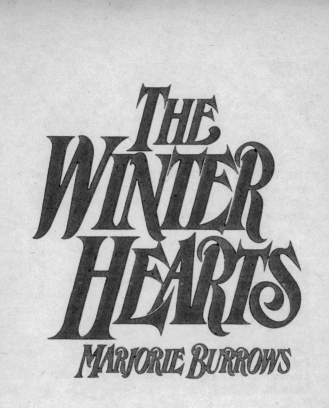

THE WINTER HEARTS

MARJORIE BURROWS

AVON
PUBLISHERS OF BARD, CAMELOT, DISCUS AND FLARE BOOKS

THE WINTER HEARTS is an original publication of Avon Books. This work has never before appeared in book form. This work is a novel. Any similarity to actual persons or events is purely coincidental.

AVON BOOKS
A division of
The Hearst Corporation
1790 Broadway
New York, New York 10019

First Avon Printing, January, 1985

AVON TRADEMARK REG. U.S. PAT. OFF. AND IN OTHER COUNTRIES, MARCA REGISTRADA, HECHO EN U.S.A.

Printed in the U.S.A.

WFH 10 9 8 7 6 5 4 3 2 1

TO JEFF

Prologue

Meg
1865

   " 'FRAID OF THE DARK, she was. I tol' that Yankee the youngun' and her lantern'd bring 'em nothin' but trouble..."

The flames reached skyward, illuminating the wagon site as brightly as the noonday sun, forcing back the onlookers who ventured to approach.

A child with windblown hair that tumbled down her back and nightclothes in wild disarray stood just beyond the circled wagons as the accusing voices condemned her. She stared at the burning wagon that had been her home for more than two months of the overland journey west, her chest heaving as she struggled to regain her breath. Her eyes widened in horror as they fell to the still form on the ground. She ran forward, falling by the singed hem of her mother's nightdress.

"Mama?" At first her voice was soft, but then her screams of "Mama! Mama! Mama!..." echoed through

1

the scorched night air until they trailed off into wretched sobs.

"Where the devil did she come from?" A harsh voice raised itself above the murmurings of the spectators who watched as she kneeled by her mother's body. "Girl, what's the meaning of this?"

Dazed, she looked up into the fearsome face of the wagon-train leader as he broke away from the crowd that had gathered around her. Standing above her, he reached down to grasp her thin shoulders. With fingers of steel, he lifted her to her feet. "My—my pony—I went to look for my pony," she stammered. "I wanted to make sure..." She fell silent, remembering to whom she spoke, remembering that this was the man who had sworn to leave her lame pony behind. It was because of him she had feared for her cherished pet; she had feared his threats enough to waken during the night and brave the terrifying darkness to look for her. From his great height, the wagon leader spoke down to her.

"Don't you know your daddy jus' burned hisself to death lookin' for you in that wagon?"

Comprehension flickered but briefly in the anguished eyes and then, mercifully, the world receded as she crumbled to the ground.

Part One

Cross Creek

Chapter One

FOR MOST OF MY LIFE, a cloud of suspicion has shadowed me. Although some called it the hand of God, others held me responsible for my parents' deaths. Tanner would say, years after it had happened, that it had been an act of the greatest cruelty for the Parker party to lay the blame on me, a six-year-old child at the time. But the fact remained, my mother and father died one night in the blazing inferno that consumed the wagon that took us west. I survived, and the suspicions and ill feelings that had plagued us from the beginning of the trip fell upon me.

When the wagon leader, Ezra Parker, cast out the unwanted orphan from his train, claiming I was not his burden, he did me a great service, although he did not know it. He handed me over to his gold-seeking nephew, Frank, and ordered him to deposit me at nearest town. A thread of decency ran through Frank, and he did not leave me at just any settle-

ment—many were not much more than a saloon,
brothel, and post office—but waited until we came
upon the town of Cross Creek.

Originally a gold town, Cross Creek was similar
to other towns that had sprung up to meet the needs
of the growing mining and ranching populations.
Like the others, Cross Creek's days as a gold town
had been short-lived as the miners had moved on to
easier diggings. But unlike the others, Cross Creek
had survived. Good grassland and fertile soil surrounded this town in the foothills of the Rocky Mountains, and some of the miners, disillusioned with the
elusive golden riches, settled there and returned to
what they knew best: the land. They raised their
stock and cultivated the soil. Others set up shop and
reaped gold-dust profits, charging exorbitant prices
in a land where demand was great and supply limited.

Although the mining communities in the upper
reaches of the mountains came to rely on Cross Creek
for provisions, the town had quieted down since the
first frenzied days of the gold rush. The settlers and
families who followed reshaped the small town, which
began to grow with law and order from a rip-roaring
mining settlement into a stable community bent on
peacefulness and prosperity.

The improvements were welcomed.

Streets were lined with wooden sidewalks, and
many of these were covered by protective overhangs.
The early dominance of Ab Monroe's general store
over the Main Street trade had been broken by Lyon's
Mercantile and Winkleman's Dry Goods store on the
north side of the street. There was a dress shop, a
millinery shop, and a bootery that catered exclu-
sively to the women of Cross Creek.

The well-heeled men of town had their clothes
custom-made by Mr. Gold, the tailor, or they purchased them at Jud Stern's haberdashery, which car-

ried an almost exclusive line of clothing from San Francisco. For the less discriminating and more ordinary folk, who comprised the bulk of the town's population, the dry goods store did a thrifty business. Two bakeries provided bread and other delicacies, while directly across the street red-streaked carcasses hung in front of the butcher shop. All this was enough to put three lawyers in fancy clothes, keep the Merchant's Bank prosperous, and satisfy the undertaker.

The people rejoiced when Dr. Seth Elliot arrived in Cross Creek and took up residence, glad he did not have the habits of a former town doctor who had fought a losing battle with the bottle. Of some concern to the God-fearing and righteous were the nine saloons and Rose's Boardinghouse, which was not a boardinghouse at all. The good ladies of Cross Creek refused to acknowledge Rose and her girls publicly, but behind their gloved hands the whispers proliferated, the rumors being more exciting than the girls themselves.

A real estate office, a barber shop, three hotels, four restaurants, a laundry, a watchmaker, a furniture maker, a saddlery, a harness and bootmaker shop, a feedstore, two livery stables, and a freight office completed the businesses in town. The lumber mill, a family run operation outside of town, provided employment for some of Cross Creek's population. There was also a courthouse, a social hall, and a stage depot. A two-story brick building housed the Cross Creek *Gazette*, the second floor being occupied by Dr. Forbes, the dentist. The jail, another one of the early brick buildings, was located on the next block. Baptist, Presbyterian, and Methodist churches each had their devout followers, and the Ladies Benevolent Society, founded just the year I came to Cross Creek, managed to take up whatever good works were left. Their last crusade had been to pro-

hibit spitting in public places but, as far as I know,
they were not taken seriously, in that cause at least.
The Ladies Benevolent Society is what saved me—
that, and the fact that there was no orphanage in
Cross Creek.

Sheriff Thatcher and his deputy, Bud Weeks, were
out chasing down an elusive criminal that day in
August 1865 when Frank Parker deposited me on
the dusty wooden sidewalk fronting the Sheriff's office just as the sun was at its fiercest. Susan Thatcher,
the sheriff's pretty young wife, had just brought dinner to Zeb Hines, who was sleeping off his disturbance of the peace. She stepped out into the glare of
the noonday sun, shutting the door to the office behind her. With her shiny brown hair gathered neatly
in a bun at the nape of her neck and the scent of
lavender emanating softly from her, an image of my
mother rose before me and I painfully swallowed the
lump in my throat.

"Can I help you, sir? The Sheriff is out right now,"
she informed us pleasantly as Frank attempted to
open the door she had just closed. Frank was not
very good with words.

"Well, Ma'am, I'm Frank Parker and I'm lookin'
for the sheriff. Or an orphan's home. Either will do
me jus' fine."

Shielding her eyes against the slanting sun with
her hand, Mrs. Thatcher looked down at me. "Well,
perhaps I can help?" she suggested gently. I can
imagine how pitifully thin and ragged I must have
appeared.

"I'd be right grateful if you could, Ma'am. I got no
time to wait around. I've kept 'er longer than I
wanted, but the first few places we come to weren't
fittin' for a girl her age, if you know what I mean."
Frank paused to catch his breath. "It was her fault,
the fire that killed her folks, the way we fig-

ured...'Course no one wanted to take 'er in after that. Ezra, he's my uncle and leader of the train, he says she's not our responsibility, no sense takin' 'er on to Oregon. She'd just land up in some orphan's asylum there, so we might as well leave 'er in one here."

I stared down at the toes of my dusty boots, not wanting to see the look in the pretty woman's face as she learned of my crime. I thought they would keep me in jail if they didn't have an orphan's home.

"What do you mean, exactly, by saying she caused the fire?" Susan Thatcher's voice was sharp.

"Well, it was the middle of the night an' they was in the wagon. Smoke got her ma, and her pa went back in lookin' for this here little girl. Thought she was still in there...he burned to death."

I cringed at Frank's words. I would never know the truth. Perhaps I had indeed knocked over the lamp, spilling oil, as I left the wagon that night. Knowing my dread of the dark and never suspecting I would venture out alone, if my father had awakened and not found me in my bed he may have lit the lamp to search the wagon, unwittingly setting off the fire that claimed his and my mother's lives. Maybe I had not set the fire, but could I ever stop blaming myself for causing it to happen?

"What's your name, child?"

I looked at her dumbly, still trapped by the haunting vision of the burning wagon.

"Her name's Meg, Ma'am. Meg Logan," Frank answered for me.

"Well, now, Meg. Is what this gentleman said true?"

I nodded miserably, still looking at my feet.

"Look at me, Meg," she commanded. "I want you to answer me." I lifted my eyes to her and some of my torment must have touched her.

"Yes, Ma'am, it's true." My voice was so soft it barely reached my own ears. Her smooth brow wrinkled with what I thought was horror.

"How did it happen, Meg," she inquired carefully.

"I don't know, Ma'am," I replied truthfully.

"But why weren't you in the wagon at that time of night, Meg?"

"I was looking for my pony, Ma'am."

"Pony?" She looked inquiringly at Frank.

"Yes'm," Frank confirmed. "She had a pony. Caused us nothin' but trouble, too. Pulled up lame. My Uncle Ez was goin' to make her get rid of it. He was pretty nervous 'bout them Injun raids. Didn't want it holdin' us up any."

A frown marred Susan Thatcher's face as she considered this information. "What about her family?" she asked finally. "Do you know where she's from, if she had any family left behind?"

"Don't rightly know much else 'bout her, Ma'am, ceptin' they came on at St. Joe and said they was from Boston. Them Logans...they kept pretty much to 'emselves. They was Yankees. Not real sociable folks, if you know what I mean?"

Susan Thatcher nodded her concurrence as I remembered the friction and the petty jealousies that had been with us from the start, since St. Joseph, Missouri, when we first joined up with the hardbitten Parker clan. They had come from the dry, rocky region of southern Missouri and made no effort to hide the hostility they bore my gently reared mother or their animosity toward my father, who had fought for the North in the war. "...No," Frank continued, "none of us ever heard 'em mention kin. Ez kept their stock," he added, rushing on. "Seein' how they'd owed us money for joinin' the train." He avoided my cold stare, as if he were afraid to be caught in this bold lie of his uncle's. "Wasn't much...jus' some oxen, a milk cow, and Logan's saddle horse."

"And the pony?" Susan Thatcher inquired thoughtfully.

"Never did find her, Ma'am. Must have took off during the night."

"I see."

"I'll be on my way, Ma'am, if that's all right with you?" Frank said cautiously, seeking to end the interview.

"Yes. Yes, of course. Thank you, Mr. Parker. It was most kind of you to bring her this far. We'll make arrangements for her." Afraid of what I might see written on Susan Thatcher's face, I watched the last of the Parkers walk out of my life forever. Then, instead of taking me into the sheriff's office, she gripped my dirt-stained hand and led me across the wide street directly into the path of the blazing sun.

By the time Sheriff Thatcher returned to his office that evening, his wife, Susan, had put the Society's brand upon me. The ladies had already met, she announced, and had decided upon this. I heard her with perfect clarity from the spare room in which she had installed me just as soon as she had given me a bath and some clean clothes from the Society's "need bag." The Society, she continued deliberately, would fight for me. I think Susan was already on her way to becoming a suffragette.

She had not found a home for me, she admitted to her husband, because of the strange circumstances surrounding my parents' death. Although I had been stared at and all but poked and prodded as the ladies took my measure and discussed my future, none of them had been willing to take me in personally, but all were ready to take on my cause. Yet Susan remained adamant. I was not to go to the territorial orphanage. I would waste away there, she claimed. It was the duty of the Ladies Benevolent Society, she said forcefully, to do their best for me.

Unfortunately, Ed Thatcher did not see it that way. While Susan defended the Society's plan for me, her husband did his best to circumvent it. It was sheer foolishness, he protested, to place me with the recently widowed and newly appointed school-teacher, Mrs. Walker, for the term, and expect me to help with chores around the schoolhouse and her home in exchange for my board and education. How could I be trusted in light of what they knew of me? I belonged in the territorial orphanage!

"Ed!" Susan spoke sternly. "The child is six years old! Who are you to pass judgment on her? No one will ever be certain of the circumstances, but she deserves a chance to prove herself." She continued my defense, undaunted. The town owed Mary Walker a favor, she said purposefully. Everyone knew that the only reason Mary had been offered the job was because she had her own house and the town would be saved the trouble of boarding her around! There would be no need for local families with no room to spare to put the teacher up this year, or worse yet, to raise the salary so that the teacher could at least afford a room at Weston's boardinghouse.

Silence followed Susan's outburst. The Sheriff was wise enough and had lived with her long enough to know when to give in to her. But he couldn't help but try to reason with her one more time. "What happens when Mary decides she doesn't want to teach anymore? We'll only be faced with the same problem again. And Meg will be older. It will be even harder for her to adjust to an orphanage," he said.

"We'll worry about that when the time comes," Susan replied with victory and finality in her voice.

If I thought I had found a friend in Susan Thatcher, I was only partially right. Intensely concerned with injustice, she had no time or affection for me after ascertaining that I would be cared for and given an opportunity to prove myself. I was lucky to be her latest cause.

In spite of the fact that I lived with Mrs. Walker in her little frame house adjacent to the schoolhouse and not in the territorial orphanage, I did not easily overcome the tragedy that had befallen me. During the daylight hours I was a solemn child, almost numb, although I learned to do the chores common to children my age. It was a tribute to Mrs. Walker's steeliness that she allowed me to handle the matches to light the schoolhouse stove, knowing how fire terrified me. I had to get over it, she said. But at night, in my little attic room tucked under the eaves of the house, the Parkers haunted me, mouthing wordless accusations, and I woke from nightmares in sweat-drenched terror. I stifled my whimpers in my pillow, fortunate that Mrs. Walker was the soundest of sleepers. I thought of the father I had barely known — for most of my short life he had been away at war — and I cried for the light of happiness that had shone so briefly in my mother's eyes at his return. I missed them dreadfully.

At school I was unable to make friends with the other children. The girls, especially, talked of all that was dear to them, of baby sisters and brothers and hair ribbons and parties. My experiences had marked me, and even at such a young age I was too old for their childish and inconsequential chatter. I had nothing in common with them and therefore nothing to share.

Mrs. Walker's tenure as teacher was short. By the end of the school session, the purpose of her weekly trips to Ab Monroe's General Store became Ab Monroe himself. They planned to marry later that summer and the search for a new teacher began.

Susan Thatcher once more came to my rescue. My position was permanently secured and voted on

unanimously by the school board and backed by the
Ladies Benevolent Society when it became apparent
that the swelling population of school-aged children
would necessitate the building of a new school, one
with boarding facilities to accommodate the needs
of the outlying ranches. While the sons of the ranchers would continue to board with families in town
during the week, the daughters and I, with a special
allowance made for me, would live at the school. The
new frame building had a kitchen at the back of the
schoolroom and three rooms upstairs, a small room
for the teacher and two larger rooms for the female
students who boarded there. The problems that a
male teacher might pose would never arise: the school
board had been prejudiced against them ever since
Mr. Crittenden had been found behind the schoolhouse with one of his female students.

The luxurious new schoolhouse was not enough
of an incentive to convince the teachers to remain
beyond the mandatory one-year commitment of their
contract, and in the ensuing years a steady stream
of teachers came and went from the Cross Creek
school. Any woman desiring matrimony, especially
a teacher, had more offers of marriage than she could
possibly choose from, but somehow they all did. The
only exception was Miss Tucker.

Esther Tucker remained two years and did her
best to make life pleasant for me. She was slim and
pretty and an unerring wisdom shone in her clear,
light-blue eyes. Her knowledge captured my imagination, and as she shared it with me I learned that
I could lift myself above the constraints of my situation. On Saturdays and holidays, when the boarding pupils had gone home, if the weather was pleasant
we would picnic in the adjoining meadow or go for
long walks through the countryside. During the winter months we would make hot chocolate and the two
of us would warm ourselves by the cookstove in the

kitchen as we pored our way through her favorite books. Together we read Shakespeare, Coleridge, Burns, Shelley, as well as The Arabian Nights, assorted histories, and whatever else caught our fancy. She brought a girlish laughter to my life. She declared my hair to be beautiful, although until then I had always thought of it as nondescript, without the brightness of yellow or the richness of brown. She further insisted that Mary Kay Simmons, the prettiest, wealthiest, and therefore most spoiled girl in our class, was jealous of my curls, which I had to fight into submission each and every day. I was to watch Mary Kay, she said, for at the age of sixteen, the slightly older girl considered me a rival for the affections of the boys in our class. I burst into laughter at this, for Mary Kay had all the older boys doting on her affected helplessness, and she flirted with them outrageously. But Miss Tucker claimed that it was my very independence that would stand me in good stead. I had the spirit, she said, to withstand life's adversities. I had already proven that, she added with a smile.

But I was not the only one who came to appreciate her kindness and gentle ways. Miss Tucker met and married an engineer, a mining expert, who had made Cross Creek his base as he traveled to and from the mines that dotted the hills and mountains around us. In the early days of their courtship I often accompanied them, for she had been reluctant to give up her outings with me and also reluctant to have her feelings for the engineer known. But gradually he came to replace me in her spare hours, as it should have been. I never told anyone of my secret dream that they would marry and take me with them when they returned to his company headquarters. I knew better than to believe in fairy tales.

Her leaving marked a turning point in my life. It was impossible for me to face once again the reign of a new teacher who would be summarily informed of my dark history. Only Esther Tucker had been able to see beyond the past I could not escape. To be fair, I waited until the new teacher arrived. As the dark eyes of Miss Philippa Henry marked my future, I made my decision. For the first time, with the fledgling independence and spirit Miss Tucker claimed I had, I assumed responsibility for my own life.

Chapter Two

THAT I WAS RETURNED within twenty-four hours after I ran away did not matter. Irretrievably, the die was cast. To this day, events bear the consequences of that time in May when I decided to leave Cross Creek.

Tommy Henderson, whose schoolboy pranks and deviltry were the bane of every teacher and all his classmates, provided me with just the opportunity to put my plan into action. I caught him in the kitchen late one afternoon, his hands and mouth full of the gingerbread intended for supper that night. I quickly determined that he and I were of a like size, and I struck my bargain. He would go blameless in exchange for some of his old, cast-off clothing. Grinning sheepishly at me, Tommy agreed. I doubt he believed that I intended to report his infraction, but he was a sympathic soul.

The schoolhouse was quiet that night. Only the Beechum sisters—Mary, Francis, and Allie—remained for the weekend. There was illness in their

family at home; their mother had just undergone her
ninth lying-in. But their presence suited my purposes well. They would unwittingly keep Miss Henry
occupied as I went about my preparations. That evening, after supper, as I scrubbed down the kitchen
floor, Tommy returned with a small pile of clothing,
winking at me as he deposited it by the back door.

I retired early and, after making certain that no
one was about to observe my furtive labors, I stole
into Miss Henry's room and rummaged through her
sewing basket until I found her scissors. Then, retreating to my own room, I stood before the mirror
in the fading light from the window and hacked away
at my long, thick braids. Freed from the restraining
weight, my hair sprung in riotous curls about my
head, emphasizing the brown eyes flecked with green
and gold, a delicately shaped nose, a mouth tightened by determination, and a pointed chin. If anything, the effect heightened my girlish appearance,
but there was no turning back now. Desperately, I
pulled the shapeless slouch hat that Tommy had provided down over my ears. The result was somewhat
better, but it would not bear close inspection. I swept
up the cuttings, meaning to leave no clues behind
as to my changed appearance, and wrapped them in
one of my two school dresses, to discard along the
way. While they searched for a girl with braids wearing a brown plaid pinafore, my identity would be
safely hidden beneath the frayed and patched clothing of a young boy with a somewhat straggly haircut.

I returned the scissors to Miss Henry's sewing
basket. Tommy's shirt fit well enough over my slender shoulders, hiding the gentle swells of my shape,
and I was grateful that I lacked Mary Kay Simmons's more grandiose proportions. The breeches
needed suspenders, but a length of rope at the waist
did just as well. I made a small bundle of Tommy's
jacket and my dress with the telltale clippings of

hair, and I included a wedge of cheese and some leftover biscuits I had secreted from the kitchen earlier in the day. I drew my nightdress over my clothing just as the voices of Mary, Francis, and Allie came to my ears; quickly, I jumped beneath the covers of my bed and lay quiet, feigning sleep. They giggled at my still form as I held my breath. In my haste, I had left my bundle of belongings in the middle of the floor. Worse, Tommy's hat still covered my head. I burrowed down deeper under the bedclothes and waited.

The moon climbed high above my window and my roommates gave themselves up to sleep, leaving the telling bundle undiscovered where it rested. The night stretched endlessly before me as the light from Miss Henry's room spilled across the hall floor, warning me of her restlessness. No matter what, I had to leave that very night. Otherwise all would be lost, for there would be no way to explain my cropped hair come morning. Finally, the light at the end of the corridor dimmed, leaving the entire floor in darkness.

I did not waste a minute. Throwing off my shift and taking up my bundle and Tommy's boots, I made my way through the night-shadowed room. Pausing at the doorway, I turned my head toward Miss Henry's door at the end of the hall. The entire schoolhouse was silent. I crossed the corridor to the landing and gingerly descended the creaking stairs that seemed to scream of my escape. Still, no one stirred.

Below, the rooms were awash with moonlight. I hesitated briefly at the door to the empty classroom and stared about the room where I had spent more than half my life. The room was eerily quiet without the restless rustlings and voices of students at their lessons. No traces of my presence remained. Most of the children who passed through the doors of the schoolhouse would scratch their initials into a wooden desktop, but that would not have been fitting be-

havior for a child sponsored by the charity of the
Benevolent Society. A dark shape took form at the
corner of my eye and I froze, but it was only a forgotten cloak hanging from a wooden peg. Shouldering my sack, I turned from the room and soundlessly
made my way to the door and into the night.

I welcomed the daylight as I cursed Tommy's boots.
Several sizes too large, they slipped painfully up and
down with every step I took, but I stopped only long
enough to wedge some grass between my heels and
the offending leather. The first pale blue of daybreak
faded to pink as the sky above lightened, chasing
down the glowing spectacle of sunrise. My predawn
departure had placed me well past town and it was
only now, with the daylight, that I needed to seek
the cover of the trees bordering the road.

The worst was behind me, I told myself, as the
dew-laden grass brushed wetly against my trousered
legs. I had made good my escape. I refused to dwell
on the uncertainty and necessity of making my own
way. I would pose as a boy, and if I was thought to
be a runaway, so much the better. Runaway boys of
my age were often left to themselves. I planned to
do a day's chores in exchange for a meal and perhaps
a bed of straw in a barn at night when I came across
a likely enough place to stop.

As the sun climbed higher, I welcomed the shade
of the cottonwoods, although I would have made better time if I had traveled the road. But I didn't dare
risk the exposure. My absence had surely been discovered by now, and a rider on horseback would be
able to overtake me easily. I smiled at the thought
of Francis Beechum, always first to arrive in the
kitchen for her breakfast, discerning something was
amiss. She would tell Miss Henry that I had not lit
the cookstove nor done any of my early morning
chores, and they would all troop to the room I shared

with the sisters and search it for clues. They would spot my second dress hanging on its peg and assume I wore the other. The word would pass around. Meg Logan was missing! What had happened to her?

It was noon when the pain of my blistered heels forced me to stop. The grass had not lessened the smarting rub of raw skin. Climbing a gradual rise to a rocky ledge overlooking the road, I checked the direction from which I had come. The road was deserted. Seating myself behind a sun-warmed boulder, I eased off the annoying boots with care as I considered my situation. If I rested for just a short while, it would not cut my lead by much. Brushing aside a fly that buzzed lazily at my head, I settled back against the hard cushion of rock and closed my eyes.

The sound of a horse's hoofbeats penetrated the thick fog of drowsiness. I drew into the shadow of the rock, listening for the sound to pass and fade away into the distance. But instead, the horse stopped. Someone had been sent after me. Ignoring the gravel that bit into my hands and face, I flattened myself to the ground, silently inching myself sideways until I came to a screen of low-lying brush. Cautiously, I parted the straggly growth and peered down at the road.

The man on the horse was gazing wearily around. He took in the rise in ground to the south, where I lay hidden, then looked northward, across the road. A dark, flat-crowned hat shaded his face and features as he turned reflectively in his saddle and scanned the trail ahead. I suspected that this man was Sheriff Thatcher's newly arrived deputy, because I did not recognize him. Ed Thatcher had chosen well; the sheriff's expanding girth had slowed him down considerably during the past few years. Without a doubt, I could have outrun and outmaneuvered the portly

sheriff, but I stood no chance against this new deputy. He was tall—I could tell from his height in the
saddle—and he had wide shoulders that tapered
down into a lean but powerful build. He sat his horse
well, as if he had been born to it. He needed only to
turn in my direction and I would see his badge glinting in the sunlight. And then with the sharp crack
of a rifle the stillness of noon exploded, and bright
droplets of blood splashed to the ground. The man
in the saddle winced in pain and surprise, but leaning forward, he drew his carbine as he held in his
nervous mount. As quick as he was, he was not fast
enough, for a second blast of gunfire knocked him
from the saddle. There was a dull thud as his body
hit the ground.

Instantly I realized that what had happened below
was not my fault. The man who lay sprawled in the
dust was not the deputy of Cross Creek, but a stranger
whose murder I had just witnessed. A sudden fear
seized me. Whoever ambushed him would unhesitatingly do the same to me if I was discovered as a
witness. My approach through the screen of trees
along the side of the road must have been missed,
but the murderer would surely spot me if I attempted
to escape. More than my freedom was at stake—I
was risking my life.

A smattering of loose rock trickled down the slope
from above. Scarcely breathing, I heard the short,
quick steps of a man leading a horse down the rock-
strewn rise past my hiding place. The footsteps and
the clattering of the horse's hooves stopped as they
came to the bottom. Cautiously I raised my head.
The man who stooped by the body was a well dressed
man, his black frock coat only lightly smudged by
the dust of his recent activity. Satisfied that his aim
had been true, he dragged the dead man across the
road, through the tall grass, and into the woods where
the body would be hidden from view. Returning to

the road, he withdrew a snowy white handkerchief from his breast pocket and fastidiously wiped his soiled hands, then refolded it and returned it to his pocket. He mounted his horse unhurriedly. For a moment, he turned in my direction, and I saw a thin, chilling smile of a reckoning on his face. Then, riding close to the dead man's horse, he gave it a vicious cut with his quirt. Startled, the animal bolted down the road. His work completed, the man in the black coat put his spurs to his own mount and disappeared in a westerly direction before a floating trail of dust clouds.

It was then that I made my first mistake. I forgot the pressing need to be gone and instead let the violent act I had just witnessed interfere with my plans. It never occurred to me that I should continue my journey and leave the man to be discovered by time, or a passerby. His kin or those who cared for him might never learn of his fate. I put aside all thoughts of escape as I descended the hill.

Except for the blurred tracks of the horses' hooves and the blood-soaked stains on the ground, there was little evidence on the now-quiet road of the savage violence that had taken place moments ago. I crossed the road and followed the path I had watched the killer take. My heart pounded and I swallowed hard, shaken by the impending confrontation with a bullet-shattered body and death. Entering the shaded woods, I searched the tangled underbrush for the tall man's body. I found it not far from the streambed, lying facedown in the brush. A dark stain spread across his back; another stain ran down the side of his leg, where the first shot, the one that had struck low, had alerted him to his danger. The side of his face, too, was streaked by blood where he had grazed it in the fall from his horse. I was struck by an over-whelming sense of loss at his death, even though I did not know him. He had been killed in the prime of his manhood, and it seemed such a terrible waste. Foolishly, for one does strange things under strange circumstances, I spoke to the body. "I'm sorry, Mister," I heard myself say.

At the sudden sound of a horse crashing through the trees I froze in terror, but it was only the murdered man's horse returning to him, the sting of the lash forgotten. He stared at me for an instant, blowing through distended nostrils, his sides slick with sweat. When he saw that I made no move toward him, he ambled closer. Then, spotting some lush foliage, he lowered his head to nibble at the greenery. I gazed at the fine animal reflectively. If I had a horse like the chestnut gelding, no one would ever catch me. But then reason asserted itself. I didn't know if taking a dead man's horse was a hanging offense, but the possession of so fine an animal by a ragamuffin boy was bound to attract attention. It was just too risky. I turned away from the gelding regretfully and once again looked to the body half-hidden in the brush. A shiver traced its way up my spine.

It was impossible, I told myself. His hand had not moved. It was only my imagination. I stared hard at the man's body. In an effort to chase the impression away, I knelt down beside him and regarded him intently. His skin had a gray-white pallor, and a short growth of beard covered the lower portion of his face, as if he had been clean-shaven until just a short time ago. His features were strongly cast, from what I could see. Detecting the shallowest and most irregular of breaths, I raised a tentative hand to his brow, carefully avoiding the scalp wound and the blood soaked hair, and drew back at the cold, clammy sensation. If he was not dead he was close to it. The least I could do was keep him warm. Rising to my feet, I went to his horse.

His bedroll held little: a blanket, a slicker, and a few utensils. He was a man used to living simply. Taking up the blanket and leaving the rest behind, I surveyed our surroundings. There was a flattish ridge between us and the water that was well screened by a small grove of cottonwoods, which would serve to shelter us from the wind. I had to move him there.

There remained only my squeamishness to conquer. Gritting my teeth, I lifted and pulled at the inert form until enough force was exerted to turn him over. His face was a surprise. Beneath the pallor, he looked strangely defenseless. Ignoring the twinge of pity, I squatted by his head and secured a good grip beneath his arms. Tugging at the deadweight until his body finally gave in to the persistent force, inch by inch I dragged him down the bank to the shelter of trees. My muscles protested at the test of strength, but I lost my footing only once and then quickly recovered.

If the move didn't kill him, surely the cold dampness of the falling night would. Covering him with his blanket, I built up a small fire close by. I checked his belongings again and found a small pouch of jerked beef. It would do for a broth if it were heated in boiling water. I had only cheese and biscuits, hardly fare for a dying man. I wasn't expert enough to tell if the red-brown stains on his clothing were the same or if his blood continued to seep away. There was nothing for bandages except my shirt, so, tearing the sleeves into strips, I packed them gently against his wounds, trying not to think of the cold night that lay ahead. Then, as he lay quiet, I retrieved my small sack of provisions and Tommy's boots from across the road and, returning to his side, began my vigil.

It was not that I wished him dead. I did not. But alive, he posed nothing but problems. How was I to explain my involvement when I went for help? I could not go to Cross Creek, which was the closest town, and in all likelihood he would die once I left him no matter what town I headed for. If I were too evasive when I related the incident, people would be suspicious, and I ran off afterward, they would come after me. Had he been dead, as I had at first thought, I had only to leave word with someone in the next place I stopped as to the whereabouts of a body. Alive, he was a great risk to my safety.

His stirring wakened me to the chill in the air. Twilight had deepened into a starry sky and I added more wood to the fire. It flared briefly, then died down to a steady burn. Heating some water in the tin cup I had found among his belongings, I stirred in the jerked beef while studying the still shape next to me. Almost imperceptibly the eyelids flickered. I touched his shoulder lightly, mindful of his injury. "How about some soup, Mister?" I asked him in a quiet voice.

His eyes opened slowly, reluctantly, as if he did not wish to waken. It took him even longer to focus his sight on the spreading branches of the cottonwood above us. I read the confusion in his face. Raising him slightly, using my shoulder and arm as a brace, his head heavy against me, I supported him as he tried to sit up. "Easy does it," I said to him. "You don't want to start those wounds bleeding again."

An involuntary moan of pain broke from his lips as he tried to move his leg. "You were hit twice," I volunteered, trying to forestall his questions and any further movement on his part. "In the chest and your left leg." Bringing the cup to his lips, I held it for him as he tried to steady his hands around it. The broth had cooled enough for him to get down a few swallows.

"No more." His voice was a harsh, choked whisper.

I set the cup aside and then very gently eased him back down.

His hair lay in sweat-soaked strands and the pupils of his half-shut, feverish eyes were dark in the flushed, angular face. It was hard to determine his age in his condition, but I thought him to be somewhere between twenty and thirty. Even in his severely weakened state I was strongly aware of his physical presence, and I thought I would have found him threatening had he been well. He carried a Colt .45 Peacemaker that was shiny with wear in his gunbelt. I had removed it to make him more comfortable but had left it by his side, thinking that should he regain consciousness he might want it handy.

"How long have I been like this?" I started at the voice. It was weak, but sharp.

"Since midday. Must be a few hours past sunset by now," I said.

"How'd you find me?" His voice shook a little from the effort to speak.

"I...I..." The bite of the night air at the back of my neck, newly bare of hair, left me feeling peculiarly naked and defenseless. There was no reason to tell him of my masquerade. I knew nothing about him. I had no cause to believe he was any different from the man who had ambushed him. Perhaps he was a killer, too—an unlucky killer who had been at the receiving end of a bullet.

He didn't wait for my answer. He carried on as if I had spoken. "You could have been killed," he stated unemotionally.

"Yes, I suppose so," I answered, and in my mind I saw him fall again from his saddle. It occurred to me that although he had not seen his attacker, he had known exactly who the man was. Then, because I feared he might recognize my girlish voice if we should talk longer, I lied deftly. "But you see, I came along after it happened. I didn't see a thing." I was happy when he fell silent. Shortly afterward the sound of his shallow breathing told me he had fallen asleep or lost consciousness again. I drew the blanket to his shoulders and stared at the fire.

A small noise, like the chitter-chatter of little chipmunks, wove itself into my dream as I slept and then woke me. The sound persisted as I lay huddled beneath the inadequate length of Tommy's jacket, striving for a warmth that was not there. Poking my head above the threadbare folds of my cover, I realized the noise came from the stranger. Cursing my luck, I crawled to his side and saw that his teeth chattered alarmingly. His color, if possible, looked worse. I built up the fire, knowing it would not warm him soon enough. I picked up his hand. It was cold to my touch. In spite of the flaming heat as the dry wood caught and burned, he remained deathly cold as the tremors shook his body. I knew of only one thing to do. Brushing aside all thoughts of propriety, I edged myself under his blanket. Mindful of his injuries, I held myself stiffly at his side, fighting a natural impulse to recoil at a stranger's closeness. A moment passed. My breath quickened as he stirred slightly. I was acutely aware of him, and it seemed my skin burned where we touched. Surely the heat of it would reach him. The stars leaped down at me as I lay beside him; the night noises became a crescendo of sounds. The chill in the air disappeared as we shared the single blanket. I lent him my warmth until, at last, our combined body heat lulled me to sleep.

It was daybreak when I awoke to find my head nestled against his uninjured shoulder and my body curled up at the stranger's side. Surprised by the soundness with which I had slept, I was curiously refreshed despite the compromising situation. At the wayward thought, I turned to glance at the man I knew so little about, glad to see that his breathing was deeper and more even. Taking care not to disturb him, I eased myself from beneath the blanket. My body was still warm where it had pressed against his. In a shrinking freshet of water, all that was left of the creek's spring overflow, I washed thoroughly. There was an odor of blood about my clothes. I stared at the stains that marked them, the proof of an intimate closeness the night before. Then, as a sense of propriety returned to me, I flushed guiltily. A smile came to my lips, for although I knew that what I had done would have terrible repercussions if ever it were found out, I had not minded it a bit.

The sky lightened and my reflection rippled in the water, startling me with the image of my shorn hair. I ran my fingers through the short ends that barely reached my collar. With the taming weight gone, it refused to lie straight but framed my face with soft shiny curls the color of dark honey in the early light. I wondered what Mary Kay Simmons would think of me now, and of my latest escapade. Then my thoughts returned to where they rightfully belonged. I clamped Tommy's hat down over my head and filled the cup with water for the stranger in case he should want a drink.

The morning shadows flickered over the chestnut gelding as he grazed in a small patch of sunlight on a rise of ground above the stream. Raising his head suddenly, he snorted a warning, but it was too late. Even as I darted up the bank, I heard the voices. I never made it to the cover of the trees. A firm hand reached out to my shoulder, stopping me quicker than a gun to my back. I was slowly turned around so that I came to stare straight into the broad chest of a man wearing a badge.

Chapter Three

I WAS BROUGHT BACK to Cross Creek that same day, riding double behind the sheriff of the nearby town of Stanton, and I knew I was a spectacle as we proceeded down Main Street to Ed Thatcher's office. Defiantly, I held my head high as we passed the schoolyard. One by one, the pupils lined up along the street to gawk until Miss Henry ran from the schoolhouse to call them in, no doubt to protect them from my sinful ways. I heard her gasp aloud at my cropped hair.

It had been bad luck, pure and simple, that had placed me with the wounded stranger, for he was the one Sheriff Baker and his deputy had sought, not me. He was wanted in another county, further north, for a killing. They said I was fortunate to be alive. Sheriff Baker, responding to the telegraph dispatch warning him that the killer was heading his way, had also received word of a runaway from Cross Creek, the town twenty miles due east of Stanton.

He didn't mind returning me; he was an old acquaintance of Ed Thatcher's. On the way back to Cross Creek, we stopped at Rube Johnson's livery, and Baker made arrangements for a wagon to be sent back for his deputy and the wounded prisoner for transportation back to Stanton. No one seemed concerned about the gunman who had shot him, as if the injured man had only gotten his due. Before we left for Cross Creek, I heard Sheriff Baker tell his deputy that with a little luck one of those bullets would have saved the county the expense of a hanging. Nothing was said about the nature of the man's crime. They probably thought it wasn't fitting for my ears.

Sheriff Thatcher greeted us at the door, his disapproval clear on his florid face. "Well, here she is, Ed," Sheriff Baker said by way of a greeting. "What are you gonna do with this little runaway now?"

I hated Sheriff Thatcher's office, because it never failed to remind me of my arrival in Cross Creek. There would be no Susan Thatcher to stand up for me this time. I had disgraced the Ladies Benevolent Society. Miss Henry would never take me back. There remained only the territorial orphanage. I closed my ears to what the sheriffs were saying, trying very hard not to think of my future. The stale smoke of Ed Thatcher's cigar hung heavy in the small, airless front room. The office held the barest of essentials: a desk and chair, a stove, a cot for sleeping, a gun rack, and coat pegs by the door. Against the back wall, near the door to the jail cells at the rear of the building, hung the dog-eared "Wanted" notices. I wondered if the stranger's face would be among them, or if this had been his first brush with the law.

A sudden noise startled me; I turned about and my eyes came to rest on the figure of Doc Elliot, reclining casually in the swivel-backed wooden armchair, his feet propped unceremoniously on top of Ed

Thatcher's desk. Doc Elliot was gazing at me thoughtfully. He was a gruff man—crusty, they called him—but he was known to be fair and hard-working. He would not stop to pass the time of day, but he was reputed to have never refused a summons to the bedside of an ailing patient, no matter how trivial he believed the complaint to be or how far the distance.

At Sheriff Baker's departure, Ed Thatcher took up a seat in one of the spare wooden chairs, not at all concerned that Doc Elliot had claimed his. The chair squeaked under his weight as he leaned forward.

"Miss Henry doesn't want you back, Meg."

"I didn't expect that she would, Sheriff Thatcher," I said, raising my head to accept the consequences of my actions.

"She thinks you would be a corrupting influence on the rest of the pupils," he continued.

"Yes, sir," I acknowledged respectfully.

"You know there's only one place I can send you now, Meg. There's no one else that'd have you."

"Yes, sir."

"In a way, I'm sorry. Because contrary to what I had first believed, I think Susan was right. I think it worked out just fine until that Henry woman took over the school. She's a bad tempered woman. Now, mind you, she does a fine job of teaching, and it doesn't hurt the youngsters any to toe the mark. No siree. I just wish you had tried a little harder to get along with her."

I stared down at the dusty floor, my rebellious feelings undiminished, regretting only that I had been caught. I wished myself back by the side of the wounded stranger, an accused killer, fearing him far less than my future at the orphanage. In an instant of straying fancy, I imagined that he and I had escaped together into the unknown. Then I brought myself back to the present. In all likelihood, he would not survive his wounds, and if he did, there remained the hanging Sheriff Baker had predicted. I tried to convince myself that, in spite of the territorial orphanage, I was more fortunate than he.

"I'll make the arrangements with the orphanage sometime today," he continued. "We can have you on a stage in that direction the day after tomorrow." Then he added, almost kindly, "The jail's empty now and I'm not expecting any trouble tonight, so I guess we can have you stay here. That suit you?"

"Yes, sir."

I bit my lip to stop it from trembling and wiped at my eyes with the sleeve of Tommy's jacket. Glancing back up at the sheriff, I found him and Doc Elliot deep in conversation. My gaze fell to the unwatched front door, but before my feet could act on my impulse Doc Elliot's heated words stopped me.

"Oh, hell, Ed, I know what she did," he said, removing his feet from the desktop. His dark, piercing eyes fixed themselves on the large bulk of Sheriff Thatcher. He was not a man of convention. There was little he respected, and Ed Thatcher's authority was not apparently one of those things. This was the doctor who had single-handedly mobilized the town during the diptheria epidemic even as the Ladies Benevolent Society floundered in the wake of their own sickness and that of their loved ones. No one had ever found fault with the unsmiling doctor of Cross Creek again.

"Seth, you're a crazy fool," Ed said to him. "I tell you, it won't work. Why do you think she's in this mess? You're gone more than half the time. She needs supervision, not a free rein. And she's too young for what you've got in mind!"

"Well, now, Ed. I heard you talkin' with Baker before he left. I know what she did. Seems to me she showed some good presence of mind. Can't think of many girls that would've done what Meg here did to save a life."

"Seth, if she knew what she was about, she wouldn't have done it! Any self-respecting girl would've gone for help, not spent the night with him. That man's a killer. You're ignoring that fact!"

"She did the right thing, Ed." Doc Elliot's voice was cold. "That's all that counts to my way of thinkin'." He gave the sheriff a steely look. "It took guts, Ed. And it took guts leavin' that witch of a woman, Henry. Now I'm seein' this through and I don't want you interruptin', you hear me?"

Seth Elliot didn't wait for Sheriff Thatcher's accordance. He swiveled his chair around and addressed me without preamble.

"Meg Logan, Sheriff Baker says you may have saved that man's life." The doctor's eyes were steady with purpose, but I did not understand what he wanted of me.

"He was alive this morning, Doc Elliot, but I don't know about now. He was in a pretty bad way."

"Must have been a lot of blood," he said, ignoring my conjecture. "Most girls your age wouldn't have done so well. Might have lost their heads."

I responded truthfully. "I didn't think of it at the time, sir." It had been my physical closeness to the wounded man as we slept, not the blood, that had left a far greater impression on me. I didn't dare admit that to him.

"Did it bother you any to find out he was wanted for murder?" This time Doc's voice was pained. I assumed it was because he had no love for criminals.

"Well, I didn't know it at the time, but seeing how it happened, it doesn't surprise me. Someone must have hated him an awful lot to ambush him like that. So I guess I figured he might have done something wrong."

"Would you help him again, Meg, knowing that he had killed somebody?"

"Yes, I suppose I would," I said. "But I don't think Sheriff Baker was too pleased with me. He said I could have saved them the cost of a hanging if I'd just let the man be."

"Hah!" Sheriff Thatcher's voice broke in. "That man will never hang. Why his family..."

"That's enough, Ed!" Doc Elliot's voice cracked sharper than a whip. Ed Thatcher closed his mouth, and for a moment, we all wondered who was the sheriff and who was the doctor. It would be years before I learned why Doc Elliot had been so vehement just then.

Doc Elliot rose from his seat. He was not a large man, but he was well proportioned. It was his hair that aged him. The once-dark head was generously sprayed with silver, so that his eyes were a surprise—they were not old, just hard in a rather forbidding face. His gaze bore straight through me and his voice was stern. "The way I see it, Meg, you've got two choices. I can let the sheriff here go ahead with his plans and let him board you on that stage the day after tomorrow, or... you can come stay with me."

I stared at him in astonishment, unable to speak. But he had not finished. "Now don't you go thinkin' that this is some act of charity or an easy way out of this mess, because it isn't. I need someone who can look after things for me. I'm gone most of the time. The sheriff here says you're too young. And that I can't trust you. I have stock that needs carin' for. I need someone to see to my meals when I'm around. And I need someone with a good sensible head in case of an emergency. And that makes what you did yesterday look like a Sunday picnic. I'd need to count on you.

"In exchange, you can stay with me and consider

my place your home. I want you to think it over. If
you go to the orphanage, you'd be taken care of.
You'd go to school and have some chores to do, maybe
lookin' after the younger children. It'd be a whole
lot easier on you."

There was no gentleness in his eyes, nothing to
tell me that he wanted me because he cared what
happened to Meg Logan. He wanted a servant. But
I didn't need to think it over.

"Yes, sir, I'll do it."

"Good," he said, instantly affirming my acceptance. "We won't mention this incident again. No
sense having the town know how you spent the night.
I think we can assume that Sheriff Baker and Ed,
here, won't speak of it. I admire what you did, but
it won't do your reputation any good," he added, taking in my bloodstained clothing with a curious glint
in his eye. "You know where I live. I'll expect you
there after you pick up your belongings at the schoolhouse." Without a backward glance at me or Sheriff
Thatcher, he strode out the door.

The sheriff shook his head slowly. "Don't you forget, Meg. I had nothing to do with this!"

Doc Elliot's house fronted a crossroad at the east
end of town. From the seat of the old wooden rocker
on the porch of the frame house, a clear view could
be had of the entire length of Main Street. On the
north side of the house, the once-white paint had
been turned a soft, weathered gray by the changing
seasons and passing years. The house's exterior had
been neglected since the time years ago when it had
been readied for an eastern doctor and his new bride.
The neat picket fence and the well tended yard had
not impressed his wife, nor had the new but ordinary
furnishings inside. Unable to abide the unsophisti-
cated society of Cross Creek, she unheedingly affronted all who did their best to welcome the new

couple to town. Within two months of their arrival,
they departed, with no regret on the part of the
townspeople.

Mere chance had brought Seth Elliot to Cross
Creek. Newly retired from the military, the doctor
had given little thought to settling down. But, too
long without the services of a reliable physician, the
townspeople found the taciturn doctor a reassuring
figure. While no one would ever get close enough to
Doc Elliot to find out if he qualified for a position in
society, the people of Cross Creek needed him. To
make their offer more attractive, they bestowed upon
him the frame house, which boasted both living
quarters and office space. Thus, Doc Elliot benefited
from the eastern physician's defection.

The house was set far back enough from the road
to allow for a small, unkempt front yard. The second
spring I lived with Doc Elliot, I ousted the weeds
that had grown during years of neglect and planted
a border of pansies with seeds purchased from Ab
Monroe's General Store.

The house itself was modest. A central hallway
ran the width of it, separating the living quarters
from the office on the first floor of the one-and-a-half
story structure, and a narrow stairway led to the two
bedchambers tucked beneath the eaves. Lace curtains framed the windows and the walls were painted
a pale green, a shade whose only redeeming quality
was that it never needed repainting because it was
impossible to tell whether it was a fresh or faded
color. A stiff horsehair sofa and two equally uncomfortable chairs presided over the unused front parlor.
In his rare free time at home, Doc could be found in
the more comfortable surroundings of the kitchen,
reading the Cross Creek *Gazette*.

Doc Elliot's offer to me had not been motivated by
kindness, but by practicality. My strong stomach and
level-headedness under adverse conditions had al-

ready been proved to him. I knew he admired my
courage and perhaps he recognized my stubbornness
as a trait akin to his own. He did not know that,
given this chance, I not only intended to make a place
for myself in his practice and house, but in his life
as well. Blithely, on my first full day with him, I
went out of my way to prove my worth to Doc.

I had learned my lessons well in the Cross Creek
schoolhouse kitchen—nothing was to be wasted.
Therefore, it was with great pleasure that I found,
in my immediate exploration of my new home, the
one-hundred-pound sack of beans stored away as if
forgotten. Since he received a good portion of his fees
in produce, it never occurred to me that Doc might
not wish to use up the foodstuffs he had acquired. I
was extra generous with the pieces of pork I added
to the pot for flavor. Proudly, I set a bowl before Doc
Elliot for our first supper together and waited for his
approval. Doc leaned forward and sniffed the contents of the bowl, flaring his nostrils slightly as if
he did not believe his eyes. He barely glanced at the
plate of creamed carrots I set on the table—I had
found nearly a bushel of them in the root cellar and
had tried to use them up also.

"Beans?" he inquired in a peculiar voice.

"Beans, Doc Elliot," I replied, puzzled by the
strange look on his face. "And at least one half pound
of salt pork. And some molasses and green pepper.
I didn't need to buy a thing. You had all the fixings
right here," I added falteringly, sensing now that all
was not right. I never realized that after all his years
in the army Doc Elliot couldn't abide the thought of
beans.

Rising from the table, Doc excused himself. "I'll
be at the Gold Dust if anyone comes looking for me,"
he said, his words coming back at me as he left for
the saloon. My cheeks flushed with defeat in a kitchen
suddenly grown overly warm. He hadn't wanted to

hurt my feelings, I told myself. It was just that he was not very good at hiding his.

But the very next morning, as I shaved soap slithers into the wash water heating over the stove, I observed him through the kitchen window with some curiosity as he dropped an odd-sized object from the shed into a battered tub filled with water. "You were right," he said gruffly upon entering the kitchen. "We should be using our stores. Saved that piece of venison long enough. You let it soak and we'll have a good meal from it," he promised, letting his hand drop to my shoulder in an awkward but reassuring pat. My heart swelled with gratitude at his effort on my behalf and I knew that, as set in his ways as he was, a link had been forged between me and Doc Elliot that day in Sheriff Thatcher's office. Events that might have turned censuring people away from me had brought the ex-army doctor and me together.

This is not to say that things progressed smoothly. When he balked at my next suggestion of a vegetable garden, claiming it would take up too much of my time, I said nothing and, waiting an entire year, wisely refrained from asking his permission before I laid one in. All that summer he refused to acknowledge that the fresh greens he enjoyed came from our garden, but his eyes twinkled when I served him a freshly baked pumpkin pie that fall.

After some weeks, Doc finally summoned me to assist him as he drained the ear of a fractious child, the boy's mother being more in need of calming than the child. But it was later that summer, during the typhoid epidemic, that I became indispensable to Doc Elliot.

It was useless to talk about preventatives. Doc's insistence that the drinking water be boiled went unheeded. Patients swore that the streams they drank from had been sparkling and pure. Once they were stricken, insensibly their neighbors repeated their folly. Doc cursed under his breath some of the time and aloud most of the time at their ignorance. Each of the patients had to be visited by Doc or me at least once daily. Often, if there were no family to care for them, I remained. As the crusted lips of the sick gave voice to the delirium that claimed the mind, only hours of cold sponging would temporarily relieve the fever. When the epidemic was at a peak, patients were wrapped in wet sheets in an effort to lower their body temperature. Even when a patient seemed well on the road to recovery, there was danger of relapse. Doc was tireless and I was determined to follow his example. But he saved me from complete exhaustion by insisting that I rest, for typhoid was contagious and if the disease took hold in a weak or tired victim it sapped the very strength needed to withstand its ravages. He may have rested while I slept, but for six long weeks he never did give himself up to the comfort of his bed.

But it was nature and foolhardiness that provided Doc with most of his patients. Not a winter passed without the inevitable amputations necessitated by frostbite. Miners suffered eye injuries from flying rock and debris, and cowboys came with broken bones. Doc swore that some of the home remedies people used on themselves were worse than their ailments, although he did have a healthy respect for some of the Indian cures. If Doc thought I might be of some help to him, I accompanied him on his calls. Once the outlying homesteads and ranches got wind of his visit, a single call often grew to a dozen within a fifty-mile radius. It was not an easy life, and I wondered if he had retired from the army in pursuit of a simpler existence.

In spite of Doc's flinty manner, on several occasions I noticed him openly return the salutations of Rose's girls. This must have caused great speculation among the ladies of Cross Creek, for even I wondered about it. I could not associate him with those men with the sheepish expressions who visited him furtively at the oddest hours. As a courtesy to them, I remained as far from the consultation room as possible and offered no words of farewell as they departed by the kitchen door, so their privacy was not invaded by the seemingly curious eyes of Doc Elliot's young female assistant.

Many times that first year I recalled the strange circumstances that had brought me to Doc's side. It was usually late at night, just before I dropped off to sleep in my little room under the eaves, that I remembered him, and although my memory of his features had faded, the feeling of a hard body next to mine and the strange comfort the wounded stranger had brought to me that bright starry night had not. I never asked Doc about it; I was afraid to. I remembered all too well how cold his voice had become when Ed Thatcher spoke of the man, and I was afraid that I would incur that same coldness if I brought it up. I avoided the Cross Creek *Gazette*, fearing it would confirm my suspicions with a picture of him hanging from the gallows in some town north of Cross Creek, as Sheriff Baker had predicted.

For the first time since I had come to Cross Creek, I wanted for nothing. I allowed myself to forget the past, and the circumstances that had brought me to Cross Creek, and all the years I was the burden of the Ladies Benevolent Society. I had Doc Elliot, and as cantankerous as he was at times, we suited each other well. He patently ignored the advice Sheriff Thatcher had given him and offered me as much freedom as I wanted. Of course, it wasn't freedom I craved; I longed to be needed and wanted for myself. Besides providing me with a home, Doc insisted on giving me an allowance, saying that I more than

earned it. He encouraged me to be independent much
as Esther Tucker once had done.

In his own rough way, Doc looked after me, much
as I did him. "You looked peaked," he exclaimed
brusquely one late summer afternoon as I finished
putting up the season's preserves. "Take Nutmeg for
a ride. Some fresh air'll do you good." Taken aback
by his concern, I retreated to the privacy of my room
and gazed at my image in the mirror. What did peaked
look like? My hair, having grown out after my aborted
escapade, skimmed the top of my shoulders and
gleamed softly in the muted light from the small
window. My skin was smooth, my brow clear, my
wide-set eyes alert, reflecting golden lights captured
from the last rays of the late afternoon sun. Perhaps
it was my cheekbones, emphasized by the slight hollows beneath them and almost alabaster in the fading light, that had Doc concerned. The paleness was
unusual. But it was not just the subtle changes of
my face I noticed. Even though I remained as slim
as ever, I would no longer find it quite so easy to
pose as a boy, I decided. While I would never possess
a figure as curvacious as Mary Kay's, I did not mind,
for I was quite happy with the image reflected back
at me. It showed a capable young woman who was
Doc's assistant, and who had made a place for herself
in the town, despite an uncertain background. My
eyes no longer possessed the searching look that had
been there during the years I had sought an elusive
happiness. I had found it at Doc's side. I loved the
brusque-mannered doctor and, although I could see
no reason for alarm, to please him I cut short my
thoughts and changed into my riding clothes. Sad-
dling Nutmeg, I galloped off for a ride through the
countryside.

Chapter Four

✒ I CAN RECALL my eighteenth birthday with perfect clarity. Not because it was a special day, because none of my birthdays were. They only marked the passing of another year with Doc Elliot. Rather, it was the circumstances that preceded that birthday that foreshadowed ever so slightly the gathering maelstrom that would eventually alter all our lives.

My birthday was in the springtime. Spring did more than just green the land and charge the air with the fragrance of flowers and give rise to a new crop of animal offspring. It surged through a dormant winter body and churned the blood into an awakening frenzy. Like frozen streams breaking up under the warming touch of the sun, so did human passions erupt come the spring thaw.

It was in the very early morning hours of one such day that a sharp sound startled me awake. Reaching for my dressing robe, I heard the noise again, like the spray of gravel against a window. I belted my robe hurriedly, going to the door of my room in time to see Doc Elliot, his clothes hastily drawn on, pass by me with a Colt tightly gripped in his hand. "Stay where you are!" he snapped at me. "I'll see to this!" Just having returned from a patient's deathbed a few hours earlier, he was none too pleased at this disturbance, somehow sensing it was not a birthing he was being called to.

I did as he said, waiting at the top of the landing for the familiar sound of his exit through a silent kitchen. The door opened but instead of his hurried footsteps departing into the fading night shadows I heard the clamor of a falling chair, and I rushed down the stairs. Seizing the shotgun from its corner at the back of the stairs, I quickly made my way through the hall to the rear of the house, my nostrils catching the odor of gunpowder and blood even before my eyes came to rest on Doc and the bloodied cowboy he was supporting as he led him across the passageway to his office. Putting my weapon down, I ran to the other side of the wounded man and, placing his arm about my shoulder, helped him to the examining table.

Illumination flooded the room as Doc lit a lamp, and my attention fell back to the cowboy. His face was sharply cast in the harsh light and his discomfort showed plainly in his dark features. He had a bullet in his side. Although nothing vital had been struck, he was weak from loss of blood. He removed his hat and a shock of dark hair fell forward. He brushed it back, giving me an appraising look as he did. I flushed under his scrutiny and busied myself with the bandages I knew Doc would need.

"From the looks of this, you were shot hours ago," Doc Elliot said ill-temperedly. "You sure took your time getting here."

The man remained strangely silent.

"The law after you?" Doc asked bluntly.

The cowboy's hand fell to his holstered gun. Doc continued to clean the wound. The room echoed the man's silent answer.

"You're one of Rinehart's new hands, aren't you?" Doc went on, treating the cowboy's mute reply as if it were conversation. "I saw you at the Gold Dust early last night. You and your friends were riding that homesteader pretty hard." Doc probed deep into the wound. The man grimaced. "He do this to you?" Doc inquired casually. The cowboy grunted.

Beneath the weathered skin, his features were ordinary. There was nothing to distinguish him from any of the other drifters or hands who frequented the streets and saloons of Cross Creek. Their number had grown recently. With nothing holding them to a job but money, they embroiled themselves in the growing dispute between the ranchers and the homesteaders to sanction their own wildness. Hank Rinehart, one of the big ranchers, was this man's employer.

"Look, friend," Doc spoke sharply. "Whoever did this to you has got you worried. You're lying low or you would have come to me before this."

Still, the man said nothing. It was customary for doctors to report any kind of incident involving firearms to the sheriff, in case an investigation was warranted. It was clear that this cowboy had no fondness for the law. He swung himself upright as Doc wrapped the bandages around him.

"Mister," Doc said when he was through, "I've seen this kind of trouble before. Now I suggest that you pack up your gear at Rinehart's and then you ride out of here. The sheriff's bound to get wind of this and come nosing around. Do yourself a favor and leave these parts while you can."

The cowboy gave a derisive snort. "Well, now, thank you Doc," he said, his tone cutting. "I'm pleased you feel that way and I surely do 'preciate your advice. Think I just might follow it—"

"You young fool!" Doc snapped at him. "I'm not doing it for you, so spare me your thanks. I know your kind well enough. The sheriff more than likely won't find anything to pin on you or whoever did this to you. And it'll just fester inside of you 'til you set your sights on revenge. Then you'll start pickin' off anyone you think had something to do with it. You'll get your friends to help you. The list will grow. And those fool nesters won't know any better either, because they don't like what Rinehart's doing to 'em and they sure don't like the men he's hired. They won't take your harassment sitting down. No, I'm doing the favor for them as much as you, but it might just happen to save your hide. Just get out of here as quick as you can."

Doc spoke to me over his shoulder. "Meg, you get this man a shirt. No sense advertising he's had trouble." I did as he said, going to the small chest where we kept a supply of washed and mended clothing, those articles that had been left behind from time to time when patients found it easier to replace their belongings than trouble with the washing and repairing of them. Digging through the assortment, I picked a faded cotton shirt that was likely to fit him. It bore the stitches that marked the previous owner's injury.

"Why, thank you, Ma'am," he said as I handed it to him, boldly letting his eyes rove up and down my body suggestively, making me uncomfortably aware of my night attire and of the thick, sleep-loosened braid that tumbled down my back. My hand went protectively to the ruffle at my throat, as if it could ward off the eyes that penetrated my clothes.

"You be on your way!" Doc said sharply, catching the exchange. The wounded cowboy obliged, but not before flashing me a impudent grin. With an impatient frown, Doc ushered him to the door.

The instruments had been cleaned and the soiled clothing picked up by the time Doc returned.

"You'd best be off to bed, Meg," he spoke harshly. Without a word, I left him, used to his moods by this time.

Doc made no mention of the early morning visitor or of my birthday later at breakfast, before leaving for his calls that day. I was working in the garden patch at the back of the house in the late afternoon, carefully extracting the weeds before they choked the life from the delicate seedlings, when he finally returned. I brushed aside the stray wisps of hair from my brow with the back of my wrist, having misplaced my gardening gloves and not daring to use the hands creased with the rich, dark soil, and I waved as he rode Coalie around back. I smiled appreciatively at the spare horse he led alongside of him.

"She's real pretty, Doc," I said, admiring the looks of the clean-limbed filly. "Can she run?"

"She does all right." He spoke rather blandly for an astute observer of horseflesh and for a person who had more than a passing interest in them. Although it was customary for doctors to rent their horses and rigs from the livery stable, Doc claimed that the livery teams were undependable because doctors were, on the whole, good drivers and were therefore assigned the animals considered unsafe for the inexperienced. He owned Nutmeg and Coalie, both trained to ride and drive. Coalie, although not flashy, possessed a surprising speed. Doc relied on his horses. It was not unusual for either of them to return with Doc asleep in the saddle or buggy after a long day of doctoring in the countryside. But this high-bred filly looked like she would need some mellowing before she could match Nutmeg and Coalie's dependability. "Do you want to try her?" he asked, offering me the opportunity I had hoped for since I first saw the beautiful animal.

I smiled delightedly and, rising from the garden, went quietly to her. She was a burnished chestnut, and her face was marked with a perfect blaze. Dark, intelligent eyes looked into my own. "Is she used to skirts?" I asked him as she nudged me with her head.

"Well, she's seen 'em," he said as he handed me her lead, "but I doubt she's felt 'em."

I walked her about first and then led her over to an old, upended crate. Using it as a mounting block, I hoisted my skirts high and climbed onto her back. Letting her get the feel of me and speaking to her gently, I guided her by just the halter and my knee. I urged her faster and she circled the clearing in an effortless, floating gallop until I gradually pulled her to a stop, coming to a standstill before Doc Elliot.

"She's wonderful," I said to Doc, patting the filly's neck. "How'd you happen on her?"

"Oh, I found her over at the Robinson place. Seems that this here filly was the cause of their trouble. One of the little ones spooked her and got concussed for a thank-you. She's still pretty green. I'm not exactly sure how John came by her. He's a man with a weakness for a good-looking animal. I think she proved a little too rich for his blood. He offered her to me as a settlement for his debt. Didn't seem right to pass her up, since they couldn't have kept her and it was a way for them to wipe the slate clean."

Dismounting, I went to the filly's head and stroked her face. Doc was right. The Robinsons had a chicken-scratch homestead with nothing to spare and eight children who had a penchant for accidents. Just the past year, between five of them, there had been seven broken limbs. Mr. Robinson's wife's egg money carried them through the lean times. Occasionally, he made some extra money by racing one of his good-looking horses, the purse making up for a poor crop, but more often than not, his horses were a poor man's extravagance.

"But she must be worth more than that, Doc! They could have sold her for more than your doctoring bill."

"Well, I did throw in twenty dollars in the bargain," he admitted sheepishly.

I hid my smile at the crack in his granite exterior. "How do you think she'll take to the buggy?" I asked him as he unstrapped his saddlebag. Some horses proved to be worthless at it, and usually it was these that landed up at the livery, the bane of some unsuspecting driver.

Doc cleared his throat and did not look at me as he finished unsaddling Coalie, turning him into the corral to join Nutmeg. "She's not for driving," he said, "unless you want her to be. The filly's yours. You'll be the only one to use her."

Bewildered by the magnitude of his gift, I stared at the man who refused to meet my eye, the gruff, rude and cantankerous man who meant more to me than anyone in my life, the man who rarely offered praise or thanks even when I deserved it.

"But, Doc, she's too valuable—" I began to say.

He held up his hand, halting my protest. "Happy birthday, Meg," he said softly, and then he turned and walked to the house.

It was only after the gift of Sassy, which is what I named the filly, that I truly knew how much I had come to mean to Doc. He was not a man of extravagant gestures. I was aware of the significance of the beautiful animal: I had come to fill the emptiness in Doc's life that he had filled in mine.

I was determined to learn more about the man who was so reticent with his feelings, yet who gave so unstintingly of himself to his patients. Doc himself presented the opportunity the day he claimed that Millie Fowler's chronic complaints were no more than a product of a neglectful husband. My respect for Doc's observation and sensitivity emboldened me.

"How is it that you never married, Doc?" I asked him quickly, expecting him to ignore the question that trespassed on his past. I joined him in his office, a functionally furnished room heavy with the scent of stale tobacco and medicinal odors. Journals and circulars thickly padded the top of the desk he sat at, while correspondence and papers brimmed from the cubbyholes. An examining table and dressing screen were positioned at the center of the room but the most notable item was a large glass jar containing Doc's collection of misshapen bullet slugs that sat atop a glass-shelved bookcase. It was a useful conversation piece, he claimed. He removed the spectacles he had taken to wearing recently and rubbed his hand over his face. His thick hair was almost completely gray now. He had no pictures or items of a personal nature that gave a clue to his former years. Unlike his office, his small bedchamber that I swept and dusted once a week was methodically neat, his army habits deeply ingrained over the years. He looked at me thoughtfully and a small smile tugged at the corners of his mouth. Removing his pipe, he spoke frankly. "I almost did marry, once. Does that surprise you?"

I shook my head. "No."

"She turned me down. Couldn't see her way clear to leave her father. He was all alone and she looked after him. She was very young." A brief look of sadness crossed his face and then was gone. He elaborated no further on his lost love. Seeing the concern in my eyes, he gave me a keen look. "Now don't you go feelin' sorry for me. Wouldn't have gone to medical school otherwise."

Incurably romantic, I suffered the loss of Doc's love along with him. "Did you ever see her again?" I asked him.

"She died not too many years after that," he said shortly, and I dared not intrude further.

"Later," he continued voluntarily, "I joined the army because of the war and, after the war, I decided to stay on. It didn't seem too bad a life."

"Well, then, why did you leave, Doc?"

This time a distinctly pained expression crossed his face. "I left because I had to," he said simply. Then, seeing my confusion, he began to explain. "It was after the war. And we were all so damned tired of the killing. The enlisted men were being sent west to put down the Indian uprisings. All they wanted to do was go home. They'd seen enough fighting and dying to last them a lifetime.

"There turned out to be some bad blood between the officers and doctors, we being responsible for sending on reports to headquarters about the health and sanitary conditions of the camps. Well, I guess they turned out to be pretty damned critical, mostly because of the whiskey and the camp followers attaching themselves to the units. The commander refused to send the reports on his superiors.

"About the time the feelings were running the highest, I had a typhoid patient. He wasn't much more than a boy, really. There was an infantry private who happened to be the nurse on duty that night. I instructed him to give the patient an ounce of brandy every two hours for stimulation. When I came back at dawn, I found the private in a drunken stupor and my patient dead.

"I dragged the private to the guardhouse and entered charges of negligence against him. An hour later I saw him wandering the grounds. The charges had been dropped. The commander claimed that I didn't have the authority to make them and the private was not guilty of negligence because caring for the sick wasn't a military duty.

"That was enough for me. I was sick of it and I

wanted out. I wasn't heading any place in particular
when I came to Cross Creek. It seemed like a pretty
good offer that the town made me. So I took it. Call
it fate, if you like."

The evening light faded, leaving the room in darkening shadows. Still, the lamp remained unlit. Instead, each of us sat in silence, reflecting over the
past. Then Doc's voice broke the silence. "We all have
our ghosts, Meg," he said quietly. But a little time
still remained before I was to appreciate the wisdom
of his words.

Chapter Five

IT WAS THE GREEN DRESS that signaled the end of my four years of peace and well-being at Doc Elliot's side. The morning of my nineteenth birthday dawned a bleak gray, and through the muslin curtains that framed the kitchen window I watched the day darken as the hours passed. Even the hanging kerosene lamp over the table did not dispel the gloom. I placed the coffeepot back on the stove. Taking my seat across from Doc at the table, I spied the plainly wrapped parcel Doc had left by my plate. Ignoring the food, I glanced up at Doc, pleasure lighting my face. Again, he had not let me down; he had remembered my birthday.

I fumbled at the brown paper and string. "Oh, Doc!" I gasped aloud as I beheld the length of moss green figured silk that lay beneath it. I fingered the folds of the exquisite fabric. "It's beautiful!"

He forestalled any more of my exclamations. "You take that silk over to Verna Brown, she'll make it

up into a dress for you." Enthralled by the thought
of one of Verna's beautiful creations, I looked at the
material dreamily, until at last my sensibilities returned, retrieving me from my impractical imagin-
ings. "I've no occasion to wear the kind of dress that
Verna would make up for me, Doc," I said regretfully.
"You know she does the dressmaking for Ruth
McKenna and Mary Kay Simmons. I'd have no need
for such an elegant dress."

Doc frowned at me and then cleared his throat. "I
heard you talk about that theater company that's
coming to town next month. You said something
about Shakespeare. I thought I'd take you to see it.
You could use something pretty to wear to that."

My heart overflowed with a warm rush of love at
his thoughtfulness. Doc studiously avoided any social occasion more formal than his stops at the Gold
Dust Saloon. He looked at me awkwardly, as if he
read my thoughts.

"Every girl needs something special in her life,
Meg," he said at last, with a bit of difficulty. "You
need to get out more...to dances...picnics...things
like that. You've grown up, Meg. You're beautiful—
a damned sight more beautiful than those women I
see parading up and down Main Street. I look at you
now...well, I haven't done right by you. I wasn't
thinking. All those years I let you look after
me...keeping you to myself..."

"Doc!" I said, shocked by his words. "Can't you
understand that I'm happy with the way things are?
I like being with you. You're all I have. I don't need
anything else."

He shook his head at me knowingly. "Don't turn
away from the future, Meg. You're safe here. But
we've become too dependent on one another. I'm saying this as much for my own good as yours. I care
for you as if you were my own, but I don't want to
hold you here. It's no life for you, caring for the sick,

bandaging up the riffraff that comes by. You're a beautiful woman with your future still ahead of you."

Angrily, I shook my head. "It's good enough for you, why not for me?"

"I chose it freely, Meg. And you haven't done that. It isn't right for a girl to be wanting to spend her time looking after an old man like me."

Decidedly unhappy with the turn our conversation had taken, I stared down at the beautiful gift, confused, feeling that somehow I had failed Doc.

"Meg," he said gently, "I don't want to make you unhappy. Maybe, these past few years I thought I was protecting you. Every time one of those cowhands like Hank Rinehart's comes around, well, they make me want to hide you away, not show you off like you deserve. You haven't had much of an opportunity to involve yourself with other activities or people."

"Parties, picnics, church socials?" I asked, with my eyebrows raised.

"Yes. Humor an old man, Meg. Let me think I did my best for you."

"You mean you want me to be more like Mary Kay Simmons?" I asked with a glint of mischief in my eye, for Mary Kay, in the ensuing years, had fulfilled her early promise and had become the social belle of Cross Creek. Gossip abounded about the number of marriage proposals she had received and the last count had been twenty-two.

The corners of Doc's mouth quirked upwards. "Well, it's up to you, Meg, whether you want to do me proud, or make a horse's ass of yourself."

I laughed as Doc Elliot retreated back to his usual ornery self. But I knew how hard it must have been for him to even broach the topic of my future. I never wanted him to think poorly of me, or himself. "I'll bring the silk to Verna's this afternoon," I promised, as a low rumble of thunder sounded outside. The

storm broke and the rain fell to the earth in a heavy
downpour.

Doc nodded, accepting my decision. Later, I was
to wonder if he suspected just how much a green
dress could change my life.

Verna Brown catered to the wealthy patrons of
the town. Her small shop was sandwiched between
the watchmaker and the shoe shop, across the street
and as far away from the numerous saloons as possible. Wary of my reception, I hesitantly busied myself with the fashion plates propped upright in the
window as passersby brushed past me. Holding up
a hand to shade a small piece of glass, I peered beyond the fading glare of sunlight deep into the store
to where an ornate gown demonstrating Verna's excellent stitchery was displayed on a form. Taking a
deep breath, I entered the shop.

The tinkling bell was just loud enough to be heard
above the steady hum of her sewing machine, located
behind the partition at the back of the room. The
storefront was small. Wallpaper patterned with large
pink roses adorned the walls and a hooked rug lay
at the center of the room, over the spotlessly clean
plank flooring. Four striped side chairs were positioned around the two occasional tables neatly
stacked with fashion magazines. A large cheval mirror revealed my apprehension and I tried to compose
myself as a plain woman of middle years, dressed in
a simple shirtwaist and dark skirt, came forward to
greet me with a pleasant smile.

She looked at me closely. "You're Doc Elliot's girl,
aren't you?"

"Yes," I answered somewhat shyly under her scrutiny. "Doc gave me some silk for a birthday gift and
told me that you were to make it up into a dress." I
handed her the package that I had carefully re-
wrapped and noticed her approval as she inspected

the green silk. She held it up to the light, letting it fall free, and then draped it loosely across my shoulder.

"This is lovely," she said. "Doc has excellent taste. It goes beautifully with your coloring. It matches your eyes."

"My eyes aren't green," I corrected her. "They're brown."

"Oh, no! They're hazel, and definitely green when you wear this color."

"Oh," I replied, feeling peculiarly dull, certain that all her customers knew the color of their eyes. But she smiled at me reassuringly. "Do you have something special in mind?"

We spent the next several hours poring over the plates from Godey's Lady's book and Harper's Bazaar, searching for a dress that was fitting for the beautiful green silk. We passed over hundreds of plates, all elegantly stylish, yet none of them made me want to give up my length of silk to the ornate array of overskirts, trains, frills, and flounces. In the end, with Verna Brown's complete approval, I chose a dress that was a composite of four different plates. She was well pleased with my decision, saying that it should compliment my figure nicely. She took my measurements and I made an appointment for my next fitting.

Verna Brown had been right. When I tried on the green silk at the final fitting, I turned to her with pleasure. Although not daring, the understated elegance of the dress did much to show off the figure that had been hidden for too long under winters of serge and alpaca and summers of gingham and calico. A froth of ecru lace spilled down from a high, banded collar over the intricately tucked bodice and matched the lace cuff of the long, fitted sleeve. A plain, slim skirt fell simply from the waist, a marked departure from the ornate bustles of previous years, the soft shimmer of silk being ornament enough. As Verna marked the few additional alterations that were needed, I gratefully thanked her for her efforts, but she just brushed my thanks aside. "I enjoyed working on it for you," she confessed. "So often I make up dresses that are totally unsuitable for my customers, but I have no say in the matter. No, I should thank you. You look beautiful in your dress, Miss Logan. Doc Elliot will be very proud of you."

The town was in a flurry of excitement as the opening performance of *A Midsummer Night's Dream* drew near. It was rumored that once, when Cross Creek was in its infancy, a certain young lady of one of the most circumspect families in the then wild town had run off with the principal player of the troupe. Ever since that time, expectations ran rife during every production, and the romantically inclined were much disappointed with the sedate departure of each of the traveling shows. In shop after shop along Main Street, the play was the topic of conversation, and at the livery the best rigs had been reserved days in advance for the courting men to travel to the countryside for their eager girlfriends.

Reluctant to admit to my own fervor, I busied myself around the house and garden, accomplishing no more for my efforts than if I had simply sat back to watch the dust collect or the cabbage grow. Doc was not called out of town that day as I feared he would be, but when I could talk of nothing else he left the house early for the saneness of the Gold Dust Saloon. The kindness of his escort did not extend to my senseless chatter.

Later that night, I came to realize that Verna Brown had also been right about the color of the dress. As a pair of intent green eyes looked back at me from the mirrored dresser in the dim light of my small room, it was not the beauty that shocked me, but rather that the reflection was so different from the image I carried of myself. The slightly arched brows over the wide-set eyes accentuated a heart-shaped face, with the features lightly gilded by the sun. Completing the transformation from ordinary to magical, I wore my hair free instead of disciplining it into obedience. Taking up a length of matching ribbon, I brought it up under my hair, tying it at the top, gently persuading it to fall in waves of symmetry down my back. The soft lamplight cast a shimmering web of brilliance, dusting the undecided shades with gold, so that each strand shone with life. Only by stepping lightly upon my bed was I able to see a fuller reflection and I found myself wistfully thinking of Verna Brown's cheval mirror so that the figure standing so agilely upon the bed might have a head atop the beautiful green silk dress. But I could see that the long sweep of hair falling below the straight shoulders accented the lines of the dress perfectly. Satisfied with that, I picked up my fringed shawl and reticule and in the lightest of kid slippers tred quickly down the stairs to find Doc.

I found him dressed in the gray frock coat he had last worn to Gabe Edward's funeral and cursing up a blue streak as he struggled with his tie in front of the mantle mirror. I smiled to myself, for it was the same tie he wore day after day with no trouble at all. His coat covered a vest of black wool and his boots were freshly polished. He looked quite dashing. And then, he stood shock still at the mirrored reflection of the slim green figure standing off to the side, behind him. Silently, he stared at me.

"You're lovely, Meg," he said almost sadly.

Confused by his manner, I thought I sensed his disapproval. "You don't like the dress," I said, disappointed.

He cleared his throat. "No, you're wrong. The dress is perfect. You're a vision in it. The only trouble is that if an old coot like me can see it, so will all those others. I'm going to lose you, Meg."

"Doc! You're talking nonsense!" I scolded him. "I haven't changed any...it's just the dress...and my hair..." I saw the doubtful look in his eye. "As for me leaving you," I continued pertly, "you know how I feel about that. I have no intentions of doing so. I'm doing this to please you. Remember, you brought this on yourself!"

I should have seen it then, that the green silk would bring me nothing but trouble, for it was unlike Doc to get flustered over so little. I hadn't changed, at least I knew that. But the chaos that was to follow can be traced back to that one evening. Presenting my arm to Doc, I stepped blindly into the night in a shimmer of green silk.

Chapter Six

✍ THE PRODUCTION OF *A Midsummer Night's Dream* was a spectacular success, but I remember little of it save the laughter and applause that sounded in the Cross Creek social hall, which served as the theater that evening. Indeed, all my memory of the plot comes from my having read Shakespeare's play, not from the performance of the traveling troupe of actors. True, the hall was crowded, and the press of people filled the room to capacity, and turned the warmth of the late spring night to stifling heat, but neither that nor the pure excitement of the event was the cause of my preoccupation, although later I tried to convince myself otherwise.

Doc left my side at intermission swearing that never had he felt drier, even when operating in the infernal army field hospital tents. Giving a tug to his stiff collar, he disappeared into the crowd with the promise of a cool lemonade for me upon his return. I smiled to myself at the effort he was making

61

on my behalf—I knew full well that he'd rather be
quenching his thirst down at the Gold Dust Saloon
instead of among the perfumed people surrounding
the refreshment table.

The crush of the crowd suddenly brought me face
to face with Ray Hodges. During the first year I had
lived with Doc, Ray had worked for Ab Monroe's
General Store to support himself and the gold claim
he worked up in the hills. His diligence and hard
work had paid off, it was said, and he had made good
on his claim. He was as handsome now as he had
been when he worked as a store clerk, and perhaps
even more so, for his success seemed to have given
him an aura of quiet confidence. With a start I realized that his eyes were warm and admiring, and I
flushed in confusion, for not only was Ray handsome,
with sand-colored hair and devilish dark eyes, but
he was one of the most eligible bachelors in town.
And then I caught sight of the beautiful girl at his
side. Clinging possessively to his arm and fixing me
with a poisonous stare was Mary Kay Simmons; immediately, I knew why she had turned down her
twenty-two previous marriage proposals. As Mary
Kay's eyes inspected every last detail of my array,
from the sheen of my hair and the silk of my dress
to the kid slippers on my feet, I paled as I read her
mind. Clearly, she considered me a threat; she believed me to have designs on Ray Hodges.

Embarrassed by her silent insinuations, I stepped
backward, breaking away from Ray's lingering gaze,
only to be brought up short at the solid feel of a body
directly behind me. I turned, mumbled an awkward
"pardon me," and continued to seek my escape. Raven
hair and a curious look in a pair of clear blue eyes
barely registered.

"Wait!" called a voice and, startled, I stopped.

"I know you, don't I?" He focused a searching gaze

upon me. "Meg. Meg Logan. I didn't recognize you at first," he said. "You don't remember me, do you?"

I looked back at him uncertainly. Good-looking almost to a fault, his appearance was saved by the easy way he wore his clothes. He looked to be about my age, or maybe a little older. I looked again at the shiny black hair and intense blue eyes. His face was a trifle thin, and his well worn jacket had seen better days, but his smile was warm, showing even, white teeth. A slow dawning recognition began to play at the back of my mind.

Add Matthews! Of course, how could I have forgotten him? Add had left school just shortly before I had run away. Although his parents respected the value of education, his father had needed his help on their small spread that lay to the east of town. Just then Add's gaze shifted to the people standing behind me and, although she held fast to Ray's arm, Mary Kay flashed Add a coy smile. Quickly, Add remedied the situation. With a hand at my elbow, he guided me away from them and out of the crowd to the welcome coolness of a corner refuge.

"I'm sorry, Add," I said shyly, grateful to be away from Mary Kay at last. "If you were the same height as you were the last time I saw you, I'm sure I would have recognized you right away." But as he looked down at me, I knew that no matter how much his height might have confused me, his eyes were familiar, smiling eyes, light and clear. Once, Mary Kay had spent an entire recess describing Add's eyes to her friends. But shortly afterward, at a school dance, Add had chosen me for his partner, passing her over. As I smiled at the long-ago memory, Add caught my expression and grinned back, and I did not mind that he had sequestered me from the crowd. I had always been fond of him, and this new, older Add rekindled my feelings with ease. I felt my cheeks warm under his scrutiny.

* * *

"Guess I should have taken sick more often," I heard him say to me with a glint of humor in his eyes.

It was a moment before I gathered his meaning and this time I blushed under his admiring gaze. It wasn't at all peculiar that we hadn't seen each other in the intervening years. His family's small ranch was some twenty miles from Cross Creek, and as I had ignored the social events that would bring him to town, there were few places I was likely to run into him. But I took pleasure in his gentle teasing.

It was obvious from Doc's expression upon his return, as he handed me the watery contents of the now lukewarm lemonade, that he had jumped to conclusions about Add and me. Or had he? So quickly had the moments passed since Add's rescue that I had not realized that Doc had been gone an uncommonly long time—he had inevitably been waylaid by well-meaning townspeople suddenly wishing to discuss their various aches and pains with the town doctor.

Doc nodded his welcome to Add. "How's that brother of yours doing, Add? He been taking it easy like I told him to?"

In an instant the lightheartedness was gone and in its place was a side of Add Matthews I had never seen before. And then, with a quick glance in my direction, his grim, determined look was gone.

"He's doin' all right, Doc," he said shortly, and then I remembered that Doc had been out at the Matthews place not long ago. A gunshot wound to the elder boy, Bob, he had said without elaborating, and I had not thought to question him further, gunshot wounds being common enough and mostly due to carelessness. But I found it strange that Add had not mentioned it and the sudden change in him set fire to my curiosity.

"I don't like what's going on, Add," Doc said with a shake of his head. "You tell that brother of yours to take care of himself. There's no saying what Rinehart's men might try next."

Rinehart? The very name sent a shiver through me, and the somber expressions of the two men before me did nothing to still my apprehensions. Ever since one night about a year back, when Doc had taken care of one of his riders, it seemed that Rinehart's name cropped up more and more frequently. Any time enough of them showed their faces in town there was bound to be a ruckus in at least one of the saloons they frequented.

"It's not Rinehart who's got Bob worried, Doc," Add said guardedly. "We know what to expect from him. It's Barton we're keepin' an eye on."

"Holbrook Barton?"

Doc said the name with disbelief. Holbrook Barton was the wealthiest cattleman in the territory. His cattle grazed the sweep of land extending down from the foothills to include a wide stretch of plains. The men of Cross Creek considered him to be a cattle baron. His ranch lay about forty miles due east of town, and he also kept a house in Cross Creek. His two sons, Chad and Jay, rumored to have been hellions in their younger days, helped run his place. A man with well known political aspirations, Holbrook was a respected, law-abiding citizen and had, so far, kept himself apart from the growing hostilities between the ranchers and the homesteaders. Was it possible that Holbrook Barton had become involved in the range war, too?

But I had no chance to ask any of my questions, for the lights had dimmed and as the last of the stragglers returned to their seats, Doc and Add fell silent, putting an end to their conversation. As Doc and I turned to go, Add's eyes rested on me thoughtfully and a bemused expression briefly crossed Doc's face. Reading my benefactor's thoughts all too clearly, I looked away, confused by my own emotions. Still, the remainder of the performance held little interest for Meg Logan, who concentrated instead on unanswered questions and on the light touch of a hand she had felt earlier at her elbow.

Doc was called away just as the play ended, and thus the conversation I had hoped to have with him concerning the Matthews shooting incident was delayed. His absence extended through another day and then I no longer needed to question him about it, for just as I closed the ledger on Doc's bookkeeping that afternoon I saw Add Matthews through the window, leading his jumpy half-broke mustang up to the gate. The scent of budding lilacs lightly charged the air as I stepped out to greet him.

"I'm looking for a young lady in a fancy green dress. Don't suppose you've seen her around?" he asked, flashing me a wide smile as I approached.

"Hello, Add," I replied. "There's just me today. Maybe I can help you?" He'd have to know soon enough that the girl in the green silk dress wasn't quite real.

He appeared younger without the confining frock coat and stiff collar of the other night. I found myself strangely stirred by the tanned throat showing at his open shirt and I reached out a hand to his pony to cover my confusion.

"I had a few things to take care of in town and I thought I'd see if you might like to go ridin' with me on Sunday," he said smoothly. "I remember Doc mentionin' a while back that you had your own pony now."

I smiled at him as an unreasonable surge of happiness took possession of me. "I'd like that. Sassy's fast, too. I work her out whenever I get the chance."

"We could try racing her if you like. Two Bits here

is pretty good, though he don't look like much." He gave the mustang a fond slap. "That road by Larson's place would be a good place to run them."

"I'll pack a lunch, if you'd like," I said, trying to keep my excitement from showing.

"Why, that'd be real fine." With a pleased look he climbed into his saddle, touching his hat to me in farewell. Had he looked back, he would have seen me staring after him with shining eyes.

That Sunday I watched for Add's arrival from behind the lace curtains of the front room. I wasn't quite sure of the reason for my happiness, just that I had a strong liking for Add and took pleasure in the feeling that it was returned. Doc was right. I had been too long without friends of my own and though my dedication to him remained as strong as ever, it would do me no harm to pass a pleasant afternoon with Add Matthews. Only Jess Garfield came by to put an end to my foolish behavior as he entered the front hall and spied me by the door. He was a tall, lanky, good-natured cowboy with a mop of straw-colored hair.

"The Doc told me to come by today so he could take a look at his sewing. Said if he wasn't 'round that you could do it for him." Jess had been around Cross Creek for several years, hiring on with any outfit that needed a hand when he needed a job. Presently he was working at the Bar B, Holbrook Barton's spread.

"Sure, Jess, I'd be glad to," I replied, happy to have a useful task to concentrate on. He followed me through the waiting room into Doc's office. Rolling up his sleeve, he revealed the neat row of stitches Doc had taken in an arm that had been laid open by a vicious bronc. "Guess you got too close to him," I said, smiling.

"Nope, just wasn't watchin' him as close as I should've been. Serves me right."

The wound was healing nicely with no sign of inflammation.

"Next time I come to town, I'll show you what a gentle ole' pony Sky turned out to be."

"Sky?" I inquired at the bronc's name.

"Sure," Jess grinned affably. "That's how high he throwed me the time I rode him."

Laughing at Jess' effacing humor, I completely missed Add's entrance. I lifted my gaze from Jess's bandage to find him leaning casually against the wall in the waiting room, observing us silently. My welcoming smile passed unacknowledged as Add looked with undisguised contempt at the man rolling down his sleeve. My greeting froze on my lips. Jess turned at my sudden interest beyond his shoulder and, catching sight of Add, flushed slightly before a wiley expression came to his face. He strode away without so much as a thank you, carelessly brushing past the man who stood, unmoving, in his way.

"I'll settle with you some other time, Matthews," Jess said quietly, between his teeth, and I caught the menace behind the words as he pulled the door closed.

"Didn't mean to scare away none of your patients," Add said solemnly, as if nothing unusual had taken place.

"Don't be silly, Add," I said, relieved that Jess had left and that Add's eyes now held the warmth I remembered. "Jess was just leaving. I was only checking the stitches that Doc took the other day." I waited for him to offer an explanation for their odd behavior a moment ago. But it seemed Add was determined to throw me a false trail.

"He must've waited 'til Doc was gone so that you could do it for him. Seems to me he was watchin' you while you were watchin' those stitches. Of course, maybe he saw you in that green dress of yours and wants to get better acquainted. Not that I blame him any for that."

I was not that easily distracted despite Add's attempt at flattering banter. "Add, what was all that about? Between you and Jess, I mean," I asked in a puzzled voice.

He apologized immediately. "I'm real sorry, Meg. I didn't mean to offend you. Guess I'm a mite jealous."

It was true that I was not all that experienced with men and their ways, but I didn't believe him for an instant. Whatever had passed between Jess and Add, it had not been jealousy. As determined as Add was to keep the truth from me, I was equally determined to ferret it out. But I did not advise him of my intentions. Instead, I smiled at his admission, glad for the kind of friendship that permitted such lighthearted banter and pleased by his interest. I resolved to put my questions aside until later.

Sassy restlessly pawed the earth as I saddled her, and Add held her head as she impatiently mouthed her bit while I mounted her. Add's mustang, Two Bits, came along docilely. Appalled by Sassy's fractious behavior, I did not hold myself blameless, believing she sensed my own mood.

Add was amused by her antics. "Seems like Two Bits here is on his best behavior, like me. Of course he's already put close to twenty miles under the saddle today. Your mare will be fine once you run her a bit. High spirits is all that ails her," he said knowingly.

The road to the Larson place was a widening series of curves that flattened out by the bull pasture. Sassy settled down as we followed the twisting bends under a brilliant early summer sky. A wide-brimmed hat shielded my face from the sun and my hair was securely anchored in a bun at the nape of my neck. I wore a leather vest over a thin white shirtwaist that

left my arms free for movement while providing a
measure of warmth and protection against the wind,
and a divided riding skirt, each side containing
enough fullness for modesty's sake, that fell to my
boot tops. It was a most practical outfit, though still
considered scandalous by some of the proper townspeople who would have women riding about the
countryside perched upon a sidesaddle. Anyone who
had any degree of respect for the rugged land or for
comfort did not fault a woman for riding astride.

I glanced sideways at Add as we came upon Larson's pasture, noting the plodding mustang he rode.
The mustang did not appear to be a particularly
threatening racehorse compared to Sassy. Add
glanced my way. As if reading my thoughts, he pulled
up his gelding by the roadside and took a rock from
the ground. He handed it to me. "You throw this
rock up high and when it lands, that'll be our starting signal. We'll race to that oak down the road. You
got that?" I nodded at him. Standing in my stirrups,
I threw the fist-sized rock heavenward.

"Go, Sassy!" I screamed in her ear as the rock
touched ground, setting my heels to her side, holding
on as she leaped forward. I leaned low, close to her
neck as her mane whipped at my eyes and mouth.
My hat flew back and the wind tore at my hair as,
stride for stride, we pulled away from the sorrel mustang. Wind-stripped tears blurred my vision and the
trees and field were a brilliant patch of green as we
swept by, the road to the distant oak—and victory—
a clear stretch before us. But then a ragged beat
filtered through the rushing sound of wind and Sassy's hooves, and it seemed only too soon before the
flaring nostril and dark eye of the red mustang edged
into sight. Unflaggingly, he crept up on us until he
and Sassy were neck and neck, neither of them taking the lead. Add raised his hand, lashing once, and
the pony responded, the drumming hooves pounding

in my ears as he made his move. I gave a hoarse shout to Sassy, determined that Add should not beat us, and she answered gallantly, her muscles straining under the sweat darkened chestnut coat. She stretched out fully as I called to her, giving all she had, but gradually the mustang pulled away, dust clouding the road behind him. Her last effort was not enough to make up the lost ground. The giant oak loomed closer and I was chasing the bright tail of the mustang as we passed it.

"Congratulations," I said to Add, with a wry smile. "I'll try to be a gracious loser."

"I should have warned you," he replied, lifting his hat to wipe at his sweat-lined brow. "It's the mustang blood. It has stayin' power. If we'd have kept the distance to under a half mile, you would have beat us for sure," he generously consoled me. The red horse looked calm and complacent as he stretched his neck to nibble at the grass along the roadside. Sassy, blowing heavily, was winded by her final effort, and we continued to walk our mounts, cooling them down.

"Please don't tell Doc," I said imploringly, turning to Add. "He'd be mortified if he knew your broomtail ran the legs off Sassy!"

He laughed at the thought of Doc's indignation. "I'd offer you a rematch some other time, but I don't think it would matter," he said truthfully, looking at me, and slowing his long-legged stride to match mine. His eyes were so startling a blue it was as if they had borrowed their brightness from the sky. I saw warmth and love in his gentle expression.

It is easy to understand why I thought I loved Add. He was handsome enough and kind enough for any girl to build her dreams around, and I was a novice at relationships with men. Blooming under his admiration, and unaware of the deeper passions that lay dormant beneath the warm regard I had for him, I confused my sentiments for something more than they were.

But neither of us knew that then. Leading us back to the spot where we had left the picnic basket for safekeeping before the race, he quietly spoke his mind, filling my head with a sweetness I had missed from my years spent at Doc's side.

"You know, Meg," he said, lightly gripping my hand and holding me back before we reached the shady spot, "I couldn't believe it when I saw you the other night. It's been years since I'd laid eyes on you. You weren't at the picnics or at the big doings on the Fourth. I couldn't have missed you. No one could. You're too beautiful for that."

I was speechless, unaccustomed to such compliments, uncertain how to respond. But Add seem to understand my reticence and did not take offense.

"I hope there's no one else you're seein' right now, Meg, because what I'd like most is for—"

The sound of hoofbeats interrupted him and, distracted from our conversation, we scanned the horizon. A screen of white dust gave way to the form of a horse and rider.

Add's face hardened as he squinted into the sunlit path of the oncoming horseman, reminding me of the night of the play. And though he did not draw his gun, his hand hovered close to the holstered Remington revolver. The black horse sprayed us with dust as the rider pulled him to an abrupt halt before us.

"Howdy, Add," his rider said coolly. He was of his middle years and I wondered how he had survived his younger ones, for his posture and manner were that of a man who spent his life looking for trouble. "Ma'am," he nodded politely in my direction, but his manners did not set me at ease.

"Heard you've been lookin' in the wrong places

for your calves, Add." His voice was smooth, but he fooled no one.

"I take what's mine, Egan, nothing more," Add said tersely, but a muscle twitched in his cheek.

Egan ignored the signal. "How's your brother feelin' lately?" The words, though friendly enough, were not intended that way.

Add drew his gun.

"Add, no!" I cried in alarm. But I needn't have worried. Egan pointedly ignored the Remington.

"Now you know you ain't gonna shoot me, Add," he said in too patient a voice. "In fact, that's your problem," he continued. "You ain't a killer. You're out of your league." He narrowed his eyes against the sun as he sat his horse loosely, with all the strength of a coiled snake beneath his outwardly casual posture. He reined his horse around. "I'd be countin' those calves real careful if I was you," he warned, holding in his restive mount, and then, with a tip of his hat, he stared at my face just a shade too long before putting his spurs to the black. He disappeared as he had arrived, blowing dust in the peaceful afternoon.

It was as if Add had forgotten me. He stared off into the distance and I spoke to him twice before he finally turned back to me with an apologetic smile.

"Add, you tell me what that was about. I want to know!" I demanded stubbornly, denying him the chance to put me off this time. Even so, he didn't begin right way, but instead walked silently alongside me until he found a spot to his liking beneath an old cottonwood with good grass for the animals. We left the horses to graze and I sat down beside him. When he began to speak, his voice held a weariness I had not heard before.

"Both Pa and my brother Bob were wounded at the beginning of the war," he said, closing his eyes against the memory. "As soon as they were well enough, we all left Ohio and came west to take up land. A new start, Pa said it was. He and Bob each filed claims—Bob being over twenty-one was entitled to his own—and they planned on working 'em together. According to the Homestead Act, all you needed to do to prove 'em up was work the claims for five years 'til it was free and clear. Well, that suited us fine. We picked the best land, with water bordering the property, and then later Pa and Bob both preempted an extra quarter section. They had already proven up their claims when Hank Rinehart moved in. Not long after that, Holbrook Barton followed him.

"Things were peaceful enough at first. There weren't so many of us homesteaders back then. Then Barton and Rinehart put their heads together and decided they didn't want anyone else movin' in, they wanted the best land for themselves. Course, Barton's always let Rinehart do the strongarmin' for 'em. He likes to keep his reputation clean. But they ran into a problem. Without water, all that land out there is useless. So they filed on quarter sections with water rights for their headquarters and then had some of their hands do the same, makin' an agreement with 'em that they'd be signing their deeds over to 'em afterwards. I can't fault their thinkin'. All that government land out there that's free for grazing just isn't worth a damn without water. And that's where we figured in.

"They tried to buy us off at first. They didn't want a small spread like ours or any of the others using up the water on crops, or maybe fencing it off so their cattle couldn't get to it. Up 'til now, we've done all right for ourselves. We came out to homestead, just like the other folks. We worked hard and we were lucky. We even run about a hundred head of beef. So that makes us a little more understandin' of the way they see things. We use that public domain same as they do. Everyone has a right to it. But not everyone has a right to the water if it's running through someone else's property. There are creek beds dryin' up out there that never did before and the old timers are sayin' we're long overdue for a drought. That's what's really got 'em worried. Because there's a law on the books sayin' that the first person that lays claim along a stream has the say of how that water gets used when there's not enough to go 'round."

"But I don't understand, Add. You own your land free and clear. They just can't drive you off if you won't sell to them!"

Add gave a chilling laugh. "There's more than one way to drive a man off his land, Meg. You're right. We won't scare off. That man Egan and some of his friends were responsible for driving off the Henderson family. Killed their boy's pet dog, set fire to their barn, and scared Mrs. Henderson so bad with night raids she near went crazy. We think he had something to do with Bob's accident. Of course, we can't prove it. But they've got different ways of dealin' with folks like us, the ones that don't scare so easy."

"What do you mean?" I asked uneasily.

"They've formed a ranchers' association. Only not everyone can join. Barton and Rinehart belong and some of the other spreads do, too, the ones that were here before them and are too big to be pushed around. They decide the policy. And they decided not to let any of the small ranchers or homesteaders like us take part in the spring roundup. Our cattle run with those others, on the public domain. Spring roundup is when the winter and spring calves get branded. That means we don't get to claim our own calves, even though they're following their mama's heels and she's wearing our brand. The association declares all the unbranded stock mavericks and then at the end of the roundup, they divvy them up among themselves and put their own brand on 'em.

"Now there's even talk about a law bein' passed makin' it a crime for anyone to brand a calf between February and the spring roundup. That's when the little ones get dropped. That means that even if we came across our own stock while riding the range, we'd be arrested and accused of rustlin' if we branded 'em. If we can't take part in the roundup and claim 'em, and can't brand 'em on the range, we'll be wiped out."

"But how can they get away with that?" I demanded. "Surely it's against the law?"

"Against the law?" Add repeated bitterly. "How do you think those laws got passed? The ranchers' association is made up of the richest men in the territory. The politicians listen to them. And they get the laws passed for them. Believe me, Meg, it's all nice and legal."

"What will you do, Add?" I asked, stunned by what he had told me. There had always been rumors of trouble between the cattlemen and homesteaders, but the incidents had been small. A missing cow, dubious ownership, angry words. Never had I guessed it had reached this volatile state.

"I'm not sure yet. Bob's moved back in with us. He was worried 'bout Ma. So far, it's been petty things over at our place. They trample our crops with their cattle and we put up fences to keep 'em out. They pull down the fences. I'd say they plan to use us as an example for any newcomers that come along with thoughts on settling down in these here parts. Probably figure once they get rid of us, some of the other homesteaders will scare off, too, since we're 'bout the strongest of 'em. Guess we'll have to see what they try next."

"Can't you and some of the smaller spreads band together?" I asked.

"We tried that, right at first. But folks around here are like the Hendersons. They scare real easy.

You can't force 'em to stand up with you. Someone's gonna get killed one of these days. The association's hired stock inspectors to ride the range, making sure their orders are being followed. They're no more than hired killers. That man, Egan, was one of them. It was one of them that shot Bob."

"Is Jess Garfield part of it, too?" I asked, recalling the antagonism between them earlier.

"He's one of Barton's men," Add answered shortly.

Suddenly, I was very much afraid for Add. He sensed my thoughts. "We just take each day as it comes, Meg. That's all we can do right now."

Thickly forested mountains rose in the distance, their naked, wind-ravaged peaks worn smooth by nature and time. A hawk soared lazily above and I traced its path with my eyes, savoring the beauty of the moment, envying the bird's uncomplicated freedom.

When Add reached out to me, I went to him unhesitatingly, for as he unburdened himself to me I had felt as if he had already made me part of his life. Tracing the curve of my jaw with his fingertips, he raised my face, covering my lips with his. I came alive under his searching mouth, the sweet sensation holding me captive even more than his embrace. His kiss spoke of his need for me, and I awakened to the longing of a new kind of love. I responded with an intensity that left me shaken. Finally, I pulled away from him and stood, afraid and confused, my breath ragged.

In silence we walked together where our horses grazed the rich grass. He held Sassy's bridle as I mounted, laying a gentle hand on her burnished neck as he handed me the reins, speaking the words that to this day leave me wondering whether I was a participant or a catalyst in the events that were to occur.

"I don't know how this will all turn out, Meg. The

way things are, I've nothing to offer you because I can't promise what tomorrow will bring. Can you understand that?"

I nodded, my throat tight with unspoken words. Gratitude and love whelmed up inside me. Doc had taken me in because I had no place to go. But Add wanted me for myself. I thought that was enough. I did not know what tomorrow would bring, either, but I believed in Add.

Chapter Seven

IT WAS ALMOST TWENTY MILES from the Matthews place to town, yet in the beginning Add traveled that distance every Sunday on his tireless mustang, Two Bits. During those days, our friendship deepened. We rode and picnicked together, the companionship we shared answering needs for both of us. Add found in me a willing listener who, for a few short hours a week, helped him forget the burden he carried. Meanwhile, I continued to blossom under Add's attention, welcoming the frivolity, for it was a new experience to me. Doc took my late blooming in stride, offering only a raised eyebrow when he found me gazing idly out the kitchen window, ironing undone, with a smile on my face.

I had a real affection for Add, no mistake about it. But the mood of our first kiss under the cottonwood had not been repeated. Afterward, I thought it was because Add held himself in check, that he did not press his suit until he could declare his intentions

79

to me. I would find him at times studying me with a quiet intensity, but never when he looked at me did his eyes hold the deep burning passion that flared in them at the mention of Barton or Rinehart.

Only one incident marred our plans that summer, on the day of the Independence Day festivities. Add did not show up at all, and several days passed before I learned from his neighbor, Ed Peterson, that Add had spent the day butchering his steers that had gotten tangled up in the barbed wire his family had just strung across their property. Later, Add told me they had found fresh hoofprints of mounted horses near the downed animals, which meant the cattle had been driven into the wire. Add suspected that Rinehart or Barton was responsible, but he had no proof.

On a Sunday in the middle of the summer, the trouble assumed new proportions. When it was well past the time of Add's arrival, I saddled Sassy and went to wait for him at the edge of town.

The hoofbeats of a horse being pushed to his limit set my heart to pounding and I held Sassy in as she sidled about in the path of the oncoming mustang. Even at a distance I could see the frightening look on Add's face. He pulled up his horse at the last moment. "It's my pa, Meg. He's been shot. We need the Doc."

I wasted no time asking questions.

Doc loaned Nutmeg to Add, leaving the spent mustang behind. We headed for the Matthews place but it was only when we stopped to rest our winded horses that Add grimly told us the circumstances of his family's latest misfortune.

"Pa didn't come home last night," he stated flatly. "He'd been out looking for those injured steers, the ones that survived the run-in with the barbed wire, to see how they were doing. Bob and me, we left before sun-up to look for him. We figured he'd be somewhere along the creekbed, thinking those steers wouldn't be up to traveling far. We were right. Each one of 'em had been shot as it came down to water. We searched for Pa and found him by the willow thicket along the creek. He'd been shot in the back. Bob took Pa back to our place and I came for Doc. He was still alive when I left . . . If I ever get my hands on the murdering bastard that did this, I swear I'll kill him!"

"Hold on there, Add," Doc cautioned. "Your father may pull out of this. He's a strong man. You save that feeling of yours. You might not be needin' it."

"No! You listen to me, Doc," Add fairly shouted at him, "I don't care what happens from here on in. I'm goin' to make 'em pay for what they've done to us. They're not taking our land from us. The sooner they realize that, the better!"

Doc shook his head at me while Add stared off into the distance with a stony expression. There was no reasoning with Add while he was like this. He needed time to cool down.

The Rocker M, the Matthews family's small spread, lay in the southern half of the valley. A deep creek, flowing down from the slopes above, curved protectively about the holdings, the choicest parcel in a basin that alternated wide open spaces with patches of dense wooded growth. The creek narrowed as it worked its way through the valley, branching across the rich green floor. Sleek cattle grazed in the distance and at the boggy banks of the creek. It was easy to understand why Holbrook Barton would want this land for himself.

We rode up to the Matthews place just in time to hear Add's mother arguing with her older son in front of the low log house, entreating him to stay out of trouble. "Talk some sense into your brother, Add!"

she implored him, for the moment dispensing with
a welcome. "It might not have been Rinehart a'tall,
but Barton that done this. At least wait 'til you can
talk to your pa!"

"Oh, hell, Ma. He was shot in the back! He ain't
goin' to be able to tell us a thing 'bout this," Add
replied, dismounting as his brother Bob rode away
after no more than a brief nod at Doc and me. "Can't
hurt for him to do a little investigatin' on his own
before the sheriff gets here."

Although Add had given him the news, it was
unlikely Ed Thatcher would show up before the next
day, seeing how late it already was and given his
loyalties. Hallie Matthews wasted no more time discussing what couldn't be changed. The tall, spare
woman gave us a terse welcome and led the way
through the main room into the bedroom opening off
of it.

She had done all she could for the man lying on
the iron bedstead under the quilted coverlet. The
bullet had passed through her husband's ribs and
the bleeding had stopped. She had cleaned the wound
and bandaged it tightly. Tom Matthews's color was
poor, but that was to be expected. He did not waken
as Doc examined him. All we could do was wait.

That evening for supper Hallie Matthews served
up a thick stew that had been simmering on her
stove. Add scarcely spoke as we ate and purposefully
avoided my eye, choosing to shut me out. Trying not
to mind, I exchanged pleasantries with Mrs. Matthews and admired the few pieces of fine furniture
that had made the journey with them all the way
from Ohio. The fire in the large hearth gave the room
a false sense of cheeriness. Add paced restlessly about
until well after we retired for the night. As I lay in
the corner bed of the room, I longed to go to him, but
I knew what my reception would be. Afraid of his
rejection, I remained silent, only Doc's gentle snores

across the way breaking the quiet. At the sound of Bob's horse, Add left the house to meet his brother. From a window, I watched them as they disappeared into the yawning darkness of the barn, leading Bob's tired animal.

Tom Matthews had regained consciousness by morning and was much improved. Encouraged by this welcome news, I greeted Add in good spirits, looking across the breakfast table at him expectantly. But if Add was relieved, he hid it well. In spite of Hallie's cheerful talk, Add's gloom cast a pall over all of us.

Still, I was surprised at the depth of his feelings. I had expected Add to rail against the underhanded dealings of Rinehart and Barton, but I did not understand this cold silence.

When we were ready to leave, Add led Sassy from the corral for me.

"I'll take good care of Two Bits until you get back to town, Add." He did not answer, and I gave him a searching look. He stared out across the valley, as distant as he had been during my entire visit. And then he told me to send the mustang back with Ed Peterson, rejecting my offer to return the pony myself. Crestfallen, I listened as he explained that it wasn't safe, that he didn't know what Barton or Rinehart might be planning and he didn't want me coming back to the Rocker M and getting in the way. His blue eyes were shadowed and it was obvious he wished me gone, as if I were already an unwanted encumbrance. An unspeakable feeling of dread came over me, and I knew he planned to get his revenge.

I wanted to curse and shout at him in defiance. I had shared his burdens from the first, it was not fair of him to shut me out now. But he curtly cut me off as I expressed my fear for him. Then, as if to reassure me, he placed his hands on my shoulders and gave me a brief kiss. "I'll see you when I can," he said.

"Please thank your mother again for me, Add," I said somewhat stiffly as I saw Doc leave the house. Mounting Coalie and leading Nutmeg, Doc rode over to where I waited. I looked at Add once more, but it was no use. His mind was made up. Nothing I could say or do would change it.

I tried to tell myself that his anger would cool and that when it did he would once again be my caring friend, and that our happy times together were not over. But his coldness left me oddly bereft and somehow betrayed the closeness we had shared. Swallowing my bitterness and hurt, I rode with Doc away from the valley, leaving a stranger behind. Somehow I knew that Add had slipped beyond my reach.

I tried not to hold Add's decision against him, telling myself he was doing what he thought best. I learned from Ed Peterson, when he came by for Two Bits, that Tom Matthews was making a good, if somewhat slow, recovery. But I couldn't help worrying that Add's hot temper, so tightly under control the last time I saw him, would overwhelm his common sense. I worried over him and I damned him, too, because I wanted to be part of his life, troubles and all, not cut off from it like some child that needed cosseting. As the summer days gave way to the crispness of early fall, I tried to think kindly of him and rode to the places we had once shared, thinking to rekindle the closeness I was missing. But instead, a stubborn resentment arose in me at the way he had treated me, the way he had dismissed me from his life until my presence would once again be convenient.

I kept abreast, from town gossip, of the latest incidents in the undeclared war between the ranchers and the homesteaders. Every night I badgered Doc for information he might have picked up, until he accused me of taking him for a rumormonger. But all I wanted was to reassure myself that Add was not involved in the recent disturbances. Little did I realize how right Add's instinct for trouble had been.

It was just a coincidence, I believed, that one day I happened to overhear a small group of men standing by the potbellied stove in Ab Monroe's General Store. They were warming themselves against the chill of a crisp fall morning as they helped themselves to the crackers from a nearby barrel.

"...well, he got what was comin' to him, thinkin' he could take on Barton's riders like that. Damned homesteaders."

I froze in my tracks, blatantly eavesdropping. "Leastaways, we don't got him to worry 'bout, no more. He got what was due 'im, I say. He won't be stayin' on now. Bet them Matthews'll be gone 'fore you know it." The speaker glanced over his shoulder, his eyes falling on me knowingly.

I did not think about the stares or my forgotten purchases as I abruptly left the store and hurried down Main Street, unmindful of the people I brushed aside in my urgency to find Doc. I burst into his office, but the rooms shouted back their emptiness. I ran to the kitchen and looked out back to where Nutmeg and Coalie peacefully grazed. Doc would be close by—but then a shred of reasoning replaced my frantic thinking. Doc probably would rush off to the Matthews place, but it was just possible that he might forbid me to accompany him. He would return to the house soon enough. I would leave a note for him. If he caught up with me, fine. It would be too late to send me back. Hastily, I changed into my riding clothes and wrote Doc a brief message. I saddled Sassy and, flinging myself onto her back, headed out of town at a gallop.

The faltering stride of the winded mare returned me to my senses, and I slowed Sassy to save her for the miles that lay ahead of us. The very stillness in the air was like the calm before a storm. The mare snorted restively as I brought her to a stop. I looked around, troubled by a peculiar sensation. Something watched me from beyond the golden aspens that bordered the road and gave way to a dark stand of pine. The trees stretched skyward, screening the path from the light of day and hiding the view of the open spaces beyond it. Sassy's ears pricked forward as she, too, sensed the unknown presence.

There was no way for me to know that I had become a pawn in a game I barely understood. I urged Sassy forward uneasily, and she picked her way down the curving road. She snorted at the sight of the solitary rider who detached himself from the wooded depths. Sassy came to a standstill in a shaft of golden light that beamed through a break in the trees. The rider brought his horse a few steps closer, examining me as if he were ascertaining my identity and then brought his mount to a halt, holding him in across the road so that he blocked my passage. I almost breathed a sigh of relief. My fear had been of the unknown, not the flesh and blood person before me.

There was nothing to set him apart from any of the other cowhands who patronized Cross Creek. His face under the wide-brimmed hat had a narrow cast to it, and his dark eyes were coolly calculating. The lower portion of his face was unshaven and his faded shirt and work pants were none too clean. I had never seen him before.

"You're Matthews's girl, ain't you, on your way to see 'im?" He saw my surprise and took my silence for his answer. "Well," he continued, "I'm the fellow that found 'im. He's beat up pretty bad. I've been stayin' 'round his place, jus' helpin' to look after things an' all. Add, he thought you might hear of his trouble and get to worryin' 'bout him, so he asked me if I wouldn't mind goin' in to fetch you out to his place. Didn't want you travelin' alone. No tellin' what could happen, he said."

Overwrought, I was blind to the truth. "Can you tell me how he is?" I pleaded.

"Well, now, missy, why don't you come along an' see for yourself?"

In that instant, as he turned his horse about and reached for Sassy's bridle, my head cleared. But it was too late. Add had been right to keep me away. I was the tool they would use against him.

I reined Sassy sharply to the right, digging my heels into her sides. She responded with a lunge that nearly unseated me as I clung to the saddle. But I had broken the man's hold on her bridle and quickly had the mare running full out under me. She was not as fresh as his mount and he slowly gained ground, closing the gap between us. Neck and neck the horses raced and I swerved Sassy once more, but this time he had anticipated my move and, sticking to me like a burr, he reached over and wrapped an arm of steel around my waist. Dropping my reins, I hammered at him, but I could not compete with the sheer force of his strength. Damning the consequences, I kicked out at him as he lifted me to his saddle, not caring if he dropped me between the pounding hooves of the running horses. He resisted my flailings as if they were no more than a mere annoyance and jammed me across his saddle as if I were a weak-kneed calf. Then, reining sharply about, he plunged his horse down a sloping embankment to the bottom of a dry wash. Pulling up his mount, he allowed me to slide off into a heap on the ground and then, dismounting, he walked toward me.

Until he grinned, I hadn't known what true fear was. I did not need to hear his words to know his intentions.

"Come on, missy, you can fight me if you want. I'm goin' to deliver you to young Matthews after I'm through. Seems like he just won't learn otherwise

that it ain't healthy 'round these parts for him or
his loved ones."

Unsteadily, I rose to my feet, only to be knocked
backward by a push of his outstretched arm. Before,
I had seen only the face of an unkempt cowhand.
Now I saw the face of the devil himself. The thin lips
leered at me in anticipation. He undid his belt, and
the fear that clutched me gave way to a sudden
strength. I scrambled to my feet and aimed a crip-
pling kick to his groin. But he had seen it coming
and grabbed my leg; he threw me off balance and
onto my back. I struck out, kicking and scratching,
until with one arm he pinned both of my hands use-
lessly over my head, forcing my chin up and back
with his shoulder, while with his free hand he tore
the buttons from my vest and ripped my shirtwaist.
My breath became an agonizing gasp as his full
weight crushed my ribs and his legs pinned mine so
that I could not move at all.

At the touch of his hardness on my thighs, desperation forced a glimmer of hope to my beleaguered
mind. He was not wearing his gun. He must have
removed it when he dismounted his horse, otherwise
I would have seen him take it off when he discarded
his belt. I could not overcome his brute force, but if
I could manage to escape him long enough to reach
his horse and weapon, I'd make sure he would never
lay a hand on me again.

He fumbled and cursed at my divided riding skirt,
trying to hold me still, when suddenly I ceased struggling. In his momentary confusion I raised my chest
and shoulders closer to him, as if seeking his embrace. His hesitation provided the chance I needed.
Turning my head slightly toward him, I lunged forward and sunk my teeth into the side of his neck.
My stomach roiled at the sensation and the rank
odor of his unwashed body, but I maintained my
bulldog grip. As he pulled away from the punishing

bite, I rolled from under him, stumbling to my feet and toward his horse, which snorted in alarm at my headlong approach. Grabbing at the bridle to steady him, I saw the gunbelt draped carelessly across the saddle. I pulled the pistol from the holster and pointed it straight at him. "I'll kill you if you come any closer," I rasped out at him. The gun wavered unsteadily in my hand and I knew he did not believe me.

Heaving with exertion, he rose to his feet. Three long gashes streaked the left side of his face where I had slashed him with my nails, and blood trickled from the brand I had left on his neck. But his eyes gave no indication that he was aware of what I had done. He was a long way from giving me up and he smiled as he took a step closer.

"I know how to use this!" I warned, for Doc had instructed me in the use of firearms soon after I came to live with him, so that I'd have a means of protecting myself against the dubious moral fiber of some of his patients. Perhaps the desperation put a tremor in my voice, for he believed I lied. He reached across the remaining distance to me and wrapped a hand tightly in my streaming hair. He gave a violent tug, yanking my head toward him. I pulled the trigger and we both recoiled at the loud explosion of the gun. His smile disappeared and a stunned grimace took its place as he released his hold on my hair and gripped my shoulder instead. I fired again, and this time his knees buckled and he sank slowly to the ground.

Staggering to a nearby tree, I leaned against it for support as I became violently ill. Every instinct told me to go to the aid of my attacker, but I could not. As my tremors subsided, I caught a movement from the top of the embankment. It was Sassy. She had not strayed far. On hands and knees, I crawled up the rocky incline until I reached the top, then, fighting dizziness, I painfully dragged my bruised

body to the grazing horse. Grasping the stirrup
leather, I pulled myself up, steadying myself against
Sassy's side. With a shaking hand I held the stirrup
and, placing my foot into it, slowly climbed into the
saddle. Sassy raised her head and looked back at me
as I reached for her dangling rein. Her ears strained
forward at the sound of an oncoming horse. Panick-
ing, I looked for the gun and saw that it lay where
I had dropped it, by the body down in the wash. I
urged Sassy into the dense cover of the pines.

I watched the horse and rider advance through
the thick screen of green boughs, and when they
drew abreast, I called out to the rider. Doc rested his
hand by his scabbard and as I nudged Sassy forward,
I saw dismay register on his face. He had expected
trouble, but not this. As he assessed the damage to
my person, I grew aware of my disheveled appearance for the first time. My clothes were in tatters.

"I'm all right," I called out to him before he could
think the worst.

His face was grim as he dismounted and came
toward me.

"It was all a trick. They...they...wanted to use
me—to get to Add." Incoherent though I was, he
understood all too well what had happened. "I—I
think I killed a man, Doc," I said, looking back at
the wash. I rubbed a hand across my wet cheek as
fresh tears spilled from my eyes. Taking off his jacket,
Doc gave it to me to put over my torn clothing and
handed me Coalie's reins. Then he disappeared down
the embankment.

It seemed like a long while passed before Doc returned, leading the bay horse with the blanketed
dead man across the saddle.

"One of Barton's men," he said tersely. "I've seen
him hanging around town lately with some of his
friends. My guess is that this fellow here was waiting
for you all along, planning for this." He gave a harsh

laugh. "Looks like he bit off more than he could chew when he took you on."

I sobbed in reply and he handed me his clean handkerchief.

"Do you think you can make it back to town?"

"Of course, I can," I replied. At his insinuation that I might be in a weakened state, I regained a bit of backbone.

"Good," he said. Mounting Coalie, he led the bay horse alongside. Returning his handkerchief, I fell in next to him.

"Doc, when Add finds out about this, he'll do exactly what they wanted him to do. He'll fly off the handle. There'll be no stopping him. They'll kill him, Doc, and call it self-defense. It won't make any difference to him that I wasn't hurt."

Doc raised his eyebrows and looked pointedly at some of my bruises. "Well, not like they intended. Looks like he tangled with a wildcat, Meg. Even if we left him here, it wouldn't take long for his friends to come looking for him. He didn't plan this alone. When they get a sight of you, they'll know what happened for sure." Doc looked at my face and I raised a hand to a throbbing bruise I didn't even remember receiving.

The sun glanced down at us through the trees but I did not feel its warmth. Doc gave me a keen look and then spoke sharply. "You ride on ahead. Take that old trail heading north that comes in by the back pasture and make sure no one sees you like this. Leave Sassy for me to see to when I get back. I'll be along shortly."

Hurt by the tone of his voice, thinking he condemned me for what had happened, I lowered my eyes and put my heels to Sassy's sides, heading her back to town. I didn't realize what Doc knew—that the slightest bit of kindness would have broken me. The mare needed little guidance and I took no special

notice of the muffled retorts of a distant rifle that
shattered the silence in the direction from which we
had come.

Sickened by the touch of the dead man, I dragged
the tin washtub into the kitchen and heated water
for a bath, as I tried to shake the image of leering
eyes that seemed to follow wherever I turned. Ignoring the painful and dark discolorations that mot-
tled my shoulders, arms, and breasts, I scrubbed at
my skin with the harsh yellow soap, welcoming the
burning contact of the nearly scalding water against
the raw scrapes along my legs, vainly hoping that
it would strike the chill from my body.

By the time I joined Doc in his office, wrapped in
the heavy folds of my flannel dressing gown, he had
poured two brandies. One glass was empty. He pushed
the other across the desktop to me. "Drink that," he
ordered.

I complied. Still standing, I drained the glass of
its contents, sputtering as the fiery liquid brought
tears to my eyes.

Doc had me sit on the examining table, and with
a gentle touch he probed at the bump beneath my
hair, peered into my eyes, and looked at the assorted
scrapes and bruises. I still had not spoken, so he
began straightaway, as if he knew that it would never
be mentioned again.

"I've done all I can," he said. "He's none too pretty,
but at least your mark is gone from him."

I looked at him uncomprehendingly and seeing
my confusion, he continued in a softer voice. "That
man, Meg, met with an unfortunate accident today.
He was ambushed by a person or persons unknown.
There are three shotgun wounds, all from the same
weapon and fired at close range. I managed to hide
the evidence of the two .45 slugs. The third gunshot
destroyed part of his face, so there's no sign left of
those scratches. When his friends visit him at Hal

Selby's, which is where I left him after finding him along the roadside this afternoon, they'll see him in a pine box and will rest assured that no little girl was capable of doing that kind of damage to him."

Doc poured himself another drink. He looked tired and worn, his face even more lined than usual. He met my troubled look, acknowledging my wordless thanks with a grim smile. "The way I see it, Meg, there wasn't any choice. We could have made a big to-do about this, but what would that have gotten us? The man's dead. And no one was going to press charges against you. It was pretty obvious what happened. No sense in putting you through all that if it could be avoided. The whole plan was designed to bring Add trouble, either by making him pack it in, which any sane person would know he wasn't going to do, or by setting him off so that he was bound to do something foolish. I figure that I've saved his life and there's no saying how many others by keeping this quiet."

The unlit room grew dark with the falling night. I stirred uneasily. "But won't either Barton or Rinehart suspect something?"

"It's hard to say, but I don't think so. First of all, no matter what you think of them, I don't think that either one of them planned this, especially not Barton. That man's got a political reputation to consider. No, I'd say it was some of their hands who were behind it. There's a pretty rough bunch working for them now. And second, no one's going to be doing any bragging about this. Anyone who could tie that man's death to you isn't going to want his involvement known."

As I listened to Doc, I thought that perhaps he was right. Remembering the look the man Egan had given me the day he had come across Add and me, as if he were memorizing my face, it was just possible that he might have been behind my attack. I shook my head despondently. "Where's this all going to end, Doc?"

"There's going to be more trouble first, Meg. Ranchers like Barton and Rinehart, no matter how powerful, are in the minority. Right now, they're trying to protect their interests, because they see the way things are shaping up. More and more settlers moving in, like Add's people, the kind that don't scare off easy. But just now, there aren't enough of 'em to make a difference. I'd say the storm's just beginning to brew."

Despairingly, I thought of Add. I could not imagine that he would sit idly by as Barton and Rinehart continued their attempts to run him off his land. I was lost in thought; it was a moment before Doc's gruff voice penetrated my grim contemplations.

"...did you hear what I said? You're to stay in bed for the rest of the day. I'll bring you some food—"

"Oh, Doc! I don't have a concussion, if that's what you're thinking," I protested.

"You don't know what I'm thinking and I'm not asking for your opinion. You do as I tell you."

For once, I decided not to argue and resigned myself to following his orders, thinking all the while that I was glad I had not known him during his army days.

Chapter Eight

I DID NOT HEAR FROM ADD in the days that followed and I grew certain that he had not learned of the attack on me. I was relieved that, aside from the passing gossip in town, the body Doc brought in to the undertaker caused no undue comment. Incidents like that occurred, I heard people say. Doc later told me that the man I killed, Fenton, had been a drifter before Barton had taken him on. No one knew much else about him.

In my weakened moments after the attack, fear warred with anger that was as sharp as the knife-like pain of my bruised ribs. Defiance poured through my veins as I at last came to fully understand Add's dedication—a dedication that left no room for me in his life.

Oddly enough, it was Jay Barton, Holbrook Barton's younger son, who was the last of us to become drawn into the tragic web of circumstances. The fault was not his, for although he was a Barton, with the

Barton desire for power, it was Jay's very effort to halt the hostilities that provoked the killing.

I should have recognized Jay that morning as he headed his horse down Main Street and across Willow, riding with a lazy assurance, at ease under the curious stares that never failed to follow him. I had seen him around town often enough, mostly with his older brother, Chad, as they lingered in front of the saloon, or amongst an all-male gathering down by the livery, discussing the finer points of animal breeding or Rosie's girls or some other likely male topic of conversation. They had grown up motherless, and their pranks as youths had long been legend in town. By the ages of twenty-four and twenty-five, their reputations as troublemakers were well established. But it was not until he alighted from his horse, loosely tying him to Doc's hitching post, and our eyes met and held that I knew him to be a Barton. And then it was as much from his manner as from his features.

"Morning, Ma'am," he said, removing his hat politely.

"Morning," I responded, not bothering to stop or even slow my broom as I briskly swept the porch clear of the first dry leaves that littered the floor that season. I did not acknowledge him by name, although I knew it. It was rather rude of me, but I did not concern myself with niceties. Whether Barton or his sons had anything to do with Fenton's attack on me, I was not certain, but the memory of that day was clear in my mind. Jay Barton did not receive the benefit of my doubt.

"If you've come to see Doc, he isn't here. He's out at the Hutchins place. You can leave a message for him if you like." I offered abruptly, doubting he would, given his reception.

"Well, Ma'am, the fact is, I've come to see you."

"Me?" I queried, taken aback. "I don't understand. I'm sure Doc can help you better than I can."

But he aroused my curiosity, Jay Barton did, as the notorious often will. I looked at him more closely. His hair needed cutting, but it was clean, and his clothing was only lightly dusted with powder, as if he had recently taken the trouble to brush himself off. He did not have the distinctive odor that many of the unwashed cowboys we treated had. He lacked Holbrook Barton's size and stockiness, but in spite of a lithe build he carried that same aura of power.

"No, Doc wouldn't be able to help me a'tall," he continued with a slight smile as if he were enjoying my discomfiture. His glance seemed approving as he took in the color that the crisp morning air and my exertions had brought to my cheeks. "You see, I've come to ask you if you'd accompany me to the picnic that the Ladies' group is throwin' on Sunday."

Incredulous, certain that I had not heard him correctly, I stared at him, my broom forgotten as he awaited my response. My answer was curt and to the point.

"I really don't think so, Mr. Barton. I don't plan on attending this year."

But I had underestimated him.

"If I might ask, Ma'am," he observed shrewdly, cloaking his next question with politeness, "is it because of who I am or because of Add Matthews that you won't go with me?"

His boldness astonished me, until I reminded myself that the rich often felt they had that right. I decided to answer him in kind.

"To be truthful, Mr. Barton, you happen to be right on both counts," I replied bluntly. "First of all, I don't know you at all, and what I do know about you wouldn't encourage me to welcome your company. And as for Add Matthews, he's a good enough friend so that I care about his feelings. And I think you know what those feelings are, or you wouldn't have asked me."

"Well, I'm sorry about what you think of me, Ma'am, I truly am," he said looking more bemused than regretful, "but while we're on the subject, since I've offended you anyway, I'd like to ask you one more question. I know you think poorly of me because of who I am and what you've heard 'bout me an' my brother. But don't you think you could at least make up your own mind 'bout us Bartons?"

Dumbfounded, I looked into the beseeching brown eyes, not at all taken in by his charm. "Well, Mr. Barton," I countered shortly, "I know I am running the risk of offending you back, but perhaps you'll tell me the reason you've asked me to accompany you. Maybe that would help me make up my mind."

He hesitated but an instant. "Why, that's easy. I saw you in a green dress at that play. Springtime, it was. This is the first chance I've had. I came to town to pick up some supplies for the fall drive. I've been riding herd all summer."

"I don't believe you," I said ungraciously. "I don't think that's why you've asked me at all." The memory of my assault was too recent. I was suspicious of all the Bartons.

He gave me a rueful grin, in an attempt to disarm me. "It is true, Miss Logan. I meant what I said about the green dress. But I do have another reason. I was hoping that you could get to know me a little better."

"Why should I want to do that?"

He paused a moment and cleared his throat as if considering his own audacity. "Because I thought maybe we could use you to work a deal with the Matthews family, as a kind of go-between, if you know what I mean. They won't listen to reason. They shoot on sight if we even get close to their place. But you, now...you could do it for us."

"Mr. Barton," I said, barely controlling my rage,

"I have trouble believing what I'm hearing. But let me tell you this. I wouldn't interfere on your behalf for all the gold in those hills over there. Add doesn't trust you and neither do I. You must think me a complete fool to fall for a trick like that, especially since—" Just in time, I stopped myself, almost blurting out an accusation about Fenton's attack on me. I couldn't let Jay know of my part in the killing of the Barton hand.

"Especially since what?" he inquired curiously, reading too much into the unfinished words.

"Nothing. I won't do it," I said tersely.

A brief look of disappointment crossed his face. "I'm sorry then, to have bothered you," he responded, as if he meant it. "But I wanted to try. You may not believe this, but I admire Add and his family for all that they've accomplished. It wasn't easy for them. I know that. I could talk to my father if I thought it might do some good. He'd listen to me. He and Tom Matthews have been at each other's throats almost since the beginning. It's crazy. There's enough land in the valley so that a small spread like the Matthews's needn't be crowded out, if they could reach some kind of understanding."

My eyebrows lifted of their own accord, expressing my doubt.

"I know you have no call to trust me. An' maybe you're right in not wantin' to be seen with me." He paused, giving emphasis to his next words. "But in case you change your mind and you find yourself wantin' to go to that picnic on Sunday, I'll be there."

He set his hat back on his head and took up his pony's reins, not giving me a chance to issue another refusal. But he hadn't quite finished. "Thanks for your time, Ma'am," he said, again displaying the best of manners. "I'm awful sorry to have caused you any inconvenience."

Before I could respond, he put his spurs to his

gray's flanks and departed, cool and collected, not as if he had just lost his gamble, while I stared after him in bewilderment. But then, he was Holbrook Barton's son and he had learned his lessons well.

As much as I wanted to, all that afternoon, I could not dismiss Jay Barton from my mind. His words had not fallen on deaf ears. He was right. I had not made up my mind myself, and even Add was not certain whether it was Barton or Rinehart who was responsible for his misfortune. What if it was as Doc said in the case of my attack—that it was not Barton but his riders who caused the troubles that had befallen Add's family? Had I been wrong to assume the worst about Jay Barton? And even if the worst were true, it did not necessarily mean that Jay agreed with his father.

I did not trust Jay Barton, yet I believed that he had spoken the truth to me. The very fact that he valued my help in the very same situation that compelled Add to shut me out of his life made it difficult for me to stop thinking of him. It was not the compliments that slipped so easily from his lips that won me over, although in all honesty I, like half the women in Cross Creek, was not immune to his charm, in spite of his reputation for wildness. And even though the dress I wore that morning was of practical serge, not silk, I had been well aware that Jay's quietly assessing eye found me desirable. But simple flattery could not sway me. There was, I decided at last, an element of humanity running through Jay Barton.

Doc was spared my painful deliberations, being waylaid by calls for several days south of town. I did not know what he would have thought of my decision to go to the picnic. I packed the hickory splint basket that Sunday, knowing I did not consider my outing to be a betrayal of Add. He had shut me out so completely from his life that now we shared neither good

times nor bad. And perhaps, just perhaps, my friendship with Jay could bring about an end to the terrible
tensions between the Matthews and the Bartons.

I wore my new blue calico, sprigged with the tin-
iest of yellow flowers and adorned by a simply white
collar and cuffs. I had made it earlier that summer
but had never worn it, for all my days spent with
Add had been on horseback. For a moment, I wished
it were Add whom I was to meet that afternoon, the
Add Matthews who had first come to court me, before
circumstances had changed things between us. I
smiled fleetingly. Jay Barton would be eating Add's
favorites that day, moist slices of ham on fresh bread,
biscuits spread with tart raspberry jam, cheese from
Larson's dairy, and plenty of gingerbread cookies
and lemonade.

The picnic was an annual event sponsored by the
Ladies Benevolent Society. It did not draw as great
a crowd as the Independence Day festivities did with
a giant parade, shooting matches, and horse race,
but there were no grandiose speeches given by the
mayor and other town officials who fancied themselves eloquent orators. That was a strong point in
the picnic's favor. Its stated purpose was to raise
funds for the Society's coming season of worthwhile
endeavors. Each basket of food was put up for auction
to the highest bidder, who then was awarded the
privilege of sharing the contents with the lady who
had prepared it. Therefore, the social significance of
the picnic was far greater than the monetary benefits
accrued by the Society.

Most of the boxes sold for one or two dollars, for
no man would bid on any other than his wife's box—
not if he expected to live it down and have peace
again in his lifetime. But the competition for the
women who were unspoken for was keen. The bidding was always spirited and good-natured and oc-

casionally exorbitant. Mary Kay Simmons's box had brought the high bid of five dollars last year.

After every last crumb was devoured, athletic contests were organized, always of great interest to the courting couples. It was said that some years prior, the sack, foot, and wheelbarrow races had put too much strain on the former Susan Fuller, now Susan Thatcher, and her then-boyfriend, Jud Fitch. They had ended their courtship right after the wheelbarrow race, with Susan claiming Jud had caused them to lose because he was so damned slow. The townspeople watched the couple argue, with a mixture of shock and glee. I've always tended to think that the races hadn't caused the breakup but merely speeded it up. Jud left town that week and within a year had made a fortune with a gold strike.

I arrived at the picnic ground belatedly, after pushing aside my last minute doubts about the wisdom of my decision. Descending the grassy knoll by the back of the schoolhouse, I skirted the clusters of people gathering by the long plank tables that had been decorated for the gala event with red and white checked gingham cloth. I deposited my basket at the very edge, preferring to avoid the curious onlookers and their rough humor and well intentioned jokes. The tantalizing aroma of food filled the air; the sun beat down a hazy golden warmth that mingled with the fragrance of the dying grasses and the escaping odors of fried chicken and sweets, still oven-warm. An excited clamor arose when Tyler Prescott, the auctioneer for the day—he normally did duty at the Cross Creek *Gazette*—made his way to his position behind the table piled high with boxes and baskets of all shapes and sizes. His editorializing wit would soon be focused on the basket owners and bidders, who could look forward to jokes executed at their expense with the bite of good humor. Some said that the show Tyler put on was the highlight of the event.

Apprehensive about the coming meeting with Jay, I stood off to the side, away from the boisterous crowd. A burst of laughter emerged from the gathering as Tyler noticed Mary Kay's picnic basket. The handle was woven with gay pink and green ribbons that matched those in her hair. He picked up the fluttering, satin-covered handle, announcing, "All right, now, folks! Let's jump right in! You young fellas check your pockets right now, 'cause I'm sure this fancy basket's goin' to bring a fine price. Just remember one thing, boys. If this young lady don't like your conversation none, she's likely to jump in the pond!" A roar broke from the crowd as everyone recalled how Mary Kay had fallen into the pond last year, fully clothed. She had been rushed home minutes later under the frantic wing of her mother. The circumstances surrounding her mishap had never been fully divulged. Mary Kay looked aghast for a moment at Tyler's comment, but her expression quickly became sweet and smiling when she realized she had the amused attention of the gathering. "Smells like fried chicken, boys. Of course, if you don't like chicken, there's still the lovely young lady who goes with the basket! Let's start with the price of one dollar!"

Tyler played his audience well. Mary Kay's basket had brought the high price at the very end of the auction last year. By starting this year's bidding with her basket, Tyler freed the losing bidders to commit their money to their second choice. Also, the high price her basket brought would inspire the married men to gallant efforts to humor their wives and bid with the generous and carefree air of their courting days, while contributing to the public good at the same time. The competition for Mary Kay's basket was keen. But when Aaron Darcy called out eight dollars, with Ray Hodges's last bid standing at six, the competitors fell away, respectful of the man who went to such limits so quickly. Purposefully ignoring Ray, Mary Kay favored the winner with a smile that showed her dimples to perfection as the losers groaned audibly in unison.

The bidding slowed considerably after Mary Kay's jubilant beginning, with most of the prices hovering around the sum of three dollars. Some in the crowd began to make their way across the field, to spread blankets on which they would share their dearly purchased Sunday dinners. Children scampered about as their mothers divided the contents of the meal amongst them. All the baskets held treats that were special to the day.

It was too soon when Tyler hefted my basket way above the heads of the crowd. His voice seemed to call out clear to the next county. "Well, well, look it here, folks! We've got a new entry this year! Here's a basket for you, boys. Now most of us have had some of Meg Logan's fine bakin' 'cause she'll never pay you a visit without bringing along some sweet, but just in case the contents of this here basket don't sit well with you, why, she'll nurse you back to health afterwards!"

With laughter to spur the bidding, I was gratified to hear several voices raise themselves above the contagious humor of the crowd. More than pleased with the respectable holding bid of seven dollars, I was almost relieved when I did not recognize Jay's voice among those of the bidders. Looking up one last time, Tyler scanned the group and then, to everyones' surprise, pointed to a hand raised high by the tree-fringed border of the meadow.

"I'm bid ten dollars," Tyler called, "ten dollars ...goin' once...goin' twice...sold to the gentleman over yonder for ten dollars! Folks, seems like someone wants nursin' pretty bad. Come up here, young fella, and let's get a good look at you." And then even Tyler Prescott fell silent as he discovered what I already knew. Over the hush of the crowd he uttered what the rest of them were thinking. "Well, well, if that don't beat all. What's Add Matthews goin' to say about this, Jay Barton?"

Chapter Nine

✑ "Would you like to sit by those trees over there?" Jay asked. I nodded my agreement. Walking next to him for the first time, I was aware that he was not as tall as Add but that I could more easily meet his gaze. Jay's warm brown eyes glanced at me bemusedly. While I did not seek the privacy for the reasons the other courting couples did, I preferred to attract as little attention as possible, although by now it was inconceivable to hope that I could avoid the wagging tongues of the town.

"I'm sorry 'bout what happened back there," Jay said as he tethered his horse to a nearby thicket. "I was hopin' to avoid all that fuss. That's why I waited so long before bidding on your basket. Hope you didn't think I had forgotten you."

I could think of no fitting reply, so I remained silent. Taking a blanket from his bedroll, he gave it a shake and spread it over the bed of stalky grass. As if he were aware of the strain between us, he tried to set me at ease. "I thought you might not want the whole town knowin' 'bout our association, in case they might misunderstand. Though it wouldn't bother me none, if they did," he said with a grin. "I even left my gray at the livery, but I guess it didn't matter. They found us out anyhow."

Suddenly, I found myself warming to him. I had not expected him to be sensitive to my feelings. He was clearly aware of my situation. Although I had not seen Add recently, in the town's eyes it would be considered disloyal of me to be seen in Jay's company. My motives for being with Jay would not matter; it was appearances that counted. He took the basket from my unresisting hand and set it down. "I bet you were hoping that Matthews would show up and save you from me." The words were lightly said, but his eyes were serious.

My face warmed as he hit upon the truth. "I knew he wouldn't be here," I replied.

"He's a fool," he said bluntly.

"Please, I don't want to talk about it," I said, unwilling to discuss my feelings for Add with anyone. Abruptly, I changed the subject. "It wasn't necessary to bid so high for the basket. It never would have come close to ten dollars, you know."

"Meg," he said, in a tone that dispatched in one stroke all the formality of our curious relationship, providing a sudden intimacy that was as brusquely shocking as a kiss would have been, "did you know any of those bidders?"

"One or two," I said. "I think I recognized their voices. I'm not sure."

"You had eight men bidding for the pleasure of your company, including Ray Hodges and his seven-dollar bid. I'm not the patient sort. I intended to end it, so I did."

If he thought to win me over with grand gestures, he was mistaken. "You're awfully sure of yourself, aren't you, Jay?" I replied, unimpressed. "Maybe it comes easy if you have money or your father happens to be a big rancher. But let me warn you now, before you get any wrong ideas about me. You can't buy me or my loyalty."

A remote look came to his eyes and he retreated far more gracefully from my attack than I had any right to expect.

"Why don't we eat first and then talk?" he suggested calmly, ignoring my accusation.

He went at the contents of the basket with an enthusiasm that itself was a subtle form of flattery, but I could take no offense. True to his word, we ate in silence. Maybe if I had been more accomplished in the social graces or had more experience with the small talk every woman was supposed to have in her repertoire for occasions such as this, I would not have felt so awkward. I had had no need for contrived conversation with Add, but Jay Barton and I had no common ground between us.

I nibbled at my sandwich with little appetite, but when I started to dispose of it Jay halted my hand with his and took it from me. "Didn't anyone ever teach you that it was a sin to let good food go to waste?" he inquired as he finished off the sandwich.

"Yes, I'm only surprised that you concern yourself with sins," I responded, suspicious even of his good intentions.

"Now, Meg, is this how it's going to be between us? A battle? I may be Holbrook Barton's son but I was raised by a spinster aunt who was very concerned about that waste not, want not sort of thing. She made me and Chad clean our plates, do our lessons, and wash behind our ears. Does that make you feel any better about me?"

"Yes—no—oh, I don't know. Considering the reputation that you and your brother have, I'd have thought it unlikely. Unless I've been hearing lies, of course. A lot of people are afraid of you and Chad."

"Can't blame 'em. We sure did cut up some when we were younger. My father didn't know a thing 'bout raisin' boys. That's why he left us to my mother's sister after she died. Guess he figured we'd have more sense than we did. Of course, we didn't. We sure were hell-raisers."

"Were?" I asked skeptically.

"You're not being fair," he replied with a sheepish grin. "We don't do things like that anymore."

"Now you've got more important things to occupy your time. Like scaring off homesteaders?" The words flew out of their own accord.

A certain weariness came to his features. "All right, Meg. Let's talk now, since you're so set on it. I want you to listen to me first, though, before you go accusing me of things you don't understand.

"I know there have been some unfortunate incidents that shouldn't have happened. But it's impossible to undo them now, even if we wanted to." He saw the closed look on my face but, ignoring it, he pressed on, determined to present his side of the conflict.

"The Matthews family was here before us, I know that. But my father and some of the other ranchers have been here almost as long. My father owns some of that watered land in the valley, same as Tom Matthews."

"Only because he staked his men so they could buy it, Jay," I interrupted hotly, "and then they turned it right over to him. They never would have had any interest in buying that land if your father hadn't put them up to it!"

"That's over and done with, Meg, but you should know that he also bought some of the land outright from the homesteaders themselves."

"By what methods? Just how did he convince them to sell?" I asked angrily.

"Are you gonna listen to me or not?" He spoke sharply and I fell silent.

"We were here before most of those homesteaders," he continued forcefully. "Do you know what happens to range that gets overcrowded, Meg? The grass is killed because it's overgrazed. The cattle don't put on enough weight during the summer months and there's not enough forage to see them through the winter. They weaken and die, Meg. Every time we try and save some of the range for winter grazing, we find some farmer's cows feeding there." Jay's eyes held mine. "Then there's the water—"

"But Jay, it's public land," I argued. "You don't have the right to scare people off!"

"We can't sit back and watch our cattle die of starvation or thirst, either. Now," he added in a more kindly tone, "we've got no quarrel with Tom Matthews, Meg. He's been here a long time. He's honest and hardworking, not like these other homesteaders who think it's fine to put a long rope on one of our cows whenever they get a hankering for beef. We'd leave him alone. But he thinks he stands for every damn nester in the valley. If he'd let things be, he'd have no problem with the ranchers."

I shook my head. "You don't know the Matthews family, Jay. They don't care who was here first, but they do care about their friends. They're not about to stand by and watch you ruin the lives of their neighbors, shooting them or their stock—"

"I never said we did any of that," Jay interrupted coolly.

"So if you didn't, Rinehart's men did. What's the difference? You go along with it, don't you?"

Jay stared at me hard, but he avoided the question. "You can't solve the valley's problems, Meg. I thought we were here to talk about the Matthews family. I told you, if they mind their own business, they won't find themselves with any more trouble. I'll make sure Rinehart leaves them alone."

I looked at him sadly. "I can tell Add what you've said the next time I see him, Jay, but don't expect it to make any difference."

Jay settled himself back against the tree and regarded me seriously. "Well, you heard me out. I can't ask for any more than that."

I sighed, and my fingers smoothed the folds of my dress as a gentle wind rustled the edges of the blanket and blew lightly across my face.

"You look real fine today, Meg," Jay said, changing the direction of the conversation swiftly and with an intensity I found disconcerting. "I heard," he continued almost cautiously, "that you don't see much of Matthews anymore."

"Please don't, Jay," I responded, unwilling to explain to him what had happened between Add and me.

"It wasn't just our troubles that made me call on you the other day, Meg. I wanted to see you. You probably don't know this, but I've had my eye on you for a while... even before I saw you that night. I watched Matthews make his play for you... and, well... I don't get to town much. I couldn't do anything 'bout it just then. But I'd like to, now."

"I have to be getting back, Jay," I answered, afraid of what he was suggesting. I wanted to extricate myself from the situation. It would be folly to become involved with him, because while I respected his forthrightness, I didn't approve of what he and his family represented. And yet, in spite of all that I knew about Jay, I liked him. Although he had known that I would not be happy with what he had to say that day, he had painted no false picture of Add's situation in the valley.

Unexpectedly, he smiled at me, not at all taken

aback by my rejection. He got to his feet and reached
down to me, helping me up. Silently we gathered up
the remains of the picnic. And then, with a light
hand, he brushed aside a fallen leaf that clung to
my hair. "You know," he said at last, holding my
gaze, "I don't give up easily." I can never remember
him without wishing that he had.

I tried not to make comparisons between Jay and
Add, but inevitably, in the days following the picnic,
I found myself doing just that as Add's continued
absence worked against him. The change I had sensed
in him at the Rocker M frightened me. There was a
side to Add I knew nothing about. Add had wounded
me immeasureably; understanding his reasons did
not lessen the pain. It was no wonder that I found
Jay Barton's openness appealing. Both men thought
me attractive, but Jay valued me. I was not the sort
of woman who was content to watch things happen;
I needed to be part of them. Jay's regard for me
pointed out Add's very deficiencies.

But the biggest blow of all came at Ab's General
Store, just a week later, when Mary Kay Simmons
informed me with a smug smile that she had seen
Add in town, and she knew for a fact he had not been
to see me. I left the store hurt and angry. Any chance
Add and I had for repairing the damage done to our
friendship had been lost, I told myself.

Impatiently I waited for Doc to return that evening, seeking his counsel. Giving him no chance to
peruse the Cross Creek *Gazette*, I confronted him
with the news. He folded the paper, placed it on the
kitchen table, and went to pour himself some coffee
from the pot that heated on the stove. Instead of the
surprise I expected to see on his face, I saw an uncomfortable expression.

"You knew?" I accused him, dumbfounded.

"I should've told you, I know..." he admitted

gruffly. He looked at me kindly, as if that could soften the blow. "I saw him at the feed store, Meg," he continued. "When I told him you'd be pleased to see him again, he said he had no time for social calls."

Add Matthews had ridden more than twenty miles to town and had been unable to spare me a moment of his time. I sat down, defeated, in a chair opposite Doc's, trying to mask the wrenching sorrow I felt, realizing that up until now I had never given up the hope that we might mend our differences.

Doc spoke again. "I'd say that he'd heard 'bout your picnic lunch with the Barton boy, Meg, but I had the feeling that he didn't know about that yet. A good thing, too, knowin' how much young Barton bid on your basket." A half smile came to Doc's face for a moment, as if he were proud of me, and then he turned serious again.

"Of course, that's not what folks are going to say, Meg. They're going to blame it on you being involved with Jay Barton."

"I'm not involved with Jay, Doc!" I exclaimed in a voice louder than necessary. "I'm not seeing him again. I only agreed to listen to what he had to say about the Matthews family. I'm not the only girl who shared her lunch with a hand from the Barton outfit."

"No, but you were the only one with Barton's son. People 'round here don't need much to get 'em stirred up these days. This is a small town and we've got some small-minded folks living here. They know you've been seeing Add. That Barton's a fine looking young man, but he's known to be on the wild side. You're a beautiful young woman, Meg. It doesn't take much to set the tongues to waggin'. They could take sides and say some pretty ugly things about you."

"Well, it's none of their business what I do," I said indignantly.

The look Doc gave me was stern. "You know I'm

not one to give a damn for what people think or say, Meg. You've got a good head on your shoulders. But I'm afraid you don't know what you're getting yourself into. I don't want to see you get caught up in something that has nothing to do with you. This thing between the ranchers and homesteaders is going to split the town wide open. You mark my words. It's only a matter of time."

A maddening urge came to me just then, a flash of rebelliousness at Doc's words. For once, I stifled it. I possessed enough foresight to realized how disastrous a friendship with Jay Barton could be. The room turned cold as the heat from the stove died down. With a sigh, I started to prepare the sponge for the light bread. It was Doc's favorite—the dough held its shape without a pan so that it was good and crusty, just the way he liked it. With the autumn chill in the air, the dough would need to rise overnight.

"You know, Doc," I said at last, "I'm tired of this whole business with the ranchers and homesteaders and I'm tired of taking sides. It shouldn't make a difference to anyone whom I see. Add hasn't been the same since that time Tom Matthews was shot. I don't know what his feelings are about me anymore. I'm sorry for his troubles. I like the Matthews family. But I like Jay, too. And just because I do doesn't mean I've turned against Add and the homesteaders."

Doc regarded me carefully. "That Barton boy mean something to you?"

"No, of course not." Doc watched me as I covered the bowl of sponge with a plate and set another under it to catch the drips. "But what if he did? Does it mean I'm not supposed to like Jay because he's on the opposite side of the Matthews?"

"Don't forget it was one of Barton's men who attacked you, Meg. I told you I didn't believe that Holbrook was behind it, but I'm not sure about his boy. It pays to be careful."

I could not control an involuntary shudder at the memory of the brutal attack. "Jay had nothing to do with it, Doc," I said quietly, turning to face him.

"You can't know that for sure."

"Yes, I do...I'm not saying that he wasn't responsible for some of the other doings," I admitted, remembering that Jay had denied none of my accusations that afternoon at the picnic, "but he's not a bad person...He was kind to me...he's not the sort who would use a woman to further his own purposes."

Doc's face was thoughtful. "Well, I can't say I like what's happening. But I'm not sorry that things have cooled between you and Add."

Bewildered by Doc's revelation, I looked at him closely.

"Why on earth would you say that, Doc? I thought you approved of him."

"I tell you, Meg, I hardly recognized Add when I saw him. He has changed, like you say. He's consumed with this hatred and revenge. He barely spoke to me or anyone at the feed store. He's been pushing himself too hard, if you ask me. If I didn't know him, I couldn't say I'd be able to tell the difference between him and any one of Barton's or Rinehart's riders."

Upset by Doc's news, I looked away. It was a moment before I realized that Doc was speaking again.

"...I know how badly Add's hurt you, Meg. I don't want to be a meddlin' old fool, but if you want to try and straighten things out with him, you could come with me tomorrow. I'm heading out Mabel Smith's way. You could ride with me as far as the Matthews place and I'll stop for you on my way back. Give you a chance to tell him what Jay Barton had to say."

I shook my head. "No, Doc. What Jay had to say won't make any difference to Add. I told Jay that at

the picnic. It won't do me any good to see him now,"
I said. My wounds from Add's latest rejection were
still too raw. Indeed, I thought my hurt at Add's most
recent behavior might turn to a reckless anger if I
confronted him too soon.

Taking off my apron, I hung it on the peg by the
door. "Let's not worry about it anymore, Doc," I said,
forcing a bit of gaiety into my voice. "I'm done with
all of it."

Doc was right to look doubtful. Never had I been
more wrong.

Chapter Ten

I HAD NO WAY OF KNOWING that the stage had been set for tragedy to occur. The only warning I had was a premonition that came one morning, not long after dawn, when through the kitchen window I spied two grim-faced men casually sitting on their horses and taking in their surroundings. People often came around the back way to see Doc, but these strangers did not look as if they needed doctoring. Leaving the bacon on to fry, I went to the door.

Even in the morning shadows cast by the porch, the eyes of the man on the dun stud picked me out, and he stared at me where I stood in the shaded doorway. I was struck speechless by the intensity of his gaze and by the unreadable expression on his face. I could not miss the insolent sweep of his eyes, boldly assessing my body. Futilely, I tried to still my racing pulse as I remembered Fenton's hot eyes and lustful attack. Deliberately, I fought down my fear of the stranger, forcing myself to take in his appearance as minutely as he took in mine. His mouth tightened at my boldness, and for a fleeting moment I thought I detected a wintry amusement in his eye.

He wore his black, flat-crowned hat low, but as he angled his head in my direction, the steel-gray eyes continued to hold mine, the light striking his face and exposing the chiseled features. A short, dark growth of beard accentuated the prominent cheekbones and did nothing to mask the hard mouth and aggressive jaw. I thought it a handsome but ruthless face, devoid of emotion.

His friend, on a rangy bay horse, rested his arm across the saddle, noting our exchange. "Whoa, now, Jed," he said to him, with a slow grin and a soft southern drawl. "She's not yours yet."

Outraged by his insinuation, I saw that he was the younger of the two and that his face, covered by a sand-colored growth, had a narrow, boyish cast to it. As he pushed back the brim of his hat with a gloved hand, he exposed hair the color of sun-ripened wheat. With his holstered pistol strapped low on his leg, he reminded me very much of the young hotbloods who rode for Rinehart.

"What do you want?" I asked, angry at the slight tremor in my voice. These men made me very uneasy.

The man on the dun stud inclined his head in my direction, as if our first words—and not the intimate glance of a moment ago—were our introduction.

"This Doc Elliot's place?" he inquired coolly.

"Yes," I replied, suddenly irritated that the wind-damaged sign at the front of the house had not been replaced since the last storm. "Are you in the need of doctoring?" I asked tartly, striving for a braveness I did not feel.

A half smile came to his lips but did nothing to still my apprehensions. "No.... You might say I'm an old friend of his."

I did not try to hide my disbelief, so certain was I that he lied. It never occurred to me that I might be wrong, that my experience at Fenton's hands might have made me distrustful of any man who was a stranger to me. Convinced he meant me harm, suddenly I was certain that the ranchers had been behind my attack, and I knew without a doubt these men had been hired by Rinehart or Barton to finish the job Fenton had started.

"Our being here is quite a coincidence.... We were just passing through town," he continued, carefully watching my face. "Didn't think I was hearing right when the fellow down at the livery started to speak of him. Thought we'd stop and say hello."

"Oh," I replied, rather ungraciously, when, to my alarm, I saw him dismount. I took in the man's faded army shirt, with no rank or insignia to be seen, and noticed that his gunbelt holstered a nickel-plated Peacemaker. His buckskin breeches, the buff color darkened and stained with wear, clung loosely to a narrow waist, emphasizing the spare but rugged strength of his frame. From the top of his hat to the plain work spur at the heel of his boot he was covered with trail dust, except for an occasional dull patch of boot leather where the grit had been inadvertently brushed aside. His travel-weary appearance did nothing to detract from his imposing stature.

"What's so confounded interesting out there, Meg?"

Startled, I whirled around in the doorway to find Doc surveying the remains of the bacon I had been frying, forgotten in the pan. Frowning at the waste, he removed it from the stove before coming to join me at the door. But the reproach remained unspoken as his eyes widened in surprise and, muttering an oath, he brushed passed me and strode out to meet the strangers. In amazement I watched as he extended his hand to the tall man standing next to the weary stud horse. How was it possible that Doc could welcome such a rude and insolent man in friendship? Before I could grasp the implication of what I had just witnessed, the man introduced his friend to Doc. Doc smiled at him and nodded his head in the direction of the corral.

"You boys are more than welcome to rest your horses here," he said. "That field of Rube's by the livery is pretty thin right now. With McCreedy's burning down last week and folks coming to town for their winter provisions, things are a bit tight."

Helplessly, I watched as the stranger stripped the saddle from the stud's dust-streaked back and then, slipping off the bridle, turned him loose in the corral. Silently, his partner followed suit.

"Didn't think I heard right when they spoke of you down at the livery," the stranger said at last. "Figured you were a lifer for sure, Seth. That army blue suited you."

"You, too, I'd say, Jed," Doc spoke quietly as he took in the man's faded shirt. They exchanged a few quiet words before a look of irritation flashed across the stranger's face. I shuddered at the glimpse of something not meant for my eyes and sensed the danger that lay beneath the surface of the once again expressionless features. "Leave it alone, Seth," I heard him say bitterly. "It's got nothing to do with you."

Expectantly, I waited for Doc to reprimand him for his churlish behavior or, better yet, tell him to leave. But Doc did neither. He simply ignored it. I looked on in amazement.

And then, to my dismay, Doc called me to his side. Reluctantly I came forward into the sunlight, joining him as the older man, the one called Jed, observed me from behind a mask of casual disregard. This time, I dared not meet his gaze, for I knew I could not keep to myself exactly what I thought of this man who smelled of sweat, horses, and lord knows what else and who took pleasure in undressing me with his eyes.

"Meg? How about you throwin' some more bacon on for these boys?" He looked back at the two men. "We were just fixin' to sit down to breakfast. Be glad to have you join us." Severely breaching etiquette, I did not second Doc's invitation.

Doc ignored my lapse in manners, proceeding with the necessary introductions. "Meg, this here is Jed Tanner and his friend Tice Grayson."

I nodded at them, continuing to avoid the eyes of the man called Tanner.

"This is my assistant and ward, Meg Logan," I heard Doc say as I winced inwardly, piqued that Doc found it necessary to label our relationship so formally.

Tice Grayson spoke for the first time, his light eyes aimed straight at me. "That's a real kind offer, Doc Elliot," he said, giving me a smile that came just a shade too fast. "But Jed and I plan on headin' over to the barbershop to see 'bout getting a bath." He ran a hand over the growth on his face. "Believe we could do with a little cleaning up. We wouldn't want to offend the young lady none."

"You boys' don't need to worry on Meg's account. She's seen fellows worse off than you. Least you won't be bleeding your life's blood on the floor. That right, Meg?" Doc said with a look in my direction.

Unexpectedly, I was saved by Jed Tanner, who seemed at the moment to have as little desire for my company as I did for his. "Grayson's right," he said shortly, sparing me from a response that was bound to annoy Doc. "We've got some things to see to first before we'll feel much like eating."

I caught the light in Grayson's eye and bristled unaccountably. No doubt they'd be visiting Rose's girls as soon as they cleaned up. Their hunger wasn't for food. Rose's hours were accommodating, providing a customer had enough money.

"Well, that's fine," Doc said understandingly. "We'll expect you for supper, then."

Tice nodded his head in assent and both men shouldered their bedrolls and saddlebags. I turned aside as Jed Tanner passed me. Deception clung to him stronger than any scent.

Bracing myself for what was to come, I approached Doc almost tentatively as he stood by the corral contemplating the two horses the men had left behind. It was evident that Tanner held some mysterious sway over him.

"That man, Tanner, how well do you know him?" I asked casually, feigning indifference, as if his answer could not possibly matter.

His eyes became thoughtful and he stared at me as if he wished to evade the question.

"Why are you asking, Meg?"

I looked at Doc helplessly, determined to make him believe me, no matter what. "Please listen to me, Doc," I pleaded. "He means me harm!"

"Don't be ridiculous, Meg." Doc's voice was cold. "I know you've good reason to be uneasy around strange men, but you're letting your imagination run away with you."

Infuriated by his lack of understanding, I heatedly denied it. "You're not being fair, Doc," I said accusingly.

A peculiar look crossed Doc's features, and I was suddenly certain that he was hiding something from me.

"I knew him years ago, Meg, when he was a boy. Does that suit you?" he said finally, carefully weighing his words.

"But why are they here, Doc?" Dissatisfied with

his answer, I pressed him further. "Surely they haven't ridden all this way just to see you?"

"Of course not," he said irritably. "If you'd been listening instead of letting your suspicions cloud your thinking, Meg, you'd have heard 'em say they just finished up with the Hayden expedition, surveying the Yellowstone country. It's like they said—their horses need restin' up." He nodded his head at the gaunt animals. "The livery's full and Jed heard them mention my name. I'm happy to be able to help 'em out."

"You believe that?" I asked, dumbfounded. "That those men were part of a geological expedition? Oh, Doc..."

Never had Doc turned his anger on me before. "Use your head, girl!" he snapped. "They were provisioners and guides. Those easterners would be sitting ducks in the mountains without men like Tanner and Grayson to look after them."

The unbidden image of Jed Tanner came back to me. His appearance had given little away about him, save he was a man used to hard living. For some annoying reason I recalled the way his dark, thick hair touched the collar of his faded blue army shirt.

He looked at me cannily, his temper abating. "Does he remind you of someone, Meg?"

It was an odd question. I had met few men when I was a ward of the Cross Creek School, and Doc and I knew most of the same people. "No," I admitted, having demonstrated only that I had no basis for my fear.

"It's like I said, Meg," Doc said with finality. "I haven't seen him in years. If you have any questions, keep them for tonight. You can ask Jed yourself. Maybe he'll excuse you for pokin' your nose into his business and ease your mind when you tell him just what it is that you suspect him of."

It was then that I knew that no matter what proof

I had, and no matter what this man had done or had come here to do, Doc's loyalty belonged to Jed Tanner.

With Doc's betrayal, I lost my only ally. If Doc refused to believe me, who would? The answer struck like lightning. I did not trust Holbrook Barton, but I did trust his son. I would go to Jay Barton.

In the end, it was Jay Barton who came to me. He appeared at Doc's door later that very morning, and my undisguised look of pleasure brought a smile to his face. "I knew it," he said. "You've missed me and you've changed your mind 'bout seein' me. Well, I thought it might happen.... I've come to ask you to the dance tonight.... I know it's late, but I just got to town this very minute. Needed some last minute supplies for the drive."

It didn't matter why Jay believed I changed my mind. It was only important that I get the chance to talk with him. I glanced back at the waiting room. Mrs. Beechum was there, sitting beside her children with the mysterious blotches. Our conversation would have to wait. Quickly, I agreed to accompany him to the dance.

"I'd be pleased to go with you, Jay," I said in complete honesty, knowing that he alone had restored my balance that day and gratified that I would have an opportunity to see him again. I felt safe with him, as if this son of Holbrook Barton, of all people, would keep me from harm. My promise to myself—that I would not become involved in what did not concern me—was forgotten.

"Don't come too early for me," I warned him. "We're having guests for supper."

"I'll see you 'round eight," he said lightly, grinning broadly.

I nodded at him. There would be plenty of opportunity to ask him about Tanner and Grayson then.

* * *

The bright light cast a deceptive cheer over the kitchen that evening, emphasizing the discordant personalities seated together at the table. In all fairness, Tanner and Grayson had repaired themselves well. Tanner had replaced his worn army shirt with one of soft gray flannel, and a black neckerchief took the place of the soiled yellow one he had worn earlier. Grayson's face had a slightly glazed expression, and I suspected he had spent too much time at Rose's. He had the pleasant look of youth about him. Once cleaned up, he must have been a favorite of the girls. I did not doubt that Tanner had been equally well received.

The men spoke desultorily of their recent expedition, but even though I listened closely, I could neither tell whether they spoke the truth nor learn anything about them personally. But across the distance of the kitchen table, which was so covered by dishes and platters of tender roast, new potatoes, peas, squash, pickled plums and fragrant cream biscuits that the blue oilcloth was barely discernable, they discussed the merits of Mr. Hayden's work, and I found my chance to study Jed Tanner at leisure.

Without his hat, the thick hair was lighter than I had expected, a deep shade of chestnut brown, the ends that had escaped the shadowed brim streaked by sunlight. Bronzed skin stretched tautly over broad cheekbones and a thinly fleshed nose that, although it looked as if it had once been broken, was well formed. The rest of his features, now free of his beard, were just as strong. The angular jaw and chin were well cast, and the lips were parched by wind and sun. But it was his eyes—slate gray beneath dark slashed brows, reflecting nothing but their own flat color—that held my attention. Creased at the corners, probably by seasons of harsh weather, and shadowed by a thick brush of lashes, they looked up at me as he reached for a second helping of meat, catching me unaware. Noting my apparent interest, his lips twisted in a slow, sardonic smile and a tremor ran through me. He held my gaze as if he were aware of the effect he had on me. Flushing, I averted my face.

"Meg!" Startled, I looked up to find Doc's eyes upon me. "Go ahead and ask Jed whatever it is that's troubling you. I'm sure he won't mind."

"Doc!" Ascribing to the philosophy that it was always best to face one's fears head on, Doc deliberately forced me to confront our guest with my suspicions. Did Doc expect Tanner to admit that he had been sent to deal with me, just because I accused him of it?

"I'm sorry, Doc, I don't have the time now," I intervened hastily. "I'm going to the dance tonight—with Jay Barton." As I said Jay's name, I cast a quick glance at Tanner, but aside from a slight tightening of his features there was no indication that the Barton name might mean anything to him. I could read in Doc's face just what he thought of my decision. "I'm sure Jay won't mind waiting for you, Meg," he said, his heavy gray brows drawn together in a frown, his very calmness belying an iron will.

I gave in, but not for the reason Doc believed. Nothing I could learn about Jed Tanner would set my mind at ease, but all the same, whatever I did learn might provide evidence that could be used against him.

"What Doc meant by that, Mr. Tanner," I said, infusing my words with a forced courteousness, "is that I was wondering what you would find so interesting in the high country and how you happen to be in Cross Creek."

His voice when he answered was chillingly polite, as if he did indeed mind answering my questions.

"Well, Ma'am, we all have our reasons for the things we do. Now, Tice, here, he lost his horse in a poker game. The quartermaster at Fort Hall was short a packer, so he offered Tice the pick of the remounts if he'd join up." He nodded at the younger man, who silently agreed, his mouth full of lemon pie.

"And you, Mr. Tanner?" I inquired with an exaggerated politeness to match his own.

"Well, those surveyors do interestin' things, Ma'am. They're not just crazy rock-huntin' easterners. They do some charting for the railroad, so the engineers can plot the easiest way to lay track through the country, or maybe they'll study rocks to predict future mineral discoveries." He inclined his head in Grayson's direction. "That's what Tice was pinning his hopes on. And then they learn all they can about the land. The soil and river sources...it all helps 'em predict wet and dry cycles. That'll save some poor farmer from pouring his life into land best suited for cattle raising."

There was the proof! Veiled references to wet and dry cycles and false sympathy for the farmer. He did know of the trouble brewing in Cross Creek! I looked to Doc to confirm my discovery, only to find that Tanner's near admission of guilt had bypassed him completely! Doc had found nothing conclusive in Tanner's poorly camouflaged answer.

"Must have been a good summer for your cattle, Jed," Doc remarked conversationally. Believing Tanner to have acquitted himself of my suspicions, he changed the topic, ignoring my urgent look. "That rain shortage wouldn't have hurt your stock any. Those snow-packed peaks of yours must keep the valley from getting too dried out."

Tanner's features hardened, reminding me of the strained moment out back with Doc earlier in the day. "Wouldn't know about that, Seth," he replied.

"I expect that Caleb is watching over my interests for me." His voice lost its lazy drawl and his words were sharp and precise. Temporarily sidetracked from my objective of proving his involvement in the affairs of Cross Creek, I found myself wondering at his obvious education, who Caleb might be, and, more importantly, that he had a place of his own. A cowman did not give up his herd and lands to roam the hills or become a hired gun for another outfit. For whatever reason, Jed Tanner had become an outcast.

Doc took Tanner's latest rebuff with the same equanimity as the earlier one. "Well, that's a fine ranch you and your family own, Jed. That north valley in particular. It'll still be there when you're of a mind to settle down again," he declared with the presumptuous familiarity of an old friend.

An awkward gap rose in the conversation.

"Mr. Tanner," I said, breaking into the silence, "if you accompany those expeditions during the summer, what are your interests come winter?"

His eyes darkened, but he answered politely enough. "Why, the same thing, Ma'am. Come winter, I do the provisioning for the army."

"Why, Mr. Tanner," I responded recklessly, "aren't you eager to get back to your ranch? Perhaps in your absence some homesteaders have moved in!"

"Meg!" Doc drew his breath sharply at the affront, but Tanner met my challenge head on, a small smile toying at his lips at my audacity.

"No chance of that, Ma'am," he said calmly. "The land's mine, free and clear. No one but a rancher would want it. We're high up. The growing season's short. Much better land for farming elsewhere."

"How fortunate for you," I replied, tempering my reaction, stymied by his answer. As much as I would have liked to, I could not accuse Tanner directly of having connections with the ranchers in Cross Creek. I turned my attentions to Tice Grayson, thinking the younger man would be less practiced at deception and thus might spill their plans.

"And you, Mr. Grayson," I asked swiftly. "Will you do the same? Work for the army this winter?"

"No, Ma'am. I've had my fill of it," he said shortly.

"Oh," I replied, suppressing a smile. Tice Grayson's unembellished response had a ring of truth. "And how is it that you decided to stop in Cross Creek?" I inquired guilelessly.

"Why, the horses were pretty tuckered. We're just passin' through. Jed found out 'bout the Doc being here. Said he was an old friend of the family he'd lost track of an' all. I thought I might look around and see if I could find a fall drive to latch on to. Or maybe talk Jed into doing some trappin' this winter, but he don't seem too interested."

"I happen to know for a fact that both Hank Rinehart and Holbrook Barton are hiring on hands. I hear they're always looking for riders who are good with a gun," I offered, watching his reaction.

"Well, thank you, Ma'am, I'll keep them in mind," Grayson replied noncommitally.

Doc gave me a deep scowl, knowing exactly what I was up to. But for the time, it seemed he was prepared to ignore my unorthodox cross-examination of the guests, and was more concerned about my attending the dance with Jay Barton.

"Meg, you know I won't stop you, but maybe you should reconsider about tonight." He spoke hesitantly, reluctant to bring up personal matters before relative strangers. How had we come to such a parting of ways? He worried about Jay Barton, while I worried about Tanner and Grayson.

"I'm sorry, Doc," I said firmly, undetered and unable to explain my reasons to him in front of the two men responsible for my decision. "I want to go. I'll see to the dishes later," I said, rising determinedly from the table.

"It's been a real pleasure, Ma'am. And a mighty fine meal," Grayson said pleasantly. "Jed was talkin' 'bout pullin' out first thing in the morning. It looks like we won't be seein' you again."

My eyes flew to Tanner's face and I found myself the object of his forbidding look. For a moment, I was captured by the steely glint of his eyes. This man held some strange power over me, and I was sure that he knew it, just as I was certain that he detected my confusion. I was flirting with danger.

"You won't be staying on, then?" I said to Grayson, tearing my eyes away from Tanner with great difficulty.

"No, I don't suppose I will, Ma'am, considering your opinion of those outfits. My mama always said I was gonna die young. Can't see any sense in rushin' it," he responded matter-of-factly.

When I left the room, Doc and Tanner were gazing after me, one face apprehensive, the other an inscrutable mask. No matter what Tice Grayson claimed he and Tanner were doing come morning, I couldn't shake the feeling that I had not seen the last of them. I was certain that Jay would be able to tell me what they were up to.

Chapter Eleven

✑ JAY'S REACTION WHEN HE CAME FOR ME that night helped me to forget, for a while, the reason I had agreed to see him again. I forgot about the danger and the threatening spell Tanner had cast, losing myself to Jay's warm approval as I greeted him at the door. I was standing beneath light of the hallway lamp, which fired my hair with gold and gleamingly danced upon a dress of moss green silk. Jay's eyes traveled the length of my person, then returned to rest on my face appreciatively. I let a girlish vanity cheer me, knowing that Jay Barton, who had his pick of the most beautiful women in the territory, had chosen me, the ward of a small-town doctor, to accompany him to the last dance before the fall drive. Handsome enough to draw any girl's attention, he wore a beautifully tailored brown jacket over a snowy linen shirt and buff waistcoat, with fine wool pants tucked into shining boots. Offering me his arm with a gallant flourish, Jay led me down Main Street to the social hall. The music floated out to welcome us as dark, dancing shapes blurred past the bright windows of yellow light.

The dances of Cross Creek were not without established conventions and a certain etiquette was strictly adhered to. For instance, the first dance, the after-supper or after-refreshment dance, and the last dance were always reserved for a girl's escort. For a couple to dance more than three dances together in one evening was as good as announcing that they were courting. If a man happened to dance with someone else's girl more than three times, a fight was in order. But even though Jay would have no more than three dances with me, people would still speculate plenty about our appearance together.

A cluster of men gathered at the door, each smoking a last cigarette as if girding himself for a coming battle. They warily eyed all those crossing over the threshold into the dance, covering their shyness and uncertainty with bold talk. The stamping of booted heels and the boisterous laughter from within poured through the opened windows and doors.

I had hoped that no one would take special note of us, but of course it was not to be. Even Jim Evans's hand-clapping fiddle-playing did not keep the glances from turning our way. Mary Kay's spiteful eyes found me quickly enough, and she smiled from Aaron Darcy's side, begrudging me Jay's company. Neither of us had any way of knowing that a calamity was about to fall that would curb even her envious nature.

The dance was well under way by the time we joined in. The floor had been made slippery with a generous sprinkling of corn meal so that it was just right for dancing. Benches that were ordinarily arranged in rows had been pushed aside to accommodate the large crowd and now lined the walls of the room, providing out-of-the-way nesting spots for babies who slept soundly while their mothers danced nearby. The light scuffing of the ladies' dancing slippers sounded a rhythmic lullaby that muffled the heavier steps of their partners. I had already spied the furtive tipping of a bottle into the punch bowl.

Jay and I took our places, joining the high-stepping square dancers. As Jim Evans sung out his calls, Jay's hands clasped my own before spinning me into the arms of my next partner. Facing him once more, I lost myself to the enjoyment of the moment and the pleasure his company brought me. I felt as if I were sparkling with good spirits. We circled the floor together, my worries having taken wing, leaving me only with a carefree bouyancy.

It was only when the dancing ceased between numbers that the heat grew oppressive. But finally Jim called a break for his fiddle players and none of the winded dancers tried to talk him out of it. But instead of heading for the refreshment table, ladened with a tantalizing assortment of sweets, Jay grasped my hand firmly and led me to the rear door of the hall and out into the bracing crispness of the night. I wondered what this possessive gesture might signify to the gossips of Cross Creek. Although I did not mind Jay's attentions, I knew it was time to explain just why I had changed my mind about seeing him.

We walked along the tree-lined path and skirted a clearing at the back of the building, ignoring the bottle that passed between the outstretched hands of the cowboys lounging against the side of the hall. Leaving their casual talk behind us, we walked on until coming to a small pocket of trees that screened us from any curious eyes that might look our way.

Jay gave me a level look. "Okay, Meg. Let's have it out now. Why did you decide to come with me tonight? You can forget what I said earlier, 'bout you missing me an' all." He gave a short laugh. "That's not to say I don't wish it were true, but you were pretty strong in your feelings that day at the picnic— and you're not the sort who'd easily change her mind. Course I didn't give up hoping, but I'm no fool."

Jay mistook my silence as I struggled to find the right words.

"Is it because of Add? You're not seein' him anymore?" he asked quietly.

"No...no, it's not because of that."

He waited expectantly.

"What do you know about Jed Tanner, Jay?" I asked, straight out.

"Jed Tanner? What does Jed Tanner have to do with this?"

"Then you do know him," I said, my pulse quickening, seeing that he recognized the name.

"I know of him," he corrected. "Why should you want to know about Jed Tanner, Meg?"

"He rode into town with a man by the name of Tice Grayson early this morning," I answered shortly. "I think he's been hired by Rinehart or your father to cause trouble." Deliberately, I watched Jay's face. "And I think he plans to use me to get to Add and the Matthews family."

Disbelief crossed his face, but not the surprise that would have indicated he thought Tanner incapable of performing such a deed. Jay shook his head. "That's crazy, Meg. Why on earth would you think that of my father, or even Rinehart, for that matter? They don't use women to fight their wars."

As much as I wanted to, I could not tell Jay about Fenton. "Tell me what you know about him, Jay. It seems that Doc knew Tanner years back, but he won't say a word about him."

Jay hesitated, considering his words. "You'd do best if you left well enough alone and forgot you ever saw him, Meg," he said finally. "He's not the sort of man someone like you should be associatin' with. He's trouble."

"Then why is he here, Jay? Everyone knows how much your father wants the Matthews land. And that nothing he and Rinehart have tried has succeeded. They can't buy them out or scare them off. Maybe he was hired to ... do something about me, as a way to get to them."

Jay's face was clear. "God knows, Meg, Tanner'd be capable of doing something like that," he said evenly, "but you're wrong if you think my father would hire him for that reason. It's not his way of doing things."

"Even if your father didn't hire him, Jay," I asked unwaveringly, "how can you be so sure that Hank Rinehart didn't?"

"I'm not sure," he admitted. "But I'll find out. Most likely he's just drifting through. But I'll talk to Rinehart in the morning and see what I can learn."

At least he had not pronounced my suspicions absurd, as Doc had done. Relieved and grateful, I found myself drawn to the steady brown eyes that studied me so intently.

"Meg..." his voice trailed off as if Jay had suddenly grown unsure of himself. He cleared his throat. "I'll be gone for a spell. We'll be driving the herd to the railhead..." he paused before continuing. "I'll be thinking of you.... I think things could work out for us, Meg, but I'd like to think that you're finished with Add, first. That way, there won't be anything standing between us."

I tried hard to understand him, this man who had never been denied anything in his life. Though I faulted him his high-handed manner, I was not angry with him.

"I can't promise you anything, Jay. It's true, I cared very much for Add. A feeling like that just doesn't go away. I'm not committed to anyone, that's all I can guarantee."

"That's enough. I'm not askin' for more than that," he said. "At least it gives me a chance. I wasn't so sure the first time we spoke. I reckon you were ready to take that broom to me."

"I guess I was," I admitted. "But you've been honest with me and that means a lot. You're different from what I expected."

Then, before I could stop him, he pulled me close in a hard embrace, taking me by surprise. For a moment, I felt the quick leaping of his desire in his kiss, and then, with a shaky laugh, he put me from him. It had been a kiss that spoke of a passion held back and a promise of more to come.

"No sense in asking for something you might have refused me," Jay said, his eyes glinting with mischief. "Thought I'd help you make up your mind first." He knew he had not offended me. The thought of that last, lighthearted moment has always been of some comfort.

The foreman of the Bar B, the Barton ranch, was waiting for us at the door as we returned to the brightly lit social hall. Mumbling an embarrassed apology at his untimely interruption, he drew Jay aside. Leaving them to discuss ranch business, I made my way through the crowded room to the refreshment table to await Jay's return. It took only a moment before he came to stand next to me, claiming me for the next dance.

The silence descended slowly, so that we did not notice it right off, but later, as I recalled it, it was like a wave that began at the door and worked its way forward into the room until finally it reached the crowd of people gathered around the remnants of the refreshment table at the far side of the room. It was the only warning we had. First I looked at

Jim Evans, his fiddle and bow down by his side, standing with his boys on the platform, high above the unnatural hush of the crowd. My eyes flew to follow the direction of his gaze.

I did not recognize the man who stood there blinking in the doorway at the brilliant glare of light. It was not the Add I had known, but a stranger, his face gaunt under the shadow of a beard and his clothes soiled and bedraggled. Wordlessly, I watched him, as did the others, and we took in his altered appearance. Stunned by the change, I winced at the lines of fatigue that etched his face as his eyes searched the crowd. Without thinking, I started in his direction, but Jay's hand came out to grasp my arm, halting me in my steps. It was enough to call attention to us and Add's eyes came to rest on Jay's well dressed figure. And then they fell to me, at his side. Add's eyes narrowed and he spoke too loudly. "Damn you, Meg! So you've joined them, too, have you? I might have known. I bet you and Barton have been laughin' plenty hard over this one. Were you in on it all along?" he asked accusingly.

I gasped at his implication. I noted the desperate look on his face, a face that had looked on me before with only gentleness and affection.

"Add," I said as calmly as I could, taking a few steps forward as the crowd obligingly parted to let me pass. "You're wrong. You're not making any sense. I'm just here at the dance with Jay. You haven't called on me in more than two months. You didn't come to see me the last time you were in town and you wouldn't let me ride out to your place. We can talk if you like, only not here."

"No!" He spat back at me in anger. "I'm not here to see you. It's Barton I want!" Add fixed his eyes on Jay, who had made his way quietly to my side and stood by me protectively. "Did you know those bastards got the rest of our herd, Meg?" he asked angrily. "Bob and me, we told ourselves they just couldn't have vanished like they did. We'd been trailin' 'em for days and then we lost track of 'em. Then we found their hides. Dug up by wild animals. They had been butchered all right, but first they'd been driven off our land!"

Jay's voice was sharp and it cut through the room as he stepped in front of me, trying to reason with Add. "What makes you so sure my men did it, Matthews? We suffer losses from rustlers same as you do. We've no call to butcher your beef. We've plenty of our own."

"'An I'm sayin' the beef you serve at your table is Rocker M beef!" he fired back. "You'd like that, wouldn't you, knowin' that you were drivin' us under, eatin' the last of our steers. I found those hides on your land, Barton, and one of the horses I trailed there cast a shoe. He belongs to your foreman!"

The watching crowd gasped as Jay's face showed his surprise. The light of anticipation was on too many of the men's faces as they relished the prospect of a fight. High-spirited and befuddled by drink, they were too slow to see what I had quickly recognized. Add was beyond control. "It don't matter who gave them orders, Barton," Add said as his face twisted in contempt. "You, your brother, or your Pa. It's all the same to me."

I saw the film of sweat on Jay's brow as he made one last effort to reach Add. He took a step closer to him. "Listen, Matthews," he said firmly. "We can settle this—"

Add laughed wildly. "I'll see you in bloody hell before I let you get away with this, Barton!" Struck numb with horror, a disbelieving crowd watched as Add drew his gun and fired.

Nothing could ever have prepared me for the sight of Jay sinking slowly to his knees, the surprise still written on his face, as the small crimson stain spread across his newly washed shirt. I dropped to the floor beside him and cradled his head as his life drained away. What happened immediately after that is blurred in my memory. For a brief moment there was the shock of silence, and then the room exploded into an uproar. Frantic mothers ran to their babies and booted legs brushed past me as the hall split into two, with the ranchers and homesteaders seeking their own kind. No one dared guess at what might now erupt. Jay Barton, for one of the few times in his adult life, had been unarmed. Add had murdered him in cold blood.

Strong hands were at my back, lifting me to my feet as the room wavered alarmingly. And then, despite my protests to remain with Jay, I was pulled away from him, and with my eyes still glued to his motionless form, I was forced through the rear door and into the cold night air.

Chapter Twelve

GRASPED BY THE ELBOW, I was propelled along at such a pace that it kept me from falling to my knees. Gasping for breath, I finally faltered, only to be jerked forward by the relentless pressure on my arm. "I've got to get you away from here!" a voice shot at me.

My bearings were lost in the dark as we ducked between the shadowed buildings and skirted portions of the rutted back alleys. Only when my lungs threatened to burst from the burning passage of night air did he slow his pace, ushering me across a narrow road and against the cold frame of a dark building. My knees began to shake and I would have collapsed if not for the support of the man at my side, holding me upright. I turned my head to see who had come to my aid and gasped as the shock penetrated the numbness that had settled on me. It was Tice Grayson.

"What are you doing?" I whispered raggedly,

struggling to regain my breath, certain he meant me harm.

"You just listen to me!" he said, his voice deadly. "In another minute, those kindly people in there were goin' to be tearin' you apart. Those homesteaders for thinking you double-crossed your boyfriend and them ranchers for thinking that you just might have had something to do with that boy's death."

"I don't understand!" I said pleadingly, but he just gave me a disgusted look.

"You wait here," he commanded. "Don't move. I'm goin' to get help. I don't want to be alone with you once those folks realize you're gone and start combin' the streets for you. I'll be back."

"Wait!" I cried after him, but he disappeared into the blackness of night without a backward glance.

I looked around me, aware of the strains of music for the first time. The odor of stale beer and worse permeated the air as raucous laughter and shrill voices burst out loudly, without warning, just a little ways off from me. I was standing in the back alley of the Lucky Coin Saloon. Two dim shapes separated themselves from the shadows and I froze. With relief, I recognized them to be a saloon girl and her companion, slipping into the privacy of one of the small shacks lining the back street, where a girl might add to her evening's earnings. A yellow light flared briefly as the back door of the saloon opened and closed just ahead of me, revealing a tall loose-jointed figure casually intertwined with his lady friend. They melted together in an embrace, touched by a pool of light from a window above. I looked away.

With a loud crash, the door was pushed open again, but this time a solitary man broke loose from the sharp light into the murky darkness. He cast a look in my direction before I had time to flatten myself against the shadowed building, but paid me no mind as he spied the two people still locked in an intimate embrace. The woman turned her head away from her companion toward the intruder, and in the spill of light I recognized her to be Sally, one of the girls who had, for a time, worked for Rose. Though they still stood in darkness, I also recognized her partner, because the man who had come after him was Grayson.

"Jed!" Grayson's voice shattered the foreground of night as the backdrop of music continued behind the walls of the saloon.

"What'n the hell are you doing following me, Tice?" There was no mistaking Tanner's anger.

"There's been trouble, Jed," Grayson said. "There was a killin' at that dance tonight. Some are gonna say that Doc Elliot's girl was the cause of it."

Tanner fumbled for something in his breast pocket, then threw the three of them into sharp relief as his match flared briefly and he held it to his cigarette. Sally sidled closer, clinging possessively to his arm. He looked back at Grayson. The younger man took in the tight set of Tanner's face and then turned his head in my direction. "Hey, you, Meg, come here!"

Reluctantly, I emerged from the shadows and made my way toward the two men.

Sally swore sharply. "Sonofabitch! Listen, when you fellas mean business, you come see me then!" She stalked back to the golden lights of the Lucky Coin Saloon, the music blaring loudly as she reentered the building.

Tanner stared after her a moment before turning to me, the contempt with which he viewed me as sharp as a slap across the face. I saw his eyes fall briefly to the green silk, but they were carefully blank when they looked back at me.

"It's none of our concern, Tice," he said to the younger man. "I knew she was trouble from the minute I laid eyes on her." He spoke his words dispassionately, not caring how they might wound me, denying the intense interest he had taken in me only that morning when he had insolently disrobed me with his eyes. I was hurt by his cruelty and stung by his indifference, furious I should even care what the despicable Jed Tanner thought.

He drew on his cigarette, ignoring me. "Now, I've got some advice for you, Tice. I'm leaving at first light and you're welcome to ride along. You can see I've got some business to attend to now, and if you're smart, you'll do the same. Go inside and find yourself a woman. What happens to the girl is Seth's problem."

Grayson swore softly. "You're worse off than they say, Jed, if you can turn your back on this. There's no tellin' what a mob might do to her. It was that rancher we've been hearin' 'bout, Barton, whose son got murdered. The one the girl went to the dance with. I heard 'em say that the fella that done it was one of the valley 'steaders, and that she was pretty thick with 'im. That bein' the case, those ranchers just might say she set up the Barton boy for the killin'. If she goes back to the Doc's, Barton'll find her there for sure."

"Well, that's a real shame," he remarked in a bored tone. "But I told you before, it's got nothing to do with us. So why don't you let me go find Sally and let me be."

"Jed," Grayson tried again, "there's gonna be more killin' tonight unless she gets away from here. You know how these kinds of things can turn out. If those ranchers have a mind to, they might take it out on your friend the Doc, if they want her and he tries to stand in their way."

"Shit," Tanner said, at last staring straight at me but directing his words to Grayson. "I knew it. I knew all along she was no good." The handsome, chiseled features carefully composed, he passed sentence on me.

At that moment a new hatred took the place of my fear of him.

Grayson took no offense at the insult Tanner had bestowed upon me. "I'd say we've still got a little time. I heard 'em say they were goin' for Barton. He keeps a place at the edge of town. We can take her to Doc's now and see what he wants to do with her."

Tanner dropped his lit cigarette in reply, grinding it into the dust with his boot.

By the time we skirted Main Street and came upon Doc's, taking a narrow, beaten footpath leading to the back of the outbuildings, a small crowd had gathered at the front of the house. At least half of them were armed.

"They're watchin' for her already," Grayson said quietly, as he peered around the side of the weatherbeaten frame building.

There was a light shining at the back, from the window of Doc's office, and I caught the comforting sight of him as he moved around the room. Then he paused at the side of his examining table. I stiffened when I saw him lean over a sheet-draped body and fought down a sob. Tanner crossed the clearing to the house and, quickly opening the back door, stepped inside while Grayson and I waited in the darkness. I saw Doc look out into the night and at the slight nod of his head, Grayson put a none too gentle hand at my back, keeping me low as he pulled me along the edge of the open yard.

Doc had drawn the shades by the time I entered his office. I carefully averted my eyes from Jay's body. Grayson remained by the door and my eyes picked Tanner out of the shadows where he rested casually against a wall, his distaste for the unfolding scene obvious.

"I heard about what happened, Meg," Doc said gravely.

"Wasn't her fault," Grayson broke in, coming forward into the room. "She had nothin' to do with it. Lucky I happened by there. I heard that fiddle—it kind of reminded me of my daddy's playing when I was a boy..." The harsh flood of lamplight played across the boyish features of Grayson's face and I began to realize how much I owed him.

"What happened to Add?" I asked suddenly, realizing there had been no mention of him. "Is he all right?"

Doc gave me a peculiar look. "Add got away, Meg. He was seen heading up into the hills.... Some of Barton's men have already gone after him."

"Oh, no, Doc! If they find him—"

"—they'll string him to the nearest tree," Doc finished for me. "I know. They said some of the homesteaders went along, just to make sure that doesn't happen."

"Barton won't bring him in alive," a cool voice interrupted from the shadows of the room. Tanner's angular features were obscured but his voice was clear and sharp. "He'll want his own justice. With all those homesteaders around Cross Creek, he knows any jury's bound to be weighted in that boy's favor." Moving into the light, his face strained, Tanner gave Doc a knowing look. "Killers get off when the circumstances are right, isn't that so, Doc?"

Doc looked troubled.

"Well, I hope Add gets clean away, Doc," I spoke up defiantly. "He'd never give in without a fight. Besides," I added brokenly, "killing him won't bring Jay back."

The loud knock at the front of the house startled us all. Doc reached into his desk drawer for his army-issue Remington revolver. Tucking it into the waistband of his pants, he fastened his jacket over it. Quickly retrieving the Spencer carbine from the other room, he handed it to me. Not a word had been spoken. Straightening himself, he left the room to answer the door.

Apprehensively, I watched as Tanner positioned himself by the rear door to the room while Grayson stood guard at the entrance to the office. In the deadly silence that followed, I looked down at the carbine I clutched tightly in my hands, perceiving for the first time the seriousness of my situation. My emotions warred within me. I hated being beholden to the man who said such terrible things about me, yet Tanner's presence was also reassuring. Whoever it was at the door would have to shoot their way through him and Grayson before they got to me.

The voices carried clearly to the room at the back.

"I want to see my boy, Doc. Where is he? And then I want the girl. I know she's here. My men have been watching this place. They all saw her disappear right after Jay was killed. We know she came here, she'd have no place else to go."

"Damn it, Holbrook!" A voice broke in. It was Ed Thatcher's. "Just calm down and give the Doc a minute."

"I'm sorry about what happened, Barton," Doc replied in a steady voice. "I've got your boy in back. Of course you can see him if you want." Doc's message was clear.

His gun drawn, Tanner cracked open the rear door and, with his face rigidly set, motioned me through the dark hall. Following me silently, he and Grayson crowded me through the unlit kitchen into the black night.

The sound of footsteps echoed out across the wooden floor and there was a moment of silence as Holbrook Barton viewed his murdered son.

"Doc, I'm sorry to have to bother you with this right now," Sheriff Thatcher's voice broke through the unnatural quiet. "But Holbrook, here, wants to get started with the questioning. He seems to think

that Meg had something to do with this. We want
to take her down to my office, if you don't mind."

Doc cleared his throat. "Well, I can understand
that, Barton. But as much as you want to see Meg
right now, I can't allow it. She's asleep. I had to give
her a sedative just as soon as she returned. She was
mighty upset. She'll be fine by morning. I'll bring
her down to your office first thing. Is that all right
with you, Ed?"

There was a burst of profanity from Barton and
then, for one of the few times I can recall, Ed Thatcher
exerted his will against the powerful rancher. "He's
right, Holbrook. Listen to reason. It's past midnight.
There's no sense pushing it if we can't get anything
out of her now. We can go down to my office and
wait there. Matthews didn't have much of a start on
your boys and my deputies. Wouldn't be at all surprised if they've already caught up with him and are
bringin' him in."

"Damn it, Ed. If you say I can't see her now, I'll
have to go along with it. But I don't trust the Doc.
I'm going to leave some of my men behind, just to
make sure nothing goes wrong. That girl is going to
pay for her part in this. She won't get away."

"You do what you think best, Barton," Doc said,
unruffled by the rancher's surly manner. "I can tell
you that Meg had nothing to do with what happened
tonight, but I can see that you won't believe me.
You'll just have to find out for yourself, tomorrow,
down at Ed's. But, like I said, Meg's sleeping. There's
no need for your men to waste the night standing
guard, but suit yourself."

The disgruntled voices faded from the room and
then we heard sharp talk from around the front of
the house as Ed Thatcher finally persuaded Holbrook Barton to send all but two of his men away,
saying there would be no need for any more, that
there was no way Doc would be able to remove a

sedated girl from his house without alerting them.
The last of the Barton men departed, save for the
two who remained to watch over the house and the
long view down the length of Main Street. Evidently
moved by their plight on this brisk fall night, Doc
went out to them, generously offering them some
coffee from the pot that he had warming on the stove.
Gratefully, they accepted.

The back door swung open softly and Doc signaled
us inside. "Keep away from the window, Meg," he
said sharply as my shadow wavered on the shade.
He dimmed the light. Tanner seated himself in Doc's
chair. Leaning back, he propped his feet up on the
desk.

"Seth," he began coldly, the lamplight casting his
face into harsh angles, "you'd do best to get the girl
away from here as quick as you can." He spoke as if
I were not in the room with them. "I heard one of
Barton's men saying they were sending to his ranch
for more hands. Most likely, he'll call in some of
Rinehart's, too, from the talk. There's going to be
real trouble come morning if they don't bring the
Matthews boy in by then. Thatcher told Barton the
homesteaders were arming themselves. All they need
is one hothead to set things off."

I knew that what Jed Tanner said was true. Cross
Creek needed only a spark to ignite the fighting
instincts of men who had been held under a tight
rein for too long. But still I waited impatiently for
Doc to tell Tanner that his concern wasn't necessary.
That as bad as the situation was, I would be safe
with him. After they learned the truth, in the morning, there would be no more need to worry.

And then, as I saw the dreadful set to Doc's face,
I froze. Not until that moment did I realize the magnitude of the charade that Doc had played for Ed
Thatcher just minutes ago. He had no intention of
turning me over to the sheriff either in the morning,

as he had promised, or at any other time. I was not to have a chance to explain the circumstances of Jay Barton's death. I would not be able to tell his father how sorry I was, how much I had grown to care for Jay in so short a time, or about the future that Jay had hoped we might have together, or how preposterous it was that I could have anything at all to do with his death. I could not tell him that it had all been a terrible mistake, that Add was a man gone crazy, a man gone crazy with hate. I realized then that the truth would mean nothing to Holbrook Barton. Tanner was right. He wanted vengeance. But the true horror of the situation still awaited me.

Doc's voice was dead calm. "You were leaving in the morning, Jed. Go now, and take her with you."

"Doc, no!" I cried, outraged by his suggestion.

It was a small relief to see that Tanner was as stunned as I by Doc's words.

"No," he said, his voice steel-hard.

Grayson shifted uncomfortably as the tension rose in the overcrowded room.

"Help me, Jed," Doc continued, as if he had not heard Tanner's refusal. "I've got no other place for her. I can't hide her here for long. They'll take her and I won't be able to stop them. God knows what they'll do to her if they believe she was involved in that boy's death. This isn't going to blow over in a few days or even a few weeks. She has to be kept out of Barton's reach. You'll have no problem getting her away from here. I slipped a sedative into the coffee I gave Barton's men."

"Seth, you're a damned fool for even suggesting this! What in the hell are you trying to do?" Tanner asked harshly.

Doc looked steadily at the man whose dark eyes glinted dangerously back at him. "She'll be safe with you, Jed," he said.

"Just how in the hell do you know that?" Tanner's tone was vicious.

I shivered, not believing what was happening.

"I know," Doc said quietly.

Tanner purposefully set his eyes in my direction, giving me a brutal look. The impact was almost a physical jolt. Never had I read such condemnation in a man's eyes. The look seemed to bear years of hatred and loathing, yet only that morning I was sure he had looked on me with desire. "It won't work. I'm headed for the high country. It's time I went home, Seth, and there's no room for the girl."

I breathed a sigh of relief. Tanner would not consent to it. No matter what Doc believed, I knew I was safer with him.

"That's all the better, Jed," Doc persisted. "It won't come to them right away that she's with you. Once they figure it out, you'll have enough of a headstart to outride them. You can lose them in the hills. Once you see your way clear of town, you won't have any trouble."

Tanner met Doc head on, refusing to reconsider his decision. "If Barton's intent on finding her, he'll put two and two together," he said. "He'll head for the north valley, Seth. The risk's too great."

"Not if you head due west, Jed. You can wait him out at Rainbow Pass. You're familiar with the area. There'd be no reason for them to look for you there."

"That's crazy, Seth, and you know it! We'll get snowed in for sure. Then what? You want your innocent little girl wintering with me?"

"Believe me, Jed. There's no other way. I know what I'm asking of you. Take Tice along. He'll keep your nose clean. Besides, I heard him say he wanted to do some trapping. Here's an opportunity for him."

"Seems to me, Jed," Grayson brusquely interrupted, "we really don't have much of a choice."

I could not allow this madness to go any further.

"Doc, please! You can talk to people. They'll believe you when you say I had nothing to do with Jay's death. I'll be fine here, I know I will." I gave him a beseeching look. I was afraid of Jed Tanner. Threatening by daylight, and capable of such deeds that Doc and Jay had refused to reveal them, he seemed downright terrifying now, at night, with his anger barely held in check. It made no difference to me that I had been wrong and Tanner was not involved with Barton and Rinehart. Jay had said that the man was capable of anything, and I believed him.

Backed into a corner, Tanner turned his anger and contempt on me, lashing out viciously. "Shut your mouth, girl. I sure as hell don't want you along and it doesn't surprise me one damned bit that you don't care about Doc Elliot here, but I'm not going to give you the chance to let him get killed over you. Because you're not worth it. And that's exactly what will happen if you stay behind. I'll take you along, all right. But if you give me one bit of trouble, I'll leave you for those who want you so badly, if I don't kill you myself, first."

Shattered by the bitterness of his attack, I looked helplessly at Doc, but he did not come to my defense and I could only wonder what it was about Tanner that made Doc hold back the reproaches this man so desperately deserved. Grayson's voice was almost a relief in the stinging silence that followed.

"... You'll need clothes for hard riding, Meg. You got any pants you c'n wear?"

I nodded, remembering our supply of clean and patched clothing.

"Good. You put 'em on and we'll be waitin' for you out back."

There was no choice. I left the room and went to the storage chest, searching out the clothing best suited for my purpose, recalling an earlier time when I had donned boy's clothing to escape the hand of

Miss Henry. Now, I had no wish to escape at all. My
life had begun again when I came to live with Doc
Elliot, and leaving him was the hardest thing I ever
had to do.

I dressed as quickly as I could in the small room
tucked under the eaves of the house, not daring to
light the lamp. It would be best if all of Cross Creek
believed that Meg Logan slept a drugged sleep until
morning, when she and Doc Elliot would slowly walk
down Main Street to Sheriff Thatcher's office. The
dark flannel shirt hid the swell of my breasts well
enough and, if the breeches clung a shade too tightly
at the hips, the poncho, still smelling of horses and
tobacco despite a careful airing, would protect me
from any eyes that might prove too inquisitive. I
pushed back my hair and fastened it, making sure
that none of it escaped the confines of the broad
brimmed hat I pulled down low to shield my features.
I wrapped a few of my possessions together and then
turned my back on the room where I had spent the
most peaceful years of my life, not allowing myself
to wonder if I would ever return to it.

The dim shapes of the unwashed supper dishes
shone in the pale stream of moonlight that spilled
through the window as I passed through the kitchen.
It was cold and dark, the heat of the cookstove re-
duced to a pile of ashes. Doc awaited me by the door
and I went to him. His face was drawn with strain
and he suddenly looked as if he had aged years in a
single day. He pressed a small leather pouch into
my hands, closing my fingers about it tightly. When
I protested, he shook his head. "I want you to have
it, Meg. You needn't be beholden to anyone. It's yours.
You've earned it many times over."

For the second time that night, the tears fell from
my eyes and for the briefest of moments I rested my
head against his shoulder. But then he put me from

him and together we walked to the waiting men and horses.

Grayson extended his hand to Doc in farewell. "We'll take care of her," he said briefly. Doc nodded and turned to me.

"Meg, you listen to them, you hear? They know what's best for now. Don't let that damned stubbornness of yours get out of hand."

His face blurred. I tore my eyes away from him, and my gaze fell on the waiting horses. Sassy was not there. In her place stood Coalie. Tanner silenced my protest before I could speak. "If anyone comes looking, the mare should be here for appearances. I'm doing you a favor. She doesn't have the bottom for the kind of riding we'll be doing."

"Spare me the favors!" I snapped, venting the feelings that had built since the first time he rode into the clearing that morning, but he ignored my outburst. I stuffed my belongings into my saddlebag and mounted up.

Crossing the meadow awash with moonlight, I looked back one last time at Doc as we headed our horses toward the cover of trees bordering the edge of the field and away from town.

Part Two

Tanner

Chapter Thirteen

IT WAS AN OLD WAGON TRAIL that we traveled, underused and overgrown. It skirted town until it crossed the main road after an hour's ride and began winding its way through the foothills. Shifting veils of clouds thickened and thinned in the light wind, toying with the silvered slice of moon and throwing long shadows across the uneven terrain. A stream, hidden by the brush, gurgled frostily in the crisp air. Except for the creak of saddle leather, the jingling of bits, and the dull thud of the horses hooves on the hard-packed earth, it was quiet.

I rode behind Tanner, who held the dun stud at a checked pace, while Grayson brought up the rear. Whether this was for my protection or to keep me from running off, I was not sure. We passed a wooded section, some ten miles from town, and a near-forgotten memory of another night, a spring night, came to mind, when on the far side of the copse of trees a runaway girl had watched over a dying man.

Tonight, for the first time in several years, I wondered about him. For a moment I almost believed that Tanner caught wind of my thoughts, for he, too, looked deep into the tangle of darkness, sensing a lurking danger or perhaps some whispered secrets of the past. The dun, feeling his unease, tossed his head nervously, pricking his ears back and forth.

I tried not to think of the future. All that I had to build on was gone. With only the clothes on my back and a few of my other belongings I had taken with me, I was not much better off than I was on the night I had run away from school. Now I was afraid I might never be able to return to Cross Creek. But once free of my reluctant escorts, with the small leather pouch Doc had thrust into my hand, my own small accumulation of savings, and the serviceable serge skirt I had hastily included with my other possessions, I would make my own way until I found some suitable employment. I could not know at the time that, because of the help he had been pressed into giving, they would want Tanner almost as badly as they did me.

I never learned what it was that alerted him. But suddenly, without warning, he wheeled the dun around.

"The trees!" he barked at me. There was the sound of confusion and a rifle shot rang out.

"Hold your fire, Len," came an indistinct voice, and then, more loudly, "We don't mean you fellas any harm. Just give us the girl and we'll be on our way..."

I tried to make sense of the shrouded shapes ahead, failing utterly to follow the order that demanded instant obedience.

"Tice!" Tanner blared out into the night.

Bringing his horse alongside of mine, Grayson blocked me from the gunfire that sprayed into the darkness. Charging his bay into Coalie's side, he drove us off the trail, sheltering me from the fire with his own body. He slumped forward as a bullet found its mark and then, recovering himself with a remarkable effort, he threw himself at me, taking me with him as he fell from the saddle, rolling us clear of the nervous hooves. Stunned by the impact, I looked up in time to see Tanner dive off the dun and, landing on his off shoulder, roll over and come up crouching, his .45 drawn and spitting back fire at our assailants. Scrambling for the dun, he pulled his carbine free of the scabbard and then crossed the open road, melting into the darkness of brush.

"You know how to use this?" Grayson inquired, handing me his pistol. I nodded, my throat too dry for speech. Propping his rifle across the trunk of a downed tree to steady it, Grayson fired into the night. His sleeve, from the shoulder to his elbow, was streaked with blood.

"I think there's just two of 'em," he said between the ringing shots. "This should keep 'em busy while Jed works his way 'round back of 'em."

I nodded dumbly. Tanner had been right about everything. I had been a fool not to recognize the trouble I was in. A man who held nothing but contempt for me was risking his life to save me, and Tice Grayson had already taken a bullet because of my stupidity. How much greater a debt could I owe to two people who had never laid eyes on me before that morning and in all certainty probably wished they never had? Would Tanner ever believe me if I told him how sorry I was?

At the lull in gunfire, Grayson pulled himself up and motioned me to be quiet. The moon came out from behind the clouds, leaving the road bathed in light, but he did not wait for the return of darkness. Hunching over, he ran across the path, disappearing into the night as Tanner had done before him.

The horses grazed nearby, except for the dun, who

remained by the roadside where Tanner had left him.
As unnerving as the gunfire had been, I thought the
silence was worse, until the crack of a rifle broke the
quiet. It was followed by two more shots. There was
the sound of stampeding horses and then silence re-
claimed the night. Too cowardly to face up to the
killings that had been done on my account, I remained where I was. As much as I disliked Tanner
and Grayson, they had already saved my life tonight.
What if they had just died for me? Overcome by
despair and my grief for Jay, I lay where I was, my
head buried in my arms.

They returned for me a short time later. Grayson
was tight-lipped and tense, but Tanner's face was a
smooth mask, and I realized that killing was not new
to him. I brushed the dirt from my clothing and rose
unsteadily to my feet, reluctant to admit to myself
that I was glad to see them.

"They were Barton's men," Grayson said tersely.
"They probably spotted us as we were leavin' town
and took a chance on followin'. They might have
remembered me and Jed from earlier, at the saloon,
and remembered that we were stablin' our horses at
Doc's, or maybe they recognized Doc's gelding and
figured you might be tryin' to make a run for it. It's
hard to say. But sure enough, Barton will be madder
n'hell when he gets wind of this."

I stared out blindly across the open hills.

"Don't go feelin' sorry for 'em. They got what was
comin'. Those two had more in mind than just
bringin' you in to Barton. They was pretty well lik-
kered up," Grayson said. He did not embarrass me
with his straightforward talk.

I watched as Tanner checked the dun's saddle girth.

"He killed both of them, didn't he?" I asked Grayson suddenly.

He gave me an odd look. "No, one of 'em got away.
It's too bad. Means that Barton will find out about

this pretty quick. Would have taken longer to figure out what happened otherwise," he said, glancing down at his sleeve.

"Let me take a look at that for you. I can bandage it."

"It'll keep. It's just flesh wound. We need to keep moving," he replied in a practical tone.

Tanner brought up the horses, his dark eyes meeting mine as he handed me Coalie's reins. I stood erect and unflinching in a silence laced with recriminations. I wanted to thank him for saving my life, but I feared his acid tongue, which would surely tear me to pieces as it had before. Feeling suddenly fragile, I knew I could not bear it if he did that. He did not look at me again, and silently we mounted up and rode on into the night.

Tanner set a merciless pace in the urgent desire to lose any possible pursuers. The death of Barton's hand would spur the ranchers on to even greater efforts to find us. The circumstances under which it had occurred would mean little. I offered no complaint. I had nothing to say to the grim-faced man.

I'm not sure how far we would have traveled that night if it hadn't been for Coalie. The gelding stumbled, nearly pitching me over his head as I fought to regain my seat. At the sound of the faltering horse, Tanner pulled up the dun, casting a disparaging look in my direction. "We'll rest the horses here," he said curtly. "You see to Tice's shoulder. Then get some sleep. We'll be riding before sunup." Dismounting, he led the stud to a nearby meadow that was bordered by an aspen thicket.

I saw to Grayson's shoulder. He was right; he had just been grazed. "I'm sorry, Mr. Grayson," I said sincerely. "If I hadn't frozen like that, you wouldn't have taken that bullet. You saved my life and I'm grateful to you." Unlike Tanner, I had no difficulty apologizing to the younger man.

"You c'n call me Tice, Ma'am," he replied evenly, "an' don't worry none 'bout that bullet. It wasn't the first and most likely won't be the last that I take." I swallowed hard at his matter-of-fact manner. Afterward, I took a blanket from my bedroll and rolled myself up in it not far from where Coalie grazed. The stars glimmered weakly in the sky above. It would not be long until daybreak.

The predawn sky lightened perceptibly in the east, the dull gray giving over to the faint blush of rose, while the trail before us remained sheathed in darkness. We no longer followed a path but crossed a trackless sweep of land as we made our way higher into the hills. We were dim shapes in the dawn light against the dark landscape as we silently continued our journey.

Pushing doggedly on over the next several days, we worked our way through the foothills and began the ascent into the higher reaches of the mountains. I heard Tanner tell Tice that we had put forty miles behind us one long day. The horses were gaunt despite the grassy meadows Tanner found for them at night. The air thinned and the nights grew colder as we climbed higher. Each morning, the ground was frosted and the horses broke through the crystal edges of the pools they drank from. We saw no signs of our pursuers.

Grayson grew confident, claiming we had outdistanced them. He said that once they realized we were headed into the high country, they would turn back, being unprepared for the cold or the possibility of being trapped by an early snow. But this was not enough to reassure Tanner. He left nothing to chance. We rode as if they were one step behind us. Tanner knew men like Holbrook Barton. He said they didn't get to be big and powerful by giving up. I believed him. After all, he had been a rancher himself and they were his kind of people.

In the days that followed, our pattern never varied. Rising each morning before daybreak, we ate no breakfast and stopped only at brief intervals during the day to rest the horses. Jerky and a swallow or two of water sufficed at midday and was often taken in the saddle. Our supper consisted invariably of rabbit, pan fried with biscuits made from the limited supply of flour Grayson carried with him, and coffee. Game was plentiful and elk roamed the ridges and slopes, working their way into the valleys for winter. But we ate sparingly, just enough to satisfy our hunger, leaving nothing to waste. Neither Tanner nor Grayson felt the need to supplement the meager diet.

It was a matter of circumstance as well as intent that in all that time not a word was spoken to me except by way of command. Once we began our ascent, we rode strung out along the mountainous trail, often losing sight of one another as the trail wound tortuously around the steep inclines and numerous switchbacks. Any attempt at conversation was impossible. Towering stands of fir and pine screened the sunlight, muffling the sounds of the rushing creeks and cascading water that glinted down the steep mountains. We forded streams and climbed precarious ridges, dismounting frequently to lead our horses around the felled trees, fallen giants that stretched their lichen-encrusted trunks across our path. As the thickets and low-lying branches tore at my clothing, I was grateful for the protection of my breeches as Tanner followed a trail visible only to him. Except to brush the scattered leaves from my clothes in the morning, I took no pains with my appearance. In the evenings, overtaken by weariness, I did little but eat what was offered and sit by the fire, warding off the mountain chill, falling asleep while Tice and Tanner passed the time in quiet conversation. My body responded to the demands placed upon it, hardening until my muscles no longer ached

at the end of a long day's ride and I no longer noticed
the chill of the hard ground at night. Thinking of
neither the past nor the future, I wrapped myself in
the natural majesty of my surroundings.

Judging by the sun, it was at noon on the fifth
day that Tanner pulled the dun off the narrow ridge-
line and onto a rocky promontory that jutted off the
mountainside, affording a sweeping view over the
distance we had traveled. Instinctively, Coalie followed the stud's lead as he had all the while and
Tice came up behind us as Tanner scanned the broad,
rolling valley below. The dun lowered his head wearily, his flanks steaming in the crisp mountain air.
Tanner swung down, relieving the animal of his
weight. Behind me, Tice did the same.

There was no rational reason for my fear. There
was enough room on the small ledge for all of us.
Kicking my foot free of the stirrup, I swung my leg
over the saddle, closing my eyes as I slid downward
until my feet touched the ground. "We'll rest here,"
I heard Tanner say. Then, with my eyes still tightly
shut, I heard the sound of the horses being led away,
off the narrow shelf. All through the tortuous climb
I had managed to keep my humiliating fear of heights
to myself. But now, standing on trembling limbs, it
was as if an unseeable force of nature threatened to
suck me over the edge of the flat, treeless ledge with
the mesmerizing pull of a magnetic force. I had no
choice but to admit to my dread. With sweat beading
my brow, I forced my eyes open. Beyond the ledge,
the land fell away in an alarming swoop, creating a
vast open valley below that narrowed as the far slopes
of the mountains came together at the bottom. I buried my face in Coalie's mane, too tired to summon
up the courage to stiffen my quaking legs and lead
him away from the beckoning void, and yet still pos-
sessing too much pride to call out for help. Coalie
shifted his weight onto his near side, leaning slightly

toward the edge of the precipice, and I felt an invisible tug, pulling me backward. Gripping the saddlehorn, I fixed my gaze upon it, unable to close my eyes, for the darkness would erase my last hold on whatever small courage I had left.

I heard the sound of footsteps approach and then halt midstride, but I was unable to lift my eyes from the horn to welcome my rescuer. I knew that it was Grayson who had once more come to my aid. But neither my relief at my imminent deliverance nor my shame at my cowardice could make me relinquish my grip upon the saddle. Sensing my panic, he did not rush to my side, but slowly worked his way behind me, knowing that the least false move might tear loose the scream from my throat and cause Coalie to bolt. He edged up in back of me on the narrow strip of ground between the rim and the yawning hole beyond. Two strong hands reached around me, loosening my white-knuckled grip. The hold broken, I fell back against him, his body a strong physical shield between me and the gaping emptiness below. At the feel of him, I froze. This man was taller than Grayson and harder, his body as unyielding as steel. As his large frame sheltered me, cutting off the buffetting wind, his arms continued to brace me. My reflexes paralyzed, I longed to fight the intimate embrace, hating the comfort I took in it. At his low chuckle, I exerted all the will I had left, pulling free, but my weakened knees responded too slowly. I pitched forward directly into Coalie's side.

The gelding had been well trained. He swung his hindquarters away at the impact, but left his forelegs firmly planted on the ground. Losing my bulwark, I fell face down, scraping my palms badly as they took the brunt of my fall.

"You damned fool!" Tanner said as he reached down to me, painfully gripping my elbow, raising me to my feet while grabbing for Coalie's bridle. White-eyed and skittish, the horse's patience was at an end and he snorted a protest. Furiously, I tore myself from Tanner's grasp just as he let me go, causing me to look even a bigger fool than I felt. I glared at him, but he had already turned away from me.

"What'n hell happened to you?" I heard Tice's voice behind me. I whirled around. There was no sense in lying to him; he could see that I was upset.

"I...I don't like heights much."

I scowled at his whoop of laughter, but it was hard to stay angry at him. He meant no harm by it.

"I expect I'll get use to it. It's just that I never had occasion to before," I explained.

He looked at me doubtfully. "Some folks just don't cotton to high places. They never get use to it."

I shrugged my shoulders and wiped my stinging palms on my breeches as Tanner went to turn Coalie out to graze with the other horses in a small pocket of grass that grew beside a steep rise in the mountain wall. My eyes followed him as he climbed the sheer side with amazing ease and agility and vanished into the stand of pine that lined the ridge above us.

"From that ridge up there, you c'n see for miles. Almost clear back to Cross Creek," Tice remarked in explanation.

"Does he think they'll still be following us?" I asked.

"Yes'm. I believe he does. They'll be after him, now, for the killing of Barton's man." He spoke casually, apparently unconcerned that they would also be after him.

"You don't seem worried," I remarked. "Wouldn't they be just as likely to want you, too? They won't know for sure who did the killing."

"No, it'll be Jed they're wantin'. You see, I ain't never been in trouble with the law before, 'ceptin' for a little disturbance of the peace. No, it'll be Jed that they're after. The law's got it in for 'im."

"Why, Tice?" I asked hesitantly, almost afraid to know the answer.

He looked uncomfortable. He toyed with his hat, as if uncertain how to begin. "Well, maybe I shouldn't be tellin' you, but maybe it'd make it easier if you knew what you were up against. An' why he don't take kindly to you gettin' 'im in this mess. But, you see, there was some trouble a while back. An' because he got off for it some folks have it in for him now. Makes it easy to blame him for things he didn't do. Now, if that man of Barton's that got away said that Jed happened to shoot his friend in cold blood, why they'd never believe Jed if he said it wasn't so."

"Why not?"

"Well . . . he's done it before."

"Oh." Tice's words came as no surprise to me. I suppose I had suspected as much. But the curious, deflated feeling I had inside did surprise me. It was just that I didn't like to be beholden to a man who was a killer, I told myself. "Killers get off when the circumstances are right," I had heard him say to Doc the night we left. Perhaps he had been influential enough to have justice look the other way. Things like that happened, but people didn't take kindly to it. Still, I found myself feeling sorry that I had added to his troubles. My eyes found Tanner as he unhurriedly descended the ridge, jumping the final distance with the grace of a mountain cat—and the deadliness, too.

Chapter Fourteen

TANNER AVOIDED ME after my latest follies, my inadequacies proved to him once again. Tice tried to lift my spirits, spinning endless stories of the cantankerous mules of the Hayden expedition as we shared a midday meal of jerked beef. But all through our brief respite I found my eyes returning to the solitary figure keeping watch on an outcropping of rock over our backtrail. A well of anger built and rankled. How dare he treat me with such contempt! With his own past, he was an unlikely candidate to think harshly about my failings.

The terrain changed as we continued on that afternoon, and the stunted growth that clung to the stony mountainside above the timberline gave way to barren windswept reaches that matched the gray of the sky and the darkness of my mood. The trail was easier now, cresting wide benches that rimmed small parks below, and the horses stretched out in a comfortable walk. Occasionally, when the low-lying growth allowed, Tice pushed his bay up alongside of Coalie, but my continued ill-humor kept me from speaking.

"Somethin' wrong?" he asked pleasantly enough, after several of his attempts at conversation had failed miserably.

"No," I replied shortly, hoping to put an end to his inquisitiveness.

"You know," he said, with an irreverent gleam in his eye, ignoring my none-too-subtle message, "Jed ain't use to havin' a lady sore at him."

I gave him a withering look. "What makes you think I'm angry at him?" I asked waspishly, hating to admit that my curiosity was aroused by his comment.

"I wasn't born yesterday. I heard the things he said to you back at Cross Creek." He observed me shrewdly as I shuddered inwardly at the memory. "You haven't spoken to each other since then, 'ceptin' for maybe a cuss word or two. You know, Meg," Tice continued confidentially, "you're gonna have to get used to him, else it's gonna be a pretty uncomfortable winter."

Get used to him? To a man whose kindest words labeled me nothing but trouble, worthless, and no good? Get used to him? Never! I turned to Tice, venting the rage that had been growing in me since I left Cross Creek.

"I don't give a damn about Jed Tanner!" I stared ahead angrily at Tanner's back. "He can ride clear to hell for all I care!"

As if he possessed the power to intuit my thoughts, Tanner turned his head in my direction; swinging his horse around, he rode back to where I sat Coalie. I gripped my reins uneasily at his approach.

"We're coming on to Culley's trading post," he said, his voice a low growl, addressing Tice and paying me no attention. My anger flared anew at his latest rudeness. I told myself I didn't care, it was of no concern to me. His words at least explained why the trail we followed had widened into a respectable, well trodden path.

He turned to me. "You're not to talk with anyone. Is that clear? They speak to you, ignore them, like you're dumb."

Smarting under his words, I raised my head, meeting his eyes straight on, silently demanding to know what he intended to do with me if I disobeyed his orders.

"Get rid of that hair," he said abruptly, his eyes glittering strangely as they did whenever he looked at me. I stuffed the thick braid back under my hat, noticing he watched me until I had done so.

Tice gave me a puckish grin as Tanner rode on ahead. "Like I said before, Meg—I've never seen anyone rile him quite the way you do."

The trading post stood in a clearing that nestled in the crook of a mountain pass. Pack animals stretched out along the flat bottom, grazing the rich, sun-cured stalks that reached as high as a man's waist. Several of the horses, in the corral adjacent to the cabin, crowded the gate as we drew near. A porch fronted the small structure where a few tree stumps and one lone chair overlooked the approach that followed alongside a shallow streambed. Dismounting uncertainly, I followed Tanner inside, leaving Tice to tend to our horses.

At first, all I perceived was a cavelike darkness and musty, mingling odors of pelts, coffee, and tobacco. The only illumination was a few rays of fading daylight fighting their way through a much begrimed window. My eyes adjusted to the dimness of the interior after a moment or so. There was very little space to move about. Merchandise was crammed along the shelves and on the counter and was propped into corners of the cabin and piled high on the floor. Wooden barrels stocked with staples lined the back walls and edged forward to the center of the cabin. There was a limited assortment of dusty canned goods. Traps of varying sizes hung from pegs along the wall, and a small assortment of tools and utensils peeked out from unexpected places.

There was a sudden sound, a confusion, and from the darkest corner of the room an object suddenly took shape, as large as a hibernating bear emerging from his den. My eyes flew to Tanner, standing calmly in the path of the hairy apparition, but before I could call out a warning, he looked at me and shook his head. My fright subsided at his lack of concern, and resentfully I remembered his instructions forbidding me to speak. My pique was momentarily stymied as a burly giant of a man, thickly coated with hair but reassuringly covered by a homespun shirt and leggings, stood and yawned, rubbing the sleep from his eyes. Nearsightedly, he peered though the gloomy light at his intruders.

"Howdy, Culley."

The huge man stopped short at Tanner's voice. He shook his head as if to clear it. Like the bear, his eyesight was poor but his hearing was keen.

"Jed? Jed Tanner? That you? Well, I'll be... hell, I never thought to see you again after all these years, Jed. Last I heard you were..." He paused suddenly at the memory and then shook his head again. "...Well, never mind that now, I say." He scratched at his head. "Makes a man feel mighty old, it does, to see the changes in you. Hadn't been for your voice, I'd never have recognized you."

"It's been a long time, Culley," Tanner agreed, not elaborating.

"Let's see. The last time you was here—why, it was when your granddaddy was still alive. He brought the three of you with 'im, that time. You, Caleb, and Travis. How are those boys?"

My attention was riveted back to Tanner. Suddenly the thought of the family who had raised him, a man whose coldness only indicated he had close ties to no one, intrigued me. What had his grandfather been like? Were the names Culley mentioned those of his brothers? I recalled the name Caleb. Doc had spoken it at dinner that last night in Cross Creek. Caleb was watching over his interests, Tanner had said.

"Can't say how they are." Tanner's voice was strained, his face inscrutable.

Culley backed off. Grateful for company, he was wise enough to leave well enough alone when he had presumed too much. He and Tanner conversed quietly and I edged a bit closer, all the while listening to their words for bits of information I might find useful.

"Is that cabin still standing, Culley?" Tanner asked suddenly.

"Sure enough is, Jed. Course I ain't swearing by the roof, but there's been some folks livin' in it off an' on. Last of 'em moved on just this past spring, soon as breakup let 'em get through. One of the men, he lost a leg. Caught in a storm. Froze. Damned lucky to be alive. The other one, his partner, he kinda lost heart for it after that. They wasn't real woodsmen like you used to see 'round these parts. No one stayin' there now, that I know of. You aimin' to set a spell?"

"Maybe," Tanner answered evasively.

"Well, now, who's that you got with you, Jed?" Culley squinted across the room at me, noticing me for the first time. "Howdy, young fella," he said in my direction.

I looked at Tanner helplessly. He ignored me, determined to carry out the charade.

"Got me a partner this year, Culley," Tanner broke in, effectively interrupting any possible communication between the trader and me. "And this boy is our camp tender. Need someone to look after us and see to the skins. If we can scare any up," he said, deftly changing the topic. "How's the trapping been?"

Camp tender! Bristling at Tanner's assumption, I choked on the words I was not allowed to speak. He expected me to look after him and Grayson and see to the skins! I'd be damned if I became Jed Tanner's servant! He had decided my future without so much as a word to me!

"... The trappin's been poor, mighty poor, if you're wantin' to know the truth, Jed," Culley continued, unaware anything was amiss. "Ain't no way to make a livin' anymore. Course there are always plenty of wolves around. Depends on if you're wantin' to make a livin' or just get by. You can always get by."

The door opened and Tice Grayson entered in a shaft of gray light. He smiled affably at the trader as Culley squinted him a welcome.

"Heard what you just said," Tice told him. "But I tell you, it sure does beat line riding. You just point out what I need to see me through to spring."

Cully shook his head. "I can't stake you, boy. You give me somethin' in return, and I'll be glad to help you out. I'm sorry, Jed," Culley said, turning his head in the direction of the silent man, "but things just ain't like they used to be. Now if he had a season behind him, it'd be a different story."

"No trouble, Culley," Tanner said easily. "We've got the outlay. Just give us enough to get by. Oh, and throw in whatever you think the young'un needs. He's not too well set up. He can't talk. Something wrong with his head."

A shriek strangled itself in my throat as three pairs of eyes turned on me, two with menace and one with pity. More than likely, Culley would get the impression that I was crazy as well as mute from the bug-eyed expression on my face. No doubt, I imagined, he thought me a complete idiot, bound by charity to these two kindhearted men. I turned to Tanner and our eyes met, his steely and mine furious. Fuming, I realized that he was enjoying himself immensely at my expense.

"What a shame, now," Culley said, his big heart stricken by Tanner's tale. "Come here, lad, come to Culley. I've a peppermint stick for ye." He reached into a dusty jar on the counter behind him and handed me the stick of candy. I looked at Tanner, glaring mutinously at him, aghast at deceiving the warmhearted Culley with such lies. "It's all right, lad— Jed, here, won't mind, he had a fondness for them himself when he was your age," Culley said, pointing a finger at Tanner and pantomiming the silent man's liking for the sweet.

Wordlessly, I took the stick from Culley and walked over to Tanner and, with a little bow, presented him with the brightly colored candy.

"Well, fancy that, Jed!" Culley said, impressed by my generous act. "Simpleminded the lad may be, but he's well set on manners. Here," Culley said, taking another peppermint stick from the jar and holding it out to me. "There's enough for you and your friend, lad." I took the candy and this time put the stick in my mouth and indicated to Tanner that he should do the same. Thrown off guard by my behavior, Tanner gave me an odd look. His features held, then relaxed slightly, the creases at the corners of his eyes deepening. His mouth quirked downward as he supressed a reluctant smile. I raised my eyebrows at him irreverently, puckering my lips and smacking them noisily, making a production, for Culley's benefit, of dispatching the stick of candy. The storekeeper beamed at us.

"We'll be needing pack animals, too, Culley," Tanner said, finishing off the peppermint stick with short work and attending to business. "And nothing like that son-of-a-bitchin' walleyed mare you claimed was a packhorse last time."

Culley chuckled at the memory. "I surely did get complaints 'bout that one, I did. But she dropped the prettiest little foals come every spring." He good-naturedly ignored Tanner's insult and continued to stack the goods in the small space he cleared on the grimy counter as Tanner began to help Tice, shouldering the heaviest of the provisions and carrying them through the door.

Left alone in the room with Culley, I wandered about the cabin. A clouded mirror hanging by Culley's stock of hats caught my attention. For the first time since Cross Creek, I viewed my likeness. It was no wonder Culley had taken me for a youth. Staring back at me was a thin-faced lad with large, green-flecked eyes in a tanned face. My small, straight nose, well shaped lips, and pointed chin gave no hint of femininity, and there was no wealth of shiny hair to soften the image. I could not fault Culley for thinking me a boy. I'd have thought it myself. In a matter of a fortnight, I had managed to lose my sex, my tongue, and my wits.

"Here."

An immense bundle of fur came at me and I staggered under the weight, blindly fighting it, until I realized the animal's life had long ago departed. Unfolding it, I found it to be a buffalo coat, a scaled-down version of those issued to the Northern army troops.

"Try it on," Tanner ordered.

I struggled with the bulky skin. Then, to my surprise, it lifted of its own accord and was held so that all I had to do was reach behind to stretch my arms into the sleeves. Raised to my shoulders, it dropped into place, enveloping me with a wonderful warmth.

Through the thickness of heavy coat I felt the weight
of Tanner's hands resting on my shoulders. Confused
by the luxuriousness of his selection, for surely Culley had less grand wraps to choose from, I turned to
him.

"Thank you," I said with sincerity, but softly so
that Culley could not hear.

The grip of his hands tightened for a moment at
my words and he raised the warm, protective collar
over my ears, bringing it up under my chin. His eyes
regarded me intently. "It'll do," he said briefly, looking down to where it fell past my boot tops. He took
his hands away but I still felt them, imprinted in
the fur. My cheek burned where his fingers had accidently brushed up against it with a surprisingly
gentle touch.

"That there coat belonged to Fargo's daughter,"
Culley volunteered from behind the counter as he
stuffed a large, coarse cotton sack with the smaller
items we needed. Tanner moved off, and suddenly
disoriented, I looked to the trader. "It fits you well
enough, you being so skinny and all. He brought me
all of her belongin's and told me to sell 'em, he did.
She'ran off with that fella from North Fork that was
here last month. Some Indians took her dresses and
gewgaws real quick, but they had no call for a buffalo
robe."

I smiled my understanding at Culley. The look he
returned was one of surprise. "You're a handsome
enough lad, at that. Too bad 'bout your wits an' all,"
he mused aloud. Hastily, I removed the coat and
folded it carefully, avoiding his eyes. I could imagine
Tanner's wrath if Culley learned the truth.

While Culley worked his sums, my eyes wandered
along the cabin interior once more, until they came
to rest on the dusty bolts of fabric. Fingering my
small leather pouch, I drew his attention to the bolts
of serge and muslin. He cut the lengths I indicated

and I paid him for the material. The serge would do for another pair of breeches, and if either Tice or Tanner came across the cheap cotton, they knew enough about women to assume I would need it for personal needs. Culley would think it for bandages or perhaps a shirt. It was not uncommon for men to do patching or sewing when the need arose. As camp tender, I thought grimly, who knew what would be expected of me? I wrapped the fabric in the folds of the buffalo coat and started for the door, when Culley called after me.

"Here, boy, gimme that. I'll put it in here for ye." As I lay the purchases on the counter, something akin to pity washed over his face and once more he reached into the dusty jar for a peppermint stick. I smiled at him and held up my fingers. Two. And then I pointed out the door to where Tanner loaded the pack animals.

A loud burst of laughter came from the big man. "Laddie, Jed Tanner was a lucky man the day he came across you. You look after him, you hear?"

The pack animals, strung out on a lead, waited patiently under their burdens. There were three of them, each with a pack weighing well over two hundred pounds. They carried hundred-pound sacks of flour, cornmeal, and sugar, as well as coffee, dried fruit, canned goods, ammunition, and traps. There were even a few pots, since Tanner was unsure as to what we might find at the cabin.

We were almost beyond sight of the small trading post when Culley came lumbering after us, panting heavily from his exertions. "Here," he called, as he waved a clear bottle at us. Uncorking it, he took a long swallow before tossing it to Tanner. "For a cold night. It will keep ye warm!" He bellowed a laugh as Tanner caught it singlehandedly. Holding the bottle aloft, Tanner nodded his thanks.

* * *

Tanner pushed us hard the remainder of the afternoon, wanting to make this the last night in the open before reaching our destination. It was well past dusk before he called a halt to our travel. His mood was black. The humor he had had for a moment at Culley's was gone, as if it had never existed. With hunger gnawing at my stomach, I dismounted and saw to Coalie as the men unloaded the pack animals.

"Wait!" Tanner called after my retreating back as I headed toward the stream. Turning back to him, I saw him take his knife. Bending over the side of sowbelly he had purchased at Culley's, he cut off a piece and threw it at me. "Fry that up," he ordered. His knife followed, landing in the dirt at my feet. I looked up at him and it seemed that I recognized a challenge in his face, as if he were daring me to refuse him. He had known how terribly I had resented the designation of camp tender that afternoon. He did not know that I was more than willing to pull my weight and fully expected to do my share of the work. I was not used to being idle. What I resented was his high-handed manner of ordering me about. Still, remembering that moment of silent laughter at Culley's, I knew I wanted to be at peace with him. I picked up the knife, denying him the satisfaction of goading me to anger. Giving him an even look, I went to do his bidding.

It wasn't until later that night, while I doctored Coalie's saddle sores, that I overheard the rough voices and recognized that the tenor of the conversation between Tice and Tanner had changed. Stubbornly, Tice belabored his point and, stubbornly, Tanner resisted it. An awkward silence followed. And then Tice's wrath exploded.

"Damn it, Jed, mark my words, you'll regret this!" Throwing his coffee dregs to the ground, he stalked off into the darkness. Even without hearing my name, I knew who they had argued about.

"It was about me, wasn't it?" I accused Tice, catching up to his angry stride.

He kept walking and then halted in disgust. He took the fixings from his pocket and rolled himself a cigarette.

"Damn it, Tice, I have a right to know why!"

He stared at me and then drew on his cigarette. "It's for his own good, Meg. I tol' him hidin' out here with us is crazy. It's gonna make it harder for him. I told him he needs to steer clear of you. He's already seen us safely up here. Now, he needs to get it straightened out with the law before they get it in their minds that what happened back at Cross Creek was all his doin'."

"He's in trouble because of me is what you're saying." I said softly.

"That's right," he said, not mincing words to spare my feelings. "Told 'im the Doc wouldn't expect him to sit the winter out up here knowin' that was the case, 'specially since I could do it for him, but he sure as hell won't listen to me. Says he'll take his chances."

The burden of Tanner's decision rested heavily on me. Why didn't he do as Tice suggested? Surely I'd be safe with him.

"I'll talk to him myself," I told Tice slowly, wondering at the turmoil of my emotions. Of course I wanted him to leave, I reminded myself sternly. There had been nothing but animosity between us from the very first. Except for today. Except for the lighthearted moment at Culley's. And how quickly that mood had passed. Sometimes I thought that Tanner only had to look at me and a black mood would descend upon him.

Tice shook his head. "I don't think I'd try it, Meg. He was feelin' awful cross when I left 'im. Might be best to let 'im alone right now."

"No," I said, knowing I had to erase the odd memory I held of him as he placed my buffalo coat on my shoulders. I would be well rid of him. Without a word, I turned on my heel and went back to the campfire.

The mournful howl of a timber wolf announced my presence, but I knew that he had been aware of me even before I stood across the fire from him. Through the flickering light I looked down at his long length stretched out on the ground, his head pillowed against his saddle, his hat tilted forward so that it covered most of his face. The glowing embers were another barrier between us. He didn't bother to acknowledge me. A slight tightening of the lower portion of his face was all that betrayed the disturbance to his calm. The bark of the wolf's mate sounded in the distance.

"I agree with Tice," I began abruptly, without preliminaries, knowing they would be wasted on him. "I think you should go back to Cross Creek and explain what happened. I know it will make things easier for you."

"Is that so?" His voice had a lazy, mocking quality to it.

"Yes," I said, realizing he found my concern amusing. Did he believe everyone to be as heartless as he? I tried again. "I'm grateful to you for what you've done for me. But there's no need for you to do any more. Tice told me about the trouble I've caused..." My voice wavered and I wondered why his mere presence was enough to put a tremor in my speech.

"Did he now?" he asked, and an undercurrent of hostility ran through his words. Slowly, he sat up, pushing back his hat to reveal eyes that glinted black in the night.

"So you want to get rid of me," he said softly, capturing my eyes with his. My pulse began to hammer at the gaze that held me prisoner. He is dangerous and he plays with me like a cat with a mouse, I thought wildly. In his eyes I read a deadly invitation that flickered like the flame of the fire and I suddenly admitted the truth to myself. I didn't want him to leave. I wanted him to stay. Then, just as swiftly, I buried the absurd thought. No self-respecting woman would respond to such a man as he. He treated me despicably. He was a killer.

"No," I said shortly. "There's no need for you stay on now. I'll be quite safe with Tice."

"Tice?" He laughed, a short, unpleasant sound. "You know Barton's men. How long do you think Tice would last against them, if they make it up here?"

Resentfully I stared at him, reminded again of the danger I had placed all of us in.

"So I'll leave," I shot back at him hotly. "Take me to the nearest town. They won't expect it. I'll take a new name."

"Assume a new identity?" he inquired sardonically.

"Yes," I nodded. "That's what I'll do."

"Well, you're a bigger fool than I thought you were," he replied caustically. "Do you think anyone could ever forget what you look like?" His eyes branded my features. "Do you think you could disguise a face like yours?" I tore my gaze away from his, uncomfortable under his scrutiny. I had been told I was beautiful before, but never like this. Coming from Tanner it seemed to hold a new, ominous meaning.

"Listen to me," he said, his tone biting. "If Barton's men find you, they'll string you up. Now, I'll tell you, folks don't take kindly to seein' a woman killed, no matter what the reason, deserving or not. If they hang you, you'll only be a martyr for those poor homesteaders and more killing will be done in your name. Dead or alive, girl, you're poison."

His words devastated me. I was as much an outcast as Jed Tanner was. Eyes as cold as gun metal flashed at me across the fire and I felt his damning judgment of me. As the pain of my future overcame me, I blinked back the brightness in my eyes, knowing that he watched me all the while. Tears did not soften Jed Tanner. "Now go get some sleep," he said roughly. "We're pulling out at first light."

I turned away from him and sought the comfort of my blanket nearby. But I did not sleep that night. By morning, the ache in my heart had receded until all that remained was despair.

Chapter Fifteen

✒ THE CABIN WAS SET in the curving arm of
the mountain pass, framed against a backdrop of
lodgepole pines that climbed the granite face behind
it. A shimmering fence of gilded aspens hemmed in
the green forest, leaving a grassy meadow to front
the small cabin and adjoining corral. In spite of the
magnificent setting, it was a trapper's abode and
nothing more. Constructed of unhewn logs, without
even a porch to grace it, the harsh mountain weather
had worn the sides smooth except for the scabs of
bark adhering at the junctures and along the north
side.

We followed a stream that meandered its way
through a gravelly creekbed, approaching the cabin
from the south, as the loneliness of the land wrestled
with its beauty. The cabin faced east, but the sun
would be a long time rising before it climbed high
enough over the mountains to warm the small cabin
in the clearing. As we drew up our horses in front

of the log structure, I was left with a sense of utter desolation as I faced the bleak future. At the very least, I was to spend a winter confined within these four walls, with two men, Jed Tanner and Tice Grayson. Stifling a wild laugh, I wondered what the good ladies of Cross Creek would have to say of my latest predicament. I actually longed to be back in their censoring midst.

The crude plank door stood ajar, offering an empty welcome. Carefully schooling my face, I entered. Mercifully, the dimness spared me an immediate realization of the dismal interior. The simple furnishings slowly took shape as light filtered through a window covered by newspaper that had been coated with bear grease for transparency: two beds built into the rear corners of the cabin with a small shelf nailed above each for personal effects, a scarred plank table in the center of the room, and a small bench and three-legged stool that lay where they had fallen upon their sides. Dirt-encrusted skins, chewed into tatters by mountain creatures that had made the abandoned cabin their home, served as coverings for the rough puncheon floor. A small furry animal in a noxious state of deterioration lay in the hearth of the fireplace on the far wall. A live rodent, alarmed by my intrusion, scurried across the floor. The musty odor of filth and animal leavings was unendurable. Fighting my repugnance, I sought my escape in a headlong flight from the room.

Blinded by the brilliant stream of sunlight at the entrance, I did not see Tanner until it was too late. Unable to halt my impetuous rush, he threw out his hands, grabbing at my arms to break the impact of my body as I hurtled into him. The clean, pure fragrance of pine mingling with the comforting smell of horses and the warm scent of his skin was such a relief that I was not aware at first of his firm hold on me as I gasped in the fresh air. He did not loosen his grip nor did he move aside to break the contact between us but instead, remaining where he was, continued to block my passage in the narrow confines of the doorway. So stunned was I at that moment by the impact of his closeness that I might just as well have tried to move a mountain as move him aside. I dared not look at him and held my face averted, lest he see the confusion play across it, for much greater than the strength of his arms was the force that held me there. At last summoning the power to break his hold, I pulled backward, freeing myself. I pushed past him, running for the freedom of the sunlight. Not even Tice's curious call after me brought me to a stop.

It took two days until the cabin was clean enough to meet my standards, which had been lowered accordingly, for otherwise I might never have had a shelter that winter. Only after every moveable object had been dragged into the clearing did I begin hauling countless buckets of water from the stream, scrubbing until every last bit of dried mud, dirt, and grime was either washed or swept away. Tice questioned my wastefulness when I removed and burned the bedding, but I had been with Doc too long. As much as possible would be fresh and clean. When there was nothing more to be done, there was the inevitable to be faced: settling in for a long, hard winter.

During the days that followed I looked after the stock, tended the fire, provided the meals, and daily swept the cabin clean with the broom I had fashioned from dried stalks and a tree limb. My bed was one of pine boughs, blankets, and skins, both men having laid claim to the beds soon after our arrival. Resentfully I had dragged in the thick pine branches, realizing only afterward how luxurious was the sharp fragrance of the bed of needles that cradled me ever so gently beneath my blankets.

From the first, Tanner prowled the ridgelines with the instincts of the hunted, casting a watchful eye over the floor of the pass. But in spite of Tanner's expertise in the wilderness, it was Tice who took to the mountain life best. In fact, he was hard put to contain his enthusiasm.

"It sure do beat riding the grub line" he said, during one of our first meals together, his mouth filled with loin steak from a fresh-killed deer. He referred to the common way laid-off cowboys spent their winter months, drifting from ranch to ranch for a meal and bed in exchange for the lowliest of chores.

Tanner avoided the cabin whenever I was about and just looking at me within the confines of those walls was enough to bring the familiar scowl to his face. "Makes Jed edgy, just sittin' 'round," Tice said to me once, intuiting my thoughts. "We make 'im nervous." I rather thought that he did not mean "we" but me. But the inevitable was bound to occur and did one evening. Tanner joined us, dismantling his carbine across the table for cleaning. Tice's words were like those of a songbird that night, cheerfully ignoring Tanner's saturnine face and my own quiet mood. Knowing that only the necessity of a clean firearm had forced Tanner to suffer my company, I enjoyed Tice's expansiveness with a contrary fancy.

"... The most excitement I ever had that winter," Tice continued, with a wink in my direction, "was countin' bullet holes in the bunkhouse ceiling. 'An I ain't very good with numbers, but I was better 'n anyone else there. I didn't stay long, even though they'd offer'd me a steady job." Tice grinned at me. "It was the rancher's wife's fault. She didn't want no card playin' and such. Her man abided by ev'rythin' she said. Henpecked, he was. So I told 'em nope, they could keep their job, thank you. Had to. Even her cookin' couldn't keep me on.

"Course, even that job surely beats workin' at the livery or tendin' shop," Tice admitted somewhat expertly. While Tanner scowled anew at this foolishness, because Tice could neither read nor write and there was little likelihood of him getting hired on as a store clerk, Tice's eye caught mine from across the room. Laughter and good spirit shone from their depths as he regarded me warmly. For an instant my mind flashed to Rose's girls and how handsome they must have found him.

As if he read my thoughts, the lines of Tanner's face deepened, accentuating his stony features. Our winter in the mountains had barely begun and already the discordant personalities rubbed each other raw. Tanner's forbearance was at its worst when Tice directed his conversation to me and I knew he resented my part as Tice's willing audience. I didn't know how the long months away from civilization might affect Tice, but I had never forgotten the look in Tanner's eyes when he first saw me at Doc's. Although I was aware that Tanner harbored no liking for me, I also knew that he was not indifferent to my presence. I had helped Doc patch up too many cut-up and shot-up men not to learn about the passions that sometimes drove even the meekest of them to violence during a winter's isolation. Hardened men had brawled and died over a lady's favors.

"Now wolf huntin'," Tice began afresh, "that's somethin' else again. Leastaways it used to be. Time was, all a man had to do was lay out his traps and then collect his money. An' maybe worry 'bout freezin' to death or havin' his horse break a leg an' die on 'im miles from nowhere. Of course, it's easier on the plains. All you got to do is put out your poison. After they'd eat their fill and drop, it's a snap to find 'em. But it can't be done in timber country. Too hard to find 'em in the trees. By the time you c'n get to 'em, more 'n likely the pelts been spoilt."

Tice cast a devilish eye upon an unsuspecting Tanner. "What ranchers do now is hire a wolfer. That's what I call a first-rate job. They've got their own string o' dogs and feed 'em only bacon and cornmeal, 'cause fresh meat spoils their noses and 'ndurance. They lay their traps 'long a twenty-mile stretch or so and check 'em ev'ry day. They draw top wages, 'cluding their horses an' feed. An' they get a five-dollar bounty on each wolf scalp from the county."

Tice looked at me solemnly. "Bet you didn't know that Jed don't hold with hirin' wolfers. Him bein' a rancher an' all, I find it mighty odd." His cigarette aglow, Tice leaned over and looked at me conspiratorially. "Why don't you ask 'im 'bout it, Meg?"

I shook my head silently, my eyes on Tanner, unwilling to aid Tice in provoking his displeasure any further. My contrariness did not run to destroying the calm of our first evening spent together.

"Well, then, I'll tell you," Tice replied, not at all deterred by my lack of interest. "Jed, here, has got a soft spot for wolves—guess he thinks they're just big dogs—"

"Damn you, Tice!" Tanner grunted as he finished his work on the carbine. "I never said I was against hunting wolves if it has to be done. I've seen their work. They're no damned good. They'll rip an udder right off a cow or take a chunk out of their sides and leave 'em to die. Or cripple 'em bad enough so that they die of starvation. I did say that I wasn't taking you north with me to go wolfing. But that was 'cause I find your company mighty tiresome. In fact, you drive a man near crazy with all your talk." Rising from the table, without even a thought to his coat, Tanner left the cabin.

"Guess he won't be goin' far," Tice observed. He

lay back in his bed, staring at a ceiling that had no bullet holes.

I sighed wearily. It would be a long winter.

It did seem though, that Tice thrived on orneryness, taking great pleasure in getting a rise out of Tanner. He was older than me, but he was quite a bit younger than Tanner and did not take orders well. He returned late one afternoon, having been gone since sunup, on the day Tanner applied new shakes to the roof. With amusement I watched his latest rebellion as Tanner ordered him about from the rooftop even before he had chance to dismount and unload the bulging sacks he had tied to his saddle.

"Damn you, Jed!" He shouted up at the man perched atop the cabin. "I ain't your slave, you know!"

"Never said you were, Tice. Just do like I tell you to. If you feel like eating, leastaways." Tanner's laconic answer made Tice's anger all the more irrational. He strode over to the lean-to at the side of the cabin, took up the pick, and stalked over to the north face of the dwelling and attacked the ground with a fury.

Curious, I wrung the excess water from the shirt I had been washing in the stream and ambled over to watch Tice as he worked.

"What are you doing?" I inquired innocently.

"What does it look like I'm doin'?" he snapped back at me. "Jed's crazy. This ground is too damned hard for such foolishness. It's half froze already." He gave a vicious swing to the pick.

Knowing I would get little else from him, I left and went to the sacks he had left by the giant spruce tree. They were filled with root crops. I turned and called out to him excitedly. "Where'd you get these, Tice?"

"Widow McGrath's. In exchange for fresh meat.

She and Jed agreed to it," he panted, swinging the pick high above him.

"Widow McGrath?" I repeated, puzzled by this latest information. "Is she someone he knew when he was a boy up here?" I inquired curiously.

Tice gave a whoop of laughter. "Hell, no...sorry, Meg. You've got it all wrong. Culley told us 'bout her livin' on the mountain," he explained, already putting the pick down for a rest. "She's not old at all, she's got two youngin's...she's a fine cook...an' real pretty, too."

Grimly, I took this into account. Tice liked her, that much was obvious—and Tanner, too, I was willing to bet, suddenly remembering a day that he, like Tice, had been absent from sunup to late afternoon. I looked up at the roof, catching sight of the thick brush of chestnut hair falling over his brow as he bent to his work.

"Where does she live, Tice?" I asked, thinking that no matter what, it would be nice to have a woman's company on the mountain.

"Shut your mouth, Tice, and keep digging that root cellar!" Tanner barked from above.

I whirled about and looked up at the roof. Damn him! Standing tall on the rooftop, glaring down at me, he dared me to make trouble, liking nothing better than to find a reason to vent his prickly temper on me. I saw his eyes fall to my shirt, where inadvertently I had clutched the clothing I had washed, suddenly aware that the wet fabric clung to my chest. I turned away from him, my cheeks flaming. Understanding his reasons for not wanting me to meet the Widow McGrath did not make it easier. I knew Tanner insisted that the masquerade continue, in case someone was still on our trail. The fewer people who knew of the young woman living on the mountain with two men, he believed, the better. My disguise had fooled Culley but would never fool another woman. I was a prisoner in the mountains and Tanner was my keeper. Clutching the wet wash tightly, I gave him a defiant look and walked away, knowing that he watched me until I disappeared from sight.

If Tanner worried that we had been followed, he kept it to himself, and although I knew the delay in the expected snow troubled him, as several weeks passed I grew confident that the danger was over. Therefore, I was only curious, not alarmed, the day Tice returned empty-handed from his rabbit hunt. Spying him as he conferred with Tanner by the woodpile, I sensed the urgency of their talk.

I met them at the cabin door. I refused to recognize the obvious. "Where are the rabbits?" I asked Tice shortly.

Tice met my gaze, then quickly looked away. "Didn't see any, Meg," he said, removing his coat.

Then suddenly I shifted my eyes to Tanner just in time to catch him watching me. His face was again bearded, but this time as a protection against the approaching winter. It softened the hard, uncompromising lines of his face just a bit, masking the usual grim set of his mouth. Above it, his eyes appeared lighter, the color of the wintry sky outside. He did not look away from me. My apprehension rose. Jed Tanner did not often grace me with penetrating looks.

"What's wrong?" I asked, feeling as though I held my breath. It had been Tice who had brought Tanner the news, yet it was not Tice I turned to now but Tanner. My fear of him had gradually evolved into a reluctant trust. He had sacrificed too much for me not to realize how much I depended on him.

For the first time, he looked at me as if he were weighing what he saw. Going to the hearth, he reached over to the crudely made mantle shelf for a cup and then poured himself some coffee. He walked over to the table and sat down, sipping the steaming liquid slowly. I caught the strain in the room.

"Christ, Jed!" Tice burst out. "Tell her the truth! There's no sense hiding it from her!"

I knew it was not Tice's admonitions that persuaded Tanner to tell me. He had already made up his mind to do so.

"There's trouble," he said finally.

"What kind of trouble?" I asked softly as my thoughts began to race. I dropped into the seat across the table from him.

"Tice found traces of someone nosin' around on that ridge that overlooks the clearing. It's not the first time." I caught Tice's surprise; evidently Tanner had chosen not to tell him before. "It was a couple of days ago—I didn't want to jump to conclusions. Thought it'd be better if everyone seemed to act natural around here."

"I don't understand!" I said, trying to keep the panic from my voice. "You said yourself that no one came up the pass after us. You've watched over it almost day and night since we've been here!"

"Well, I was wrong," he admitted bluntly.

"How do you know it's not someone from around here?" I asked desperately. "Maybe it's just a curious neighbor?"

"It's not," he replied curtly. "According to Culley, there's only Ada McGrath and Ben Trew living on the mountain. And Ben hasn't returned yet, he was summering below. Unless he came by way of the south face. Anyway that's not his style. No neighbor's going to spy on us from some ridge. No one from around here would pass up the chance of company and a meal. Whoever it is, he's keeping his distance on purpose, that's for damned sure."

"But why? Why would they wait if they know we're here?"

"Can't say for sure. Maybe it's because you've never been left alone. One of us has always kept pretty close to you. Whoever it is might just want to make a try for you and not risk a shootout. Or maybe he's just waiting to get all of us together before he tries anything. That way, there'd be no one following him after he leaves."

Shaken, I rose from the table and paced the small cabin restlessly.

"I wouldn't be believin' every word Jed here goes spoutin' off, Meg," Tice said suddenly. "He's just bein' careful, expectin' the worst to happen. Now I took a look at those very same tracks today and didn't get that impression at all."

Both Tanner and I looked at Tice, me with hopefulness, Tanner with curiosity.

"You didn't?" I asked, encouraged, wanting desperately to believe him.

"Nope. No sane person is gonna come up that mountain 'fore the snow and just hide out, watchin' and waitin'. It doesn't make sense. None of Barton's men'd be that crazy. You've gotta remember that whoever it is would be stuck up here for the winter just like us.

"Nope, I'm sayin' that Jed's mind is workin' overtime, if you know what I mean. And on the chance that he's right, that there is someone out there, it just might be that whoever it is, is after him an' not you. Hell, Jed's done a whole lot more livin' than you, an' I just bet he's offended a damned sight more people, too. So if there is someone out there, they could be after him, and you won't have to worry none 'bout this bein' your fault. Because he can take care of his own hide, believe me."

I expected Tanner to call Tice a fool, to tell him what he had just said was ridiculous. But he didn't. Instead, he appeared to give Tice's words some thought. I didn't believe that either of them had ever lied to me before, and I didn't see any reason for them to do so now. But the words did not bring me the expected relief Tice had intended them to. Instead, I found myself watching Tanner, wondering what it was that he had done in the past that would make his enemies seek him out. Had it been the killing he got off for? Or was it, as Tice had suggested before, that trouble dogged him no matter where he happened to be? I told myself that the worry I felt for him was only natural. My life depended on his safety.

"You could be right," Tanner said after a while, addressing Tice with a fathomless expression on his face. "But just the same, we're not taking any chances. You keep an eye on the girl and don't let her out of your sight. From now on, one of us stays with her, here, and we'll keep a watch on the place from the ridge, too, as often as we can."

"And you," he said, turning to me with a harsh look, "you keep that hair of yours hidden. You hear me? No sense making you more of a target than you already are."

I stared at him angrily, my fingers reaching for the strands of hair that had escaped the confines of my stocking cap.

"Don't I get to say anything about this?" I asked bitterly, hating the habit he had of reducing me to a small child. "I only want—" I started to say.

"Nobody cares what you want!" he snapped, silencing me abruptly with his words. Stiffening under his unexpected attack, I met his pointed stare, then turned and went outside.

He sent Tice after me, of course, because I was no longer to be left alone.

Tanner left early the next morning to lay in a good supply of meat for Ada before the full thrust of winter descended on the mountain. I upbraided myself for my irritation. Game would be scarcer later on, I reasoned; that was the explanation behind Tanner's quick departure, not the bitterness from the day before which had not subsided even with nightfall. Still, I could not shake the image of a beautiful widow welcoming him with open arms. Where Tanner went and what he did was of no concern to me, I reminded myself sharply.

I was grateful for Tice's company. A casual comradery had developed between us despite his teasing ways. He fashioned snowshoes for each of us from the steamed boughs and rawhide strips, to use when the snows became deeper, and we went for long walks along the snow-dusted ridges and meadows. Although he did not speak of it, I knew he looked for signs of an intruder's tracks, but we saw nothing. Relieved, I began to believe that Tanner was being overly cautious. Buoyed by this thought, I grew cheerful.

Tice, smiling at my high spirits, decided the time had come for me to learn hunting skills. He turned aside my protests, taking it upon himself to teach me.

"It's just plain crazy for you to be out here and not know what you're about," he admonished me, bringing down the stag I had missed. I remained prone on the ground as he jumped to his feet and went to inspect his kill. Reluctantly, I rose to my feet and joined him.

"You've got to put aside those squeamish feelings of yours, Meg," he said as he made his first cut along the underside of the deer.

"I'm not squeamish, Tice," I replied rather unconvincingly. "How can you think that I am? I fixed up your arm and God knows how much worse I've seen at Doc's."

"Aw, Meg, look at you! You're almost as white as snow!" he said, looking up from his work.

"It's just that I'd rather be patching things up, Tice, not cutting them apart."

"Well, just you wait until you taste these steaks tonight, Meg. You're gonna change your mind. You wait and see."

Tice was right in a way. I did get used to it, but I never took pleasure in it and I was never able to conquer the cold pit in my stomach when my animal went down. It reminded me too much of Jay, and Fenton, too. Human or animal, I didn't like killing.

We spied Tanner in the doorway of the cabin late the next afternoon as we lightheartedly descended the rise at the edge of the clearing, our rifles and catch of rabbits in hand. His eyes squinted against the harsh glare of sun and snow as he observed us draw nearer. The color of his skin had weathered to that of well worn leather. Under the cold stare of those wintry eyes, the cheer his appearance brought to me drained away. I turned silent and uncertain under his fixed gaze.

"Glad you're back, Jed," Tice said. "Look at these here rabbits. Meg took 'em herself," Tice continued, proud of my achievements. "She's quite a shot."

"I'm not surprised," he remarked, his gray eyes holding mine. "I'd think she'd be real good at it." His words condemned me for no reason, and then I wondered if Doc had told him that I had killed a man. Would he fault me for protecting myself? Would the incident reinforce his already low opinion of me? Seeing that my prowess with a rifle did not improve Tanner's humor, Tice willingly dropped the subject.

"Didn't think you'd ever get back," he said to Tanner over his plate of fried rabbit later that evening, referring to the fact Jed had stayed away an extra day. Tanner sat hunched over his plate, wiping away the last traces of his meal with a chunk of bread.

"Couldn't help it," he said, pushing it aside. "Ada's

youngest took sick. Happened just as I was getting ready to leave."

"That Timmie. He's a cute 'un all right," Tice agreed. "An' he sure has a way of gettin' under your skin. Guess he's been doin' a mite poorly. Ada worries 'bout 'im."

"He'll be all right," Tanner said, reaching for his cup.

Tanner's consideration for Ada McGrath's boy surprised me. I hadn't thought him a man to be moved by the plight of a sick child. His kindness to Ada and her boy should have worked in his favor, proving that there was some basis for the strange attraction he held for me, that he was not entirely the cold-hearted man I assumed him to be. But instead I found myself wondering about Ada McGrath. Tanner did not have the look of a man who had suffered through an unpleasant, dutiful visit to a poor widow and her two children. I found myself very much wanting to meet the woman he and Tice found so intriguing.

"Can I visit her?" I asked Tanner suddenly, sure the danger of my discovery was over by now.

"No." His reply was swift and to the point.

"Why not?" I demanded, angry that his refusal should wound me so. "Or is it that you just take pleasure in denying me what I ask?"

"I don't want her involved." His calm reply made my accusation look all the more unreasonable, but it did nothing to stem my outburst.

"Damn you, Tanner!" I cried at him across the table. "You still think that someone's out there? Then why haven't Tice or I seen any signs of him? We combed these ridges while you were gone. And what did we find? Nothing! I think it's just like Tice says. Your mind is working overtime!"

He gave me a withering stare as he set down his cup. Abruptly, he rose from table. "I'm not risking a good woman and her two kids just because you've got a hankering for woman talk. Is that clear?" he asked. Leaving the room, he slammed the door behind him, convinced of my selfishness. Despairingly, I stared unseeingly across the room.

"He's right, you know, Meg," Tice ventured in the hostile silence that followed.

I glared at him accusingly. "You'd agree with just about anything he'd say, Tice."

He studied his hands reflectively. "Well, maybe what you say is true. But then again, usually he's right in how he figures things."

Exasperated with them both, I cleared the supper dishes from the table, thinking all the while about Ada McGrath.

"It must be hard on her," I said finally, "living up here alone, with just her children."

"She don't talk much 'bout it," Tice leaned back in his seat as he concentrated on the memory of the pretty widow. "She's got lots o' books and things. She teaches the kids their lessons. Jed thinks mighty highly of her."

"Oh," I said casually, trying not to let Tice know how much it mattered to me. "How can you tell?"

"Just a feelin'," Tice replied somewhat carefully. I poured myself some coffee and sat down across the table from him. "I didn't think he thought highly of any woman," I managed to say lightly. "Or is it just me that he takes pleasure in hurting?"

"You judge him harshly, Meg. Without knowin' anythin' about him."

I gave Tice a hard stare. "What do you mean?"

He looked uncomfortable. "Well, I know he hasn't treated you kindly, Meg," he said hesitantly. "But you've got to realize somethin'. No man's born mean. It takes some doin' to get 'im that way."

Tice shut up tighter than a clam after that and no amount of questioning would shed any further light on his cryptic remark. It seemed that the more I learned about Jed Tanner, the less I knew about him. And both Tice and Tanner himself were trying to keep it that way.

Chapter Sixteen

MY FRIENDSHIP WITH TICE DEEPENED during the intervals when Tanner was away keeping a lookout on the ridge and it was easy to see that this displeased him on his return. He glowered so at our shared laughter that he reminded me of the grimfaced Miss Henry at the Cross Creek School, and my accomplishments in hunting and tracking that Tice boasted of so proudly were regarded as of little account.

But only when I caught him observing us unexpectedly, a look of speculation on his face, did I perceive the reason for his behavior. He believed the attachment between Tice and me to be a romantic one. Reserved at best, Tanner misinterpreted Tice's caring ways and my response to them. He mistook the fun we shared for something more. I stifled the desire to tell him the truth, for he would call me a fool to think it mattered to him at all. I was glad my friendship with Tice annoyed him, I decided obstinately, remembering his quiet praise of Ada Mc-Grath. It seemed all I ever was destined to be was a thorn in his side.

"You didn't leave him any biscuits," I remarked to Tice the day Tanner had gone hunting for game. It was not meant to be a reprimand, only a comment on Tice's inexhaustible appetite.

"Well," Tice reasoned, "seein' how he didn't leave me none of that pie yesterday, I figured he's got it comin'."

"You just weren't fast enough for the leftovers," I commented dryly, amused at Tice's sense of fair play.

A lull in the conversation followed, but so silent was Tanner's approach that when the door burst open, without warning, we both beheld the bloodstained man as if he were a messenger from hell. It covered him so thickly it took us a moment to realize the blood was not his.

"Good God, Jed! What happened to you?" Tice exploded.

Relief at his well-being overcame all my other feelings for him. I went to the hearth and poured him some coffee. He shook his head, rejecting it, and knowingly Tice brought out the bottle of whiskey, saved for deserving occasions. Tanner lifted it to his lips and drank it straight down. Ignoring our anxious looks, he brushed away the snow that clung wetly to his jacket and went directly to the hearth, bending down and helping himself to the contents of the steaming stewpot. He spied the empty biscuit plate as he sat down at the table, but said nothing and instead fell to the hot food with a ravenous appetite. He paused only when his plate was empty.

"Grizzly spooked the packhorse," he began at last, directing his words to Tice. "She bolted, then stumbled as she tried to make it up the switchback. Fell back down to that shelf below. The pack tore... saved her hide, but I can't say as much for the meat. I cached some of it and carried back the rest." Then, for the first time, I saw his face crease in a wide smile, the strong white teeth making his face seem all the darker.

"Sure as hell scared off the bear."

With a surprising willingness no doubt spawned by relief, Tice offered to see to the meat Tanner had brought back with him.

There was a strained quiet between us once Tanner and I were left alone in the cabin. Forsaking the intimate glow of the lantern light and the warmth of the hearth, I retreated to the comforting pile of skins atop my bed. Taking up some mending in the less than adequate light, I carefully avoided looking at the man in the blood-stiffened clothing. I heard him push his plate aside. The quiet that followed was broken only by the snapping of the dry wood as it burned steadily in the hearth. Then I lifted my eyes and saw him in the dancing shadows cast by the flames. Silently stripping away his shirt, he bent over the pail of water that warmed by the fireside and washed away the blood and grime that had soaked through his clothing. The light flickered over his lean, well muscled body as he moved, accentuating the rugged strength of his frame and emphasizing the broad shoulders and powerful arms. The rest of him remained in darkened relief.

It was as he straightened and turned from the fire that I first saw the jagged scar of the bullet wound on his left shoulder, a scar that plowed diagonally across his chest for several inches. I uttered an incoherent sound and he turned toward me, his eyes staring into mine through the darkness. "The needle," I said, swallowing. "I've stuck myself." I put my finger to my mouth, my mending forgotten.

It was like a drowning wave, so swiftly did the past come rushing back, scarcely giving me a chance to think as my thoughts ran wildly together. Shoulder wounds were common, I told myself severely. I had seen enough of them at Doc Elliot's to know that. There was no reason to believe—just because this scar approximated that of the stranger I had helped that night in the woods all those years ago—that he was the same man. The thought of a man like Jed Tanner at the mercy of a ragamuffin runaway disguised as a boy was absurd.

I remembered it all, then. The man in the black frock coat, the solitary rider on a chestnut horse, the ringing blast of the rifle. The image of the stranger came back to me, but try as I would, I remembered few of his features. Not the color of his bright, fevered eyes nor the true color of his hair, matted with sweat and blood. He had not been so terribly old, but the ravages of his injury, distorting his face with pain, had aged him beyond his years. I remembered his helplessness that had kept me from fearing him and how I had placed his gun close by, to ease his mind upon waking. But although I could not recall his face, the impression left by his body as I feared for his life and lay by his side had not faded. I remembered too well the warmth we had shared that night and how, at the sheriff's office, I had fleetingly wished myself back at his side, eluding our pursuers together. Had that man even survived? Could that man have been Tanner almost five years ago? I was not certain of Tanner's age, but I judged it to be about thirty. But I didn't believe that even five years of hard living could change that helpless, dying man into the forbidding person Tanner was today.

Why did I try to make the chance mark of an angry bullet answer questions that had no answers? Perhaps it was just the wish that the man I had cared for had survived the bullet wounds and the hanging promised by Sheriff Baker.

Tanner dried himself with a piece of sacking that

hung above the pail, and rummaged through his belongings for a clean shirt. As he shrugged his shoulders into the wrinkled garment, the jagged tear across
the muscled chest was once more exposed to my eyes.
I dared not ask him if he had another scar from
another bullet wound. Through the darkness his eyes
found mine and this time I did not look away. I did
not know his thoughts, but the scar confirmed his
violent past. He was a killer, I reminded myself again,
knowing I held that fact as a barrier between us
because I was not indifferent to him. It took only
Ada McGrath's name to set fire to a jealousy I had
no right to feel. Moving away from the hearth, Tanner was once more hidden by the shadows. But the
angry brand of the bullet wound remained before
me.

It was inevitable that Tice would take his turn up
on the ridges, leaving Tanner behind with me. Without Tice's buffering presence, his remoteness was
hard to bear and at times I thought that even his
rage would be preferable to the stilted tension between us. I was confined to the cabin, permitted out
only after dark for a breath of fresh air. The memories of Cross Creek hauntingly returned during the
long hours in which there was little else to occupy
my mind.

The days had been overcast since Tice's departure,
but finally one day dawned clear and bright, with
the crispness of fall in the air. It was a day for sharing
an adventure, a romp in the snow or chasing rabbits.

It seemed perfectly natural to defy Tanner and his
edict. There had been no recent signs of an intruder
on the mountain and I dismissed his cautionary
measures as extreme. I yearned for the solitude long
denied me, and Tanner's anger seemed a small price
to pay for the privilege of an afternoon's freedom.
Slipping from the cabin, I skirted the bare aspen
thicket as the snow dust was lifted from the ground

by a light wind capturing the radiance of the sun like a sparkling diamond powder. Tanner stood with his back to me, his shirt sleeves rolled up, the corded muscles straining as he heaved the ax and attacked the stack of firewood. He split the wood cleanly with a smooth rhythm that kept his attention focused on the task before him. Under the ringing sound of the ax he took no notice of me as I made my way to the cover of pines that fringed the clearing.

Although the winds had drifted the snow into deep pockets, no new snow had fallen since Tice had left and I picked up one of our old trails easily enough, my snowshoes affording me a slow but steady gait. A wind came up, a refreshing coolness against my perspiring brow, and breaking through the stand of trees, I rested on a bare hilltop, breathing heavily from the exertion—and then I cursed myself for my stupidity. In my eagerness for solitude, I had forgotten how early the winter darkness would descend. With the fading rays of sunlight gleaming dully at my feet, I turned to go back.

Had I not stepped backward, I would not have stumbled over the barely protruding root, half hidden in the waning light. Hampered by the snowshoe, I fell, badly wrenching my ankle. Realizing that my anger at my predicament would be nothing compared to Tanner's should he find me like this, I wrapped my muffler, made from the excess material of my poncho, around my injured foot. Expecting to return victorious from my venture, proving he was wrong, that no danger lurked for me outside the cabin, I had demonstrated instead what he had known all along—except that I was a bigger fool then even Tanner believed me to be.

The fast-setting sun slipped behind the jagged peaks in the west, bathing the land in a dusk that would soon be darkness. With no hesitation, I abandoned the trail I had followed, no more than an animal trace at best, all too treacherous in the coming night. Under a clear moonless sky and a cloud of pain, I struck out directly across the floor of the little park. In the gloomy light, all the landmarks familiar to me were undefined. Stubbornly, I kept on. The time that passed had no meaning. I did not panic, for the agony of the swelling ankle did not allow me the luxury of fear. With the aid of a broken branch from a fallen tree, I finally came to the creekbed, but I did not allow myself relief at the sight of the shimmering crystalline banks. Instead, I plodded onward. At last rewarded by the glimmer of light escaping at the edges of the skin flap inside the cabin window, I shut my burning eyes weakly, bracing myself for a coming storm, and I summoned up the courage I needed to face Jed Tanner.

He did not disappoint me.

"Where in the hell have you been?" The bearded face lashed out my welcome.

I never expected to be glad to see him. As naturally as possible, I closed the door behind me, leaning against it for support. An open pack lay on the table with some hastily gathered food next to it. And the inevitable bottle of whiskey. His snowshoes were propped nearby.

"I'm sorry," I said in a subdued voice, humbled by what I saw. My defiance and restlessness were gone, evaporated during the long, painful trek back. I waited for the anger that I so richly deserved. But instead there was only silence in the cabin.

"I needed to be alone..." I tried to explain, suddenly wanting him to understand. "I knew you wouldn't approve... but I did it anyway."

"I don't expect that you'll do it again." His voice was rough, but not angry, and for that reason alone, it startled me. I looked up at him quickly, but did not find the censure I had expected to see.

"I know why you did it," he said in the same careful tone, an inscrutable expression on his face. "That's why I didn't come after you sooner...figured you knew what you were doing. Tice is a good woodsman."

I had been wrong. A need for solitude had been the one thing a man like him could understand.

"No, I won't do it again..." I heard myself repeat after his retreating back.

Overcome by the generosity with which he had forgiven me, my tension seeped away, leaving me with an overwhelming exhaustion and a painfully throbbing ankle. Unwilling to have him witness the folly of my afternoon, I made my way to the bench as inconspicuously as possible. Turning slightly so as not to draw attention to my efforts, I removed my boot and eased down the woolen stocking. I viewed the dark, swollen flesh with dismay and gingerly rotated my foot at the ankle as Doc would have done. It didn't appear to be broken, but it needed binding. Struggling to my uninjured foot, I limped over to my bed to search my belongings for some cloth to serve as bandages.

I jumped at the sound of his voice.

"Sit down," he ordered sharply.

Turning my head, I saw that he had observed my attempt to keep my mishap from him. Taking up the length of muslin, I returned to the bench. He crossed the room and rummaged through his belongings on the shelf above his bed until he found what he searched for and brought to light a small tin. In it, and meant only for the likes of the dun, was the foulest smelling salve I had ever come across, the rancid odor making up for the punishment I had escaped. He walked over to where I sat and, crouching before me, pushed the leg of my breeches out of the way, deftly applying the ointment to the discolored flesh.

His touch was cool and impersonal, but I felt the

warmth of his hands even through the heat of the injured ankle. Continuing to grip my leg, he ripped the bandages with his free hand and teeth, then bound them snugly around my foot, carefully building up the support until it encompassed my ankle. I stared down at the top of his head as he worked, embarrassed by this unexpected intimacy. Feeling curiously vulnerable, I looked away.

"I looked for tracks by the stand of pine above the south ridge," I said at last, breaking the silence between us. "But there weren't any, at least not since the last snowfall. That's where you found them, wasn't it?"

"That's where I saw them last," he answered. "Doesn't mean anything. Like Tice said, it might be nothing at all." His words were reassuring and I wanted to believe them. His voice sounded natural, as if we conversed all the time. Finishing his work, he rose to his feet, once again towering over me. I looked down at my ankle. Doc could not have done a better piece of work himself. I wasn't too sure about the salve.

"Thank you," I said rather awkwardly.

He returned the tin to his shelf and picked up the bottle that rested on the table, the same bottle he had unsparingly drunk from the night he had returned to the cabin stained with blood. Deferring to my womanhood, he poured some of the contents into a cup and pushed it in front of me.

"Drink it," he said.

The assault of the fumes was a warning, but it did not quite prepare me for the liquid fire that seared my throat, momentarily blocking out all sensation below. A warming glow in my stomach traveled the length of my extremities, easing the stiffness of my body. My ankle became a distant ache.

Wearily, with exhaustion setting in, I watched him as he moved across the room. Although the fire still burned, he had not bothered with the makings of supper. He found a tin of tomatoes among our supplies and, without taking the time to heat it, opened it and set it on the table. He reached up to the sack containing a supply of jerked venison and tossed some strips next to the tomatoes and brought out some leftover biscuits. I helped myself to the food.

Through my slightly befuddled haze, I found myself staring at him again. In the soft, flickering light of the hearth, his eyes were dark, shadowed hollows. The high-planed cheekbones captured the wavering illumination of the firelight and the remainder of his face was lost to the obscurity of darkness and the thickness of his beard. The contents of his plate remained untouched as he looked broodingly into the fire. I sensed, through the wisdom of my alcoholic musings, the turmoil of the emotions hidden within him. Desperately, I wanted to reach out to him, but I didn't know how. Even through the vapors of a drunken whim, I knew anything I offered him would be rebuffed. Yet I had to try. Slowly, mindful of my ankle, I rose to my feet and hobbled over to where my buffalo coat hung from a peg on the wall. I found the pocket and took what I wanted and made my way back to where he sat. The peppermint stick, the extra one I had taken that day from Culley, was in my hand. I held it out to him.

He looked at it, and I saw the curtain on the past drawn once again. His mouth twitched involuntarily and I knew he recalled that day at the trading post as well as I.

"You're drunk," he said softly.

I smiled.

He looked at me, his eyes glinting oddly. "It's not a good thing for a girl to be. Someone just might take advantage of her condition."

"But you're responsible for it," I reminded him mockingly.

"So I am," he recalled reflectively.

"Do you plan to take advantage of me?" I inquired politely, the last of my inhibitions banished by the whiskey.

He reached out to me, his hand under my chin.

"I don't think so."

He silenced any further inebriated questions with a finger to my lips. "You'd regret it tomorrow, Meg," he said gently.

My senses warmed to the sound of my name on his lips.

"And would you?" I asked boldly.

Our eyes met, mine questioning, his with answers I didn't want. "Not now," he replied, with only the slightest tightening of his jaw to indicate his tension, "but in the morning, yes."

I stiffened under his touch and he let his hand drop.

"What we have now, Meg, isn't the way things are between us," he said quietly. "The whiskey's clouded your thinking...and I've let myself forget..."

"Forget what?" I had to ask it, but my voice was small. I was afraid of what he would say.

He answered me, then, and what he said made me wish that he hadn't. "You remind me of someone, Meg. Someone I wish I could forget."

"Oh..." My voice trailed off. I did not know what to say, but I realized how much had been explained. He got up from his seat and looked down at me, but I averted my eyes, not wanting him to see the pain I felt.

I heard him walk away and then the cabin door opened and shut behind him. He did not reenter the cabin that night.

It was well past daybreak when I awoke, a throbbing ache penetrating the thick fog of sleep. The stuporing effect of the alcohol had worn off and my ankle was at its worst. With a grimace, the previous evening came rushing back. Stiff with pain, I dragged myself from my cramped position, mortified by the memory of my behavior. Had I really said those things to him?

It was then that I noticed the rudely constructed but perfectly adequate crutch by the cabin door. A smile came to my face. Tanner had made it for me. I was sure it was a sign that things had changed between us. His past no longer mattered to me and I thought that he, too, had put it from him for a little while the night before. Perhaps he would again. It is beyond me how I failed to perceive the truth at the time. But for this I can rightfully blame Tanner, for he had a way of blinding me to it.

The brutal truth of Jed Tanner's past came out when the crutch called Tice's attention to my injury. He stared at me with immediate dismay.

"What happened, Meg?" he demanded, frightening me with his intensity.

I hesitated, sensing his alarm. "What is it, Tice? What's wrong?"

"Did he do this to you?" he asked me harshly.

"What on earth are you talking about? It was my own fault...I fell..." I hesitated, reluctant to tell even Tice of my foolish afternoon of freedom. "He made it for me," I said, holding out the crutch for his inspection. Tice ignored it, still suspicious of my injury.

I tried to allay his fears although I did not understand them. "You don't have to worry about Tanner and me anymore, Tice," I said softly, to reassure him. "It wasn't what I thought. It's not that he doesn't care for me, it's just that I remind him of someone he used to know, someone he wants to forget."

I had thought that Tice would be pleased by this, but instead, a swift look of alarm came to his face.

He was clearly upset by my news. "Don't be getting too friendly with Jed, Meg. I'm telling you this for your own good."

"Maybe you'd better tell me what you mean, Tice. You said yourself that it'd be easier on all of us if we got along this winter."

"Well, I just changed my mind. You keep your distance from him—"

"And just who do you think you are, telling me what's good for me, Tice Grayson?" I inquired, annoyed.

"You don't understand, Meg," he said quietly. "I'll tell you this only because I think you have to know about it. Your saying that you remind Jed of someone he wants to forget is the worst thing that could happen." He shook his head. "I should've known what was eatin' him. It didn't make any sense, him not taking to you, you lookin' the way you do an' all..."

I looked at him uncomprehendingly, and then I thought I knew the truth of Tanner's past.

"It was over her, wasn't it, Tice? He killed someone because of her? And that's what's got you worried? Because I remind him of her?" I looked at him, expecting to see a reluctant admission in his eyes. But that was not what I found at all. They were curiously empty.

"You don't understand, Meg. He did kill someone, all right. But it was a woman, not a man." Tice faltered for a moment. "An' not just any woman, at that. It was his wife, Meg. An' I'm afraid it's her that you remind him of."

There was no explaining the hollowness that Tice's words brought to me. I had no reason to feel so devastated, to ache so. But the clearing we stood in receded and my eyes focused on Tice's face, begging him to be wrong. How could it be true? How could I have been so mistaken about him? I realized then just how little I knew of Jed Tanner. Believing him to be cold and unfeeling, I had wrongly assumed he had always been that way. But once he had been so driven by passion that he had killed the woman he loved. A bitter laugh welled up inside me. I reminded him of her. No wonder it seemed at times that he could scarcely stand the sight of me. It was what everyone had known about him, but I had not.

"How did it happen?" I heard myself ask Tice, my voice a foreign sound in my ears.

"I only know what the others have said. But he's never denied it. An' he's had plenty o' chances, too, while I've been around." He avoided my eyes, lifting his gaze to the distant mountain peaks. "They say he shot her in cold blood . . . because he found her with another man."

I shut my eyes against the painful images.

"Don't try an' understand him, Meg," Tice continued. "I wouldn't have told you otherwise, 'cept as a warning . . . I don't believe it's anyone else's business. You be careful 'round him, you hear?"

I nodded.

"Tice . . . do I look like her?"

"Can't say, Meg. Only heard 'em say she was one of the most beautiful women they'd ever seen."

I didn't see Tanner before he left for the ridge. He had made a point of avoiding me since our night together in the cabin. He was gone by early morning, long before Tice and I awoke, to seek out whomever it was he believed was out there.

Chapter Seventeen

IN A STRANGE WAY, I felt even more drawn to Tanner after I learned the truth. I suppose it was another example of my waywardness. Instead of being repelled by his crime and shunning him as any decent woman would have—or so I thought—I came to accept him. Knowing as little of him as I did, it was foolish of me.

Doc was well aware of Tanner's past. I realized that now, and at last I understood his reluctance to talk about the man. "She'll be safe with you," he had told Tanner on the night we fled town. Doc had trusted Tanner enough to send me away with him. But then again, what choice did he have? I was curious about Tanner's freedom, having assumed that he had bought his way clear of both judge and jury. But it was possible he needn't have done that, as the law often worked in peculiar ways. It might not fault a man for protecting his own and a wandering wife could be justification for an otherwise terrible killing. Especially if a man or his family had enough power or money, or both.

The storm that Tice had predicted on his return from his watch on the ridge descended upon us with a howling ferocity that sent the snow scuttling in through the cracks in the cabin's chinking. The bitter wind came through the walls as if they were not even there. Only a seat directly in front of the blazing hearth afforded any relief from the cold. So heavy was the snowfall that the view from the cabin door stretched out not more than an arm's distance into the obscuring sea of white. Neither Tice nor I spoke of Tanner that night, each of us grimly contemplating his whereabouts silently. I tried to rid myself of an image of him frozen in a vast, snow-swept wilderness, the dun standing close by, his head lowered against the gusting wind. I feared for him.

No one should have been out that night, so when a harsh pounding sounded at the door, Tice held a finger to his lips, silencing my questions, and quietly reached for his rifle. Motioning me aside, he aimed at the door, knowing it would be but a few seconds before it burst open.

It was a draw as to who was startled the most— Tice and I, or the shaggy giant of a man standing at the threshold of the cabin, his heavily bearded face and clothes so encrusted with snow it was impossible to discern his features.

"Who the devil are you?" he bellowed at Tice, unmindful of the raised weapon.

"I might ask the same of you, Mister." Tice's voice was as cold as I'd ever heard it.

"Trew. Ben Trew," he snapped. His voice was rough.

Tice lowered his guard. "Why didn't you say so?" he asked laconically.

"Never expected to be starin' down your rifle sight,"

the big man answered. "Not much of a greeting for
a soul needin' help."

"Sorry. Storm's made us jumpy." Tice gave me a
cautioning look. There was no need to tell Ben Trew
of the stalker who was thought to be combing the
nearby ridges. Tice put his gun aside and Ben Trew's
eyes came to rest on me.

"Meg, this here is Ben Trew. One of our neighbors.
An' I'm Tice Grayson," he said, introducing himself
to the newcomer.

"That's right. You're stayin' with Jed," he allowed.
"I'd clean forgotten that. Ada mentioned it a while
back. That rifle of yours startled the hell out of me.
Wasn't expectin' that sort of welcome. Thought I'd
find Jed here." His eyes fell on me again in una-
bashed curiosity.

Inadvertently, I raised a hand to my hair. It flowed
loose past my shoulders, the stocking cap Tanner
insisted I wear forgotten in his absence. Ada Mc-
Grath, not knowing the truth, would believe as Culley did and would have told Ben of a young boy who
accompanied Jed Tanner and his partner, not a young
woman. Tice, intuiting his thoughts, came quickly
to my rescue.

"Meg, here, is kin of Jed's. A cousin," he volunteered, leaving my reputation intact by naming me
Tanner's relation. If Ben wondered at Ada's mistaken information about my gender, he made no
mention of it just then. I came forward slowly, hin-
dered by my ankle.

"Let me set your things out to dry, Mr. Trew," I
offered. He shrugged off his jacket and handed it to
me.

Even without his coat of prime silver-gray wolf-
skins and the hat that came down well over his ears
and brow, Ben Trew was a large man and of a greater
height than even Tanner. He was the first person I
had seen aside from Jed Tanner and Tice Grayson

since early fall. With a curiosity of my own, I returned his look.

Much of his taciturn face, reddened by the biting wind, was hidden behind the mane and beard, which showed up russet under the crust of melting ice particles. His eyes were a deep blue and his nose thin and hawkish. Then, with his gaze still fixed on me, he spoke to Tice, leaving me with a strange feeling.

"I'm shy a horse, Grayson. I'd sure appreciate the loan of one of yours. Mine went down in the storm. Broke his leg an' I had to shoot him. Cached my belongings, except for what I could carry with me."

"Be glad to lend you a horse, Ben," Tice replied quickly enough. "But you sit this storm out with us. You can even have Jed's bed, seein' as he ain't back yet," he offered generously.

Ben gave his silent assent and after he seated himself by the fire I served him up a plate of stew. I studied him at leisure while he concentrated on his food. His bearish appearance had been mostly due to his outer wrappings, but the impression was not completely lost even without the heavy layers of clothing. The mane of thick red-gold hair that framed his face and wide cheekbones dropped immediately into a full growth of beard, slightly darker in color, leaving the sensation that the rest of his bulk would match the fullness of his face. This was not so. His trapper's clothing of fringed buckskin was belted at the waist, and although it dropped to mid-thigh in length and high Indian moccasins climbed his legs, it did not hide the tall, straight, powerful build. There was a steeliness to him that matched the look in his eyes. If such a man as Ben Trew, clearly no novice at mountain living, was afoot and without provisions on such a night, where might Tanner be?

"Meg?" Tice called my name. "Ben was interested in knowin' how you came to be up here with Jed 'n me."

I glanced at Ben Trew before answering. He did not look like the sort of man it would be easy to lie to.

"Well, you see, Mr. Trew," I drew a deep breath, "The doctor strongly recommended the mountain air for my condition." That much, at least, was true, I thought, not daring to look at Tice. "I'm taking the cure," I said, gathering steam, leading Ben to believe I had lung fever.

His eyes raked me over. I looked the picture of health.

"But I'm quite well now," I amended briefly.

"I'm glad to hear that, Miss Logan," he commented, deadpan. Damn Ben Trew. He was entirely too nosey. I attempted to sidetrack him.

"Have you lived in the mountains long, Mr. Trew?" I inquired politely.

"I come and go, as the mood suits me," he responded courteously.

"What do you do when you're not running a trapline?" I asked, my curiosity aroused.

He smiled a little at my questions. It was really none of my business and we were not nearly well acquainted enough for me to be so inquisitive. He did not misconstrue my interest as flattery.

"Civilian Army scout, Ma'am," he answered respectfully. "Most recently, that is. Or anything else that happens along. If it pays enough, I'll take it on."

Ben Trew was just like the rest, a man who would ride for the most money he could find.

"Well, if it's money you're after, Mr. Trew, I'm surprised you're still around here. Tice hasn't had much luck. And according to what Culley said, this area is pretty much trapped out."

"Depends on what you're looking for, Miss Logan. That's pretty true of the beaver. But there's still some sable, mink; and otter around. If you know where to look and don't care where you lay your head

at night, it's enough to get by on. Come spring, I'll
find other work to keep me busy. Last few years I've
been scouting pretty regularly."

"Is that where you met...ah...my cousin, Jed?"

"Oh, we came across each other before that. Bound
to happen. Both of us are the restless sort. Haven't
seen him in some years, though. Last time was just
before he took one of those expeditions out."

Somehow I could not see Ben Trew sheperding a
group of eastern scientists about the mountains. He
seemed to read my thoughts.

"No, I've never had anything to do with those surveying parties. I just do my scouting for the army."

"Do you live far from here, Mr. Trew?"

"Just on the other side of the ridge, Ma'am. 'Bout
eight miles or so east of here," he said. "But I see to
my traps, mostly. You'd not often find me there.
You're not far from Ada McGrath's, though. Her place
is just across the gap, maybe some fifteen miles from
here. In winter you can save time by crossing the
creek at Flat Top. It freezes over and will save you
about three miles from crossing upstream."

Ben did not refuse the bottle that Tice passed to
him, growing expansive before his small audience
by the cozy warmth of the fireside. He had a deep
voice and it sounded pleasant against the backdrop
of crackling logs. Ben Trew intrigued me, speaking
of the mountains he loved and the loneliness that
drove most people away.

"Is that why you leave the mountains so often," I
asked him curiously. "Because of the loneliness?"

"No, that's why I come back. I only leave when
the times are lean and I need to pocket some money.
I like it here. It's peaceful. It suits me."

I was grateful to Ben Trew that night. He took
the edge from the storm that raged outside and, even
given his earlier questioning of me, it was the most

peaceful evening I had spent since coming to the mountains.

We loaned Coalie to Ben the next morning, for the smaller pack animals would have foundered in the snowdrifts under his weight. We said our good-byes to him against a landscape blanketed with the pristine glitter of new snow. By then we had dispensed with formalities and had become "Ben" and "Meg," to each other, glad that a chance meeting in a storm had ended so pleasantly. His mouth lifted slightly at the corners and, turning Coalie, he headed him toward the white rise, leaving a trace of sparkling dust floating loftily to the ground as the departing horse kicked up the snow.

Tice was worried about Tanner's prolonged absence. I watched him as he scanned the mountainsides, surveyed the ridges, and gazed out over the floor of the snow-shrouded pass. He would neither leave me to search for him nor take me along.

"I can understand your not wanting to leave me behind," I argued as he inspected the corral for damage caused by the storm's high winds, "but if I went with you—"

"No, Meg," he broke in. "An' I mean it. We don't know what happened to Jed. We'd be easy targets. Hell, I don't even know where to start lookin'. Could be, you know, that he's just been delayed by the storm."

"But you don't really believe that, do you, Tice?" I asked him quietly.

He shook his head. "Can't really explain it to you. It's just a feelin'. But I think somethin's happened...he should have been back 'fore this."

I told myself that Jed Tanner could look after himself. But it was no use. I could not put him from my mind. Images of him preyed on me day and night. I remembered the first time I saw him at Doc's, and the times he had saved my life. I remembered when he greeted me with understanding rather than anger after my bid for an afternoon of freedom. I remembered the smile that a peppermint stick brought to his eyes. Two more days passed and there was still no sign of him. I knew that Tice was right. Even if we were to start a search, where would we begin? More than three feet of snow had fallen during the storm. It would cover any trace of misfortune or foul play. There'd be no sign of him or the dun horse before spring. Tice took to drinking on those long nights, when the darkness fell early and gave us too much time to think. I didn't mind. It was better than facing the questions in each other's eyes. As he lost himself to the oblivion of his bottle, I willed Jed Tanner to come walking through the cabin door. I didn't ask myself why.

I was studying Mandy, the packmare, who had gone off her feed despite my repeated attempts to cajole her with handpicked grass when I saw the dun horse coming across the clearing under a loose rein. Tanner was riding him. I took hold of the weary animal's bridle as he dismounted.

The angular face was gaunt, and even his beard, thicker now, could not hide the deep hollows beneath his cheekbones. His eyes were red-rimmed with exhaustion. He unsaddled the horse without a word and turned him into the corral.

"We were wondering when you'd turn up," I said by way of a welcome, my relief at his return marred by my pique at having worried over him. Of course Jed Tanner could look after himself. How had I ever thought otherwise? I ridiculed myself for the way I had suffered, imagining the amusement it would have provoked had he known. "Even Tice thought something might have happened to you," I said, covering up my own distress.

"Figured you'd get rid of me that easily?" His tiredness softened his sarcasm and I took no offense.

It was his way. It would only vex him to know of our concern. Men like Tanner had a habit of landing on their feet, no matter how great the difficulty.

"Where's the black?" he asked suddenly, noting Coalie's absence from the corral. Weariness would never dull his senses.

"Ben Trew borrowed him. His horse went down in the storm."

Tanner's face tightened at this disclosure. I did not know then of his suspicions, and I damned him silently for begrudging a needy man the loan of a horse. I took in his altered appearance. He looked as if he had not eaten or slept in a week and his clothes hung loosely on his frame, making him appear even taller.

"Where's Tice?" he asked sharply, bringing my perusal of his condition to an end.

"Sleeping it off."

His irritation flared, momentarily piercing his tiredness. "Damn that cowboy!"

At that, whatever goodwill I had for him deserted me in a rush. "He's sleeping it off," I lashed out, "because of you! That damned cowboy was worried about you! Being only human, he thought that whoever it is you've been watching for finally got to you. We thought you were dead! So what if he had too much to drink while sitting around waiting. You just leave him alone and forget about it!" I glared at him defiantly, ending my tirade.

Pale gray eyes regarded me intently from the sun-bronzed face. "All right," he agreed, with effort.

Tanner might as well have returned from the dead as far as Tice was concerned. He sat at the edge of his bed, his head in his hands, looking as morose as I'd ever seen him.

"Real sorry 'bout you findin' me like this, Jed," he said, apologizing in an unsteady voice. "But I thought for sure you'd gone under. Hell, it's been five days since the storm."

Tanner turned to the fire in annoyance, offering us no reason for his lateness. His face was haggard with lines I had not noticed before. Staring at the fire, he addressed us in a steely tone.

"Did it ever occur to either of you that Ben Trew might be working for Barton?"

Our stunned silence told him that we had not.

I gave him no chance to make further accusations. The cabin exploded with a vehement protest.

"I don't believe it!"

He turned from the fire, his eyes narrowing as he took in my bold denial.

"What do you know of him?" he asked me coolly.

"Not an awful lot," I admitted. Then I added, "He's not like you."

Tanner's jaw tightened perceptably, but I met his darkening eyes straight on, refusing to be intimidated by him. He dismissed me with a turn of his head.

"We don't know when he arrived at the pass," he said, ignoring my outburst. "It might have been him I found signs of up on that ridge. It could have been him watching us all that time."

"But why?" I asked, my words tight with disbelief. "Why would he do it?"

"Money," Tice volunteered soberly, rising somewhat shakily to his feet. "You heard him that night, Meg. He said he worked for the ones who paid 'im the most."

"So do a lot of men!" I shot back. "That's hardly enough to condemn him for!" I looked at Tanner. "Or do you have another reason to suspect Ben Trew?"

"Someone tried to kill me," Tanner said angrily, "and only a man who knows these mountains as well as Ben does could have gotten away with it."

"What are you sayin', Jed?" Tice's head had cleared

and his voice was sharp. "That Ben Trew set a trap
for you? He meant to kill you?"

"And damned near did!" Tanner's face was threatening in the half-shadowed light, but his voice when
he spoke was tightly controlled. "I picked up a trail,"
he began, "by that ridge where I found signs of him
the first time. It was there, plain as day. A little too
plain, maybe, considering how hard it's been to get
a fix on this person lately. I followed it over to that
rocky-sided north face. That's bad footing anytime.
In a storm..."

He didn't have to describe the hell he had been
through. It was there for us to see on his face. "But
what makes you think it was Ben?" I demanded. He
looked at me with irritation.

"The trail led up to a narrow ledge. From there it
sloped down to another shelf below where there's
enough room to make a small camp. Whoever it was
who led me there, left his horse there in plain view,
for bait." He paused, shutting his tired eyes against
the sting of the smoke-filled room. "That horse had
been left there just as the storm broke, before the
switchback leading down there was drifted over with
snow, so there wasn't any trail leading down the
enbankment. Anyone not knowing that would have
plunged down some thirty feet before coming to a
stop.

"Knowing what I did, I figured I had an edge. I
left my horse and waited until dark before I climbed
down there. As soon as I touched flat ground, he let
go with a round of bullets from that ledge above,
meaning to cut me to pieces. Only he didn't know
that mountainside like I do. My grandfather used to
take us hunting for sheep up there. There's a jagged
outcropping of rock along the side. I spent the night
there, not knowing if he was still waitin' on me. Then
I spent another two days holed up with that shot-up
horse just waiting for him to come back and check

out his work. I figured once he saw that no one had climbed up the ledge, he'd think me dead for sure and then get careless and leave me a nice trail to follow."

"But where's your proof that it was Ben?" I asked.

"I'm telling you that Ben Trew knows these mountains well enough to set up that kind of trap. And he showed up here, without a horse, the night of the storm," he answered harshly.

"It doesn't make any sense," I argued, refusing to accept his explanation. "Why show up here and leave me and Tice alone?"

"I'm not sure. He might have figured he could take the two of you anytime. Or maybe he was just being cautious, seeing as how he didn't hang around to make sure I was dead. If I wasn't, he might have thought I'd show up at the cabin that night so he came by to do his waiting in comfort. He couldn't have known I'd wait on that shelf for him to come back."

Tice did not question Tanner's thinking. It was up to me.

"Is that all you can say? Might be or could be? Well, I don't believe for a minute that it was Ben Trew who has been stalking us or who laid that trap for you. Why can't you believe that his horse went down in the storm like he said? And what makes you think that you two are the only ones who know these mountains so well? Even Culley said people come and go pretty easily from these parts."

Tanner watched me closely. My cheeks burned, whether from the warmth of the fire or his scrutiny I was not sure. I took a deep breath and went on, knowing that he was not going to like what I had to say.

"And I don't think that you believe that it was Ben, either. How can you be so suspicious of him?

You know him better than I do. Don't you trust anyone?"

The light played across his features as he turned
back musingly to the fire. He hadn't wanted to believe that Ben was the killer who watched and waited
for us. Tanner's own problems were bad enough, and
now his responsibility for me had him making enemies of the few people he might believe in. The steamy
warmth of the fire worked at his clothing, releasing
smells of woodsmoke and the dun and his own scent,
bridging the distance between us as if he stood beside
me. It was not sympathy exactly that I felt toward
him but rather a kind of softening as his tiredness
reminded me that he was a man and not some invincible being that knew no human weakness.

"You may be right," he admitted at last in a carefully restrained voice.

I looked at him, relieved. I didn't want him going
after Ben. Ben Trew had too much pride to walk
away from an accusation like that, and the consequences would be deadly.

Tanner never mentioned Ben's name again in con-
nection with his brush with death, but I didn't think
that I had totally erased the seeds of doubt from his
mind. I did not know much about men who kept the
things that troubled them most tucked away from
the light of day. As time passed, I ceased to think of
the threat made on his life, first because I did not
really believe that after all this time Holbrook Barton had sent someone into the mountains after me,
and second because the alternative, that someone
sought Tanner, was too disturbing to contemplate.

Tice displayed an unusual reluctance to leave once
Tanner had returned. He had a peculiar concern for
me that had taken root the day I learned of Tanner's
past. Tanner interpreted it as Tice's budding feelings
for me and it further fueled his churlish behavior,
but it was Ben Trew's next visit that produced the

most unforeseen of consequences, not Tice's hesitant departure.

My memory of Ben had been faulty. Without the lines of exhaustion, his face looked much younger. His eyes, in the daylight, were as blue as the sky behind him. His hair and beard had been recently trimmed. He rode in on a big rawboned gelding leading Coalie behind him. Bringing his horse to a stop by the corral, he handed down to me a flat parcel from his saddlebag.

"What's this for, Ben?" I asked in surprise, noticing for the first time that Tanner had disappeared. If Ben noted that I looked around the clearing peculiarly, he did not speak of it, but only fixed his attentive gaze on me.

"Just a way of sayin' thanks for the loan of your horse," he said, seemingly embarrassed by the exchange.

"But it isn't necessary. I was glad to help," I said, moved by his kindness. "You'll stay awhile, won't you? Jed just brought down a deer."

"No, I'm sorry, Meg. Not this time. I want to make Ada's before nightfall. But thank you."

While Ben watched with amused eyes, I fumbled at the scrap of hide tied about the gift. Beneath it lay a beautifully tanned deerskin. For a moment I was speechless.

"This is beautiful, Ben," I said sincerely. Ruefully, I looked down at my worn breeches. "I guess you knew I'd have use for it."

At the sound behind me, I looked up and turned in time to see Tanner approach, the carbine gripped loosely in his hand. His expression was dark.

"Huntin' for something special, Jed?" Ben asked by way of a greeting.

"Maybe." Tanner's reply was curt, but Ben showed no particular emotion at the surly welcome.

"Cousin," I said, trying to instill some warmth

into the word, hoping that he would catch on and that my expression would warn him, "Look what Ben brought me for the loan of Coalie!"

There was a slight thinning of Tanner's lips. Dispassionately, he examined the skin. "You know there's no need for payment, Ben," he said, handing it back to me.

"It wasn't meant in way of payment, Jed. Just a way of sayin' thanks here to Meg."

Tanner grunted an unintelligible reply.

"Thank you again, Ben," I said, apologetically, trying to make up for Tanner's brusqueness.

Taking note of the set look on my face, Tanner made an effort to curb his ill-mannered behavior. "You're welcome to stay, Ben," he said shortly.

"No," Ben replied. "I told Meg. I was on my way to see Ada. Maybe some other time." He pulled the gelding's head around.

"Be seein' you, Meg," he said. I watched him as he disappeared from sight.

"Cousin?"

It was not so much a question as a challenge. I whirled around to meet the rancor head on.

"Yes, Jed. Cousin. Tice thought it up the night Ben showed up in the storm. He thought it might save my reputation."

Tanner's voice was as cold as ice. "Why was there any need to explain at all, Meg?"

Ripping my cap off, I let the hair fall down about my shoulders. "Because this is what I am when you're not around, Jed! I only keep this damned hat on for you!"

There was a fathomless look in his eyes.

"It was kind of him to bring me the skin," I said to ease the tension. I regretted my impulsive action, but left the hat where it had fallen.

"Yes, Widow McGrath will be mighty pleased to

learn that Ben Trew is bringing you gifts!" Tanner said mockingly.

I recoiled at his implication, at the same time wondering about the remarkable qualities of Ada McGrath, to whom both Tanner and Ben were paying court. "You're being ridiculous!" I exclaimed. "How am I supposed to know anything about her and Ben? You don't tell me a damn thing about anyone on this mountain and you won't let me see anyone!"

His face flushed with anger and he turned away.

"Why is that you always walk away from me when you don't like what I have to say?"

He turned back, looking at me with narrowed eyes, his expression inscrutable. I sensed the violence and made a guess at his thoughts.

"I'm not like her, Jed, so don't think that I am," I said quietly.

He took a step closer. He didn't ask me how I knew. Maybe he didn't care. "Aren't you, Meg?" he asked me bitterly. Reaching toward me, slowly, almost reluctantly, he touched my hair where it lay upon my shoulder, playing lightly with the waving strand. The forced gentleness was unsettling.

"Her hair was dark and her eyes were blue, not at all like yours. But you remind me of her. You always did. Maybe it's the way you look at a man. Proud like. Men looked at her just the way they look at you."

"If men look at me, it's because they want to, not because I've given them reason to. From what I know of them, they cause a girl nothing but grief."

His hand rested lightly on my shoulder, smoothing the lock of hair that lay between his fingers. My mind silently screamed at him to stop, yet he persisted.

"You raised a man to violence," he said, "just like she did."

I lay my hand over his, stilling it, trying to ignore the strangely heightened awareness between us.

"I had nothing to do with that! Add hated Jay Barton long before we were friends. He used me as an excuse to kill Jay. Why can't you understand that? He poisoned himself on his hatred. He didn't even wait for an explanation because he didn't want one. He had no cause to be jealous of Jay. He drove me away himself!"

I paused for breath, holding his penetrating gaze.

"Is that what happened to you, Jed? Didn't you give her a chance to explain?"

The look that came to his eyes condemned him before he could even reply. As the torment flashed across his face, I immediately regretted my words. His hand dropped from my shoulder and he did not look back as he walked away.

I was never quite sure when it was that I began to love him. It was the hardest thing I ever had to admit to myself—that I loved a man who had destroyed the woman he loved rather than share her with another. I loved a man who saw the woman he had destroyed every time he looked at me, a man who wanted nothing more than a memory to carry as his burden for the rest of his life. Her memory was the cross he chose to bear, carrying it gladly as his punishment. He would never be over her.

Chapter Eighteen

✍ MY LOVE FOR TANNER WAS WHOLEHEARTED and totally irrational. As fierce as my hatred of him had once been, it was love that now tore me apart, infinitely more painful. It seemed doomed from the start. He avoided me after my outburst. I had trespassed unforgiveably into his past and the wall of silence closed around him once more. I did my best to hide my feelings and came to master the shuttered look that so often masked his face. The very sight of him from afar was enough to set me longing just to have him near. There was for me now an unbearably sweet torture to his presence, his very remoteness stabbing at me with each turn of his face, the aloofness damning me more than any invectives he might toss my way. The few times we spoke from necessity, I was careful not to let my eyes linger on him too long.

Ben Trew's visits were a break in my otherwise complete isolation. My sore spirit, sadly trampled by

Tanner's grim forbearance and utter unapproachability, flowered briefly in Ben's presence. The day after Tanner departed, waiting only for Tice to be within sight of the clearing before he mounted the dun horse to leave, Ben returned. And with him he brought a gangling part-wolf puppy that he promptly threatened to drown unless I promised to keep him. Happily, I rose to the bait, knowing the pup, which Ben said went by the name of Dog, would help occupy my thoughts, which at present dwelt only on Tanner's trips to Ada McGrath's.

I never changed the pup's name, perhaps suspecting he would not be with me long. On Jed's return, he ignored him, much like he did me, but I sensed that it was not really the dog that bothered him so much as his anger at Ben for giving him to me. His temper even fell on the unsuspecting Tice, who in all innocence commented upon the increased frequency of Ben's visits.

"Sure has taken a likin' to our Meg," Tice kept on with an impish smile, sorely seeking entertainment. "Can't imagine what makes a man like him so flapjawed when he comes 'round if it ain't that. Suppose, now," he added thoughtfully, "it's a good thing, since you've been takin' up the good widow's time—"

"Shut up, Tice!" Tanner's words were like a whiplash across the cabin and his face was tight with fury. Raising his brows in feigned surprise, Tice whistled a tuneless song softly.

Had I not been so stricken by scorching jealousy I might have seen the humor in the situation as Tice's barbs found their target. Instead of taking Tice to task over Ben's supposed interest in me, I settled on the implications of Tanner's relationship with Ada McGrath, torturing myself with painful images of them together. I watched as Tanner, white-lipped with anger, left the room without further word. Tice was not one to ask forgiveness. Finding Tanner even more unapproachable on his return from Ada's, he willingly removed himself rather than face his friend's continued wrath, expecting that it would blow over in time. Later, Tice was to apologize for leaving me with Tanner like that, confessing to thinking only of himself, but he had no way of knowing that this time it would be any different.

It was Dog who brought things to a head between Tanner and me. "Why's that damned animal so restless?" Tanner snapped at me the morning after his return from Ada's, as Dog looked up soulfully, jumping to his feet expectantly whenever I moved about the cramped cabin. Angry at myself for having missed him, and wounded afresh by his cutting words, I bit back my retort and forced myself to answer in a civil tone.

"There were signs of a bear. Tice thought it best to keep him inside until he was gone. He said that sometimes a dog will turn tail and bring one right back into camp. It's only to be for a few days, until he was sure the bear had gone back to its den. He said that in the meantime he'd take us up to the ridge for some exercise, but you came back."

Tanner looked at me coolly. Occasionally, a bear would break winter hibernation and emerge for a brief feed before returning to its lair. Tice was just being cautious.

"And I spoiled your fun?" he asked, one eye lifting at the sardonic question.

"Well, yes," I admitted truthfully. "But it doesn't matter, we'll be fine." I was just glad that he did not hold Tice's inopportune remarks against me. I did not want him to close me out again as he had done so often before.

He gave me a piercing look, one that I did not know how to read. "You're right," he said finally. "I guess I did drive Tice out at that. I can't make that up to him, but I can take you and the pup up to the ridge. He can find some rabbits to chase. Bears don't care much for people."

"Thank you. I'd like that," I heard myself say softly as he turned away from me.

The sky, as clear as it had ever been, was brighter that day and the trees, under the heavy draping of a recent snowfall, showed up black against the purity of the landscape. The clean, sharp fragrance of the evergreens erased all taints of the past and, for once, we rode in an easy silence. The horses followed a cobbled streambank, needing no guidance as they instinctively picked their way along the flat rise only lightly covered with wind-drifted snow. Looking back over my shoulder, I could see for miles as the land gently rolled away to the south, the far ranges standing tall at the horizon and the snow-covered peaks reflecting the brilliance of the winter sky. The lower reaches, checkered by snowy pockets and rugged slopes, caught the fiery glow of the slanting winter sun.

A slight warming in the afternoon brought the rabbits out frolicking in the small meadow and Dog madly dashed through the snow, churning the smooth white cover into a crystal froth as he chased the scampering creatures about. Panting with exhaustion, he would pause momentarily, greedily quenching his thirst on chunks of snow. Dismounting, we left our horses and walked a ways, taking in the splendid beauty of the mountains.

And then, without warning, it was upon me. Despite the hardships, the hopelessness, the empty dreams, that streak of perversity still dwelled within me, erupting with such suddenness that, even had I wanted to, there was no stemming it. I fell a step or two behind, then, reaching down, I grabbed a fistful of snow, balling it up in my hands as all the seething resentment inside of me aimed itself directly at Tanner. I threw the snowball.

I missed my mark. He turned toward me as it whizzed by his head, and I grew frightened by his fearsome look. My daring and audacity deserted me in a rush. In an effort to move away from him, I lost my balance and tumbled down the snowbank, coming to a rest at the bottom, sprawled in an ignoble heap with the wind knocked out of me. I was far from hurt. Still, due to the weight of the heavy buffalo coat and the enveloping embrace of the snow, several moments passed before I was able to work myself into a sitting position. I suppose it was that which prompted his concern. Edging and backsliding his way down the snowy slope, Tanner offered me his outstretched hand. I looked at it in amazement.

My spirit flared anew. Clasping his hand firmly, I gave a backward tug, pulling him off balance. Only by ingenious maneuvering did he manage to avert his weight as he fell, so that I did not bear the brunt of the impact as he pinned me to the ground. Within the circle of his arms, I wanted to memorize the solid feel of his powerful frame as I shut my eyes, awaiting his vengence. Never did I expect the deep burst of laughter, and I grew giddy on the joy.

It was dusk before we returned to the cabin, with the evening promising to be as clear as the day had been bright. Already, the stars glimmered weakly in the gray haze of the falling night. Wordlessly, Tanner took Coalie from me and led him to the corral. Inside, the cabin was flooded in darkness, with only the barest glow of the dying embers to distinguish the hearth from the yawning blackness of the room. With numbed fingers, I stripped off my mittens and slowly fed bits of kindling to the coals until, at last, they caught. Then I added enough wood to transform the interior from an inky darkness to dimness.

What followed came because, having once tasted the warmth of his laughter, the emptiness inside me set me yearning for more. It was not enough that we had shared a pleasant day together, unmarred by cross words between us. His laughter had awakened in me a longing greater than I had ever known. Even had I known what the outcome would be, I would not have changed the course of that night.

It was not that I did not try, but rather that the precautions I took were utterly useless. It took no more than his footsteps at the door to set my soul to singing. It didn't matter that little had changed between us, that although I had witnessed the slightest crack in his hardened exterior, a wall still remained. A small part of Jed Tanner had escaped that day. But I fully recognized the futility of wanting more, and so I put a safe distance between us that night, as if the length and breadth of the room could still my need. I chose my topic purposefully, knowing that it would set me back on the path to reality.

"I bet the Widow McGrath was real glad to see you," I said casually, watching his back as he worked, his wide shoulders moving easily as he seared the steaks in the pan. He had no way of knowing how I hung on his answer.

"She's always grateful for the company." His brief reply revealed nothing.

"I guess she gets pretty lonely up here," I ventured.

"More than likely."

"I guess we all get lonely at times." Then, testing his mood, I lifted my eyes to his face. "Do you ever get lonely, Jed?"

At least he didn't look away from me as he might have. But his face was as closed as I had ever seen it. I wondered what had possessed me to ask him such a question.

He waited a bit before answering, measuring his

words. "I'm used to being on my own. I like it that way," he said offhandedly. Hunkering down before the hearth, he turned the steaks that were sizzling in the pan juices.

The meal passed in silence. Afterward, he built up the fire, bathing the hearthside in a warm glow of golden light. I gathered up the supper remains and, pouring the pan drippings over them, took them outside to Dog, who fell to his small feast with a wagging tail. I stayed outside in the cold until it bit through my thin shirt and drove me reluctantly inside.

I found him readying his provisions for the time Tice would return and he could once again leave the encampment. With my back to him, I stood by the window, absently toying with the flap as I peered unseeingly into the darkness beyond.

"Stop that!" he said sharply. "Don't you know you can see that light for miles?"

It made no difference now in what manner he spoke to me, as long as he did. I turned from the window and went to the fire, the hurting pain looming before me no matter where I stood. I could not escape it, as I could not escape him. I ached with a feeling that had no right to exist in me. I heard him rise and come toward me, reaching past me to the coffeepot still warming by the hearth.

"I missed you when you were at Ada's, Jed. I'm glad you're back." I heard myself say to the glowing coals, not him.

The air crackled with tension. He set the coffeepot back down, his cup still empty. There was no way for me to take back my words.

I watched the rise and fall of the soft flannel shirt covering the width of his chest; I watched his breath quicken. In his hesitation, an eternity came and went. I was aware of his arousal even before I felt the heat of his hands as he laid them upon my shoulders. I shut my eyes to savor the sensation. Slowly, he turned me around to face him. He looked at me searchingly and this time I knew that he would not turn away. He had been attracted to me from the first and now there was no whiskey to cloud my thinking. His hands moved from my shoulders to my face, cupping it so that I could not look away. No longer did I care what my face revealed as I lost myself in the depths of his shadowed eyes.

I didn't care that he didn't love me, only that he wanted me. He lowered his lips to mine and kissed me. Had his kiss been gentle and undemanding, I might not have reacted the way I did, but it was not. My mouth opened under his and my tongue responded to the pressure of his until I could barely stand and I clutched at him to keep from falling. His hands left my hair and traveled downward, forcing me closer until it seemed I was fused to the punishing hardness of muscle and bone. A burning heat arose where our bodies met. I tore my mouth from his, gasping for breath, but even as I did, his lips moved to my neck. His kisses there almost made me cry with passion. He gently lifted my hair back from my shoulders, his eyes holding mine as his fingers dropped down to the fastenings of my shirt. And then he paused. His eyes narrowed, his rising need held in check. He read my acceptance of the consequences in eyes that willed him to go on. He made short work of the buttons, and I was exposed to his gaze for the first time.

Standing straight before him, I watched his face as he traced his hands across my collarbone to the hollow of my throat, and down to the fullness of my breasts, his features taut with the wanting, his eyes a liquid steel that revealed a long-denied passion. I was not prepared for the leaping of my senses as he covered the smooth, firm flesh with rough, callused hands, a sandpaper touch that made me shake with longing and weakness. I leaned against him for support and then I found myself lifted by strong arms, momentarily cradled against his chest before the softness of his bed was beneath me. His lips once again found my mouth and he drank from it as if he were a man dying of thirst, holding me close, fitting me to his body. He found the fastenings on my breeches, but his hands were shaking and his fingers fumbled. Sliding the pants over my hips, he tossed them aside and then drew my opened shirt down over my shoulders. His eyes, black as coals, traveled over me. He pulled away briefly in the darkness and I trembled, craving his nearness. He returned, the touch of his skin replacing the feel of the soft flannel of his shirt.

He sank down beside me, his face almost soft in the illuminating glow of the hearthfire. He gently lowered himself over me, covering my body with his own. I drew him closer still, and I ran my hands down the corded muscles of his back. He groaned and shifted his weight. Then the sensations that had thrilled me before intensified, setting fire to my body. A warm wetness eased Tanner's way into me, and although my muscles contracted at the penetration, I welcomed the burning heat. I felt a sharp, swift rendering of my insides as he pushed his way to my very core. Slowly and rhythmically he began to thrust until at last the burning sensation faded. Pain became pleasure as I clung to him, and my body responded with a matching, joyful rhythm as he whirled us faster and faster in the timelessness of the starry mountain night. A jubilant cry I recognized as my own pierced the heavy darkness of the room just as I felt him shudder and lay still upon me.

I must have slept. The sound of footsteps outside the cabin awakened me to the darkened interior. The fire had died out long ago. I was alone. Although the blankets kept the chill from me, I missed the feel of him as though I were suddenly incomplete without him. I did not remember his leaving, only the warmth of his body and how, without stirring or speaking, he had held me close and still in the aftermath of our lovemaking.

I guessed the time to be close to daybreak. Clutching a blanket to me, I eased myself into a sitting position, grimacing slightly at an unaccustomed soreness. I rose and went to the window. Pushing aside the flap, I stared out into the murky darkness of dawn.

The dun stood quietly at the corral, his head lowered as Tanner fastened the bedroll to the saddle. My eyes widened at the sight, the implication beginning to dawn on me. Dog sat nearby, curious. Tanner spoke and the gangling pup went to him, his tail low to the ground. Then, calling to him, he brought Dog back to the cabin, opening the door to let him in.

Our eyes met as he found me by the window. His face was ghostly pale in the grayness of dawn and his eyes shone black. In the dim light it was hard to fathom what they revealed. But there was no mistaking the bleakness of his face. I had not mistaken his hunger for me, but our passion was not to survive our night together.

I had known he hadn't loved me; the most I had hoped for was that he would see me as I was, not an elusive apparition from his past. But I was denied even that. Suddenly, I was overcome by a burning jealousy for her, his wife, who had experienced what I had only just tasted and who had known him in a way I could not. He had told me once that he would regret this, and yet, like a silly fool, without even the excuse of a drunken whim to guide me, I had gone to him with my longing plain to see. How could I fault Jed Tanner for resenting me?

"You'll be all right?" he asked, his voice rough in the quiet stillness of the waking day.

"Yes," I answered. I was not ashamed of what we had shared. At least I would be spared his pity, for he would never know of my hopeless love for him, a love that he apparently could never return. For Jed Tanner there could only be women like Ada Mc-Grath, women in whom he could seek refuge. Meg Logan only served to bring back memories of the wanton wife he had destroyed.

"I'll be up on the ridge. I can watch the cabin from there. Tice should be back sometime today," he said, and I knew that no matter how he felt about me, he would not shirk his responsibility. I nodded, knowing that my tears were only a moment away.

With his peculiar catlike grace, he swung himself into the saddle, reined the dun around, and headed him north.

Chapter Nineteen

AT THE SOUND OF THE APPROACHING HORSE I dried my eyes, hoping that Tanner had come back for me. But it was only Tice, returning as Tanner had predicted. I greeted him at the door, the disappointment etched on my face. He stood there and stared at me, his eyes taking in my swollen face and the defeat. He opened his arms and I went into them. He offered compassion, not censure.

"I should've known this was comin' Meg," he said, conscious-stricken, as he entered the cabin. "I should never have left you alone with him this last time."

"I love him," I said, admitting the truth. "It was my own damned fault."

"I wish you hadn't told me that," he said. "He worries me, Meg...you don't know Jed the way I do. I swear he ain't been right since he's been 'round you. I don't want to scare you none, but that's a fact. I just hope it ends here...but I'm afraid no good will come of this."

I gave a bitter laugh. What could happen that would be any worse? "You don't have anything to worry about, Tice," I said plainly. "He hates me now, I know he does. All I ever did was remind him of... her. He tried to tell me that..." Unable to continue, I began to cry again and he held me close, hushing me as if I were a child.

I would have done anything—I would have gladly given my own life—to prevent the tragedy that was about to befall. Nothing, not even the passage of time, has dulled the pain of those next few moments.

Tice refused to leave my side until he was satisfied as to my state. Repeatedly I assured him that I was well enough for him to see to his horse, that I had a broken heart, not a broken limb. He looked at me uncertainly and I gave him a watery smile as he left the cabin.

I heard a gunshot and froze, then realized it must be Tice warning off the troublesome bear. I went to the door and opened it—and stood stock still at the sight in the clearing. Tice layed sprawled by the corral, the bay horse pulling at his tether.

"Tice!" I screamed. I grabbed the carbine resting by the door and bolted across the clearing to where his body lay in the snow. The second shot went high, but I felt the third graze my sleeve as I hit the ground. Belly to the earth, I elbowed my way closer, but even before I reached him I could see that he was dead. Biting back my anguished cry, I raised my head in time to see the fourth bullet fly and heard Dog's pitiful yelp as it struck home. Impulsively, I stretched my hand to Tice's gunbelt and slipped his revolver free of the holster, tucking it into the waistband of my breeches. Keeping low to the ground, I turned back to the cabin just as the next bullet lodged in the wall, sending a spray of splinters flying into the air. Throwing myself over the open threshold, I landed

on the floor and slammed the door shut behind me.
Then, going to the hearth, I built up the dying fire,
blocking the entry from the chimney above.

My stomach cramped and knotted as Tice's last
warning suddenly came back to me. He believed that
Tanner meant us harm. What twisted turns had Tanner's mind taken after our night together? All along
he had resented my friendship with Tice. Had he
watched from the ridge and seen me welcome him
back, mistaking Tice's compassion for something
more? Did I remind him of his wife so much that he
had confused us in this mind, believing that I had
turned to Tice in his absence? Or had Tice, in Tanner's mind, come to take the place of the man she
had been with when he killed her? If so, he had
evened an old score. And now, he was free to take
his time with me and finally lay the ghost to rest.

It was too quiet. An eerie silence was growing with
the coming darkness, the deepening shadows keeping me as much a prisoner as the man with the gun.
The blazing fire kept the small cabin aglow, making
it impossible to crack open the door or lift the skin
flap at the window without a telltale stream of light
making me a perfect target for a gunman. Even if I
were to escape the cabin, where would I go? I had
no chance against a man like Tanner in the mountains. As he waited for darkness, I waited for him.
I missed Dog's comforting presence. The fire burned
brightly, but my wood supply was low and I would
need more soon.

At the light thud outside the cabin wall, I whirled
about. Scarcely breathing, I awaited the next sound.
Slowly, ever so slowly, came the telling noise, the
squeak of the glittering snow particles under a light
foot. I held the carbine across my knees as I sat on
the three-legged stool facing the door. Fear made my
legs weak.

"Meg!" came the faint whisper.

I jumped at the voice, so close it seemed to come from within the cabin itself. The very sound of it triggered despair in me. I hated him. He had killed Tice. The thought of facing him, knowing the pleasure I had taken in his body, the love cries I had uttered and could still hear in my mind, sickened me. I'd die before letting him get close to me again. I considered tossing out the carbine to entice him inside, hoping to place one of the bullets from Tice's revolver directly through his heart.

"Meg! Let me in!" The whisper was harsher now as he lost patience. I heard the brush of his jacket up against the door as his voice seeped through the cracks.

"Leave me be, Jed!" I called out to him. "I've got my rifle and I'll use it on you, I swear it!"

I heard him try the latch, but the door held.

"Meg! Damn it! Open the door!" His voice was louder now, and angry. "Tice is dead, Meg! I've got no time to play games with you!"

Did he think I was playing a game? "Jed, you come near me and I'll blow your damned head off and if you think I'm playing a game, you just try me!" There was a sound at the window and I aimed the carbine at the flap and fired. And then there was only silence.

I didn't think he was dead. I didn't even think I had hit him. The only thing I had done was make him more wary. The minutes stretched on endlessly. How much time passed before the gunfire began, I was not sure. On reflex, I dropped to the floor, but none of the bullets pierced the cabin walls. I listened more closely. It was the sound of crossfire. Ben! Ben was out there! I almost wept with relief until cold reality set in. What chance would Ben have against a man gone mad, a man like Jed Tanner?

The fire blazed in the hearth, the dry snapping of the wood a pale echo of the gunplay. At last the gun battle ceased. I did not allow myself to think. There was the heavy tred of footsteps. They were not Tanner's. Mingled with the relief came an aching sense of loss. It could mean only one thing. Ben. I started for the door at the sound.

"Ben?" I asked, lifting my hand to the bolt. But Ben didn't answer and neither did he wait for me to open the door to him. With a violent thrust, it burst open.

I had never seen him before. His hair was ragged and long. His eyes, a wolfish yellow, stared at me from a heavily bearded face. His outer trappings were skin, but beneath the jacket I caught a glimpse of a soiled red bandanna and in his hand and pointing straight at me was a drawn Colt .45. His lips twisted in a sneer.

"Well, now. Look what I got here. Meg Logan. Her very self."

I struggled to make sense of it.

"Bet you didn't know you was worth five thousand dollars to me, now did you?" The pale eyes gleamed at me.

"Who are you?" I demanded, the carbine feeding me courage. I pointed it at the middle of the filthy man. "What do you want with me?"

"Why, the reward money," he said with a broad smile. "Barton says you can be either dead or alive. Makes no difference to me. Makes it easier if you was dead, 'cause I got the feelin' you're gonna be a real spitfire. Then agin, it might be more interestin' if you was alive. Guess it all depends on you, Meggie."

I shuddered. Meggie had been my father's pet name for me. "You work for Barton. It was you all along." My head was spinning with the realization.

He grinned at my despair. "That's right, Missy."

Oh, Jed, I thought, what have I done? I remembered him as he tried to reason with me through the cabin wall.

"It was you that Jed was watching for all this time," I stated flatly.

"Yup. A fine game we had. He's a smart one, jus' like they tol' me. I heard 'bout him. That's what took me so long. I wanted all of you. If I'd took jus' you, why then they'd be after me. So I had to wait. Had to make sure you was all separated. That way I could pick you off one at a time. Course it wasn't easy. All that waitin'. An he was watchin' for me, too. Made it all the harder. Had me a few good opportunities. But no sense in riskin' my own hide."

The crossfire. It had been between Jed and this hired killer. Not Ben. And he had killed Jed, just like he had Tice. It was all because of me. Both Jed and Tice were dead because of me.

"Now, Missy, you jus' put down that rifle..."

I waved the carbine at him, my finger on the trigger. "Don't be stupid. I'm not going anywhere with you. I'll use this on you first. In fact, you won't be the first man I've killed. You'd be smart to back out that door right now, Mister, before I pay you back for what you did to Jed and Tice."

"You ain't gonna use that. You see, you do and my finger will squeeze this here trigger an' you'll be dead, too, Missy."

"You think I care?" I laughed harshly as I raised the carbine higher, aiming at him.

He called my bluff, advancing a step closer. Dying did not bother me, but I could not summon the courage to kill the fiendish man. Fenton's wavering image, and then Jay's, the surprise still on their faces while the life slipped away from them, was the nightmare I lived with. Even the knowledge of what I faced at this man's hands brought not a quiver to the deadened nerves of my finger. The broken stumps of his teeth shone wetly and I smelled the foul odor of his mouth. I closed my eyes against the sight.

"You shuttin' those pretty green eyes of yours ain't goin' to make me go 'way," he crowed triumphantly.

Defeated, I lowered the carbine, and a wide grin split the ugly face. He reached forward to take it. Then there was a sound behind him, from the darkness beyond the open door.

"Drop, Meg!"

The blast rang clear as I hit the floor, throwing myself out of the path of the gunfire.

A stream of blood spurted from a hole in the man's chest. Dazed, I remained huddled in the corner, unaware of what had happened. The dying man tried to focus on the blackness of night just beyond the threshold to the cabin, and I, too, looked out into the emptiness, seeing only booted feet in the dim light that spilled out over the snow-covered ground. Another shot rang out, and the slug spun the man into a motionless heap upon the floor.

I held my breath as the tall form entered the cabin and took shape.

"Jed!"

"Are you all right, Meg?" he asked.

"Yes, I think so."

I could not let him see how weak I had suddenly become. I did not try to stand but remained where I was, drawing myself into a sitting position. I had no right to look at Jed ever again, but still, I let my eyes rest on him. He knelt by the body, confirming what he already knew. Tanner's face was dark and lined with fatigue. The brows were drawn in a straight line over the shadowed slash of eyes, his mouth tight-lipped in a forbidding face. I thought of how easily he had pulled the trigger of his rifle, killing the man who lay at his feet. I never felt safer than I did at that moment.

"He's dead, Meg," he said, looking across the body to me. "He won't be bothering you anymore."

I gazed at him dumbly. With something akin to

pity, he came over to me. Reaching down with his achingly familiar grip, he helped me to my feet.

"I thought he killed you, too, Jed," I said to him, finding my voice. "After what he did to Tice—"

"I wanted him to think that. He got careless. He saw me go down, like I meant him to...but he didn't bother to check for a body. I waited a few minutes and then I followed him."

I looked at the man on the floor. Another death. When would it be over?

"He got what he deserved, Meg," Tanner said shortly, understanding my thoughts. "I owed him for Tice."

"He said it was him all along, Jed, that he was Barton's hand." I looked at him squarely. "You knew that whoever it was wasn't after you. Why did you let me think he might be?"

"When Tice suggested it that day, I thought it was all right to go along with it. You had enough on your mind. Figured you'd rest easier thinking it was me someone wanted."

Blindly, I looked away as my composure broke at his intended kindness. I felt Tanner touch my shoulder with a reluctant hand. I turned to him, seeking comfort, and he suffered my closeness wordlessly. I knew his feelings for me—or rather, his lack of feelings—had not changed. But I was past caring. He was alive and I had been wrong about him. That was enough. But I still owed him an apology, one that I was not sure he would accept.

"I'm sorry about what happened before, Jed," I said plainly, owning up to my terrible mistake. "But I—I thought it was you that had killed Tice. I didn't know there was anyone else out there. You see, Tice told me about your wife and then—" I broke off as I felt him stiffen almost imperceptibly.

"You don't owe me any apologies," he answered

roughly. "You had your reasons for thinking what you did. I can't fault you for that."

"But I should have known." I looked up at him. "You saved my life again. That night we left Cross Creek. And now." But he wanted none of my sentimentality. With his hands at my shoulders, he pushed me down to the bench by the scarred table.

"I've some things to see to. Unless you want to share this room with him tonight"—he glanced down at the body—"I'll be removing him from your company. Then I'll be seeing to Tice."

I nodded, my insides twisting with grief.

It might have been mere minutes or as much as several hours that he was gone.

He came back, bearing a large furry bundle that gave me a weak wag of its tail for a greeting.

"Dog!" I cried, as he laid him down gently on a warm spot before the hearth.

"He'll be all right," Tanner assured me. "Looks like he's got a bullet lodged beneath his ribs. The bleeding's stopped. He needs rest and food. Time will take care of the healing."

He fixed a light supper for us later, making a broth from some tinned tomatoes and dried venison. I sipped at my own steaming cup until I felt myself grow warm.

That night I dozed fitfully as Dog whimpered in his sleep. My eyes traveled the interior of the darkened cabin, coming to rest on Tanner as he reclined on his bed, his back braced against the cabin wall. The telltale light of his cigarette disclosed his restlessness. As his brooding features came to life in the occasional draught of firelight, he saw that I was awake, but he did not break the heavy cloak of silence.

I spoke through the darkness to him. "I'm sorry, Jed. I never meant for you to get caught up in my troubles like this."

He continued to draw upon his cigarette, giving no indication he had heard me.

"It wasn't fair of Doc to saddle you with me. Tice would be alive today if it hadn't been for me. Even you said I was trouble back at Cross Creek."

His voice was low and his words came slowly. "I wasn't seeing things too clearly in the beginning, Meg. Do you hear what I'm saying to you? I had my reasons, but they were wrong. None of what happened was of your making. You got caught in something that was bigger than you and all the rest of those people. You couldn't help what happened any more than you could have stopped it."

Oh, how I wanted to believe him. And because of that, I let his words soothe me as he meant them to. I let them erase the guilt I had carried with me in the darkest corners of my mind. But what he did not know was that my need for him, so tenuous at first, had become so strong that I could not believe it had not always been a part of me. I turned my face away so that he could not read the thoughts written so plainly across it. My love was a consuming passion. I would never fully understand my attraction to him. Certainly, there were men who were kinder or more handsome or more suited to my rebellious nature. And certainly, there were those who could return my feelings in kind. I was destined to bear my love for him in silence. Then, suddenly realizing that there was no longer anything to fear beyond the confining walls of the cabin, I threw aside my covers to escape the suffocating tension of hopeless love.

The vast sky seemed so close that I felt as if I had only to climb the north ridge to touch the shimmering stars. I welcomed the bite of the cold dry air as I surveyed the small clearing, carefully avoiding the spot where Tice had fallen. I felt the sting of tears at my eyes.

"Meg."

I turned in surprise. I had not heard his approach. The pale wash of luminous snow at our feet exaggerated the austerity of the angles and planes that formed the lean structure of his features. I looked away, in an effort to hide my vulnerability.

"Meg," he said again. "Please look at me."

My defenses crumbled at the sound of his voice and I turned to him. I slowly lifted my eyes to his. The steeliness was gone. But had anything changed? He regarded me narrowly and I knew he was seeing the shadowed eyes in a face too sharply hollowed from the nights I had lain awake thinking of him and from the days when the memories were the food for my hunger of him. He did not know what I suffered from, only that I did, and he could not have known that it was not his touch that devastated me, only the lack of it.

Slowly I raised my hand, reaching across the open space to touch his cheek. His lips tightened at the light stroke and he hesitantly gripped my fingers, stilling them against the bearded softness of his face. I freed my hand from his, as if to prove that it was no mindless passion that drove us together now, but something much stronger. I stepped closer so that I was only inches from him. I felt the heat from his body reach out to me; I was lost in the heady smell of him.

It was I who brought my lips to his rough and chafed ones, and the pressure of his was as warm and gentle as a spring rain. And when I pulled away from him, he made no move to stop me. I willed myself to have the sense to leave it at that, but I was like the flame of a candle, fluttering helplessly under the onslaught of a strong wind. Of my own accord, I found myself enfolded within his arms, and as his mouth fastened on mine I was lost in the magic of him. Our bodies pressed together so tightly that I felt the buttons of his shirt against the skin of my breasts and waist as we molded ourselves to each other. The stars seemed to speed around us as I stared into his shining eyes. Clasping my arms around his neck, I locked my fingers in the silky texture of his chestnut hair.

I don't remember moving inside, only that I welcomed the comfort of his bed. He pulled back to remove his clothing, but I brushed aside his hands, working at his shirt myself as my eyes traced the beauty of the thickly corded neck that flowed so smoothly into the wide breadth of his shoulders. He shrugged the loosened shirt off and then turned his attention to me, not with a sense of discovery but with an urgency that set a fire in my blood. Quickly he undressed me. Hungering for his touch, I welcomed him. His fingers and lips blazed a path over my flesh, stirring me to wantonness, never ceasing their exploring and caressing until I moved in a heated passion, aching to be possessed by him. Only then did he enter me, and my body responded, straining to hold him deep within me, the pleasure even greater than I remembered as each movement sparked explosions of exquisite delight. His hands held my head prisoner and he looked into my face, measuring my response as he held himself back so that when my back arched under a final assault he was ready for me, and ecstasy came to us together. That night we slept as one, the warmth of his skin the softest comfort I had ever known.

I had come to terms with myself. With my eyes wide open, I had no expectations of Jed Tanner and there were no more decisions for me to make.

Chapter Twenty

DURING THE VERY EARLY HOURS OF MORNING I grew aware that he no longer lay by my side, and I became suddenly alert. Instinctively, my eyes began to search him out in the morning gloom. Hearing me stir, he halted at his task across the room and straightened to his full height, but he did not look my way. "Get dressed," he said coolly. "We're pulling out."

I could not make out his features in the darkness, but I detected the rigidity of his stance. He was in no mood for talk. I was alarmed at the return of the implacable Jed Tanner.

"Where are we headed?" I asked him, as if it were of no great importance to me. My eyes lowered, I dressed within the lonely reach of his averted gaze. A surge of warmth flooded my cheeks as I vividly recalled his intimate touch. Silence filled the cabin.

"Ada's," he answered at last, in a voice devoid of emotion.

Ada's! I stiffened at the sound of her name. I opened my mouth to protest and then caught myself. I decided to bide my time. Until I had some inkling of his plan, I would get nowhere with him.

We traveled the better part of the day through a steep-walled canyon that led into the next basin, making a slow descent by way of a rocky ledge that widened and narrowed at will. Wading through the deep snowdrifts, we broke trail for the pack animals, with Tice's bay and Barton's man's gelding following in the single-file procession. I carried Dog a good part of the way, except when the going was easiest; then he would follow stiffly behind us.

All through the plodding pace of the snowy trek I tried to console myself, taking a small measure of comfort in the knowledge that this time it was not something I had done that had turned Tanner against me. He could not deny the pleasure he had taken the night before; he was not fool enough to give lie to the fact. And he cared for me. I felt that as strongly as I had felt the desire that had propelled us through most of the night. What had happened then, as I slept by his side in the early hours of morning, to change him so? Despairingly, I realized I was no closer to understanding him.

The forested slopes were fading into the darkness of evening before we finally spied the yellow glimmer of Ada McGrath's cabin from a flat-topped ridge a short distance away. Situated on a tree-dotted swatch of land, the cabin and outbuildings were nestled within the arms of a stand of fir trees on the snowy meadow floor. Ada's buried garden plot and neat pole corral abutted the cabin like a snow-white checkerboard. Try as I would, I could think of no reason for Tanner to introduce us now. He stopped to tighten the girth of the dun's saddle before swinging himself onto the stud's back, as fresh as he had been at the day's start. Knowing that I would soon face the woman I resented so greatly, I composed myself, hoping the jealousy I felt did not show. I feared that somehow Ada McGrath, a woman experienced in ways that I was not, would know exactly what my feelings were for Jed Tanner.

As we drew near the cabin, a dog began to bark, sounding the alarm and alerting the inhabitants of our approach. A door cracked open and against the narrow strip of backlight there appeared the figure of a woman, her rifle pointed soberly in our direction.

"It's Jed, Ada. No need for alarm," Tanner's voice rang out across the clearing and above the barking dog.

"Hey you, Mollie, hush up!" The light, lilting words floated through the murkiness of nightfall and the dog, a border collie mix, trotted to her side. In the faint light by the cabin door, she squinted into the mist. "Who's that with you, Jed?"

With one swift blow Jed shattered the dream I had clung to all through the grueling day.

"I've brought Meg to you, Ada. She needs a place to stay 'til spring."

With a cry of outrage, I twisted around in my saddle, jerking Coalie's head as I did. "I will not stay here, Jed Tanner!" I shot out at him.

He never had chance to answer, as Ada herself interrupted our exchange.

"Meg! At last!" she said warmly, as if I were a long-lost friend, "I'm glad you're here. I've been wanting to meet you ever since Ben first spoke of you. Imagine Jed keeping a secret like that! You just come right on in. We'll sort this all out later."

With a mixture of outright jealousy and seething anger, I turned to look at the woman I so greatly resented and I caught sight of a small figure with a white halo of curls clinging to her skirt. Without warning, he burst past her, running toward us. "Jed! Jed!" he cried, his small face beaming with delight at the silent man still atop his giant horse. Then, unexpectedly, he veered toward me, pointing a stubby finger at Dog, who lay bandaged and panting by Coalie's hooves. "Is your dog sick, Miss Meg?" he asked with an angelic smile. Dog wagged his tail weakly at the attention.

"Timmie! You get back inside!" The boy gave us a regretful look but obeyed his mother without argument. Ada turned her attention back to us.

"Jed, you'll find Ethan in the barn. He'll help you with your horses." Tanner, like Timmie, followed her orders without question. Wordlessly, I dismounted, handing him Coalie's reins. Jed led the horse away as Ada came forward to greet me.

She was smaller than I had expected, and her upturned face held a look of pure welcome. Her red hair was pulled back from the perfect oval of her face and worn in a smooth coil at the nape of her neck. Even under the thickness of heavy wool, she had an alluring, womanly shape, and I felt a schoolgirl in comparison, my tall, slender body and youthfulness measuring up unfavorably to the mature attraction of her older years. I had been prepared to dislike her on sight, so her kindness was disconcerting, giving me further cause for resentment. Ada McGrath was a fine, decent woman.

"I've been waiting ever so long for this," she said sincerely. Linking her arm through mine, she drew me into the cabin.

As my eyes accustomed themselves to the brightness of the room, she took my heavy buffalo coat from me and led me to the chair drawn closest to the fire. Leaving me there, she went to prepare me a supper plate. I looked around the room, which was filled with her loving touches. In the haze of the lantern light shining across the tabletop, the bright calico curtains at the window and the colorful rag rugs covering the plank floor took on a muted quality, lending a richness to the dark log walls of the interior. Firelight danced upon the far walls of the cabin, leaving a pine cupboard gleaming in the reflected light as it displayed an assortment of crockery and tin plates. Opposite this and across from the table, a bed was positioned against the wall. There was a loft above us, beneath the pitched roof of the cabin.

Carving off a thick slice of venison roast, Ada spooned out the baby potatoes and squash alongside of it and, smothering the entire plate in a rich gravy, placed it on the table. "You'd better eat this while it's hot," she advised, pouring me a cup of coffee. I glanced anxiously at the door.

"You don't have to worry about Jed," she commented knowingly. "He won't leave before he eats." She had guessed my thoughts. My gaze went to her face and suddenly I recognized that she was all that I was not: kindhearted, patient, and even-tempered. It was no wonder a man like Jed was drawn to her. She was a balm to his restive nature. She would not stir up ugly memories.

"I've been after Jed to bring you by," she said, as she cleared away the remains of her family's supper dishes and seated herself across the table from me. "But you know how it is with menfolk. They don't understand a woman's craving for another woman's company." My eyes wandered over to the door again. It did not escape her notice. I picked up my fork and began to eat.

"It sure did surprise me when Ben told me that the young fella that Jed and Tice had with them was a woman, and Jed's cousin at that." She regarded me calmly across the table, too honest to hide her curiosity.

I could not respond to Ada's kindness by evading the truth. Aware that she would soon find out about Tice's death and the reason behind it, I disclosed the story of my charade. From my escape from Cross Creek and Doc's enlistment of Jed Tanner to see me to safety until Tice's death, I told her what had occurred, leaving out only my feelings for Tanner and what had happened between us.

At the sound of voices at the door, Timmie jumped up from his seat, rushing to greet his old friend as he entered the room. In amazement, I watched Tanner's grim face soften and smile as the boy threw his arms about his legs. A tall, thin redheaded boy having much of Ada's looks about him detached himself from Tanner's side and went to sit by the warmth of the fire as Ada ordered the tall man to the table and placed a heaping plate of food before him.

Ada laid a fond hand on Tanner's shoulder as she freshened his coffee. I winced inwardly at the proprietary gesture, my face a careful blank. "You see, Meg," she said familiarly, "I take good care of Jed. I wasn't about to let him leave here yet. There's eggs for breakfast, too," she added with a congenial smile.

The corners of Tanner's mouth tightened. He gave me an impersonal look, and the last of what we had shared together disintegrated before my eyes. I put down my fork, unable to eat another bite of the dessert Ada had pressed upon me.

"Look at that poor girl, Jed! She's exhausted. She's hardly eaten any of her supper and she's not touching that cobbler of mine. I can understand her being upset about Tice and all, but just you look at her. She didn't get that way overnight. She's worn down pure to the bone. If it weren't for her hair, I'd take her for a boy Ethan's age!" Tanner averted his eyes, annoyed at the turn in conversation.

To be taken as a boy, especially after the hours I had spent in Jed's arms, wrecked the slim rein of control I held over myself. I began to giggle helplessly.

"Surely, Meg, it's nothing to joke about," Ada admonished as she further noted my complexion, reddened by exposure to the wind and cold, and the streaks of lightness in my hair from the sun. She ran her eyes over my loose shirt, belted at the waist and hiding the curves beneath it, and then to my breeches, covering legs that surely did not resemble the fleshy ones men were suppose to fancy. To my surprise, Tanner interrupted her critical perusal.

"She'll do, Ada. Leave her be," he said forcefully.

She took no offense at his brusqueness and I envied her her easy way with him. And somehow, too, she managed to cut through his wariness, a wariness he had always displayed around me. I realized the full extent of the grave injustice I had done her. She provided him a port in the storm, more treasured by him than any of our impassioned moments. Certainly, she gave him more than I could ever offer.

It wasn't until the boys had retired for the night that Ada spoke her mind. "Aren't you afraid Barton will send someone else after Meg?" she inquired of Tanner as if she regarded me a child in need of mothering. Despite her lithe figure, Ethan's age and the slight crinkling at the corner of her eyes revealed her years to be close to Tanner's.

Tanner rose abruptly. Going to the window, he stared out of a frosted pane of glass, ignoring me as he addressed his response to Ada.

"I don't think so. If Barton's killer couldn't get her, and he sure as hell was wise to the mountains, I don't think there's anyone left fool enough to try, no matter how much money he was offered. She'll be safe enough here, at least until spring. And I'm betting the Matthews boy will have shown up by then and he'll have set them straight. Once they get hold of him, they won't have much interest left in Meg. And if they haven't found him, enough time will have passed so their tempers will have cooled.

"Of course," he continued dryly, finally turning to

me, "I don't advise your going back to Cross Creek, whether you've been cleared or not. It wouldn't be very comfortable for you around there. Just pick yourself a nice place to start over," he suggested.

My voice shaking with emotion, I brushed aside all implications but one. "You can't do this to me, Jed. I won't let you leave me behind," I said, my eyes flashing a challenge to him.

"You'll do exactly as I say, Meg." His words were icy, dashing all my hopes to bits. After all that had passed between us, I still meant nothing to him. I did not expect him to love me, but neither did I expect to be discarded like a shirt he had grown tired of.

I glared at him mutinously, my anger giving me courage. "You have no right to tell me what to do, where to go, or who to stay with!"

Ignoring Ada's surprised face, Tanner turned a cold eye on me as he spun back from the window, silently damning me for the trouble I was causing. He regarded me almost savagely, chilling me to the bone. I felt Ada's pitying glance, but I did not care.

Suddenly, the reason became clear and I didn't know why I hadn't seen it sooner.

"You're leaving, aren't you? You won't be back," I said dumbly.

"I thought you understood," he answered, a hard note entering his voice. "This was a favor I did for Doc Elliot. I owed him, Meg. I did what I had to. But you're safe now and there's no point in me staying on. Ada's glad to have the company and Ben can take you off the mountain come spring."

I thought I would drown in the hurt of his words.

"You can't leave yet, Jed. Barton's men will still be looking for you—"

"I can take care of myself, Meg," he interrupted curtly. "But I'll stop in Cross Creek and let Doc know you're all right."

I stared at him wordlessly. Silently he returned

my stare, and for a moment I thought I saw regret
flicker across his face. But he did nothing to take
back his words, nothing to show that he had changed
his mind. An eternity passed before I acknowledged
that he would not.

Jed Tanner intended to salve his conscience by
pawning me off on Ada and Ben, counting on their
good natures to provide for me. And he expected me
to be able to start over elsewhere as easily as a tum-
bleweed. Didn't he realize that we were not all made
like him? Well, I would have no part of his plans for
me.

"I'm sorry, Jed," I said bitterly. "I won't stay here.
I'm going back to the cabin in the morning. And
nothing you can do or say will stop me."

He swore at me in vexation. I knew Ada guessed
the truth. But she said nothing. I went to help her
with the supper dishes.

I'll never know if Tanner would have tried to argue me into staying at the McGrath cabin, because
at that late hour of the night Ben Trew came storm-
ing through the door, the worry carved in the hard
lines of his face. His voice was a welcome thunder
across the strained silence in the room.

"What 'n hell happened at your place, Jed? Meg,
thank God you're safe. I wasn't sure what to think
when I rode by today. I found Tice's grave in that
cavern below the south ridge. Who was that with
him?" Ben demanded without pausing for breath.

Jed told Ben, from the beginning, what had taken
place, much as I had told Ada earlier. I listened
shamelessly as I stacked the clean plates while Jed
spoke of me impersonally. I looked up to find Ben
eyeing me speculatively.

"Damn it, Ben! I'm not some freak!" I scowled at
him. He laughed at me. "Don't get your dander up,
Meg. I never said that you were. But I happen to
agree with Jed. You stay here with Ada. There's no

sense in you being by yourself. I can take you down the mountain come spring if you're still of a mind to go."

Although this was just what Tanner had counted on, Ben's willingness to help did nothing to improve his mood. He was still annoyed with me.

There was no point in Ben misunderstanding the situation. I turned to face the red-bearded man.

"I don't think you understand, Ben. I'm not staying with Ada. Not for Jed, not for you. But since I have to wait until spring before I can leave," I said stiffly, avoiding Tanner's cold eye, "I'll take you up on your offer as an escort. It seems I have no other choice."

Ben gave me a wide grin. "It sure will be nice having you around this winter. I don't feel badly about that at all," he continued cheerily, missing Tanner's black scowl. "I tell you what. I'll even bring you over to Ada's any time you've a notion for a visit. You might even change your mind about stayin'."

I paid no mind to Ben's last comment. I was not prepared to do battle with him also that night. Ben threw Tanner a charitable look. "I can take Meg back to the cabin in the morning for you, if you'd like."

Jed cut him off coldly. "Don't trouble yourself, Ben. I'll take her back and make sure she's got enough stores to see her through. You'll have time enough to check on her after I'm gone."

"Suit yourself," Ben responded, lapsing into silence. By the light of the dying fire, he resembled one of the vikings of old that I had read about in Miss Tucker's books. I saw him turn his head in my direction, but I could not see the expression on his shadowed face.

I never asked myself why Tanner insisted on accompanying me back to the cabin, supposing it had something to do with his peculiar sense of obligation to me—that and his wariness of Ben Trew. Sometimes some men just did not take to one another. No more pleased with Tanner's plan than I had been with Ben's, I bid them all a tart good night and climbed up to the loft where I lay cosseted between Timmie's warm little body and the cold wall, listening far into the night as the soft murmur of voices continued, trying hard not to think of Tanner's eyes on Ada's beautiful face and the emptiness of my life without him.

Chapter Twenty-One

I AWOKE TO THE DEEP SOUND of Tanner's voice drifting up to the loft and steeled myself for the day ahead of me. At the breakfast table, Ada gave a disapproving look at my plate as I made a sad pretense of picking at the food. The others piled their dishes high with steaming stacks of pancakes, bacon from one of her own hogs, and enough fried eggs from her cherished flock of chickens to feed a small army. My own face, brittle as a mask, threatened to break at the least provocation. Thankfully, Ada did not press me about my appetite.

Timmie was brokenhearted at our leaving. He gave Dog a last, loving hug, too young to hide the tears in his eyes. "Mollie loves Ethan best, but I can tell Dog likes me the most," he said solemnly. The gangling pup gave Timmie an affectionate lick. Kneeling beside the two of them, I comforted Timmie, taking his small hands between mine.

"Timmie, come spring I'll be leaving the mountain

for good. Would you like it if Dog came to stay with
you then? He would be yours for keeps."

A tremulous smile broke through his tears. "But
it's such a long time 'til then, Miss Meg."

"I know that, Timmie," I said. "But you see, I'll
be alone until then and I need Dog for company. And
besides," I added, looking up at Ada, "in the meantime you need to rest up so you'll be strong enough
to follow him wherever he goes. He loves to chase
rabbits and you wouldn't want to be left behind, would
you?"

He shook his head manfully and I wished I could
be as easily consoled.

As a light flurry of snow began, Ada handed me
a sack heavy with provisions. I could guess at the
delicacies she had packed in it. Her mothering instincts ran to wayward and stubborn women. Tanner
and the stud waited for us, the horse still as a statue,
the rider a dark shape sitting tall upon the animal's
back. By the dun's flank, the dead man's horse
dropped his head against the wind; Tanner was taking him on to Cross Creek, leaving the rest of the
pack animals for Ben to dispose of. I heard him tell
Ada that Tice's bay was for Ethan. Then, turning
our horses away from the small group of people in
the clearing, we headed into the gloomy winter day.

I followed Tanner across the level white floor of
the park into the upper reaches of the mountain all
that morning without a word passing between us.
Large, wet flakes of snow fell at an alarming rate,
pelting us with a stinging fury, obscuring all beyond
Coalie's drooping ears. Pulling up my collar, I tied
my muffler about my head, wrapping the ends so
that they covered the lower portion of my face, leaving only my eyes exposed. I strained to see Tanner's
faint shape ahead of me. My eyes burned sharply in
the onslaught of wind. I closed them for long moments, trusting Coalie to follow the dun's lead. In

that lonely space of time as Coalie slowly plodded on in the stud's invisible wake, I forced myself to face the bleak truth. Jed had never promised any part of himself to me. Sharing his bed was not enough to hold a man like him. It had been foolish of me to think it could change anything between us. My vehemence at his impending departure had, no doubt, been a surprise. He had probably never guessed at my feelings for him. But it was better this way, I told myself. He would have left anyway.

Coalie's sudden stop jolted me back into the swirling white world of reality and, with stiffening fingers, I took up the reins, urging him forward until we were abreast of the dun. The stud's coat steamed sweated vapor as his silent rider scanned the white thickness around us. There was a growing accumulation of snow on Tanner's shoulders and his face was a bearded white mask framing reddened skin. "The trail's wiped out," he said bluntly. "Usually it's the warming weather that'll trigger an avalanche, but this snow is heavy and wet." He pointed up from the narrow shelf on which we stood to a flat ridge from where the wall of snow had fallen.

I closed my eyes in an attempt to clear them of the blinding snowflakes, trying to fathom how he could see anything in the blizzard of white, let alone know where the trail was supposed to be.

"What do we do?" I asked him calmly, blissfully unaware of his plan. He seemed not at all concerned about our predicament.

"We'll have to hole up until the storm passes," he replied.

"Over there?" I asked, peering several feet ahead and unable to see anything beyond an inadequate fringe of trees at the base of the wall.

"That'll do for the animals." He dismounted, stroking the stud's head absently. Dog, with his own good wisdom, had already made his way into the little shelter, curling up with his nose to his tail behind one of the small boulders that littered the bottom of the canyon wall. The cold did not seem to bother Tanner. Unhurriedly, he removed the stud's saddle and bridle. An unnamed fear clutched at my insides as I watched him work and then, in growing horror, I let my eyes travel up the shoulder of the cliff.

"Can you do it?" With a start, I realized he had been watching me all along. The ridge above us was deep and well protected from the wind and snow by a stand of pines. It would be an excellent cover during a storm. His question had been a formality; I found it little consolation that he had remembered my fear of heights. Fright kept me rigid in my saddle, numbing my legs as I continued to gaze upward through the snow, paralyzed by the enormity of the feat I would have to accomplish. Certainly I would fall, leaving behind all the worldly problems of one Meg Logan.

Tanner took up the sack of provisions Ada had given to me, dumping the contents into a blanket he had removed from my bedroll. I kicked my feet free of my stirrups and slid down the saddle. "Take off your coat," he instructed. I did as he said, shivering in the bite of the wind. "You'll be warm enough, once you start moving," he said brusquely. Turning me around, he lashed the pack he had fashioned onto my back. It was heavy, but not too uncomfortable.

He balanced his own bedroll along his broad shoulders, fastening it with a length of rope that he brought forward and then under his arms to form a makeshift harness at the back. He tied another length of rope to his waist. Pulling my reluctant form closer to him, he tied the long end about me in a similiar manner. Taking up his saddlebags, he threw them over his shoulder and I followed behind him, remaining out of his way as he led the horses to their sparse shelter, stowing their gear behind a small fall of rock and covering it with pine branches.

Mercifully, he waded through the snow to a place where the slope did not rise as a sheer wall above us but instead climbed at a steep angle. Not a tree graced the rugged incline. With the umbilical cord of rope between us, any misstep on my part would hurl us both to our deaths. With Tanner's last breath, he would be cursing me for the inept fool that I was. No matter what, I decided, that would not be my last role in life.

I remember little of the actual climb. With my eyes riveted to the spot before them, I reached for a handhold, grasping at the rough surface as it scored and scraped my fingers, struggling for a foothold as the two halves of my body worked independently, striving for survival. After a while, a stiff and awkward rhythm replaced the frenzied reaches and the pulling of the rope about my waist became less of a binding restraint and more of a reassuring pressure. Ahead of me, Tanner hoisted himself over the edge and then, dropping to his knees, stretched himself flat across the surface of the slippery ledge, reaching down for me. As his eyes darkened in concentration, they inadvertently met mine. I was so jolted by their intensity that it was as if I had received a physical blow; involuntarily, I wrenched my gaze away. Losing my footing, I plunged downward.

His hands were iron bands, capturing my wrists, bringing me up short. My body swayed as my senses reeled; my arms were stretched to their limit by the pulling force of his grasp. The rope was useless. If he altered his position even slightly, my weight would bring him sliding over the edge. He spoke through clenched teeth, straining under the effort.

"Meg, don't freeze up on me. Relax."

I tried to do as he said and he continued the smooth flow of talk.

"Easy now, bend your right leg. There's a grip for you."

I edged a numb foot upward and found the footing I had lost.

"Good. Now the left leg. Reach for it. Higher. That's right."

I rested my cheek against the cold side of the cliff, taking comfort in the solid feel of rock. But he did not allow me to take my ease for long. With a final heave, he pulled me over the edge.

I lay there weakly, unable to move in the fresh falling snow, my muscles locked in contractions. Picking me up in his arms, Tanner carried me to the shelter of the pines, placing me gently on the ground and removing my pack. Shrugging himself free of his own burden, he took his jacket, warm from his body, and wrapped it around my shoulders.

"That was a stupid thing to do."

"Yes," I agreed in a shaky voice, but he wasted no more time on me, instead retreating further back into the trees where he found a sufficient amount of dry wood for a fire.

The sky was a thick wash of colorless mist, darkening with the approach of nightfall. Recovering enough to sit by the fire and sip at the coffee Tanner had made with melted snow, I put aside the thought of our descent the next day. I watched mutely as he stirred the coals of the fire and emptied the provisions Ada had given me onto the ground, finding the elk meat, a wedge of cheese, a crock of jam, biscuits, and a leftover portion of ashcake. Taking up the meat, he sliced some into a pan, and after it began sizzling loudly, he added the biscuits for warming. He seemed to have forgotten the harsh words we had exchanged at Ada's. As he lounged by the warmth of the fire, the flames flickered brightly, painting his skin the color of mahogany and shadowing his eyes dark. Expectantly, I waited to be chastised for my obstinance at Ada's and for the trouble I had just caused him, but it never came.

He never anticipated that I would refuse him that night. I had gone to him willingly enough before. It made no difference to him that he had plans to cast me off the very next day so that he could get on with his life. Arrogantly, he wanted me as long as I was with him.

"Come here," he said to me from across the fire, as if it were the most natural thing in the world.

"No," I answered, not wanting to say more, sensing his determination. I was not afraid.

Not a glimmer of emotion crossed his face, but when he spoke, his voice had a hard edge to it, as if I had tested him once too often. "Come here," he repeated, more strongly.

Quickly, I looked away so that he could not see the depth of my longing for him. And then, as if he suddenly understood the cruelty of his demand, he stood up, taking a step toward me. I looked up at him and our eyes locked together. I did want him, no matter what the morning would bring. In denying him I would only deny myself. I rose to my feet. Slowly I went to him, hiding nothing, my love in my eyes for him to see if he chose to. His arms finally came around me in a gentle embrace as his lips lightly touched my hair. I was locked in the security of his arms, in our own little world. I wanted the moment never to end.

"Lie with me, Meg," he said quietly. The simple words touched my heart, and he brought me down to the softness of the pine-bough bed. However he meant those words, to me they sang of his need for me. His nearness chased away the snowy chill as I lay facing him. Drawing me closer, the strong arms brought me gently up against him. He brushed a strand of hair away from my cheek with rough fingers and gripped my face lightly with his hands so that I could not look away, and the gray depths of his eyes seemed to search straight through to my heart for some kind of answer. I forgot about all that was wrong between us.

I lay still, unwilling to break this fragile link between us, mesmerized by his closeness. He lowered his face to mine, and under the assault of his open lips my mouth responded, melding passionately to his. My inhibitions were swept away, as if instinct told me that the discovery of my touch might change his feelings for me. I ran my fingers lightly over his shoulders and chest, faltering over the scar I had noticed the night he had washed by the firelight. Gently, he took hold of my roaming fingers and kissed them, seeking to distract them from their wanderings. But that did not deter me. I traced a path with my hands and lips down the taut flesh of his waist and belly. He tensed with growing urgency and groaned when I bypassed his straining manhood; my mouth and fingers continued to tease along his hard, muscled thigh until I found what I sought: the ropey scar tissue of another bullet wound. This was from the one that had struck him first, before the second bullet had sent him falling from his horse that day I had run away from the Cross Creek school. The scar burned my hand like a familiar brand. But he had had enough of my straying passion. Loosening my breeches just enough, he turned suddenly so that I lay beneath him, and he took possession of me with a violent thrust. I welcomed the long-ago stranger home with my body, the fierceness of his desire stirring me to a quivering ecstasy. He rode me wildly, holding back only until my frenzied spasms peaked before his urgency exploded, freeing both of us for a time of the haunting memories that kept us apart.

"You might have been killed," I said to him later,

tracing the bullet wound again and moving closer to him for warmth. His arms tightened around me.

"And been denied this pleasure," he replied. He was amused by my concern, but his eyes did not smile.

"How did it happen, Jed?"

He withdrew from me. "It was a family matter," he said at last, without elaborating, thinking I had enough sense to leave it at that.

"One of your family did that to you?" I asked in shocked disbelief. "Why, Jed?"

"I deserved it," he said, in a curiously empty voice.

I looked at him in amazement. "I don't believe that!"

"Oh, no?" He lifted his eyebrows in mock surprise, then, seeing that I remembered about his wife, looked away.

"Was it because of her?" I asked him softly, so afraid of bringing the memory back to him and so desperately needing to know. It was hard for me to mention her. I had never even learned her name.

He didn't reply, but that was answer enough.

"Who did this to you, Jed? Who hated you enough to try to kill you?"

He laughed harshly. The lines in his face were deep grooves. "Travis, my brother," he said bitterly. "I found him with Julie. I was like a man gone crazy. I killed her and then ran away like a coward. He came after me."

"I don't believe you," I said flatly, instinctively knowing that if what he said was true, then he had left a great deal out of the telling.

The gray eyes narrowed, giving me a measuring look. "Why not?" he said oddly.

"I know you, Jed." I said, staring at him. "At least as well as you let me. You're not a coward. You've never been a coward."

His face was grim. "Don't make me into something

I'm not, Meg. I'm no hero. I killed a woman. My wife.
Don't ever forget that. The rest of it doesn't matter
much."

"It doesn't matter that your own brother tried to
kill you? That he waited to ambush you? It doesn't
say an awful lot for your family, Jed."

His eyes pierced mine, puzzling over what I had
said. "How did you know about that?"

I lowered my eyes. It was bad enough that I possessed some elusive quality that reminded him of his
dead wife. How would he feel about me when he
learned the truth about that day?

"I was there," I admitted in a low voice.

The hard lines turned his face cold. "Don't fool
with me, Meg," he said harshly. "No one was there.
Except for later. Some runaway kid found me. I spent
a lot of time cursing him. He saved my life, they
said. Well, I didn't want saving. When I realized that
it was Travis who had come after me, I was glad.
He'll put me out of my misery for sure, I told myself.
Of course, I would have been more than happy to
have taken him with me, but it didn't work out that
way. When I came to, I was in Stanton, in the county
jail."

I was quiet, afraid to tell him about the part I had
unwittingly played in his life, afraid that it would
give him new reason to hate me.

"I suppose you heard about it then," he continued,
trying to make sense out of my confession. "Cross
Creek wasn't all that far from where it happened.
Word like that passes pretty quick. I guess you
weren't so young that a story like that'd be kept from
you."

"I didn't hear about it from the others, Jed," I said
steadily. And then I told him about the day I had
run away.

His laughter held a brittle sound. "Christ. I suppose I should thank you."

Bitterness toyed with the features of his face. I did not find it strange that I had not recognized him. Little of the person Jed Tanner had once been still remained. The man I had tended all those years back had, in his fevered confusion, displayed a vestige of vulnerability. In his place was a man honed by hard living, a driven man with a ravaged past. But the features of this man I had lately thought ruthless were as familiar to me as my own. I wanted to ease his pain, but I was unable to do so.

"You changed my life, too, Jed," I said quietly. "Because of what I did for you, Doc Elliot took me in. He said he needed someone to help him who wouldn't faint dead away at the sight of blood. But he never said that he knew you, even when I badgered him with questions about you that morning you rode into town. But he did ask me," I mused, "if I thought you reminded me of someone I might have known. I never guessed what he was getting at."

But he wasn't really listening to me. He pulled himself up and stared into my face, taking a long, hard look. "You know, I dreamed about her that night. I never understood it. But she came back to me and held me close, as if none of it had happened. She acted as though she had forgiven me, when I couldn't forgive myself. But I'll be damned, it was you all along."

"I didn't know, Jed, until now. One night when you washed up by the fire, I saw the scar." I touched it lightly with my hand. "And I thought about it then, for the first time in a long while. But those kinds of wounds are pretty common. I didn't think too much about it. I couldn't very well ask you if you had another scar someplace else. Besides," I added, "you looked a lot different then."

"Yeah, I'm much prettier now."

I smiled at his attempted humor, but sobered at his expression, realizing how much his second chance at life had exacted from him. Having had enough of the past, I gently traced the hard line of his cheek with my hand. He pulled me to him. We still had the night to ourselves.

Chapter Twenty-Two

✍ THE REST OF THE TIME WE SPENT in the mountains was a time worth remembering, if only for the fact that Tanner had somehow relegated his bitterness to the deep corners of his mind. While he was not carefree, for he could never be that, he was a welcome companion, sharing in the pleasure of our snowbound days. When we finally left the little ridge three days later, his eyes were clear, and at times a bemused expression crossed his face at something I had said or done. Those were the moments that raised my hopes and made me believe I could offer him what no one else could—a chance at a future, with the pain of the past dulled forever. No one but me could have built a life of dreams around the final days I spent with Tanner.

After we returned from Ada's, Tanner did not talk of his intention to leave. Because of this, I deceived myself into thinking that we would both return to Cross Creek in the spring, once the town's temper had cooled. I welcomed Jed's desire for fresh game as another indication that he planned to stay with me. He had left early on the day Ben Trew came to visit.

It was purely a social call. Ben had no way of knowing that Tanner had decided to stay on with me. The conversation began inauspiciously enough as we traded pleasantries, until I saw his searching look upon my face and realized he had noticed Tanner's belongings in their usual place. He recognized then what the situation was.

He looked at me regretfully. "Meg," he said kindly, ignoring the fresh bread I had put before him and the crock of Ada's jam beside it, "I know I'm out of line saying this, but no matter what you think, he's not for you. Jed Tanner will kill you with grief."

My face blanched at this unexpected opposition. "You're right, Ben," I said coolly. "It's none of your business." Then, seeing his honest distress, I relented and came to sit by his side. "I can understand why you feel that way, Ben, but it's just not true. Jed's been through a lot and it's soured him. But he cares for me. I know he does."

Ben picked up my hand, swallowing it in his mammoth grip. "You're making a mistake, Meg."

"You're wrong, Ben," I said, aware that he could not know of the small changes that had already taken place in Tanner. I wanted to convince him that he needn't worry about me.

Neither of us could know that Tanner had descended the south ridge and spotted Ben's gelding running loose in the corral. All his jealousy and mistrust came rushing back, unchecked. It was too late for me even before he abruptly opened the cabin door and observed us from the threshold. In an honest show of innocence I had not thought to retreat from Ben when I sought to convince him that he was wrong about Tanner. But he was not wrong. And fool that

I was, I smiled at Tanner, oblivious to the conclusions he had drawn.

"Jed, I'm glad you're back in time to see..."

The cold, stony face he turned on me froze the rest of the words in my throat. "It seems I've interrupted your social hour," he said, his voice tightly formal. I gasped at his insinuation. "Ben Trew is a friend of mine," I replied tartly.

"How good a friend, Meg?" His tone was deceptively pleasant but the transformation was complete. The Tanner I had been with the past few days might just as well have been conjured up by my imagination. Nothing that I could say to him would matter now.

Ben, his face as dark as a thundercloud, saw the pleading look in my eyes as I silently begged him to leave. Restraining himself mightily, he went to the door.

"I'll be seeing you some other time, Meg. Maybe after Jed, here, comes to his senses." I couldn't look at him again, afraid of the pity I would see in his face.

"It wouldn't matter to you, Jed," I said after the door closed, leaving us alone. "You'll believe what you will."

"Try me," he said calculatingly, planning my destruction and in the process destroying part of himself.

"I was telling Ben about us—I wanted him to know how it is—"

"You're being a fool again, Meg," he said softly. "I think you're misjudging Ben Trew if you think he'll get used to the idea that the girl he's sweet on might like being with another man."

Ben had been right, of course. I had not seen the truth. Tanner had not changed at all. I had let myself believe our time together had meant something to him because I wanted to. But he was leaving me, just as he had planned all along. He had wanted me and had had me. I was something to be left along the wayside and now Ben could take his place. I fought back with the only weapon I had, damning words.

"You hypocrite!" The words spewed forth uncontrolled. "You couldn't share Julie, but you'll pass me on, now that you've had your fill! I guess it's my fault because I was crazy enough to think I mattered to you, that you cared for me." An incredible ache tightened my throat, yet still I lashed out at him, unable to measure the effect of my accusations. "It's no wonder she did what she did, Jed, married to you!" Tanner's eye's narrowed threateningly, but I was not afraid. "Did you tell Travis he could have her and then change your mind once you found them together?"

He stood as still as a statue as I hurled my invectives at him, as the sweet memories of what had been between us turned to ashes. I would never be able to reach him again. In the briefest of moments, before the inpenetrable mask slipped back into place, I saw his suffering, but then it, too, was gone. And when I looked up again, the cabin was empty.

I fell to my knees and wept until there were no more tears left, and then I made my way outside and there, gripping the wall for support, retched until nothing remained and my insides were as empty as my heart. Shivering, I returned to the cabin and covered myself with a blanket, my ragged sobbing echoing in my ears.

Warmth turned to searing heat as flames danced by my bed and I screamed for Tanner. I had to warn him about the fire before it was too late. But he turned away from me just as he had before. He didn't hear me. He wouldn't listen to what I said. I shouted to him above the roar of the blaze but he walked away with the flames racing after him.

I was sobbing as Ben's touch broke through the veil of the nightmare. Bracing me from behind, he placed my hands around a cup of hot liquid, guiding it to my mouth and forcing me to drink as I stared wildly about, searching for the blackened ruins of a covered wagon. But there was only the darkened interior of the cheerless cabin.

I awoke the following day to find myself under Ben's silent scrutiny. He was sitting at the table with a cool assurance, and it was evident that he had been watching me for a long while. I turned my head away from his knowing look.

"How long have you been here, Ben?" I asked him listlessly.

"Two days," he said briefly. In the silence that followed, each of us thought of Tanner but Ben, thankfully, didn't mention him.

"I don't want your pity," I said in a small voice.

"Hell, who's offering you pity? If you were dumb enough to get mixed up with him, you got what you had coming, believe me. But we shouldn't be talking of those things now. You need your rest."

"I don't ever want to talk about it," I replied dully, wetting my parched lips and grimacing at the feverish ache that racked my muscles as I shifted my position slightly. Burrowing myself deeper under the covers, I slept again.

This time the nightmares were not of flames but of horrifying reality. Again I spat out those damning words, witnessing over and over the bleakness of his face and the emptiness in his eyes. Only this time, I begged him to take me with him, and he laughed at me, mocking laughter that echoed in my ears.

Ben stayed with me until the end of the week. By then, I was strong enough to convince him to leave. I wanted to be alone, I told him. I needed to sort out my feelings. He argued with me, but I remained

adamant, and rather than upset me further, he reluctantly gave in to my wishes.

In the days and weeks that went by, I added my
recent torment to the past I kept locked within me.
Gradually, my anguish at Tanner's departure subsided into desolation, which greeted me each morning upon wakening and manifested itself during the
day by unpredictable spells of weeping. During this
time, I came to realize how Tanner and I had been
at cross purposes all along, how my need to love and
to be loved in return had blinded me to his ways. I
had experienced his indifference, rage, and, in his
weaker moments, his tenderness. But even in our
most intimate moments he had kept himself apart
from me. I knew very little about his past. I had
believed my outburst justified at the time, but what
really lay behind his accusing words when he came
upon Ben and me that day? Naively, I had convinced
myself that together we could wipe away his past,
but I should have recognized the futility of that
hope—I had had little enough success with my own
life. But none of my reflections brought me any comfort. I hungered painfully for what was gone forever.

Because winter falls so swiftly in the mountains,
Tanner's departure left the longest and hardest of
those months still to be endured. I did not mark the
days. Christmas would have passed unnoticed but
for Ben's gift of a turkey for a simple dinner. After
that, the days again sank into a sameness, with only
the slightest lengthening of the days to indicate that
the frozen mantle would not last forever. During the
coldest days, I fashioned a vest of the squirrel skins
Tice had saved, spotting the fur with soundless tears
from eyes grown weary with strain in the winter
gloom of the cabin. I saved the ashes from the hearth,
and later, when I had enough, I soaked them in a
bucket and, through the hole bored at the bottom,

collected the leeched lye drippings, adding rendered tallow to it and boiling it until it became hard. In this way, I made enough soap for Ada, hoping in a small way to repay her kindness to me. The soap was dark and lacked the fragrance of the store-bought variety, but with the piney scent of the forest in the air, it seemed of little importance.

My robust good health was slow in returning. Ben, noticing the dark smudges beneath my eyes, cautioned me about taking on too much. He tempered his words, knowing how much I disliked his show of concern, saying only that the severity of my fever had been such that I was bound to suffer from tiredness for a spell. He could not know that only after I worked myself to exhaustion would sleep come to me at night. I ignored the troubling bouts of weakness, and in time they disappeared.

It was my lack of spirit that bothered Ben most. Growing impatient with my wan demeanor, he insisted that a visit to Ada's was in order. Through Ben, she had regularly sent me specially baked treats during my convalescence, and I wondered at my reluctance to see her as I crossly protested Ben's suggestion.

"That's just it!" Ben jumped on me, halting my further objections. "Cabin fever. That's what you've got. You've been by yourself too much. You need to see someone before you get too taken with your own company."

"I'm not alone," I said irritably. "I've got Dog for company."

"A hell of a job he's done. Pack your gear. We're leaving now, while we still have a good start on the day."

Ben refused to take no for an answer. Lacking the will necessary for further argument, I did as he said, taking along a few of my things, including the soap I had made for Ada. Once more I rode Coalie down

the mountainside and across the snow-covered pass
to Ada McGrath's cabin.

Ada could only guess at the reason for my low
spirits. Ben had told her that I had been ill, but no
more than that. But she knew that Tanner had left
the mountain. Perhaps she recalled my stormy outburst when he had arranged for me to stay with her
and recognized it as a profession of a stronger feeling.
She did her best by me, enticing my appetite with
her wonderful cooking and cautioning both Timmie
and Ethan to be on their best behavior. At night,
she would tell us tales of her earlier days in the gold
fields with Michael McGrath, captivating Timmie
with stories of a father he did not remember and
setting a shining example in Ethan's eyes. It was
more than a week before Ben returned for me and,
over Ada's vigorous pleadings, I went back to the
quiet solitude of my own little cabin. Within my
loneliness, I believed, lay the elusive peace I was
seeking. I needed to come to terms with myself. But
Ben had been right. I did feel better since I had been
with Ada.

It was not until I returned from Ada's that the
truth finally dawned on me. Reaching for my small
bag of scraps, I searched among them for one suitable
for mending a tear in my threadbare shirt. Comprehension came with a numbing slowness as I stared
at my small collection of fabric, realizing that there
had been no need to use it for my monthly courses
since before I had taken ill. Just once, shortly after
the fever, had I thought of it. But it had not surprised
me that my time was late. It was, I had told myself,
a lingering effect of the illness and I had not thought
of it since. Now, raising a tentative hand to my stomach, I felt the reassuring flatness and chose to ignore
the slight tenderness of my breasts. But I think I
knew then that the sickness was not the reason.

The passage of time marked my future. Daily, my

suspicions grew stronger. I was to bear Tanner's child. Tanner had left something behind besides heartbreak; he had left a part of himself, and I carried that within me. My panic gave way to a calm acceptance. I wanted his child.

I could not bring myself to tell Ben. Several times I started to during one of his visits, only to falter at the last moment. I told myself it was because I was not ready yet to share my news with anyone, but the truth was that I was afraid to tell him. Patiently, and without words, he was biding his time, waiting for me to turn to him. In my own way, I cared for Ben deeply, but I could not return his feelings. All my thoughts were for the child.

I began taking better care of myself, and instead of growing weary on tasks meant to keep my mind and hands busy, I took long walks in the cold mountain air, rebuilding the strength I had lost and would now need more than ever. I even ate more, and Ben, stopping by for a visit one day, noticed the difference right away. "You're looking better," he remarked. "You're not as pale as you were the last time." I should have told him then, but I didn't. He thought my improved health and renewed interest in life was due to his efforts. I let him keep his dream.

It was a teasing time of year. Across the high plains and along the southern face of the rolling foothills, the earth was stirring under the first golden rays of spring as the mountain remained deep within a wintry embrace. But gradually the temperatures warmed. The crystalline snow, forged in the most delicate of crusts, began to melt, the drifts losing ground daily under the gentle persuasion of a strengthening sun. The snow dwindled from the rooftop, quickening to a steady drip in the sun's unrelenting glare, pulsing a silvered path to the frozen ground below. Water trickled down the sun-warmed boulders, nourishing the awakening earth, swelling the streams as they coursed between the rocks and crevices of the creekbeds.

It made no difference to Ben that each afternoon, as the sun sank below the western ridges, winter returned to the mountains, freezing the earth again. And it certainly made no difference that winter still endured proudly in the higher reaches with an invincible hold on the loftiest peaks. Ben had waited out the long months with a quiet acceptance, holding back until he believed my wounds had had a chance to heal. With the promise of spring in the air, he figured he had allowed me enough time.

He came for his answer on a day when the wind whipped through the pass, chilling the damp air with a savage bite. His determination was evident in the set of his shoulders as he swung down from his horse and stood his ground against the gusting wind, his hair a waving banner as he made his way to the cabin. For the first time since I had known Ben, I shrank from him as he entered the small room. The fire snapped behind me, the flame biting into the dry bark of the split log before settling down to feed on the heart of the wood. Brightly, I tried to think of things to say. He saw through my attempt to forestall him with idle chatter; with a sharp look, he crossed the short distance between us and gripped my upper arms with his hands, forcing me to meet his steady gaze. My troubled eyes blurred with tears and his touch, which I had not felt since my illness, brought no comfort.

"What is it, Meg?" The gentleness in his voice belied the roughness of his hold. Suddenly realizing that he might be frightening me, with a low laugh he let his hands fall away.

"Oh, Ben," I said miserably. "I'm sorry."

"Meg"—his voice was quietly composed—"I've tried to give you as much time as you need."

"It's not that, Ben," I answered, shutting my eyes against him. There was no way he could know that I did care for him, but in a way that could never be enough for a man like him. I turned away, unable to face him, sinking to a seat by the hearth, and stared into the leaping flames. The heat of his eyes on my averted face burned hotter than the fire.

Ben was not one for small talk. Even during my illness, when he had cared for me, the time was filled with long silences. It had only been after some weeks that he had talked of himself, with the purpose of winning me to him. The air was charged with the feelings he had held back until now.

"I know you don't love me, Meg," he said quietly. "But you care for me. The rest can come later."

"Please don't, Ben," I whispered. "You'll spoil things between us."

"You're wrong about that."

I looked up at him. "It can't work, Ben. Not with me feeling the way I do about Jed. It wouldn't be fair to you."

He stared down at me, as if taking stock of what he saw in my face. "I want you, Meg. I can live with your feelings for him. And you'll forget him. Maybe not right away; I wouldn't expect that. But you will."

I did not try to hide my amazement. "Why, Ben? Why settle for someone like me? You've loved before. Your wife..." I said, protesting softly, for Ben had told me about his brief marriage. A diptheria epidemic had claimed his young wife and newborn child.

"My wife is dead," he replied curtly. It was a statement of fact. Unlike Tanner, he had buried Rebecca in the past. He was not bound to her by an everlasting damnation. He wanted me, maybe even loved me. That was enough for him. How could I fault him for that? I'd have taken Tanner the same way if he had only let me. But Ben believed that in time I would come to feel love for him. It would be cruel to give him hope when there was none. The fondness I had for Ben could not compare to my love for Tanner.

"I'm sorry, Ben," I repeated, meeting his gaze. "It's impossible."

But he was not discouraged. The firelight cast his features into hard angles of determination. Purposefully, he extended a hand to my face, my eyes widening at his overture, but it was only to tuck a wayward strand of hair behind my ear. His gaze swept my features, ignoring my unease. Taking my hand in his, he raised me to my feet.

"Let me change your mind, Meg," he said simply, as he lightly brushed his lips against mine. With an aching heart, I shut my eyes and let my complete lack of response answer for me.

Ben wore a stubborn look that was not in the least bit reassuring.

I cursed Tanner for what he had done to me and for what I was doing to Ben. It was then that I reached my decision, knowing that unless I did so the hateful words I had uttered to Tanner the day he had left would ring in my ears for the lifetime to come.

"I have to see Jed again, Ben."

His eyes widened slightly but the stubborn set never left his face. It would make little difference to him what my reasons were, but I owed him an explanation.

"I need to talk to him, Ben. I accused him of things that weren't true. I didn't mean them. He needs to know that."

"Meg," he said severely, "it's finished between you and Jed. Nothing you say now is going to change that."

"It's not just him I'm doing it for, Ben, it's for me, too. My words haunt me, Ben, I can't forget them. I'll never have any peace until I explain that it was just because I was so angry..." I looked at him, desperate for his understanding.

His features softened slightly. "Telling him you're sorry for what you said won't make any difference, Meg. It's not going to matter to him."

"Ben, I have to do this!"

He moved closer to me and tightly clasped my hands in his so that I could not withdraw them. "Listen to what I'm saying to you, Meg. Jed was dried up a long time ago. Long before you ever knew him. You can't bring feeling back to a man like that. He carries the past around with him—his own living hell. He's got nothing left to give anyone. You don't want to go after him, Meg. Don't go after someone who thinks as little of you as he does."

"It doesn't matter, Ben," I said. "I'm going to have his child."

Ben's face stiffened as the impact of my words sank in. His eyes traveled over me, seeking the proof he had missed.

"You couldn't have known," I said gently. "There hasn't been much change yet."

"When?" His manner was curt.

"The end of the summer."

"I suppose that's why you want to see him again," he said darkly. "You know it won't make any difference to him, don't you? I remember what he said to you before he left, that day he found us together. He won't believe it's his." Ben's voice was harsh. I had put that harshness there. For a moment it reminded me of Tanner's.

"Ben, listen to me! That's not the reason! I know he won't believe the baby's his. It'll only give him more excuse to hate me."

He gave a stinging laugh, shaking his head. "You sure do beat all, Meg. You don't even known where he is! Hell, he was going by way of Cross Creek. Something might have happened to him...maybe your friend Barton got a hold of him."

I felt my face grow pale but I refused to consider

Ben's words. "He's alive. I know he is. He'll have cleared himself. Then he was heading north," I said, recalling his conversation with Doc Elliot the night we left Cross Creek. "He was going home."

"To the north valley?" Ben's face clearly registered his opinion of my proposal. "That must be close to five hundred miles from here! Maybe he changed his mind. You could be on a wild goose chase!" Ben's nearly unending patience was exhausted. "God damn it, Meg! Be reasonable! You can't travel in your condition. Not all that distance!"

I gave him a small smile, my determination unshaken. "That's why I have to leave right away, Ben. While I can still ride. I can make it there, see him, and be on my way again well before my time comes."

Ben frowned, the creases in his face pulling downward in severe lines, disappearing into his red-gold beard. He made no attempt to hide his displeasure.

"All right," he said finally. "But I'm going along with you." He raised a hand to silence my shocked protest. "Hear me out," he growled. "You need me, whether you're willing to admit it or not. I promised I'd take you where you wanted to go come spring. I'm keeping my word. It's too long a trip for you to make by yourself. You don't know if Barton's men are still out there, waiting for you to show yourself. At least consider the baby you're carrying if you're too stubborn to think about your own neck."

"But Jed—"

"It won't make a damned bit of difference to him whether I'm there or not."

I was not so willful that I did not see the wisdom of his words. "All right," I conceded, somewhat ungraciously.

"That's not all I want from you, Meg," he continued quietly. "After you've had your say and he's out of your system, like you claim he'll be, you're going to marry me." He looked deeply into my stunned face.

"Believe me, Meg. You'll wish you had never set eyes on him again. He'll make sure of that."

Mutely, I stared at him. Despite everything I had told him, Ben still wanted me. I wanted to refuse him, but reason intervened. There had been too many years that I had belonged nowhere and to no one. Ben was willing to accept me, knowing how I felt about Tanner. To me, life was worth nothing without Jed, but now there was the child to think of. Ben would be a good father. Could I deny the baby his love and security? He watched me, waiting for my answer.

"We could never be what your wife and daughter were to you," I said gravely.

"I'm not asking you to be," he answered in a low voice.

"Then I'll consider it, Ben. That's all I can do right now."

"That's good enough," he said with a confident smile, never doubting the outcome.

Chapter Twenty-Three

✍ I CAME TO KNOW ANOTHER SIDE of Ben Trew as we traveled together. After we said our good-byes to Ada, leaving Dog with Timmie as I had promised, and stopped at Culley's for provisions, he left me to myself, by day and night, as if that time in the cabin had never occurred. Never once did he press his suit on me as we rode the long trail, nor did he speak of it during the quiet supper we shared each night. It was the wisest course he could have followed. His tranquility soothed me in a way that Tanner's nature never could have.

With the mountain streams spouting liquid silver into fast-rising creekbeds that stretched like long fingers through the foothills, the heavy moist air of the fertile land broke with the fragrance of new life. Broad sweeps of winter-browned valleys were brushed with the lightest strokes of green that widened daily until the land caught fire with the brightness of spring. With the sun riding on our shoulders, we directed our horses to a flat, well watered strip of land we had spied earlier from above. Free from the shadow of the surrounding hills, the unspoiled southern exposure gave rise to a thicker carpet of grass, the tender shoots a delicate feast for our mounts.

Ben was cautions. To be safe, we skirted the closest of the settlements, heading directly for Redmonton. It was impossible to second-guess Holbrook Barton's intentions. Even if Tanner had cleared himself, he might still want me. We made camp by a willow-bordered stream one day's ride from town and I made what repairs I could after the long, hard weeks of riding by splashing in the swiftly flowing water, washing away the most obvious of travel stains. I let my hair hang free. With my thickened waist it would be difficult to hide my condition much longer, and thinking on it, Ben agreed. It was my best defense. Even a rich man's vengeance and money would be hard-pressed to find a man who would take the life of a woman and her unborn child.

The main street of Redmonton was a dark ribbon of mud when we rode into town under the soft but persistent rain that had been with us since early morning. Skirting the churning mire, we headed our mounts past the congestion of patient farm horses and wagons by the feed and supply stores, toward the center of town. Occasionally, a storekeeper could be seen attacking the muddy walkways with an aggressive sweep of his broom, but most had given in to the wet hold of spring so that the sight of a woman sidestepping her way across the muddy street with her skirt held above her ankles was of no special interest, even to the randiest of observers.

As we tied our horses to the hitching post, my mud-splattered attire attracted more than one curious look, but with Ben's tall, bearded presence by my side, I did not worry overly about unwanted ad-

vances. Only on close inspection could my condition
be detected.

Ben chose our hotel wisely. Farleigh's Hotel was
not the best in town, but a more modest structure,
an unpretentious two-storied square wooden building that had seen better days. It stood near an invisible line between the respectable and somewhat
more questionable section of town.

After the weeks of travel, it was the stuffy air,
heavy with stale cigar smoke, that I noticed first, as
my eyes strained at the dim interior of the small
hotel lobby. The sun, breaking through the thick
layer of clouds, poured weakly through the window-
panes of the hotel front, illuminating the dust motes
as they floated loftily through the room. Red wallpaper, faded by years of slanting rays of afternoon
sunlight, covered the walls above the dulled varnish
of the wainscoting. Several stuffed chairs, dusty
where the friction of wear had not brushed them
clean, were placed conveniently around the room.

The pale young clerk barely looked our way as
Ben registered us for two rooms, his curiosity already
dulled by the time spent behind the scarred hotel
desk. Ben deposited my belongings in my room with
a certain grimness, and stated his intentions to see
to the stabling of the horses and then find out whatever he could about Tanner's whereabouts. I watched
him leave, confused, with only his promise to come
for me at supper time to see me through the strange-
ness of the unfamiliar town.

The bath I had arranged for surpassed all my expectations. I had almost forgotten the wonderful
comfort of heated water. I worked the scented soap
through my hair, rinsing it clean before I lathered
my skin. Trying not to think of what Ben might
already have discovered, I viewed the plain furnishings of the room as I soaked away the hardships of
the journey. The ironstead bed with a dingy coverlet,

the nightstand with a kerosene lamp placed conveniently upon it, the cracked bowl and pitcher atop a mirrored pine chest, and the lone straight-back chair all seemed luxurious extravagances to a person so used to the barest of essentials. Only when my skin threatened to pucker permanently did I emerge from the water and dress in the clean but crushed shirt-waist and skirt that I had carried with me all the way from Cross Creek. The clothes were a tight fit; I would not be able to wear them much longer. Then, taking the stiff, yellowed towel that had been brought along with the bathwater, I dried my hair as I waited for Ben.

He escorted me to dinner at a small restaurant three blocks from the hotel. No matter how much I pleaded, he refused to tell me anything of what he had learned until after I had eaten. Fearing the worst, I began to eat, and the meal passed in silence until our plates were empty. I begged off the thick wedge of apple pie for dessert and waited impatiently for Ben to finish his. As eager as I was, I did not push him. There was a darkness to Ben that night that I did not understand. Finally, he pushed his plate away and signaled the waitress for more coffee.

"He came through here two, maybe three months ago," he said, staring down at the dark liquid in his cup as if he had never seen coffee before. "So I guess you were right. He made it through Barton's range without getting shot up. They say he hasn't been back this way since. A puncher I was talking to said that the ST—that's his father's outfit—did their spring hiring more than a week ago but it wasn't Jed that was doing it, at least according to the man's description. Seems to think he might be holed up at his place in the north valley, the land that was left to him by his mother years back. It adjoins the family spread."

"So he did go back," I said to myself more than to

Ben, feeling very much an intruder about to make
her way into an enemy camp.

"Well, that's what this old gezer at the bar was
sayin' when he heard me asking about the Tanners.
The puncher I was talking with didn't know much
about Jed at all. The old man was more than half
gone from drink, but he seemed to know what he
was talking about."

"I guess he's worked things out with his family,"
I said, thinking of the brother in the black frock coat
who had lain in ambush for him.

"Looks that way," Ben's eyes held mine and he
continued, "but from what this old fella was saying,
the Tanners always stood behind him, at least publicly."

The relief I expected to feel once I knew for certain
that I would see Tanner never came. Instead, filled
with apprehension, I was overwhelmed by my te-
merity. How could I ever have believed that I could
face him again, and in the midst of a family that
claimed to support him and all the while had lain
in wait for him? If Tanner had believed that they
were behind him, would he have waited this long
before returning?

"...Meg?"

I looked up at the sound of my name and found
Ben's searching eyes on me.

"You don't have to go through with this. We can
turn around and head in any direction you like. There
are a lot of places out there.... We never did talk
about where we'd be going afterwards."

"No, Ben," I said resolutely. "I have to see this
through. There'll be time enough later to talk about
the rest. How much farther is it?" I asked, glad that
my voice remained steady.

"That depends. Three, maybe four days ride from
here to the ST. But I think we should rest up for a
few days, first. You've been pushing yourself too hard

and you haven't been eating enough. The rest will do you good. You're looking a mite peaked."

"I'm fine," I said more sharply than I intended, angry that Ben had seen the exhaustion I had tried so hard to keep from him. Each morning I found it harder to rise and by evening I had to force myself to eat the food he had prepared, wanting only the comfort of the hard ground and the soft weight of my blankets. The truth was, I was afraid to rest. It was imperative that we continue while I still had the strength. Ben's face tightened at my response.

"Don't be angry with me, Ben. Please," I pleaded, suddenly aware of just how much I owed him and admitting to myself just how much I needed him. He shook his head at me disgustedly. "I'm a fool for letting you do this, you know that?"

I laid my hand over his. "You're doing this because you're my friend, Ben," I said, answering him sincerely. It was the wrong thing to say. He scowled at me, his face darkening with emotion. Settling up with the waitress, he walked me back to the hotel.

At the door to my room, I turned to bid him good night and there in his face was all of his hunger and his longing, but I shut my eyes on his need. He wanted loving and I wanted comforting. It was too easy to get them confused on a night like this, when I was so tired and so afraid of what lay ahead of me and he was there, reassuring and strong, smelling slightly of the barbershop and bay rum. Despite my love for Tanner, Ben Trew held his own special appeal. Clearing the cobwebs of confusion from my mind and realizing the extent of my weakness, I said good night, closing the door behind me with a shaking hand. A moment passed before his footsteps retreated. They hesitated briefly at his door to the next room before continuing down the corridor and rapidly descending the stairway. I heard the soft tinkle of a bell as the hotel door opened and he went out into the street.

In spite of my weariness, it was a good while before sleep came to me.

Ben was gone by the time I knocked on his door the next morning, but there was a message waiting for me with the desk clerk, telling me he had some business to take care of and that he would return shortly. I collected my things and walked to the general store, already open for business despite the early hour. There was only a small selection of women's clothing, although the storekeeper told me kindly that anything I needed could be ordered from the catalog. Declining his offer with a shake of my head, I chose, instead, some boys' shirts and a pair of rugged pants that I could take in or let out as my girth demanded. At the last moment I included a calico wrapper that he had in stock, using the money Doc had given me before I left Cross Creek.

Ben had the horses saddled and waiting at the hotel by the time I returned. I smiled up at him, glad to be on our way again, restless with the day's delay. He took my bedroll and saddlebag and lashed them behind the saddle, but put a restraining hand on my arm as I went to take Coalie's reins to mount. Although he was perfectly sober, his eyes were slightly bleary from drink and from whatever other release he might have sought the night before.

"Breakfast, Meg?"

I shook my head, impatient to be on our way.

A knowing look came to his face and I twisted my wrist free. He did not seem to notice, so intently did his eyes burn into mine. "Suit yourself, Meg," he said, his voice strained. "But I'm telling you now, you're going to see once and for all exactly the kind of man Jed Tanner is. Because he's not for you. And he's smart enough to know that. I can wait until then."

Grimly, I mounted up, knowing that whatever re-

lief Ben had found the night before, it had not been
enough.

We headed our horses north, fording a muddy river
before swinging them westerly across the grass-
lands. Our horses made good time over the level
plain. The distance fell away and we drifted across
the landscape under an endless sky of blue. The nights
were clear and cool and we camped along stream-
beds fringed with scrub willow and oak. Sometimes,
when I lay quietly just before sleep, the baby would
stir, almost in answer to the calling of the night
creatures with whom we shared the stars. It was a
peaceful time, and I promised myself that I would
survive Tanner's inevitable rejection, finding in it
my release. I did not think about the ordeal that lay
ahead of me but instead concentrated on the love I
would share with my child and the future we would
have together.

The storm clouds gathered warningly the day we
approached Tanner land, the warm wind rippling the
long grass in undulating waves. Tethering our horses
in a small stand of trees, we took up our rain gear
and scanned the rocks overlooking the dry wash for
shelter. With the wind tearing the words from Ben's
mouth, he pointed the way across the outcropping
and I scrambled after him over the uneven ground
as the deluge broke, pummeling the earth with its
fury. At the front of a cavelike depression of rock,
Ben rigged the slickers as flaps against the driving
torrent. The water streamed down his hair and face
and his soaked clothing lay plastered to his skin.
With the slickers providing a small relief from the
buffeting downpour, he crouched beside me as I sat
huddled in our cramped shelter and the scent of the
rain mingled with the damp press of our bodies. As
the rain dripped from his face, his eyes pierced mine

and I could not look away, so great was their drawing power. Beneath the darkness of rimrock, they steadied me with their forcefulness, their bright blue color deepening as they sensed my vulnerability. It is sometimes in weakness that the truth is finally revealed. Pulled by two forces so that my heart came near to bursting with love for one who did not care enough and for one who cared too much, I began to understand that my only freedom lay with neither Tanner nor Ben, but within myself. Suddenly, I longed to be free of both of them, to ease the torment of the loving. In the fury of the storm, my resolution was born. I closed myself to Ben, hiding my need for him. I would find the strength to do the same with Tanner. When he spurned me this final time, my heart would be hardened, the ache inside of me would nourish the love I had for my child until it surpassed all the others. That alone would be my comfort.

The storm ended as quickly as it began. As we continued to make our way over the gentle swells that gave rise to the hillier terrain marking the beginning of the Tanner domain, I had no idea that no matter what my intentions, fate would lay waste to my plans.

Part Three

The North Valley

Chapter Twenty-Four

THE WIDE, WINDING PASS THAT CLIMBED through
the hills overlooking Sam Tanner's holdings was, if
not the most direct route into the valley, the most
traveled. From above, the valley appeared to be a
narrow slash, stretching some forty miles from east
to west and perhaps a little more than half that
distance in width. Bounded on four sides by mountain slopes and traversed by bright blue ribbons that
meandered their way across the floor, the valley extended beyond the north tip, narrowing for several
miles before it adjoined a small, saucer shaped basin,
slightly higher in altitude.

The Tanner ranch was nestled midway between
the southern corner and the northwest entrance to
the smaller valley. The rutted trace we followed cut
a swath down the grassy tree-dotted slope and across
the bottomland, where it ran along a creekbed before
disappearing through a stand of timber. It emerged
some distance upstream as a well traveled road and

wound its way toward the small collection of buildings. We pushed on in the graying dusk, the shining lights of the ranch drawing us like moths to a flame, eager to reach our destination before nightfall. The darkening sky could not obscure the imposing grandeur of the Tanner ranch house as it sat apart from the clustered outbuildings on a small rise, glowing softly in the bath of rising moonlight. An inquisitive horse nickered a greeting from the corral and the sound of muted laughter floated across the grounds as we headed our horses toward the house.

It was a handsome log structure, two stories tall, its lines straight and clean. It was topped by a steep-pitched shake roof. Silvered light glanced back from the darkened windows above a dropped roof porch while below, framed through the sturdy porch railing, brightly lit windows flanked each side of an impressive paneled door. Hitching rails were planted on both sides of the walkway extending along the front of the house. The porch railing would soon be a trellis of budding roses. Despite the chill in the air, a film of moisture lightly beaded my brow. As a coldness snaked through me, Ben took the reins from my stiffened fingers and helped me down from Coalie's back. I leaned against the horse's side until I could steady myself on solid ground. I received no sympathy from Ben. Written on his face was the impatient desire for this night to be over and done with.

I mounted the porch steps slowly, a large lump at the pit of my stomach and so great the wish to be gone from this place that it overrode the sense of purpose that had brought me there. As our footsteps rang out across the wooden porch, a burst of spirited laughter broke from within the house and I felt as much an intruder as a thief in the night. Ben waited for the revelry to die down and then knocked loudly. The laughter picked up again and I wondered if he had been heard, but just as he raised his fist to the door again, it suddenly opened.

Golden light framed the woman who came to the door. "Yes?" she said. As I blinked back at the brightness from the depths of the nighttime shadows, I observed the disagreeable set of her features. A tight bonnet of iron-gray hair framed her face and she wore a work-stained apron over her dress. Kitchen odors clung to her. "Yes," she repeated again, this time with a sharp edge to her voice.

At the silence, she shifted her gaze from Ben to me. I stood quietly at his side and looked up at him in mute appeal. Ben answered for both of us.

"We're here to see Jed Tanner, Ma'am," he said, his deep voice announcing our purpose.

She raised her head slightly, as if taken aback. "Well, he ain't here," she answered huffily, with the impertinence of a long-time family servant. She peered out at us suspiciously. "What would you be wantin' with him anyways?"

Ben's lips thinned. "Personal matter, you might say, Ma'am." He would tell her no more. A blatant hostility settled upon her, and despairingly I realized we would get no further information from this woman.

It was then, only, that I began to appreciate Ben's staunch support. He took a step forward. "Maybe someone inside can tell us where to find him," he suggested, forcing a polite civility into his words.

She rose to her full height, which was well below Ben's bearded chin, as if seeking to protect her brood of employers from the presence of this uncouth giant.

"Sylvie! Who's that at the door?" a man asked from within the depths of the house. Almost meekly, she turned aside at the sound of the gravelly voice. "Company wantin' to see Mr. Jed, Mr. Tanner," she called back toward the room from which we had heard the laughter.

At her words, the light tinkling sound of fine crystal and the heavier sounds of silver and tableware abruptly ceased. Heavy footsteps sounded across a carpeted surface and then rang out across a bare wooden floor. Sylvie fell back with a satisfied look as the door was thrown open wide and we fell beneath the glaring countenance of a tall, silver-haired man who could be no one but Sam Tanner.

His eyes glared out at us from a craggy face, the frowning dark brows and the thick mustache lightly threaded with gray. The square chin had only a hint of a jowl beneath the jaw and although he was of Jed's height, time had thickened him much as it does an old tree, gnarling it with age but leaving its strength undiminished. We were not welcome. The message was written clearly across his features. He, like Sylvie, focused his attention on Ben's commanding presence.

"What do you want with my son?" he asked abruptly.

"Business, Mr. Tanner. We were told in Redmondton that we'd find him here," Ben responded coolly, undeterred by the man's manner.

"He's not here," he answered harshly. I flinched inadvertently at the animosity in his voice, wondering if he had somehow been alerted to the purpose of our visit, and his eyes dropped to me. He hesitated just a fraction too long as he took in my thickened waist. His eyes, rising back to my face, narrowed speculatively, but he had no idea who I was.

"Well, Mr. Tanner, we'll just have to find out where he is then," Ben said almost mildly, but leaving no doubt as to his intentions. There was a quiet assurance to his words. He was more than Sam Tanner's match in size with the advantage of fewer years on his frame. I don't think that Sam seriously considered the threat in Ben's voice, but glancing back at me, he seemed to reach a decision. "Come in," he said finally, his voice cold, reminding me all too clearly of his son.

The soft yellow haze sharpened into a brightly lit hall as we passed through the entryway into the house, revealing it to be one decorated with an extravagance not often found within log structures of a similar kind. Freshly papered walls, the large floral pattern untainted by the smoke of the kerosene lamps, ran from the top of the honey-colored wainscoting to the ceiling molding, providing a rich backdrop for the furnishings in the wide hallway. The most striking item was an exceptionally large, mirrored walnut hat rack obscured by a collection of dusty hats, jackets, reins and spurs, the bottom portion conspicuously devoid of umbrellas. Across the way, a large bowl of spring wildflowers rested on a table of inlaid satinwood, behind which hung a gilt-edged mirror that reproduced the image of the brilliant blossoms as well as the reflected spill of light from the room opposite it. Several doorways led off each side of the scarred but highly polished wooden floor of the hall. The passage narrowed as it continued past the stairway toward the back of the house. I could only guess at the rooms that lay beyond it.

Without a backward glance, Sam Tanner left us, crossing the hall to the threshold of the room he had left earlier. He made no effort to hide the ire in his voice as he addressed the occupants.

"Sorry 'bout this interruption, Alice...boys. I've some business to attend to. It won't take long."

"Don't you worry none about it, Sam," a masculine voice responded. "Alice, here, can do a fine job of amusing us." A light note of feminine laughter followed the speaker's words and then, as Sam Tanner turned away, I was afforded an unencumbered view of a formal dining room and of the beautiful woman who presided over one end of the linen-covered table. For a moment, our glances caught, and she gazed at me with soft blue eyes that brimmed with curiosity, before I joined Ben in following Jed's father into the library across the hall.

Although more plainly furnished, this room, too, bore the signs of recent acquisitions. An overwhelming certainty came to me that it was the young blonde woman who had been responsible for the recent changes in the Tanner ranch house. A boldly patterned carpet, lacking signs of wear, and two matching wing chairs of deep rose brocade, their cushions still stiff with newness, stood out in the room. She had met resistance here, however; it was the paneled walls and large, scarred oak desk behind which Sam Tanner now seated himself in a worn leather chair that set the tone of the room. He gestured to the chairs positioned by the massive stone fireplace, but by unspoken accord Ben and I remained standing. Sam Tanner wasted no more time on amenities.

"Who are you and what do you want with Jed?" he asked bluntly. I could see by the tense set of Ben's face that he did not take kindly to the questioning.

"I'm Ben Trew and this here is Meg Logan," Ben replied curtly, wasting little time. "It's a matter that needs Jed's attention. You can be sure that it won't take long." In anger, Ben's bearing was even more imposing.

Sam Tanner regarded us intently. "I'm sorry," he said at last, although his tone indicated that he was not, "but Jed has made it clear that he doesn't care to see anyone except for his family and I intend to make sure his feelings are respected."

Ben drew a breath and I laid my hand upon his arm to still his sorely tried temper. My action did not go unnoticed by the man behind the desk.

"But," Sam Tanner continued, offering a grudging compromise, "if you'd like to get a message to him, well, I could see about doing that much for you."

My eyes flew to Ben's. I could not let that happen.

I had to see Tanner myself. I had not come all this distance to be turned away by this self-righteous old man. With weariness clouding my thinking, I took a desperate gamble.

"Mr. Tanner," I said, addressing him in a strong voice that displayed none of my inner turmoil, "we've come a very long way to see your son. I'm afraid that a message won't do at all." I met his probing stare squarely. "I will see Jed, one way or another."

Sam Tanner's expression hardened at my affront, and he stared calculatingly at the swell of my stomach, again noting the hand resting on Ben's arm. As powerful a man as he was, he was not about to use bodily force to remove a pregnant woman and her escort from his property for simply wanting to see his son. His shrewd eyes studied me carefully.

"All right, Miss Logan," he said, suddenly acquiescing. "If you've ridden as far as you say, I'll assume you'll have no objection to another day's ride." A frown pulled at his mouth. "I'll have someone take you to him tomorrow. He's at the north valley."

I nodded wordlessly, my victory taking its toll in exhaustion.

"You can spend the night here with us in the house," he said, with no hint of welcome in his offer. He turned to Ben. "There's an empty bed at the bunkhouse. You can use that."

Ben looked at me. "I'll take care of the horses, Meg, and see you in the morning." I nodded at him gratefully. I caught the concern in his voice. He liked leaving me in Sam Tanner's house as little as I liked being there myself. I watched him go, feeling bereft without him. Aware of Sam Tanner's scrutiny, I turned back to him.

"Would you care for some supper, Miss Logan?" he asked in a voice only thinly veiled with politeness.

"No, thank you, Mr. Tanner. I'm not very hungry."

I was certain that I'd never be able to swallow a bite at his table.

"Then maybe you'd like to join some of my family and friends for the evening. Alice, my daughter-in-law, is an accomplished pianist." I suspected he was speaking of the young woman I had seen seated at the table. "No, thank you. It's very kind of you, but I'm rather tired. Perhaps I could be shown to my room?"

He smiled at me, but it did not reach his eyes. "Why of course, Miss Logan. How remiss of me. I should have realized that sooner. I'll have Alice show you the way." I thought I detected a hint of disappointment in his voice. Did he feel thwarted because I had escaped him so easily?

Alice did not need to be summoned. Before Sam could even call to her, she floated into the library, a breathtaking vision in an evening dress of rose and cream satin, with a simple low-cut bodice and with enough overskirts to test even Verna Brown's expertise. Her hair, a shiny mass of pale gold, curved softly about her face and was drawn up and fastened at the nape. Around her neck she wore a ribbon from which hung a beautiful cameo. Never had I been so aware of my disheveled and inappropriate attire. Yet the censure I expected to find in her eyes was not there, just the same vibrant curiosity that I had seen before.

Sam Tanner made the introductions with a minimum of fuss and then excused himself to return to his guests.

"Yes, of course, I'm sorry to have interrupted your supper hour, Mr. Tanner," I demurely offered my apology. I thought I caught a peculiar glint in his eye as he left, but then Alice lightly touched my hand, chasing away all further thought of Jed's father from my mind. Turning to follow her from the room,

I found myself wondering which of the Tanner sons she was married to.

She led the way back across the hall and then quickly took the stairway to the upper floor of the house. "Don't worry about spoiling our meal, Miss Logan," she said lightly as we passed through a corridor papered in the same pattern as the main floor. "It's just Mr. Randolph from the bank. He's a dreadful bore and I'm quite grateful to you for rescuing me from his company."

Astonished by her admission, I looked at her, only to find her gaze fixed upon me assessingly. "I have some nightclothes that will suit you," she offered generously. We came to the end of the corridor and she paused before the door to a room facing the back of the house. "I'll have Christina bring you some bathwater, if you like."

"That's very kind of you."

She looked almost apologetic as she turned the knob of the door. "I hope you don't mind this room. It's the only one that's been made up recently. I'm afraid Mr. Randolph is occupying the guest room while he's here." She opened the door and in the flood of moonlight I made out the dark shapes of a single bed, a dresser, and a nightstand. A braided rug, the colors indistinguishable in the shadows, lay at the center of the floor and there was the faint outline of a wooden rocker in a corner. Alice glided into the room and, taking up a match from the dresser top, lit the plain brass kerosene lamp, throwing the room into shadowed relief. As she surveyed the scene before her, a slight frown creased her smooth brow. "I've redone the whole house except for this room," she explained. "You see, it's Jed's. He had been away for such a long time I didn't think it right to change it without consulting him first. He might not have liked it." She went to the window and tugged at it. It opened with a protesting groan. As she spoke, I thought I discerned the barest trace of the East in her speech beneath the carefully cultivated finishing school voice. She smiled at me then. "I'll see to your bath and the clothes," she said, leaving in her wake the faint scent of violets as she closed the door behind her.

Alone, I dropped my pretense of well-being, letting my exhaustion emerge. Wearily, I sank into the rocker as I surveyed Jed's room. Pegs along the walls were conspicuously empty of clothing and the dresser top was swept clean of any personal effects. A clothes closet stood opposite the window wall, but I had a feeling that it, too, would be empty. How long had he spent in this room before returning to his north valley, I wondered. With fatigue playing on my every thought, I shivered slightly as I recalled Sam Tanner's antagonism. Even Sylvie, the Tanner servant, knowing nothing of us, had treated us with hostility. It was only Alice, Sam's beautiful daughter-in-law, who had exhibited any warmth or friendliness. That was even more baffling. The impersonal room seemed to echo Jed's solitary nature, and I recognized some of Sam Tanner's coldness in his son. It had not been just his problems with Julie that had marked Jed, but something before her. Had she also been unable to reach him? But thinking of Julie only made me wonder about Travis. Was it possible that Alice was married to the brother who had ambushed Jed?

A soft knock at the door banished my preoccupation and, at my bidding, it opened on the figure of a young girl and a large tin tub. As she poured the steaming water into it, Alice returned, a nightdress over her arm.

"Christina, we'll use the rainwater for Miss Logan's hair." I looked at Alice curiously. There was an unwonted reserve in her voice when she spoke to Christina that was wholly unexpected, for she had treated me, an unknown stranger, with more warmth than she did the girl. Christina inclined her head toward Alice in assent and as she lifted the last pail of water our eyes met. With a shock I realized that she was not the plain girl I had first taken her for, but rather a very beautiful young woman. In spite of her simple work dress, she had an exotic beauty that was even more stunning than Alice's. Her glossy black hair was worn pulled back, revealing a triangular face and wide blue eyes. Suddenly, I knew that Jed had not been immune to her. It was as if she carried his mark. As we stared at each other across the rising steam of the bathwater, I knew she was taking my measure just I had taken hers, and without a spoken word it was as if Jed had become our common battleground. Only much later, when I was to think back on it, did I realize that Christina and I had more in common than either of us knew.

Alice returned later, peeking her head around the door to the room before entering at my welcome as I rubbed the thick toweling through my hair. She carried an assortment of garments to the chair and dropped them down with a conspiratorial gleam in her eye. I watched, bewildered, as she selected two items and held them up for my inspection, one an exquisitely worked shirtwaist and the other a beautifully made buff-colored riding skirt. There was a soft shine in her blue eyes.

"These were made for me before I came west and, well, they just don't fit right anymore. I guess I've been enjoying Sylvie's cooking too much."

It was an act of charity, pure and simple. Alice's figure was as near to perfection as any I had ever seen. Her extraordinary generosity brought a tightness to my throat, but I would have none of it. I refused to be beholden to any of the Tanners, even Alice.

"That's very kind of you," I said, at last finding my voice. "But I can't accept them."

Perhaps she noted my confusion.

There was a determined look in her eye and I could see the argument coming. After all, if she had persuaded Sam Tanner to turn his house over to her for renovations, what chance did I have against her?

Rising from where I was seated at the edge of the bed, I let the loose folds of the nightdress fall gracefully about me, clearly outlining my shape. "They wouldn't fit me for long, Alice," I explained gently.

Just for a moment, I thought I detected a wistful look in her eyes. She turned away from me and walked over to the dresser. She toyed with the creams and lotions she had left for me earlier. "It gets awfully lonely here, sometimes," she said quietly, with her back to me. Glancing up, she caught my reflection in the mirror before her.

I saw the forlornness she could not hide and, inexplicably, felt a bond grow between us, in spite of the strange circumstances under which we had met. She gave a small laugh as she turned back from the mirror. "I'm not complaining, really. Cal takes me on all his business trips, he knows I like that. Why, this winter we went all the way to St. Louis."

I was strangely relieved to find that it was Jed's brother Caleb whom Alice had married, not Travis. But that did not stop me from again noting the differences between us. While she was in St. Louis, Tice might have been choking out his life in the blood-spattered clearing in the mountains. Alice sensed my troubled thoughts, but mistook the reason for them.

"I heard what Sam said to you," she said carefully. I gave her a startled look as she readily admitted to eavesdropping on my high-handed conversation with Sam Tanner. "He can be as ornery as an old bull when he wants to be. I guess that's how he gets his pleasure these days."

"I'm afraid I wasn't very polite to him," I said

apologetically. I was embarrassed to think she had overheard our exchange. But how else could she have come into the library at just the right moment?

"Why should you have been? He was very rude to you. We all heard him."

"It doesn't matter. I'm leaving tomorrow. It was kind of him to let me stay here," I replied uncomfortably.

She gave a small laugh. "I know you didn't want to spend the night with us, Meg."

I didn't acknowledge her comment, but instead looked down awkwardly at my callused hands. She handed me a jar of scented hand cream. Absently, I rubbed it into my skin. "I know that you've come to see Jed, Meg." Schooling my face into an expressionless blank, I handed her back the cream.

"I'm glad you're here," she said softly, as if she knew how deeply she trespassed into my life. Speechlessly, I looked up at her, taken aback by her forthright manner. It seemed that she understood all too much about me.

"Alice—" I started to say, not at all sure how I was to finish, but with great sensitivity, she stopped me.

"You see, Meg...I became worried when I saw Sam's mood, when your friend, Ben, said you had come to see Jed. You looked so tired—I thought maybe I could help. I watched from the doorway." She cleared her throat. "I heard you tell Sam that you intended to see Jed, no matter what." She let her silence fill in the rest. "And I saw Ben look at you.... He loves you, Meg." She glanced down at my hand, bare of the gold band that would have sanctioned my condition. This woman, whom I had never seen before, in a few brief minutes had pieced together the most intimate parts of my life. There was no point denying what she already knew.

"I only came to talk to him, Alice, nothing more,"

I told her honestly. I saw a flicker of disappointment cross her face.

"Oh." She moved away from the dresser. "I'm sorry, I didn't really mean to pry. It's just that I care for Jed." Going to the window, she stared out into the darkness. "They say he's not a very likeable person, you know. Hard, is what they call him. I've only met him a few times. When he first returned to the ST and then again when he came back from the north valley for some of his stock. But he was kind to me both times," she said, looking over her shoulder at me. "I haven't been here all that long, Meg, but I do know Sam and, well, I can understand how it must have been for Jed when he lived here all those years ago. And," she said, with a rueful smile, "Jed has a way of making Sam uncomfortable, and I like that. He's the only one I know who can manage it. Although," she added as an afterthought, "you came pretty close to doing that yourself, tonight."

"That wasn't my intention, Alice," I replied.

"I know that."

I smiled at her then, and despite my intention to have as little to do with the Tanners as possible, my curiosity won out. "Alice," I began, slowly, "is Travis here?"

I had surprised her with my question, I could see.

"No, he's not. I've never even met him. Someone in town had told Cal that he had seen Travis around not too long ago. Of course, he hasn't been out to the ranch and Cal hasn't seen him since he ran into him accidently in San Francisco a few years back." She frowned. "You know, they never talk about what happened. About Jed, Travis and Julie, I mean. If it hadn't been for one of those parties that Sam threw right after I came to the ST, I wouldn't know about it at all. It was a welcome-home dance, since Cal and I had been married back east. The women there started asking me questions about Jed and if Sam ever heard from him. They didn't mean any harm by it, I can see that now, but it was rather shocking to hear it that way. I'm afraid I didn't react very well. I felt rather foolish, with strangers knowing more about the family than I did. I asked Cal about it later. He wouldn't talk about it. That was the first time I really saw him angry. He did tell me, though, never to mention it to Sam. He said that Jed and Sam never got on, even when Jed was a boy. I do know that Jed just disappeared after it happened, and they hadn't heard from him until he turned up a few months ago."

True to her words, Alice did not mean to pry. She asked none of the questions I knew she had for me. She bid me good night, leaving me alone in Jed's room. I turned down the light and smoothed the coverlet over me as I lay in his bed. Sleep would not come. As the moonlight danced along the walls and the tree outside rustled lightly in the wind, I was overwhelmed by his presence. The pillow that cushioned my head became his shoulder and the quilted coverlet his body as it had lain over mine. I tossed restlessly, trying to put the images from my mind. Purposefully, I tortured myself by thinking of Christina's beauty and Sam Tanner's coldness, reminding myself that it was they who now had claim to Jed's life. I tried to summon back the resolve with which I had decided that my only peace lay far away from both Jed and Ben. I had thought that the leaving would be hard, but I had not anticipated that the ache would start so long beforehand. The hard kick I felt from within brought a grim satisfaction to me. At least this time I had something he could not take away from me.

Chapter Twenty-Five

𝒪 THE EARLY MORNING CLAMOR OF THE RANCH drifted through the opened window, waking me gently. I stirred lazily, and then memory intruded and I sat bolt upright. This was the day I was to see Tanner again.

Rising, I discovered that my clothes had been laundered and returned and lay neatly folded upon the chair. A rainbow of color caught my eye from across the dresser top, and I found the hair ribbons that Alice had left for me the night before. Not wanting to reject this gesture of friendship, I tied the dark blue one around my hair. I dressed hurriedly, eager to be on my way.

The sounds from the dining room drew me to the entrance and in the cheery morning light it appeared a pleasant but formal room. The deep-blue velvet curtains had been drawn back to let in the daylight, and a sheer white curtain muted the strong sunlight that spilled across a Wilton carpet and the large mahogany dining table. But this morning the table was free of its linen cover and the chairs with their satin cushons were empty. Disappointed, I realized that I would not see Alice again before I left.

"Good morning, Miss Logan. Please help yourself to some breakfast."

Startled, I looked up to see a stocky but well proportioned man standing by the sideboard, filling his plate with an assortment of food from the covered silver trays.

"We're pretty much informal around here at breakfast. Alice sleeps late." His comment was not meant as a criticism, only a statement of fact. "We didn't have a chance to be introduced last night. I'm Caleb Tanner." I did not miss the ring of authority behind the courteousness. Crossing the room to join him, I passed up the covered platters in favor of a cup of steaming coffee and a warm biscuit. "Your friend is down at the bunkhouse," he said, dispensing with the pleasantries. "I had Sylvie pack a lunch for you."

"That's very kind of you, Mr. Tanner," I replied, "I want to thank your father—"

"He left at sunup. We're busy with the spring roundup just about now. The fact is, if it weren't for me having to take Mr. Randolph into town for the stage to Redmonton, I'd be with him."

I seated myself, glancing at Caleb Tanner across the highly polished surface of the long table, two strangers fencing warily with each other.

"Please thank Alice for me, Mr. Tanner."

He softened momentarily. There was nothing of Jed's looks about him. His face, like his brother's, was permanantly creased by the elements, but he was smooth shaven and his weathered skin was fairer than Jed's. Noticing his blunt, work roughened hands, it was hard to imagine Alice's pampered beauty beside him. Still, for all his roughness, he lacked his father's abrupt manner and spoke pleasantly enough. But it was equally clear that all of the Tanners, with the exception of Alice, harbored suspicions about me.

I had little appetite that morning, but I forced down the rest of the biscuit before rising and excusing myself from the table.

"You'll find Christina waiting for you at the corral," he said, looking up at me.

I stopped short. "Christina?"

"Yes, she'll be taking you through to the valley."

"Please, couldn't you just give us directions? We don't want to trouble anyone. You've been kind enough already."

Caleb smiled at me and suddenly I saw the resemblance to his father. I think my discomfort amused him. "Don't worry about Christina," he said. "She's been wanting to bring some things out to Jed anyway."

I stared at him but he mistook my reaction.

"I could point you in the right direction, all right, but you wouldn't make it through, not this time of year at least. The creekbed's been flooding all month. You've got to head up through the canyon and work your way around it. It can be confusing. There are plenty of false trails that don't go all the way through. You'll be safe with Christina. She could lead the way blindfolded if she had to."

"Yes, well, then, thank you," I said, swallowing hard under his bemused expression as I turned to leave the room.

I was not to be spared even a moment alone with Ben. I found him and Christina awaiting me at the corral almost companionably. The niggling burr of resentment that I had managed to contain the previous evening began to grow, and furiously I reprimanded myself. I had no right to mind either Jed's or Ben's friendship with her. If I planned to make a new start, this was as good a way as any to test my ability to let go of the past. Ben smiled a welcome as I joined them while Christina cast a discerning eye upon my form, her lips turning up slightly at the corners. The beauty of her face was heightened by the blue-black hair, simply tied back with a yellow ribbon that emphasized her warm, almost dusky skin tone. Next to her, I felt much like a faded summer rose. Awkwardly, I mounted Coalie, relishing the feel of the morning air, hoping the cool wind would restore my humor.

It was a beautiful day. The sky was a deep, clear blue and the emerald grass shimmered like quicksilver under the morning coat of dew. Christina led the way on a small chestnut mare and, as we fell in behind her, Ben noted my set expression. "Did Sam give you any trouble after I left last night?" he asked, concerned about my well-being.

"No," I replied shortly.

Sensing my irritability, he did not attempt to humor me into better spirits. "You'd better prepare yourself for this, Meg," he said warningly. "His family doesn't want you around and they don't even know why you're here. Jed's welcome is going to be a mite stronger, I'd say."

"Damn it, Ben! I know what I'm up against!" I looked at him angrily. "I never expected anyone to welcome me with open arms! I don't happen to care what his family thinks. This is between Jed and me. When I've said what I've come to say, we can leave. Does that suit you?"

Ben abandoned the conversation without another word. I stared straight ahead at Christina's lithe back as we rode on in silence.

"Who is she, Ben?" I asked suddenly.

"Christina?"

"Yes, Christina." I answered testily.

"Well, from what the boys in the bunkhouse said, she practically grew up here. She's known Jed a long time. When he came back, she started doggin' his heels and they say he hasn't exactly pushed her away."

I suffered his information silently. "Well, Alice doesn't care for her," I said pointedly, as if that could make me feel better. "She didn't say anything, but I could sense it."

"Alice? She sure does have some fancy ways. Maybe she thinks Christina isn't good enough for her."

I looked at him, appalled, and immediately came to Alice's defense. "She's not like that at all, Ben! She was nicer to me than either Sam or Caleb. And she certainly didn't have to be."

"I'll take your word for it," Ben responded, easily enough. "I just know what the boys said. They say she's only been here a year or so. She and Cal had a whirlwind courtship back east and some of the hands say she was mighty unhappy when she first came to the ST. Homesick, maybe. Sam gave her free rein to do what she wanted with the house to keep her busy. The place hadn't changed a lick since Sam's first wife died. Even his second wife never lifted a hand to it. Cal wanted to please her, so they had all this fancy furniture shipped to the ranch. Hell of a time getting it here, too. The boys had to haul it all the way up to the house from where the freighters left it. They're still complaining about it."

I repressed a smile at the thought of cowhands moving furniture about the house, cussing up a blue streak under their breath beneath Alice's watchful blue eyes.

"Did you find out anything else, Ben?" I asked, hoping he would not make too much of my sudden absorption in the Tanner family.

"Nope," he said, and then thinking a bit, he added casually, "Oh, they did make mention of another brother, Travis." My attention sparked, he continued in an offhanded manner. "It turns out he's not Jed's brother at all, but the son of Sam's first wife from another marriage. I guess he's the one Jed found with his wife. They're laying bets on what might happen if those two ever meet up again, even though there's not much chance of that. From what they say, Travis doesn't stay in one place very long and Jed hasn't been off the ST since he's come back."

We ate in the saddle, not pausing for a rest, allowing the horses only short breathers along the way. Ben looked at me questioningly, and I tried not to let him see the difficulty I had breathing the thin air. "I'm fine," I said to him when he asked, ashamed to admit that I was nearly exhausted. My back ached and my legs cramped painfully, but I was afraid that if we should stop I would not be able to continue on.

The trail narrowed as we climbed the stony steps of the canyon and made our way from the valley of the main ranch up around the steep gorge. I battled my fatigue as we crossed over into the north valley, and although Ben was at my side, it was as if I rode alone. All my resolve and determination deserted me, leaving me to worry about the inescapable consequences of my journey. The setting sun cast cold shadows on us as we crested the skyline and descended a final, grassy knoll. We worked our way across the floor of the valley, dipping between the curves of the gently rolling land, and my rising trepidation made me forget my exhaustion.

It did not happen as I expected. I did not see him first, nor did I catch any sign of emotion that might have crossed his face. Christina, in her eagerness, spurred her mount ahead, swallowing up the last remaining mile between our slow-moving horses and the small group of buildings barely visible in the evening twilight. Her voice carried clearly as she called out to him. In the distance, we saw him approach the winded horse and rider, with a loosely clasped rifle in his hand. He had not expected visitors.

I watched the two dark figures in the deepening dusk as Christina pulled the chestnut to a stop and Jed caught up the mare's bridle. Sliding down from her saddle, she possessively linked her arm through his in an intimate gesture, pointing at us, telling him of our arrival so that when we rode out of the shadows into the clearing he was already unsaddling the mare with his back to us. Even in the softness of the falling night I could make out the hard profile of his face. Clean-shaven, his features had been burned brown by the intense mountain sun and his jaw was clamped tight in displeasure. His hat was worn low, but I felt his eyes pass over us as we drew nearer. Without a word, he turned the mare into the corral as Christina emerged from the cabin where she had placed her belongings. She would be an eager witness to what was about to take place.

I realized my blunder immediately. It had been wrong of me to come after him, no matter how good my intentions. What I had to say didn't matter; my parting words had haunted me, not him. Ben had been right all along. I had been a silly, obstinate fool to come all this way to see him. I would have gladly faced Holbrook Barton, Hank Rinehart, or anyone else rather than this rigid man who would not even look at me. At that moment, what I wanted to do most was to turn Coalie and run.

"Get it over with, Meg," Ben urged, "and we can be on our way first thing in the morning." I nodded. I had no choice. Even if I tried to escape, Ben sat his horse directly behind me. He would never let me leave until I finished what I had set out to do. I walked Coalie to the corral, dismounting on legs that trembled from weariness. Steadying myself against the saddle, I turned to face the man I had come such a long way to find.

As Jed shut the gate on the mare, he turned to face me. His look became a physical blow as the shadowed eyes froze upon my shape. He looked up at Ben, who quietly watched us from his horse.

"Is it yours?" he asked coldly.

"No."

I heard the bridled note in Ben's voice, a sure sign of rage held in check. A smug smile played on Christina's lips as she watched our exchange. Suddenly, all the words I had readied for him vanished. I was crushed by the blinding truth of his feelings for me. It was then that the ache that had gnawed at me since noon sharpened and the dullness was replaced by a searing pain. I tried to find Jed's eyes in his shadowed face, wanting to tell him that I hurt, but instead my knees gave way and I sank to the hard cushion of ground.

Slowly, the swirling fog lifted. Ben's face, creased with worry, hovered over me and I saw that I lay on a cot in a small, unlit room.

"You gave us a scare, Meg. How are you feeling?"

"I'm fine, Ben. I just pushed a little hard today."

"I'll tell the others you're all right."

"No!" At his sharp look, I spoke more calmly. "I mean, all right if you want to, but don't tell him anything else, Ben," I pleaded. "I've had enough. I don't need to talk to him anymore."

"Damn it! I didn't ride all this way for you to turn around and go back without saying what's on your mind!"

I pushed myself into a sitting position and blazed a misdirected fury at him. "Do you know what he thinks of me? Meg, the girl with so many lovers she can't be sure who the father of her child is! But of course you know that. You told me what would happen and you were right."

Ben took my hand in his. "I'll never force you to do another thing, Meg. But you will talk to him. He's a bastard. You know it now. This is ending here and you'll leave it behind you when we ride out of here tomorrow."

"I can never leave it behind, Ben! There's still the baby!"

"The baby will be mine." Gently he touched my shoulder. "Don't hate him, Meg. Hate's too strong a feeling to waste on the likes of him. He isn't worth it."

My head pounded alarmingly and I wanted to be alone, away from Ben's searching eyes. "Please Ben, I'm tired now. I don't want to talk anymore."

"All right, Meg," he said, easily enough. But when he stood up to leave, his face was grim.

Chapter Twenty-Six

 I AWAKENED TO THE SMELL OF FRESH COFFEE and the clatter of tinware at the cookstove. Turning my head slightly, I saw Christina reaching for some plates, in an obvious ill humor. Viewing the rumpled bedding on the spare cot, I suspected that she had slept inside with me, leaving Ben to share the barn with Jed. I wondered who'd had the mistaken notion that I might find it comforting to have a woman's presence close by during the night, especially in light of Christina's feelings for me. Looking around the small cabin, I noted a surprising number of feminine touches. The gingham-checked curtains at the window were bright and new as was the red oilcloth on the table, although it was littered by plates and the hardened remains of past meals. It had not been Alice's fine hand that had brought the changes to Jed's home in the north valley, but Christina's, and she possessed a proprietary air that suggested I was trespassing on her domain. At the sight of the tall,

familiar shape shouldering his way through the
doorway, his arms loaded down with firewood, I
struggled to sit up. It was time to leave.

The pains began as soon as I rose to my feet.
Clutching at my waist, I doubled over helplessly,
unable to stem a cry of pain. There was a loud crash
nearby as the firewood dropped to the floor and then
Jed was at my side, helping me back to the cot. With
strong arms, he tried to force me down, but I could
not straighten my body from its contorted position.
The sweat streaked my face as I sat at the edge of
the mattress, unable to move.

"Damn it, Christina! I told you yesterday, you
pushed her too hard getting here!" Jed's anger was
unmistakable, but I did not misconstrue it. It was
not my well-being that motivated his concern. He
only wanted me out of the north valley.

"How was I to know that, Jed? She never said a
word of complaint!" Smarting under his reprimand,
Christina's voice was sullen.

"She wouldn't!" he snapped at her. I was not allowed to take solace in his criticism of Christina. "I
thought you said you didn't want her here?" I heard
her ask him plaintively.

"I don't, damn it, but that doesn't mean I wish her
harm."

A moan broke through my clenched lips.

"She's losing the baby," Christina announced
knowingly.

"No!" I gasped at the cold pronouncement. "I am
not!"

She pointedly ignored me. "It's much too soon for
her. There's nothing you can do, Jed. Just let nature
have its way."

"Jed, please," I heard myself beg him. "Get her
out of here!"

He didn't argue with me. "Go find Ben, Christina.
Tell him what's happened." Tears streamed from be-

hind my closed eyes. The cabin was quiet. Christina had left.

The sharp, stabbing pains subsided and with Jed's support I was able to lie back on the cot. The comfort I took from his closeness was mocked by the impersonal, rigid set to his face. However, he did not leave my side.

"That would make you happy, wouldn't it?" I asked him rhetorically.

"What would?" The dark brows raised at the question and he wore a quizzical expression. For a moment I almost believed him confused.

"To have me lose the baby."

"Don't talk crazy. Why would I want that?" Without thinking, he held my hand between his.

"Because it's yours and you don't want me to have any claim on you," I said honestly.

He dropped my hand abruptly and the comforting pressure where his body had rested briefly by my side was gone. He moved across the room to stare out the window.

"Ben's on his way," he said tonelessly.

The worry loosened my tongue much like whiskey had once before. "Jed, I'm sorry for what I just said." He heard the contriteness in my voice and looked at me suspiciously. "Just what is it that you want from me, Meg?"

I wet my lips, wondering if he had any idea of what I would ask of him. "I've seen this happen before, just after I came to Doc's. It was Clara Stewart. Doc said she needed bed rest and it worked for her that time, it really did." But I didn't tell him there had been only four or five weeks left to Clara's confinement. Even though a month had passed since Ben had first learned of my condition and reluctantly agreed to see me safely to the Tanner ranch, there was more than three months left of my term. Until now, time had worked in my favor, allowing me an interval in which I could find a place to settle to await the baby's arrival. But now it turned against me. With the threat of miscarriage, I didn't dare ride a horse. The only way I would be able to leave the north valley now was if I lost the baby. Apprehension ran through me. Given my circumstances and weakened condition, miscarriage was a strong possibility.

"Just let me stay here for a time, Jed. That's all I ask of you," I said, leaving my worst fears unspoken.

He didn't even look at me. "Stay as long as you need to," he replied curtly, going to the door and closing it abruptly behind him.

In the days that immediately followed, I was beset with worry, for the baby had not moved since the pains began. I could not be comforted and irrationally I turned away from Ben. I tried to tell myself it was because I slept so much of the time, most of the day and all but the very small hours of night when I would awaken to the quiet of the darkened room.

After Jed had walked out my first morning in the valley, he did not return to the cabin. I did not need to ask Ben where Christina was. I knew she was with Jed.

It was on the beginning of the fourth day, just as the sun glazed the eastern ridge, that I awoke to the stirring inside me. Scarcely breathing, afraid that I had dreamed the ghost of a flutter, I waited. This time I was rewarded by an impatient kick. Ben came in just as the joy in my heart stretched itself into a smile on my face. His eyes radiated his pleasure and he planted a firm kiss on my lips. But I found myself wondering if his exuberance were simply for my sake or because he believed that without the baby there would be no future for us.

Jed returned a few days later, but I did not see him. From Ben I learned that he had escorted Christina back to the Tanner ranch house and had remained there until he saw fit to return to the valley. Daily, Ben grew more foul-tempered, and I knew without his telling me that he and Jed were not getting on. The north valley was a prison to him, ruled by a man he could barely tolerate. Their avoidance of one another did not help to ease the tension.

"Why don't you go back to the main ranch, Ben?" I suggested, unable to think of another way to deal with his restlessness. "You did tell me that Jed said they were shorthanded there. It's bound to be easier on you than staying on here."

"No," he replied vehemently. "I'm not leaving you here alone with him."

I gave a short laugh. "You're being ridiculous, Ben. He can't stand the sight of me. I haven't even seen him since he's been back. He'd probably move back to the main house himself if it weren't for those army remounts he's been breaking. You'd have nothing to worry about." Neither of us found it necessary to say that Jed despised me so much that he had disappeared without even knowing if I had miscarried his child. Ben recognized that my disillusionment was complete. There was nothing for me to gain by being alone with Jed.

"It won't be for long, Ben," I continued gently. "I wouldn't be surprised if my time comes early." I did not speak of my fears for the baby, but Ben read them all too clearly.

"The baby will live, Meg. And the name it will carry will be Trew, and so will yours." He looked at me perceptively. "I know you don't want to marry me, Meg. You never did and now you're sure of it. But you will. You'll do it for the baby."

I turned away from him, upset that he knew me so well and unable to fight what very well might be the truth.

"But you'll be glad you did, Meg. I promise you

that," he added in a kinder tone. "And I'll be back here with you when it's time. I'll be right here with you."

Before he left the valley, Ben waited until I had taken my first few shakey steps and had progressed to short walks around the outbuildings. There were only a few: the house, which had been there long before Jed took over the valley, a shed, and a much newer barn, constructed of milled lumber. Several corrals adjoined the front and back of the barn and these were usually filled with assorted stock, mostly horses, although a rather strange looking, stocky, white-faced bull stood dociley at the center, watching us the day Ben and I said our good-byes.

"Take care of yourself, Meg," he said warmly. I nodded, not trusting myself to speak, and he lay a hand intimately over the swell of my stomach and kissed my brow lightly. I watched him ride away with a curious mingling of loss and relief.

The rising storm of dust from the next corral kept me from dwelling on Ben's departure. I peered into the thick cloud but I did not see the lone figure among the whirling horseflesh until the bright glitter of sand thrown up by the dancing hooves had settled. And then I discovered it was just one horse, a handsome bay gelding, that flailed against a taut rope. At the other end was Jed Tanner, pitting his strength against the unbroken animal. Mesmerized, I watched him work the animal. He did not throw him or even snub him as was customary. Instead, he maneuvered as close to the horse as he could, always allowing the gelding some play in the rope as the nervous animal backed away from him, seeking his freedom. It was almost a dance, as Jed moved with him, following the gelding's every step until at last the bay worked himself into a corner of the corral. They seemed to get no further than this. With his back avenue of escape closed to him, the animal edged his way sideways, but found himself approaching Jed, who remained steadfastly at his head. After his third attempt to sidle past him, the bay rested in the corner, his sides and neck lathered with sweat. White-eyed, he riveted his attention on the two-legged creature that stretched out a hand toward his neck. With his nostrils distended and his eyes wild, he suffered the touch. Another moment passed and Jed moved in closer. The horse raised his head higher, his eye still closely following the man who now stroked him reassuringly, working his way to the base of his ears, as the gelding stood stock still with his tail low to the ground. Then, suddenly, the horse's ears pricked forward as a natural curiosity began to replace his instinct to escape. By the end of the long morning, the bay followed Jed willingly on a lead, and when he walked away from the horse, lifting the gate of the corral and swinging it shut behind him, the gelding came to the fence and, lifting his head over the railing, stared at the departing back almost wistfully. I thought, with a painful smile, that Jed Tanner worked the same magic on his wild horses that he had on me; he had left us both wanting more.

He walked toward the water trough, his flannel shirt stained with the sweat of his efforts, his shirt-tails hanging down loosely. A pair of buckskin gloves dangled from a back pocket of the grit-covered Levi's. His hands, scarred with old and new scratches, left me weakened by sudden emotion. Removing a powder-caked hat, he leaned over, dousing his head in the water. He came up refreshed, his half-buttoned shirt soaked, the water pouring down his neck and carving a wet track down his dusty chest. He mopped his eyes with his sleeve and wiped his hands on the hanging shirttails. He saw me by the far end of the corral but made no move toward me. Without the obscuring growth of beard that I was accustomed to, he appeared younger, and I had never seen him look better than he did just then, with his skin tanned and dusty, his body lean and hard. Apparently, he had passed through Holbrook Barton's land unscathed. Suddenly, I wanted very much to know what had happened.

He strolled back over to the watching bay, giving the animal a reassuring pat. As I hesitantly approached him, the gelding snorted at me but remained where he was under the steadying hand. Jed kept his attention on the horse, ignoring me.

"Can I talk to you," I asked, directing my question to the broad, water-soaked back.

"What is it?" His voice was quiet, as if he were untroubled by my presence. I gathered it was more for the sake of the horse than for me. I didn't try to make idle conversation with him but directed my question to the information I sought.

"What did you find out in Cross Creek?" I asked him bluntly.

He turned his face toward me, the full sun intensifying the deep bronze of his skin. The wet hair was dark, but the tips that escaped his hat were shot with golden glints in the blazing sunlight. Close up, he was thinner than I remembered and his tanned forearms were laced with sinew that had come from long hours of struggling against more than a half ton of straining horseflesh.

"You shouldn't be standing in the sun like that," he remarked casually. I brushed a flyaway strand of hair from my face. I wore no hat and the sun burned strong and steady. Soothingly, he continued to stroke the bay. "Ben told me you wanted to talk to me. You came all this way to ask me about Cross Creek?"

I caught the disbelief in his voice, and as he watched me he saw the hesitation in my eyes. But what had once seemed so important to me didn't matter anymore. He didn't need any words from me to ease the pain I thought I had caused him. An image of him and Christina together flashed before me and I realized that she took care of him well enough to ease whatever hurts he had.

"No, what I came to say doesn't need to be said anymore, Jed. I want to know about Doc—and Add."

He glanced up at the sun and then back at me and wordlessly walked off in the direction of the shady oak trees that stood on a grassy strip just beyond the corrals and outbuildings. Silently, I followed him. He came to a halt and rested a shoulder against the trunk of a sun-dappled tree. "Sit down," he said, his tone mild, but I felt my heart constrict at the words as I did what he said.

"Add never turned up, Meg. I suppose he could be anywhere now...Canada, Mexico...who knows. At one time Barton had thirty men after him, not counting the one he sent after you—the one who killed Tice."

I winced at the memory and for a moment I saw a brief look of compassion on his face.

"But I'd say you don't have too much to worry about anymore."

I looked at him, confused. "But I don't understand. If Add never cleared me—"

"Barton had the notion that Add's brother might know of his whereabouts. He sent his oldest boy, Chad, after him. The next thing everyone knew was that Bob Matthews turned up missing. They never found his body so they couldn't pin anything on Barton. But it was enough to stir up the homesteaders. Within a week, Chad was found strung up to a tree and later they found over two hundred head of Barton's cattle, dead. They'd all been shot. Not even their hides had been lifted. With both sons dead and sensing the climate in Cross Creek wasn't to his liking anymore, Barton sold out at the first offer he received from some foreign investors.

"After folks cooled down, there weren't a whole lot of them believing you planned young Barton's murder with Add. Besides, it would have made Doc an accessory to the fact for helping you escape, and no one wanted that. I'd say they've lost interest in you."

"Then it's finally over?" I asked unbelievingly.

"I didn't say that. It depends on what kind of line this foreign company takes. Rumor was they were putting it under Hank Rinehart's control, a sort of joint venture. You'd do best to stay away from there until Cross Creek settles down."

"How's Doc?" I asked him softly, missing Seth Elliot more lately than ever.

"I didn't see him...he was away at the time. I left word for him that you were safe."

I understood why Jed had not waited to see Doc. Doc had entrusted me to his care and things had not gone well between us. I did not press him further for information. We stood there in silence, but Jed did not turn to leave. This last encounter between us had been curiously peaceful. It would be a small consolation to know that my last contact with the father of my baby lacked the anger of our previous times together. It was as much as I could hope for. I had seen too many of Jed Tanner's sides. To probe any deeper would destroy the thin veneer that cloaked my stubbornness and his destructiveness.

Awkwardly, I got to my feet, but I didn't look at him.

"Meg..." he began.

But I walked away, afraid to stay longer, unsure as to how long I could subdue the emotions he always managed to evoke, no matter how great my resolutions.

Chapter Twenty-Seven

✐ AFTER THE DAY JED GENTLED THE BAY gelding, there was little reason to continue with the elaborate pains we had taken to avoid each other. Our conversation had done more than free me from Holbrook Barton; I believed it had proved that my feelings for Jed were dead. Not even my anger remained. It was as if all my caring for him had been drained from me. I finally understood why Ben had gone along with my idea of coming to the valley. I had worn out my passion. Everything Ben foretold had come to pass.

I wore one of Alice's dresses now, with the waist let out. She had generously packed up some of her own clothing, the simple, light summer dresses that she thought would suit me best, and had given them to Jed during his trip back to the main ranch with Christina.

My strength returned with the plentiful food and rest. I experienced occasional bouts of restlessness but the walks I took seemed to act as a cure, although there were still times I was bothered by wakefulness at night. It seemed, then, that the baby would wake from its daytime slumbering to comfort me, as if to tell me that it would not be long before I would be holding it in my arms. Jed managed to avoid notice of my growing girth with an effort that bordered on humorous, if I was disposed to regard it in that light— but I was not. He tried to avert his gaze when we met or, if that was impossible, he would meet my eyes, that being preferable to acknowledging the physical proof of what we had once been to one another. It was one more thing that ingrained itself in my mind, hardening me even further as my stomach grew big with his child.

Even so, he was never far from my side. As I stared from the window of the cabin into the clear, starry nights, I would find him smoking a cigarette under a curtain of sheltering trees, only the infrequent spot of light to indicate his presence as he wrestled with his thoughts. But it was on the rainy nights, the inky dark evenings that could be cold and damp or hold a bit of pleasant warmth, that he would spend inside the cabin with me, entering only after I had fallen asleep. In the early hours, after he had gone, some small trace of him would remain behind, a bench that was not quite positioned as I had left it or a rumpled blanket by the foot of the spare cot. He would have preferred to seek shelter in the barn, but there he would not have heard me if I needed help. He considered it his duty to watch over me, but his solicitude was no greater than it had ever been.

On one of those rare days when not a breeze could be found to tease at the glare of the noonday sun, Jed decided to wean the winter colt from his dam. She had begun to lose weight alarmingly, with no apparent cause. The mare was prized for her thor-

oughbred bloodlines, and Jed considered that enough
of a reason to separate her from her colt.

Seeking the shade of a nearby oak, I found some
relief from the heat, but as the heartbreaking squeals
of the young colt rose above the frantic whinny of
the mare, I followed the path to the creek. Removing
my shoes, I alternated between splashing in the icy
water and walking along the pebbled bank until I
could no longer hear the anguished cries of the horses,
finally coming to rest beside a gravelly bed by a
shallow bend in the creek. The bank sloped gently
down to the water's edge and I watched the creek
tumble over the rocks and tangles of wood in its
course. A light, cooling breeze lifted itself across the
water and played about the edge of my pale cotton
frock. Sitting back against a rock, I sunned myself
in the relaxing warmth, drifting off to sleep under
the cloudless sky.

A darkness blanketed the sun and then the golden
caress was gone. The absence of the warmth slowly
cut through my drowsiness. Unwillingly, I opened
my eyes.

"Jed?"

With his back to the sun, his features were so dark
that at first I did not discern his anger.

"Damn it, Meg! Tell me before you go wandering
off like that!" he said harshly.

Sitting up, I rubbed at the stiffness in my back,
confused. "I haven't done anything wrong, Jed. Why
are you shouting at me? I'm all right."

"Because you could have gotten hurt, you fool.
You could fall or—"

"You make me sound like I'm one of your damned
brood mares!" I snapped, suddenly losing patience
with his manner and his rude intrusion. "Well, I'm
not. I'm pregnant, not helpless!"

Then, seeing his set expression, I knew that he
had worried about me. "It was the mare and colt," I

admitted grudgingly. "It was terrible, Jed. I didn't want to listen to them anymore."

There was contempt in the gray eyes and I should have taken it as a warning. "That bothered you?"

"Of course it did!" I said angrily as an accusing look came to his eyes. What had I done now? Putting a hand to the rock, I slowly rose to my feet, but he didn't move from where he stood. His eyes locked with mine.

"Tell me something, Meg," he said coolly, as if he already knew the answer. "Just why is it that you've come here?" There was a ridiculing smile on his lips, and I hated him for it.

"Well?"

Nervously, I squinted up at him in the harsh glare of sunlight. I'd never tell him of the need and love and regret that had drawn me after him, especially now that it was gone, leaving me with a void so large I didn't think I'd ever feel such passion again, or even want to.

"You didn't come here to find out what happened back at Cross Creek."

"No."

"Then why, damn it!"

With a patience I had only recently learned, I refused to give in to my waspish temper. "Why do you think I've come, Jed?" I asked him at last, in a reasonable voice. "You seem to think you've figured it out for yourself."

His jaw tightened and his eyes blazed with a sudden fierceness. "Not at first, I didn't," he said, turning the full weight of his contempt upon me. "But it didn't take me long to see through your plan. Obviously, you plan to leave the baby here."

I was speechless with astonishment. What on earth had made him think that?

"That's interesting, Jed," I finally said, forcing

casualness into my voice. "Whatever gave you that idea?"

Jed Tanner did not see the danger signals.

"Why else would you come all this way? Ben told me he has plans for the two of you. If the child is mine, like you claim it is, you wouldn't want to be saddled with it. You've been hoping your taking sick would work out for you, that if you managed to stay on here until the baby is born, I'd have no choice but to take it."

"And would you?" I asked him softly, not missing the hard edge in his voice.

"Yes."

"Well, it's real interesting that you figured that out all by yourself. But I hope you're not counting too much on keeping the baby, because I won't even let you touch it. You're crazy, Jed. You're so twisted you'll believe almost anything, as long as it's the worst about me."

Instead of lashing back at me, as I expected, he looked relieved. Yes, he would have taken the baby because it had his blood, but he didn't want it.

He took a step closer, forcing me back up against the rock. Leaning forward, he put a hand at either side of my head, blocking my passage.

"Then why did you follow me here?" he spat savagely. "God damn it! Tell me why, so I can understand why I have to see your face everywhere I turn!"

I gasped under his attack and his bitterness finally released the words I had dammed up inside of me.

"I came all this way, Jed," I answered fiercely, "to talk to you, just like Ben said! And he's here with me because he wouldn't let me come alone. I came because I regretted the things I said to you the last time we were together. I said them because I was hurt and angry. Later, when I had a chance to think about them, I knew they weren't true, that I had been wrong. Not wrong about how I felt at the time, but wrong because I didn't know what was making you turn on me like that. And because I said those terrible things, I wanted to apologize to you."

"You came here to make an apology?"

I practically sputtered as I glared at him.

"No, that wasn't the only reason, but it's the only reason that could still matter. So I've cleared my conscience. I apologize. I'm sorry, Jed, for the hateful things I said to you. Though I don't know why I should be, for you've said and thought far worse about me."

He ignored my last comment and a canny look came to his face. He did not believe me.

"That's not good enough, Meg," he said, with a dangerous light in his eye. "You didn't come all this way just to say you were sorry. Damn it, I want to know why!"

He was so close I could reach out to touch his cheek. It didn't matter if he knew the truth now. I had cured myself of him.

"I came because I loved you, Jed! God knows why I thought I could love anyone who has as low an opinion of me as you do. How on earth could you ever think, even for an instant, that I would give you my baby? If I didn't know it before, I know it now. You've gone a long way to convince me of my mistake, Jed. The sooner I can leave here, the better. I hope I never see you again!"

Having spoken my mind, there remained nothing left to be said. I pushed aside his arm with all the dignity that was left to me and walked away.

I made a pet of the winter colt. I called him Ash because of his dark, smoky color and cheerfully turned a blind eye to Jed's disapproving profile while I lingered evenings by the corral, feeding him leftover biscuits from my plate. Jed kept his distance from me now, and I was sure it was because of the admission of my feelings for him. He ran from a love that lay in shattered ruins.

A rider from the ranch arrived weekly that summer, delivering the mail and supplies along with messages from the Tanner family. Alice had written me, in a beautifully penned note, of her intentions to come to the north valley with Ben for my confinement. She always managed to include a package for me, either entirely frivolous, such as scented soap, or eminently practical, such as the soft flannel for baby clothes, and her considerable kindness led me to believe she was glad that circumstances required my staying on these additional months. Jed never once displayed any interest in Alice's generosity but he must have wondered what it was that had made her take to me so. It was from the ST rider, too, that I learned that Ben had been assigned to pick up a small herd of new breeding stock at the railhead.

During one of these weekly visits, when I was concentrating on a package Alice had sent me, I missed the beginning of Jed's conversation with Wes, the rider, but I caught the swift change in his usually implacable face. A murderous expression tightened his features as the man from the ST leaned forward in his saddle, passing the news to him, and I drew closer to listen. "Cal said to be sure I told you, first thing," Wes said.

Jed went to the packhorse, unloading the supplies with white-knuckled hands. "You let them all know," he hissed, "that if he so much as shows his face here, I'll kill the bastard!" He strode into the cabin, the sack of supplies over his shoulder.

I went after him.

"It's Travis, isn't it?" I questioned him boldly from the door, watching him as he dropped the bag of provisions on the table. He half turned at the sound of my voice. "Sort this stuff," he said, ignoring my question. Brusquely, he turned on his heel and brushed past me in the narrow doorway. I heard him tell Wes to help himself to whatever he wanted before heading back to the ranch. In the dry weather, the trip between the north valley and the main ranch took no more than half a day. I left the cabin and followed him to the corral where he selected a mare to ride.

"Would you really, Jed?" I called to him, as he led the mare outside the enclosure. "Kill him, I mean."

He didn't answer.

I watched him with curious detachment as he saddled the horse.

"He's in Redmonton," he answered at last, as if that explained it.

"So?"

"So, he's got no reason to be around these parts," he said, swinging himself into the saddle.

"Just because he's in Redmonton doesn't mean he'll come here," I argued.

"No," he agreed. The mare stretched her head around curiously as I stood at her side.

"Is that where you're going?" I dared to ask him, holding my breath as I waited for his answer.

"No, I'm going to the south section." His voice softened a bit. "I wouldn't leave you alone here, Meg," he said, as he attempted to allay what he thought was my fear.

"I wasn't worried about being alone," I replied testily. "I figured you would tell Wes to stay with me if you decide to leave."

Jed laughed outright at my words.

"No," he said at last. "Wes wouldn't be much good around a pregnant mare, never mind you."

I bristled at his words and turned away, but at his mirthful chuckle I looked back to watch as he headed the mare through the waving meadow of bunchgrass.

* * *

I grew anxious at the end, awaiting Ben's return to the valley, and I took to scanning the hilltops during the late summer days for the sight of his familiar figure riding the rawboned gelding into the valley, with Alice by his side. Then, finally, on an unusually warm afternoon, I spotted two riders cresting a distant rise. The shapes were dark, moving specks upon the horizon, then they began to descend the slope, disappearing between the gentle curves and stands of timber that dotted the valley floor. Apprehension flooded me as I waited for the riders to reappear, for although I recognized Alice, it was not Ben who accompanied her, but Christina.

Hurrying to the dusty riders as they pulled up their horses, I forget everything else, even my dislike of the beautiful Christina, in my concern for Ben.

"Alice! Where's Ben? Why isn't he here?" I struggled for breath, ignoring Christina's baleful look.

Looking coolly efficient in her tailored riding habit of dove gray, Alice refused to be rushed into an explanation. Her forced calm in the face of my distress only heightened my anxiety.

"Where's Jed, Meg?" she asked me gently as she dismounted. With a series of impatient flicks of her hand, she brushed away the accumulation of dust from her skirt and jacket.

"I don't know," I burst out. "Tell me what's wrong, Alice! Why isn't Ben with you?"

"Yes, Alice," the deep voice growled from behind me, with Christina's face lighting up at his approach, "let's end Meg's suspense. What happened to Ben? Don't tell me that after all this time, his feelings for her have changed."

Stung by Jed's attack, I angrily whirled around to defend Ben, not needing an accounting from Alice to be certain of his kindness and devotion.

"He's not like that at all, Jed! Ben wouldn't have left me here at all if he didn't have to!"

Jed's eyes darkened ominously and I knew he misread my reaction. To him it was a reminder of my betrayal and of the possibility that it was Ben's child I carried. But it was only out of fear—not of childbirth, but of myself—that I wanted Ben in the valley. His presence would keep Jed far from my side when my time came and would, perhaps, anchor my mind to reality so that I would not call out in my pain for the man whose child I bore.

Disregarding my rising temper and Jed's black look, Christina dismounted and went to him, a careful smile on her face as she managed to dismiss my presence with an indifferent shrug. Nevertheless, Jed, instead of welcoming her, looked at Alice. She came forward and put an arm about my shoulder. "Look, Meg, Ben is going to be all right—"

"What happened?" I demanded.

"He had an accident."

"An accident?" I replied, stricken.

"Damn it, Alice! Spit it out! Can't you see you're scaring Meg half to death?" Jed said, his voice rough.

Christina frowned, the line marring the smooth perfection of her forehead at Jed's attention to me.

"He'll be fine, Meg. Really. That's what I'm trying to tell you." Alice looked up at Jed indignantly, not at all intimidated by his rebuke. "It's nothing to be worried about. He'll be laid up a bit...he was roping a steer, when the cinch on his saddle snapped. He got dragged and stepped on—"

"Oh, no!" I closed my eyes, horrified. It was all my fault. If I had listened to Ben we never would have made this wasted journey.

"He's all right, Meg. Really he is. He broke a leg and a few ribs. We even had Doc Bennett to see him. Sam said we better not trust Sandy even though he does a lot of doctoring for the boys. He set Jim's leg last year and it healed straight as can be."

"When did it happen?" I asked dully.

"A few days ago. He's in an awful state now, feeling that he's let you down. He said he promised to be with you, no matter what. We moved him up to the big house. Sylvie will be looking after him while Christina and I are here in the valley."

"Well," I said with a forced brightness to the small group of people standing about me. "It really doesn't matter. I'll be fine." Alice watched me closely, seeing through my thin attempt at cheeriness, and I did not look at the others. Rather than struggle to keep up the pretense, I excused myself and quickly walked away. I heard Alice start after me and then Jed's stern command for her to let me be. At least, he knew me well enough to recognize my need to be alone.

Alice waited just long enough to slip away undetected before coming after me. I turned as I heard her light step tripping up the stony path along the creekbed. I waited for her as she caught up to me.

"I'm sorry Christina had to come with me, Meg," Alice said. "I knew from the time Jed brought her back to the ranch and told her she wasn't to return to the north valley under any circumstances that you hadn't gotten on. But Cal wouldn't let me make the trip by myself and he couldn't spare any other riders just now."

So that had been the explanation behind Christina's continued absence these past months and the reason for her flagrant hostility. Jed's consideration for my feelings at a time when I had believed the worst about him touched me, and I felt a surge of conflicting emotions. Disturbed, I sternly told myself that he had done no more than show me a little kindness.

"She's been madder than a wet hen ever since," Alice continued with a wry smile, unaware of my state of mind as we seated ourselves under one of the trees that lined the bank. "You know, she's jealous of you."

"Jealous of me?" I said, taken aback and unable to disguise my astonishment. "What on earth for?"

"The baby," Alice said bluntly, not mincing words. "Maybe Sam and the rest of them think the baby is Ben's, but men are blind to the truth sometimes. Christina knows that it's Jed's.

I gave a bitter laugh. "Jed's not even sure of that." Alice looked at me with a troubled face.

"He feels something for you, Meg, I'm sure of it. He never took his eyes off you, even with Christina—"

"Oh, Alice, he's just watching over me..." I interrupted quickly, and then told her how hurt I had been when Jed had believed I would abandon the baby so that I could leave the valley unencumbered with Ben. A shocked look came to her face and then, more surprisingly, a knowing one. Seeing my curiosity, she looked away quickly. Whatever her thoughts were, Alice did not choose to share them.

But I did not dwell on Alice's suppositions. Something much greater had been worrying me since Wes, the ST rider, had last been to the valley.

"Alice," I said, "has there been any further word about Travis?"

Her eyes clouded. "He hasn't shown up at the ST, if that's what you're wondering, Meg. Wes told us what Jed said. I'd hate to see all that start up again." Then abruptly, she fell silent.

It seemed that she had been right about what she'd told me my first night at the ST: no one, not even her husband, Cal, felt comfortable discussing a past that had ripped the family apart. This time, seeing the expression on her face, I was afraid to venture a guess at her thoughts.

* * *

The supper we shared that night was the most elegant meal ever served in the cabin. After several bottles of wine smuggled from the ranch pantry had been consumed, Alice regaled us with her tales of petty thievery and how she had managed to take whatever she could find that would withstand the rigors of the trip, including what Sylvie had prepared for the evening meal at the main house. "I decided to let them worry about it," she said with a hint of mischief. "But Sylvie did have a fit when she saw me eyeing her meringue pie. As if I would have taken that! She offered to make me the strawberry cobbler instead," Alice said, referring to the dessert of which only a few crumbs remained.

I pushed myself away from the table. I had eaten little and taken nothing to drink. As the odor of the food turned cloying, I made my way outside and walked a little ways from the fading voices in the cabin, watching the sun paint the sky orange as it dropped behind a black-shadowed wall of mountains. I heard the dull scraping of a chair from within and a moment later saw Jed's lean frame as he stood at the cabin door, surveying his domain in the deepening dusk. I watched him as he reached a decision and strode into the graying darkness, heading down toward the stream. Not a moment passed before Christina, too, stood at the door and, spotting him in the dimming light, slipped into the night after him. She followed him until he grew aware of her light step and hurried to him as he turned to wait for her. And then they both disappeared into the obscuring curtain of trees.

Sleep did not come that night. As Alice slumbered soundly, wrapped in blankets on the cot, the bare floor that Christina was to occupy remained conspicuously empty and I lay awake staring out at a moonshine almost as bright as the light of day. I told myself it was no concern of mine how and with whom he chose to spend his nights, but it was no use. With a sudden rage, I threw aside my covers, and then quietly, so that I would not awaken Alice, I went out into the crisp night air.

From the doorway, I looked out over the corral, but the horses were quiet, and I began to walk in the opposite direction, toward the stream. The heavy chirping of the crickets hid the sound of my bare feet as they moved quickly over the bed of twigs and sharp stones. I welcomed the sensation, for it had a calming effect on me. I knew what I would find, yet it did not stop me. The image I carried of them together was so strong that when I finally came upon them I had to shut my eyes and look again to make sure I was not dreaming.

Resting against the wide, ridged trunk of an old willow, Jed was staring out over the creek, which sparkled under the blanket of stars. Christina lay asleep, curled up under her shawl on the grassy bank a short distance away. A gentle wind toyed with the gossamer folds of my nightdress, blowing them softly about me. I shivered slightly, not with cold, but from the unbroken gaze he fastened on me.

"You shouldn't be here," he said finally.

"No, I suppose it will be a relief to you once I've gone," I answered, deliberately misinterpreting his remark as I seated myself on the damp grass.

"Ben will take care of you," he said, as if he had given thought to it before.

I said nothing.

"He loves you." He spoke the words forcefully, as if that made a difference.

"I'll leave here with Ben, Jed. But I won't marry him."

The moonlight revealed his annoyance. Frowning, he turned his narrowed eyes on me, as if I had upset his plans. "What will you do?" His voice was curt.

"I'm not sure. I thought I might return to Cross

Creek, just for a little while. I miss Doc. I know there'll be gossip if I show up, but I won't let it bother me. They should be used to my ways," I added wryly. "I never led an exemplary existence while I lived there."

I thought I saw the ghost of a smile as he remembered the circumstances under which he had rescued me from Cross Creek. And I remembered, too, the time I had been returned to Cross Creek, riding double behind the sheriff of Stanton, my clothes stiff with the dried blood of Jed Tanner.

And then I saw a hunger in his eyes as they lingered on my face, and my heart quickened, but as the breeze shaped the softly billowing fabric against me, revealing the swell of my figure, his look hardened. His face told me all I needed to know. He was comparing me to Julie, remembering her betrayal of him. While he acknowledged that my child might be his, he would never be certain. Somewhere in the night, a wolf howled mournfully. Christina had not stirred from her position. Wordlessly, he rose and gave me his hand, helping me to stand. Together we walked back to the cabin, remaining close, but not touching, and he watched as I went inside. I went to the window, my eyes searching for him under a star-studded sky, and saw him lead a pale horse from the corral. With nothing more than a handhold of mane for a grip, he slipped onto the horse and, riding him bareback, headed him across the rippling grass to pound out his demons in a moonlight ride.

At a slight noise, I turned and found Alice standing behind me, wraithlike in the long flow of her nightdress, a strange look glittering in her pale blue eyes.

Chapter Twenty-Eight

* * "I FOUND HIM WITH CHRISTINA," I said to her, in a carefully composed voice, aware of my night attire, the hem of my gown limp and bedraggled from the dew and my moonlight excursion. "Of course," I added pointedly, unaware of what my face gave away, "that's exactly what I expected. Perhaps that will cure you of your romantic notions about me and Jed."

Alice took up the blanket from the end of my bed and wrapped it around my shoulders for warmth. Then she escorted me to the straight-back chair. Leaving the lamp unlit, she paced the room restlessly, her pale gold hair gleaming in the stream of white light from the window. She looked at me with determined eyes. "This has gone on long enough," she said, coming to a decision. "I shouldn't be telling you this. It's not my place. It's betraying a trust." She paused. "But I don't care anymore because it isn't fair to you. I know the truth about Jed, Meg. All of it. And I think you should know, too."

Intrigue, it seemed, destroyed Alice's serenity. She continued to walk the floor of the cabin until, exasperated, I spoke to her sharply. "Alice, for heaven's sake, sit down! It can't be that bad."

She did as I said; facing me, she took a seat at the edge of the bed.

"It bothered me, Meg, all those questions I had about what had happened between Jed, Travis, and Julie, before I arrived at the ST. After you left the ranch to go to the valley, I asked Cal about it again. I insisted that he tell me this time. He didn't want to...I think he was afraid I'd believe that he could have done something to stop it." She looked up at me. "You see, he said the story began way before Julie. It began when Jed was born."

The chill of the cabin penetrated the thin blanket about my shoulders, but that had nothing to do with the coldness within me. Alice's eyes softened with compassion as she sensed my turmoil. Now that I would finally learn the truth, I was afraid of it. She lay her hand over mine, lightly clenched in my lap. "It explains so much, Meg. If you knew it all, perhaps you wouldn't judge him so harshly.

"Jed and Travis aren't related by blood," she said soberly. "Travis was the son of Sam's first wife, Amanda. Travis was three when Amanda came to the ST to marry Sam and six when she died in a fall from a horse, just a year after Cal was born. From what everyone says, Travis was a handful even then. It was just a year later that Sam married Rachel, his second wife. He was forty, she was seventeen. She was young and beautiful, but I think there must have been problems from the start. But maybe it would have worked if she hadn't found out that Sam had married her just to get possession of the north valley, where she lived with her father. She learned that when she was carrying Jed. She left three weeks after he was born. Sam was furious that she had run

off. He wouldn't even let anyone look for her. Years
later, Cal said, they got word that she had died in
some gold camp in Colorado. She was twenty-six at
the time.

"Sam never took to Jed. I guess Jed reminded him
too much of Rachel. They say though that even as a
boy, Travis always had it in for Jed. I'm not sure
why. But he made it known to Jed that his own
mother, Amanda, had died, leaving him and Cal
alone, but she had never deserted them, like Rachel
had done to Jed. A child can't judge the truth, but
Jed knew Sam refused to let Rachel's name be mentioned in the house and had all the pictures of her
destroyed. He couldn't have known that it was his
father who had driven Rachel away, and I think
maybe he blamed himself. With Sam doing his best
to avoid him and spending his time grooming Cal to
run the ranch, even though he was only a boy, that
left Travis pretty free to torment Jed. He grew up
lonely and unwanted.

"Sam kept a tutor for the boys and, as soon as he
was old enough, he sent Cal away to school. Cal says
that that probably saved him, because although he
was Sam's favorite, the old man never was much of
a father, even to him. He sent Travis to school, too,
but mostly because he was wild and always getting
into trouble. His teachers couldn't handle him either,
because he was asked to leave every place Sam en-
rolled him in. Jed didn't want to leave the ranch, so
Sam let him be, until he and Travis got into a fight
after Travis killed Jed's prized colt. Jed almost killed
him, even with Travis being six years older than
him. Jed claimed Travis had done it on purpose. Cal
says it was probably true. But Sam couldn't do a
thing with Travis and he felt he had to punish Jed.
He knew how much being on the ranch meant to
him, so he sent him away to a school back east.

"Things ran smoothly at the ranch with Jed gone,

so Sam decided he would be better off keeping the boys apart. But Jed hated school and when he learned that Sam wasn't going to let him back right away, he ran off and worked his way south, heading for Texas. He waited four years before coming back to the ST. He was twenty at the time.

"Cal says that Sam was amused by Jed's show of independence. Things were even peaceful around the ST. Travis had left the ranch. He'd show up from time to time, then he'd be off again. He claimed he was having some luck with cards. He wore fine clothes and rode a flashy horse. Then Sam did a surprising thing. He deeded the north valley to Jed. Cal thinks Sam did it to make it up to Rachel, thinking that after all those years he had a guilty conscience about what had happened. Jed bought a stud and started breeding horses, like he always wanted to do. They began having trouble with rustlers about that time. They suspected that whoever was responsible for it had help from the inside, but they had trouble proving it. Then Julie showed up."

Alice's eyes met mine and she drew a deep breath before continuing. "Sam had met her and her family in Denver on business. Cattle raising and railroading went hand in hand. Sam invited them out to the ranch to stay for a while. Cal says that she was beautiful. She had long, silky dark hair and the brightest blue eyes he had ever seen. He said she had that sparkle you don't find very often. He also said that she had been doted on all her life and was terribly spoiled. She dressed like she had never imagined what life on a ranch would be like, in rustling silks and ruffles and lace and she was the envy of all the women around these parts. Travis returned about the time she was here and he stayed on until she left. Everyone thought she fancied him. They had a flamboyance that suited one another. Cal says that both he and Sam were taken with her, too. But

Cal had enough sense to realize she'd never make a good rancher's wife. Jed, he said, was in the valley most of that summer and the only romance that was on his mind was between his stallion and his brood mares.

"Julie's parents would have been happy to see a match between her and Cal, but Travis was another story. Not being a Tanner by blood, his prospects weren't as good as Cal's and his gambling didn't work in his favor, either. The next thing they all knew was that Julie and her family had packed up and gone. They got word of her from time to time, mostly through her father's business with Sam. She spent the next few years in England and France and then, out of the blue, with no warning, she showed up again.

"She told them she had come back west to find some real men. Sam was real pleased to have her back. Cal said her personality reminded Sam of Amanda. Cal still admired her, but he kept his distance. The cattle rustling had grown worse and he was gone a lot of the time. No one knew it then, but he suspected that Travis might be connected to it in one way or another. With Cal and Sam gone most of the time, that left Jed at the ranch.

"He was at the valley most of that summer until Sam asked him as a favor one day to take Julie out riding with him. Cal says something must have happened that afternoon, because Jed seemed like a changed man when he came back. He said that Julie was different when she was around Jed, too. More serious. He said they talked a lot. It must have been a new experience for Jed. I don't think there had ever been anyone around like that for him before, he was such a loner. The next thing they all knew was that Jed had asked Julie to marry him and she said yes. Cal said they were all surprised, even Jed, that Julie accepted him. They got married at the ranch and it was the biggest wedding ever held in these parts.

"Afterward, Cal said he supposed that Julie had been waiting for Travis to return for her all along. That she was just playing with Jed, and got bored waiting for Travis to come back." This time, Alice looked away from me, and at her next words, I knew why. "When Jed found out she was going to have a child, he was overjoyed. He had to go on a stock-buying trip for some mares shortly after that, and he expected to be gone about six or eight weeks. Julie wanted to go, but he wouldn't let her. He said that most likely the accommodations wouldn't be fitting for a woman. He said he'd make it up to her some other time with a trip to whatever city she wanted to go to. Sam agreed with him. Jed warned her to stay off the horses and Sam said he'd help look after her while Jed was gone.

"Jed came back a little earlier than he expected, but it wasn't soon enough. While he was still in Redmonton he learned that Julie had suffered a miscarriage after being thrown from a loco horse, almost immediately after he'd left. He rode two horses into the ground, riding day and night to get back to the ranch. He had seen the doctor in town, who had said Julie was making a good recovery, but he was worried sick. You can imagine his surprise when he finally arrived at the ranch to find the house empty. Sam and Cal were off chasing rustlers, and Julie had gone riding, with Travis."

Knowing what was coming was no help. I felt sick as I listened to Alice's soft voice relate the events that led up to Julie's killing.

"He trailed them to the north valley, to the site where he had been building a house for Julie. It was almost finished. He found them there." Alice looked up at me with tears in her eyes. "The rest is known because of the inquest."

"Travis hated him so much...he told Jed that Julie had only married him because he, Travis, had been gone at the time. But now that he was back, he intended to take Julie away with him. Julie didn't say anything to deny it, and Jed knew then that it was all true, that it made perfect sense. But what Travis also told Jed was that Julie had ridden that crazy pinto on purpose, that she wanted to lose the baby. He told Jed not to feel bad, that Julie wasn't the mothering sort, and that she would have left the baby just like Rachel had left him.

"Jed told them later at the inquest that no matter what Julie had done, he knew he had to get her away from Travis. When he went to pull her out of Travis's reach, he found himself staring down the barrel of Travis's gun. As Jed went for his, Julie, seeing his intent, threw herself across Travis. Travis's shot went wild, while Jed's hit her, instead. He hadn't meant to kill her, but he did. Travis was hit, too. It was just a flesh wound, but Jed didn't know at the time whether he was dead or alive.

"That's when Cal found him. He and Sam had seen him riding hell-bent for the valley and Cal had followed him down. He said that Jed was crazed with grief. Remembering how Cal had once been attracted by Julie, Jed even accused him of having had her. He dared Cal to come after him, telling him he'd kill him if Cal didn't get him first. Of course, Cal let him go. You know the rest. Travis wasn't hurt badly. After he got patched up he took after Jed, and ambushed him outside of Cross Creek.

"Jed pleaded guilty to Julie's killing. The judge was lenient, though, and being Sam's son probably didn't hurt. People don't think much of unfaithful wives around here. And everyone knew what Julie had done...about the baby. The lawyer even had Doc Bennet testify at the inquest. The judge released Jed right after that. Sam wouldn't speak to him; Cal thinks it was because he was so taken with Julie that he couldn't believe he had been wrong about her. It finally forced Sam to confront his feelings about Rachel—if he had been wrong about Julie, he could have been wrong about her, too, and maybe Rachel's leaving had been Sam's fault and his injured pride had kept him from going after her. Jed left the ST, and no one heard from him until he showed up this winter. He holed himself up here in the valley and doesn't say much to anyone."

Neither of us spoke. The silence lay heavy in the cabin, the noises of the night creatures a distant sound.

"I know Jed's been unfair to you, Meg," Alice said gently, "but maybe you can understand why, now. It's not you. I don't think he can help it. He doesn't trust anyone."

I spoke brokenly, giving her a sad smile. "In a way, Alice, it was easier not knowing the truth. That way, I suppose, there might have been the hope that someday he would change his mind. But this way, don't you see what it proves? He's incapable of recognizing love and loving in return. I'm not Rachel and I'm not Julie, but Jed believed that I would desert my own child. I can't fight that kind of past. He has nothing left for anyone. His emotions were spent long ago, with the bullet that killed Julie."

For once, Alice was silent, offering no protest. I rose from my bed and went to the window. I looked out and saw nothing but the empty night.

Alice remained close by the next few days, a mother hen tending to her wayward offspring, certain my time was near. She accompanied me on my walks, her own brow beading with perspiration as she cautioned me on the foolishness of my exertions, begging me to return to the cabin to rest.

Although I noted with some satisfaction that

Christina's next few nights were spent on the rough floor of the little cabin, during the days she determinedly followed Jed from task to task. He never sent her away. Wisely, he kept himself out of our way, occupying himself in the far reaches of the valley, watching over his strange breed of white-faced cattle.

But the day I climbed the flat-topped bluff for a view of the valley and gazed, spellbound, out at the mountains and lake, I wished I had listened to Alice. It was there, in a clearing well protected from winter winds by the thick stand of spruce that encircled it, that I saw the large plot of blackened ground. Not a sign of life marched across it, nor were the edges of the dark image blurred by the faint breeze that lifted the nearby grass. Almost reluctantly, I drew closer, recognizing the charred cinders and the scorched rubble of a chimney, the final remains of what had once been a house. Breathlessly, Alice caught up to me. She stood speechless by my side. It was where Jed had found Julie and Travis. Jed had fired the house himself.

"I think we ought to go back now, Meg," Alice said in a strong voice as I stared down at the destruction. "Christina will be starting supper soon." She looked at me oddly, and then, withdrawing a lacy, violet-scented handkerchief from her pocket, she gently wiped my brow. "It's time we headed back, Meg," she said again, this time more sharply.

"No!"

Her eyebrows lifted and a knowing look came to her eyes. "I should have known you'd do something like this," she said with an indignant frown.

"I still have some time, Alice. Please. I'd rather not go back just yet." I took a series of deep breaths as a spasm came over me and then smiled at her weakly. "Really, Alice, I'm fine. You can't imagine how many times I've seen these things through with Doc. First babies take ages."

Alice kept at me as the sun slipped lower in the sky but I would not listen to her. Several times she came close to leaving me behind, and I knew that she planned to return with Jed. Only then did I lose the tight control I held over myself. "No, Alice!" I heard myself cry out, the fear of having Jed with me far greater than the fear of giving birth under a dimming sky. Irrationally, I fought her, badly misjudging the time that was left to me. Leaning against her for support, I wanted only to sink down into the soft bed of grass.

Alice fell aside as we heard his voice and then I found then sun-streaked horizon swimming behind the angry face of Jed Tanner.

"Get away from me!" I cried out at him. His face tightened, but as another wave of pain overtook me and low moans escaped my lips, he picked me up in his arms and carried me back to the cabin, gently laying me down upon the bed. Christina's face wavered behind us. If Jed was awaiting a sign of my appreciation, he got none from me. Violently, the hurt, anger, and helplessness came together and poured from my lips as I caught sight of Christina's beautifully poised and unruffled features. Thwarted passion exploded from within me. "I hate you, Jed! Get the hell out of here!" His face disappeared as I turned my head into the pillow to stifle my cries. With Alice's cool hand at my brow, Christina's poison carried through the walls of the cabin.

"What other proof do you need?" she asked him with a low laugh. "She never would have sent you from her at a time like this if you were the father of the baby. Every woman would want her man around...even if it was just to show him how much she has suffered for him."

My numbing exhaustion fell away with her words.

Suddenly renewed, I pushed with all the strength that was left in me, pushing away the past with the future. With a cry of pain that became one of victory, my baby was born. All that mattered now was that she be surrounded by love, and I had enough of that to last her a lifetime.

Within days of Jessica's arrival, Jed arranged for the delivery of the army horses, making sure he would be away from the valley until after I had left. I did not dwell on his inevitable departure; I had expected it. Even doubting Jessica's parentage, he had remained in the valley until her birth, fulfilling, as he had in the mountains that fall what he believed to be his obligation. Instead, I concentrated on Alice's parting, for it had been decided from the outset that she would return to the ranch at the first opportunity and that Christina would remain in the north valley until Ben was well enough to come for me. I was not at all pleased by these arrangements.

"I don't see why Christina has to stay with me at all," I said gloomily to Alice on her last night in the valley. "Jessica and I will be fine. We don't need her to watch over us." Fervently, I hoped that Alice would agree with me.

"Those are Sam's orders, Meg. He said that under no circumstances were you to be left alone here." Then, seeing my face, she added more gently. "You know that if it weren't for Cal, I'd be glad to stay."

"I'm sorry, Alice. I didn't mean to sound ungrateful. You've been away from him long enough as it is. I just can't understand what harm Sam thinks I'd come to being here with Jessica."

She shrugged her shoulders as she piled wood into the stove. "Christina's no happier about it than you are, I can tell you that much. But at least she can help out with the chores until you get your strength back."

At the slight whimper from the makeshift cradle, I went to where Jessica slept by my bed. She was a mewling red mite of a thing and I felt my heart swell with a protective love for her. I had found the cradle the morning after her birth and assumed Jed had made it. True to my last words to him, he kept well away from us and had not even ventured inside to see his daughter. Only once in the past week, when Jessica had awakened from her sleep with a lusty wail, demanding to be fed, did I look up to see his tall figure shadow the doorway, observing us intently. The next time I lifted my eyes, he was gone.

"He probably remembers what you said to him the night Jessica was born, Meg. That's why he's avoiding you."

I flushed guiltily, disconcerted by the transparency of my thoughts, and looked up to find Alice's penetrating gaze upon Jessica and me.

"He does care, Meg, no matter what you think about him."

"How can you say that, Alice? You saw him at the door that day. He turned away from his own child."

"Oh, Meg. He's hurt you so much that you can't see beyond your own pain. He's suffering, too. He's denying himself the very love that you and Jessica have to offer him. He's still punishing himself after all this time."

But I wanted none of Alice's excuses for Jed's behavior just then. Since Jessica's birth I was recovering more than my strength. I had a sense of purpose, and for the first time I was able to view Jed dispassionately, as if he had already become a bittersweet memory. But the image of the empty doorway remained and rankled in my thoughts.

Alice and I said our good-byes early the next morning. Taking Jessica in my arms, I left the cabin and wandered along the creekbed until I found a likely spot to settle down as I awaited their departure. I had always thought that my final meeting with Jed would be difficult, and now that time had come, I chose to avoid it entirely. I had no desire to witness his farewell to Christina, nor have him go through the motions of one with me. All that could possibly be said between us had been said. Ben would be happy, at least, that our venture had been successful in that respect.

I hadn't expected him to come after me, but I didn't turn away from him when his footsteps announced his approach, for there was no point in it. I did not bother to rise and he looked down at me, but although I held the sleeping baby in my arms, his eyes did not fall to her. The farewell was to be a mere formality.

"Most likely I won't be back by the time Ben comes for you, Meg. I wanted to say good-bye," he said tersely.

"That's surprising, Jed. And not at all like you," I said, hurt anew by his coolness toward Jessica. "I tell you what... I'll make it easier. I'll pretend that we've already made our farewells and you can just disappear as it's your habit to do. There's nothing either one of us can say that would make a bit of difference about the way we feel about each other."

His eyes, silver gray in the bright morning sunshine, narrowed slightly under my attack but he did not repay me in kind. His words came slowly, as if he had trouble forming them, and they lacked the casual drawl or the impatient tightness that most often marked his speech. In fact, I didn't recognize the tone at all and as I returned his look it seemed that once again I was allowed a glimpse of the man who had once existed beneath the shell.

"If you or the baby ever need anything, Meg, you get word to me or Alice and we'll do what we can to help."

A chill settled over me, although I realized what these words cost him. "Do you mean money, Jed? For a baby you can't ever be sure is yours? You'd allow us to come back into your life if we needed that kind of help? Well, that's a very generous offer, but no thank you, we won't be wanting anything at all from you." My voice was cold and he remained where he was, stiff and unmoving. In the morning shadows his face seemed sharply chiseled. Looking at him I remembered how I had feared him at first. At my reply, his eyes had turned hard. We had hurt each other. I had brought the past back to him, and he had flamed a love in me that was never meant to be. He had a winter heart, one that no one could touch. It was the worst possible time for the willful part of me to surface, but at this final parting of our ways I was struck by the overwhelming unfairness of it all and I wanted to strike back at Jed Tanner one more time. I wanted to break through the wall between us, to make him feel again, to wipe the cold formality from his face. It mattered only that my last memory of him not be one of indifference. And so very gently I laid Jessica beside me and rose to my feet.

He stood his ground, with an almost soldierly determination, as I came toward him, crossing the invisible boundary of space that allowed him to remain comfortably distant, until I was so close he had to look down to see my face. As I lifted my gaze to his stern features, he closed his eyes against me and then I knew that I had won, after all, as he attempted to hide his vulnerability. Encouraged, I touched his face with my fingers and his eyes opened, his expression unreadable in the gray depths. He held himself steady as if what I did was to be endured. But as I drew my fingers down his cheekbone, tracing the curve of his jaw and the tight line of his mouth, I detected the faintest of tremors. At that moment,

Jessica stirred, cooing softly. His eyes blazed at the sound and, as I dropped my hand, he gripped it tightly with his own. The pain of his grasp shot upward but I paid it no heed. The wounds that I had struck within him had begun to fester, but instead of the gladness I expected to feel there was only sorrow. The resentment slowly drained from me. As I lowered my head, his arms came around me, gathering me to him in a devastating farewell. The warmth of his body beneath the softness of his shirt turned me weak. His arms pressed me to him and I made no move to break his hold as we said our last good-byes. And then I came to my senses, gently withdrawing from his embrace.

"Good-bye, Jed."

The haunting eyes held mine a moment longer, and then he touched the brim of his hat and was gone.

Chapter Twenty-Nine

✏ AS THE CRISP AIR COLORED THE SUMMER'S END with autumn colors, the antagonism that brewed between Christina and me while I awaited Ben's arrival came to a head. Spitefully, she refused to answer my questions about Ben's condition, and the worry began to gnaw at me that Alice had not revealed the true extent of Ben's injuries.

"Why don't you leave the valley, Christina?" I asked her reasonably, after I had scanned the ridgetop for a sign of Ben late one afternoon. I dearly wished to put as much distance between Jessica and me and all of the Tanner holdings as I could.

She gave me a sullen look. "Because both Jed and Sam told me I was to stay with you!"

I looked at her curiously. "I can understand Sam thinking I might need looking after, but not Jed. Besides, he knows we don't get along. Why would he ask you to stay on with me?"

I drew back at the enmity in her face. Her blue

eyes thinned into slits, reminding me of a spitting cat. She looked at me haughtily. "There's a lot you don't understand, Meg," she said significantly.

I looked at her suspiciously, sensing a ruse. Christina wished to do battle with me. I turned away from her.

"You never should have come here, Meg," she said smoothly to my back. "It was a mistake. You can't have Jed, you know."

I froze at her brazenness, but when I turned to her my face was guarded.

"I don't want Jed, Christina," I responded calmly. "You're more than welcome to him."

She smiled at me. "He's always been mine. He may not realize it just yet, but he will. I waited a long time for him to come back. You never had a chance against me."

"Oh?" I said, arching my eyebrows. Christina was beautiful, but such conceit was unwarranted, even ludicrous. Her eyes gleamed and her lips twitched with a repressed excitement.

"You still don't know, do you?" she said goadingly. "They all managed to keep it from you, though I thought for sure that Alice would let it out. She can't stand me," she assessed proudly. A sly smile came to Christina's generous mouth, the only full feature of her delicate face, as she carefully watched my reaction to her words.

"Did you ever wonder, Meg, why Alice never got rid me?"

"What are you trying to tell me, Christina?" I asked, exasperated by the game she played.

"She runs the house, you know...but she knew, right from the start, that she couldn't ask me to leave. You might say that I'm part of the family."

She gave me a superior look, taking in my puzzlement.

"The last time Jed saw me, he wouldn't have noticed how alike we were. I was only twelve and he didn't have eyes for anyone but her."

"I don't understand, Christina. What does Julie have to do with this?"

"Why, it's simple, Meg," she said, giving me a challenging look. "I'm her sister."

Her resemblance to Julie had always astounded her father, she explained in the aftermath of my shock, mocking my surprise with a triumphant expression. Her mother had been a servant in his house, and when she had died, her father had taken Christina in to raise alongside his legitimate daughter. His wife was long used to his indiscretions. He had planned on sending her away to school, but Christina had attached herself to her older half-sister and refused to go. She had been too young to accompany Julie on her first visit to the ST and too young to go with her to Europe, but Julie had missed her and insisted on Christina joining her at the ST once she had married Jed. Julie was very sophisticated about some things, Christina claimed. No one was ashamed of those kinds of relationships on the continent and Julie had become a devotee of European custom. But then Christina's face hardened at the memory of her sister.

"She wasn't very smart when it came to Travis and Jed. I told her so, but she wouldn't listen to me. Julie said I was too young to understand such things." Christina's blue eyes held mine. "I didn't care if she did run off with Travis. I knew I was too young for Jed then, but it would have given him plenty of time to get over her and I planned to be here when he did. I felt badly when she was killed, but I never held it against either of them. She was as much to blame as they were.

"I stayed on at the ST after Julie died. I had no place to go. My father had died and Julie's mother had put up with me only for his sake. The Tanners continued to make me welcome. I ran things well enough until Cal brought Alice back to the ranch.

"It was my idea to move into the little cabin behind the main ranch house, the one Sam had lived in before he built the big house. I'd have a perfect view of Jed's window when he'd come back. I always knew he'd be back some day," she continued smugly, watching my face carefully.

I didn't want to hear anymore. It was all over. Settled. Nothing remained between Jed and me. Suddenly, I needed to be away from her and I reached up for my shawl. But Christina had several long months to make up for and she was determined to pay me back. She blocked my way as I went to retrieve Jessica from her cradle.

"You can't compete with me, Meg. You should have left long ago."

"That would have suited you, wouldn't it?" I said drily. "To have me lose the baby? You guessed right about Jessica, Christina. But if you worried about me coming between you and Jed, you were worried about the wrong woman."

She looked at me uneasily. "What do you mean?"

I felt the corners of my mouth quirk upward in what must have seemed to be a smile. "Does he ever call you by her name late at night when he holds you in his arms?" I asked her softly.

She looked at me with a murderous expression.

I shook my head at her. "He'll never marry you, Christina, if that's what you're waiting for. He wants to forget Julie. He could never do that with you."

Her face wore a mask of rage. "I don't believe you! You're just saying that because you couldn't hold him. Even with his baby!"

I winced at the hatred in her voice as I brushed her aside and picked up Jessica. Furious, she whirled me about, and then drew back at the expression on my face. The look must have been dreadful to have stopped her as it did, but my only concern was for my daughter.

She regained her composure with a shaky laugh. "You're lying, Meg. I know you are. But I won't do a thing to stop you. I'll leave you here, just like you want me to, and I don't give a damn what happens to you when he finds out."

I laid my hand on her arm and she pulled away from the touch. "What are you talking about, Christina? Jed's nowhere near here. How will he find out that you've left me here alone?"

"Jed?" Christina's wild laughter pealed through the room. "I'm not talking about Jed! It's Travis you have to worry about, Meg! He's been waiting a long time now to pay Jed back. And knowing Travis, I think you'll serve his purpose just fine. How very touching! The mother of Jed's baby!" With a sob, she turned and ran from the cabin. I watched from the window as she saddled her mare in the dusk that had settled over the valley. She would have no difficulty making her way back to the main ranch. Not the darkness nor all the forces of nature would venture to cross Christina tonight.

My suspicion that Christina had gone to Redmonton to seek out Travis became a certainty in the days that followed, for had she returned to the ranch, I knew Sam or Alice would have sent someone to stay with me. But they knew neither that I was alone in the valley with Jessica nor that Christina intended me to be the victim of Travis's long-sought revenge. In the clear gold days of autumn I awaited him, quietly coming to terms with the inevitable encounter. How could I not have expected it to take place? Travis had figured into my life since the very first time I saw Jed sitting on his horse by the road outside Cross Creek, just moments before the bullets struck.

So much a part of Jed's life, he was fated to become part of mine. Now I would pay the price of saving Jed's life. Christina would never bother to inform him that Jed would not mourn my loss.

I toyed with the idea of taking Jessica and riding for help before dismissing it as foolhardy and unwise. I wanted no one else to come to harm protecting me, as Tice had. And so I awaited Travis alone in the valley with nothing more than a fighting spirit, an infant daughter, and a loaded carbine.

In the end, I left the carbine in the cabin. It was not, as Alice suggested later, that I knew no fear. I had plenty of that, but it was all for Jessica. It was rather that I felt my best chances lay in catching Travis off-guard. At no time did I believe he would kill me on sight but rather I thought that he would toy with me first. Greeting him with my weapon would only alert him to my determination. I intended that Jessica and I would remain alive at any cost.

At sunset, just one week later, he finally arrived. I stared as he crested the ridge, a small black dot under fading ribbons of orange and red, losing him to the gentle swells of the valley as he urged his horse across the shadowed landscape. He sat on his horse erectly, without Ben's loose rein or Jed's easy grace. They drew closer, rising above the deep grass as they made their way toward me. I went to greet him empty-handed, standing resolutely in the swirl of dust stirred up by his horse. Travis dismounted easily, as if he had come from a neighboring house for a social call.

There was no reason to have believed that Travis would remind me of any of the Tanners. He was not related to them by blood. But somehow I thought he would carry some small resemblance, as if no one could live under Sam Tanner's roof for long without bearing his stamp upon his person. Travis did not. He was tall and dark and his skin did not have the pasty pall of the gamblers I had come across. He was tanned, but without the weathered quality that marked his brothers. There were no lines of weariness about the strong features of his face. Although he was six years older than Jed, he looked younger. But it was his eyes that drew my attention. They were dark, not black nor the deepest of browns, but rather opaque in color, so that the only life that would shine from them would be that of a reflected light. They were eyes that compelled one to silence.

He returned my look, making me uncomfortably conscious of Alice's simple dress, rather poorly taken in since Jessica's birth. I lifted my head under his studied look.

"Well, green-eyes," he said, as if suddenly amused by what he saw. "I think this is long overdue, don't you?"

"No, not especially." His voice was not unpleasant, but the smoothness was like a blank page. Underneath would be duplicity. I noted the holstered gun he wore strapped on his leg. His eyes followed the path of mine and when they met again he dismissed my self-possession with a casual nonchalance as if it were no more than a front.

"This is hardly the way to greet your—why, I guess we're nothing to each other, are we?" His tone was agreeable. It chilled me.

"And not likely to be," I retorted. I made just one vain attempt to dissuade him from his course. "You and I have nothing to say to each other, Travis. So why don't you turn around and ride out of here?"

"On the contrary, green-eyes. I think you and I have a lot to say to each other. After all, I'm sure you've heard a lot about me. And I've been waiting a long time for the pleasure of meeting you."

A long time. Yes, it had been a long time since Julie had died.

"My name is Meg Logan," I said disagreeably.

Civility would be a waste of time; it would get me nowhere. Inside the cabin, Jessica stirred. I raised my head at the sound but I did not go to her. He smiled at what he saw and I flashed him a challenging look.

"Why don't you see to your daughter, Meg Logan?" he suggested evenly. Taking his horse by the reins, he led him to the corral.

I tended to Jessica's needs, blotting all thoughts from my mind. I counted all her fingers and toes and buried my face in her sweet-smelling swaddling clothes as she gripped my finger with her little hand. I lit the lamp in the darkened cabin and went to the window. There was no sign of Travis, but his horse had been stripped of its gear and put in with the other horses. And then I started at the sound of his footsteps, even though I was expecting him. I returned Jessica to her cradle, trying not to stiffen as he entered the room. He walked over to us unhesitatingly and stared down at her small form. It was almost as if he were the father, so interested was he in her. Her blue-gray eyes were alert. She met his gaze with one of equal intensity.

"She's Jed's all right," he said, with no trace of doubt in his voice. I looked up at him, over the cradle. "How can you be so sure of that? He's not."

The dark features revealed nothing. "She looks like he did."

I looked at him in amazement. "You remember what Jed looked like when he was a baby? You were only a boy yourself!"

"I was six years old at the time and I've never forgotten it." He moved away from Jessica and went to the window, staring out at the dim shapes of the horses in the corral. "Why don't you fix me something to eat, Meg?" he asked abruptly. Grimly, I turned to the cookstove and ladled out a portion of

the supper stew. He removed his black frock coat
and seated himself at the table. Above the brocaded
waistcoat his shirt was a snowy white. My eyes fell
to his well cared-for hands and he took note of my
observation.

"You've heard about my penchant for cards?" he
asked.

"Yes."

"And cattle stealing?"

"Yes."

"Don't feel badly about it, it's all true." He didn't
say anything more but quietly ate what I placed
before him. When he emptied his bowl, I refilled it
without him asking me to. Finishing his second helping, he pushed away the dish and watched me with
an unwavering intensity as I poured him more coffee.

"Pour some of that for yourself," he commanded.
"I don't like to drink alone."

I was glad to see that my hand was steady as I
did what he said. He took a thin flask from an inside
pocket of his waistcoat and poured a measure into
the cup. Holding the flask out to me, he offered me
some, but I declined, shaking my hand, and he returned it to his pocket.

Sitting down across the table from him, I took a
deep breath, no longer content to await his next move.

"Travis," I began, looking at him directly, almost
desperately. His opaque eyes met mine with no difficulty. "How did all this begin? Why do you hate
Jed so? Why him and not Caleb?"

He gave me a cold look. "You forget, green-eyes,
that Caleb is my brother. Jed is nothing to me."

"So? Is that supposed to mean something to me?
What could Jed do to you? He couldn't have hurt
you. You've hated him all your life."

"You're wrong. He hurt me in a way that mattered
very much to me. He was a Tanner. What little interest Sam took in me died when he was born. There

was no more room in the house for Amanda's child. There was Caleb, and I suppose it was only right that he came first, though it's hard for a boy to understand by the mere circumstances of his birth that he'll be tolerated, but no more than that. It wasn't too bad until Jed came along. I was old enough to see how it was going to be, from then on. Sam may have despised his mother, but right away he started building up the south section for him, for the future, he said. Once I was older, I started to make up for it. I took the cattle I figured I had coming to me. But never more that I thought was my due," he added with an ironic note.

"That's a poor excuse, Travis," I said with a hard edge in my voice. "Maybe growing up among the Tanners wasn't easy for you, but don't expect any pity from me. You weren't the only one to grow up orphaned or alone."

"No? Then I suppose we have even more in common than I thought, green-eyes."

"Don't call me that!" I snapped at him. "I don't feel sorry for you, Travis. I feel sorry for myself, for ever having crossed with the Tanners and that includes you, too. And I'll tell you something else. If you think you can get back at Jed through me, you're wrong. He can't stand the sight of me. The baby means nothing to him. And if you think otherwise, you've been listening to Christina, and she's lying!"

"Ah," he said knowingly, "Well, I can see you feel the same way about each other. Tell me, Meg. Why should I believe you over Christina?"

"Because she loves Jed. She'd do anything to protect him. From you and me."

"And you don't?" he asked shrewdly, watching me closely. "You'd trade his life for your own? Because you know I'm going to pay him back. You'd save your own skin, is that what you're telling me?"

"No." I felt as if I were debating the devil himself.

"That's not quite right. You see, Travis, I don't think you intend to kill Jed, even if you tried to before. I think you intend to use me to make him suffer, to get him back for killing Julie."

An uneasy quiet fell over the small room. In the soft haze of the lantern light, it was obvious that Travis was still a handsome man. In a few years he would be forty. It was a long time to carry such a hate. He scrutinized me carefully.

"Why don't you let me be, Travis," I said at last, hating the pleading note in my voice. "I've done nothing to you."

He silenced me with a look. "Don't, Meg. You know I can't do that. He took from me the one person in this world that I cared about. In a way, I'm sorry, because I do like you."

"Damn it! You're sorry? That's not good enough, Travis! I have a baby to raise! By myself! Do you think that the Tanners would take her? And if, out of pity, they did, what would happen to her? They'd raise her to be like you and Jed. Twisted! Jed's no better off than you are, Travis. He's the coldest man I'd ever met until you came along. How you can sit there and tell me you're going to take your revenge out on me is something I'll never understand!"

Jessica, awakened from her sleep, began to cry at the sound by my harsh voice. I went to her and soothed her as Travis's cold eyes glittered at me. When at last she quieted, I returned to the table, but I did not sit down. I stood my ground and directed my words to him.

"You're a cruel man, Travis."

He smiled, as if I had offered him a compliment. "You have spirit, Meg. You remind me of Julie."

"Damn you! Don't say that!" I spat at him. "I'm not like her at all. I don't play with people, Travis. If I had loved you, you can be damned sure I wouldn't have married someone else because I got bored wait-

ing for you to come back! I wouldn't have played with
another man's feelings!"

This time he didn't smile. "No, you're right. I'm
sure you wouldn't have."

Why was he agreeing with me? Why did he toy
with me? I stared at him pensively, recalling all that
I remembered about him, and then I thought I knew.
He wanted an audience for his deed. Did he mean to
wait until Jed had returned to be a witness? I wet
my lips nervously, knowing I could not allow that to
happen. I sat down, trying to keep the knowledge
from my eyes.

"Travis?"

"Hmm?" His eyes lit on my face.

"There's just one more thing I want to know." Our
gazes held as I tried to determine the depth of his
hatred for Jed. "Was it your idea that Julie ride that
pinto? Did you hate Jed that much, even before he
shot Julie?"

His features darkened and his flat eyes did not
waver from mine. "What do you think, green-eyes?"
he asked, his voice fierce.

I ignored the goad, instead focusing intently on
his bitter face. "I don't think so, Travis. I don't think
that even you could do such a horrible thing."

His laugh was harsh. "You're wrong there. I did.
She claimed she could ride anything on the ranch. I
picked the pinto and she didn't even blink an eye.
We had to blindfold him and snub him to get him
saddled and Julie mounted on him. I turned him
loose and he pitched straight up into the air. She
stayed with him for two, maybe three jumps and then
it looked like she just let go." His voice turned quiet
and he ran his hand across his face as if trying to
erase the memory. "Christ, I thought she was dying.
There was the blood. I thought she had broken something inside. I didn't know about the baby until Doc

Bennett came out to the ranch. Damn it! I didn't know about it!"

I closed my eyes at the worst of Julie's betrayals and when I opened them again, I found Travis staring at me. "Then why, Travis, if she was like that, are you doing this? Is she worth it?"

"Yes! Damn it! She was flawed, like me. Am I worth it, Meg?" His torment demanded an answer.

"You're worth whatever price you put on yourself, Travis," I said. Somehow, I spoke calmly. "You know that Jed won't let you get away with this. It has nothing to do with me, does it? You just want to give Jed a reason to come after you. That's why you were waiting in Redmonton all this time, but he didn't take the bait. So you'll use me, instead. You want him to kill you, Travis. You want to die, because you, too, blame yourself for Julie's death."

He pushed back his chair and abruptly rose to his feet. Reaching across the table, he grabbed my arms, pulling me toward him.

"Do you have anything else you want to say to me?" His voice was a low growl.

"Yes!" I cried, wincing at the pain of his punishing grip. "Why don't you turn to Christina, like he does? Then maybe Julie will come back to you, too!"

He gave a cutting laugh. "You poor little fool. He doesn't go to her because of Julie. He goes to her to forget you!"

"What are you saying?" I gasped.

"Did he tell you once, like I did, that you reminded him of her?"

I nodded.

"It's not her he was remembering. You brought back to him the feeling of love. He was attracted to you and he wanted you. It scared the hell out of him."

"How do you know this?" I demanded.

"Damn it, haven't you been listening to what I've been saying? It's because we're alike, Jed and me.

You've seen that for yourself. I was orphaned and he might as well have been. Jed and I have always wanted the same thing."

I whimpered slightly under his burning gaze. How could I ever have thought his eyes lifeless? He released my arms and I fell back to my seat across the table, my face in my hands.

"You're right, Meg. It was an unlucky day when you ran into us. You're paying a hard price for it."

I looked up to find the same bleakness in his eyes that I had seen so often in Jed's. "That's not true," I said softly. "I've got Jessica." He saw the mute appeal in my face. "She doesn't have to grow up like the rest of us, Travis. It's up to you."

I never told him that my feelings for the man I fought for so desperately were no more than a heart-breaking memory. Travis was gone before either Jessica or I stirred the next morning.

Chapter Thirty

CHRISTINA'S PLAN MAY HAVE FAILED in her intended purpose, but it succeeded only too well in bringing Jed and me to final blows. His honest concern and good intentions exploded into violent anger, destroying my last hope that Travis's interpretation of Jed's feelings for me had been accurate.

Ben filled in the details when I returned to the main ranch. Christina, suffering from a belated fit of conscience, had confessed the part she played in bringing Travis to the valley. She had remained behind in Redmonton so that no one would tie her visit to town with Travis's sudden appearance in the north valley. Within twenty-four hours of his departure, unaccountably guilt-stricken, she had ridden back to the ST hoping to salvage anything she could of the situation she had helped to create. She was unaware of the fact that Jed, having had a premonition of trouble, had left his consignment of army horses with his men and turned back, purposely riding through Redmonton looking for Travis. What he learned there had sent the sparks flying under his horse's hooves as he headed back to the ST.

Although Christina was more than half a day's ride ahead of Jed, she had scarcely more than an hour's lead when she returned to the ranch house and spilled her tale to Ben. Wasting no time once he found out what Christina had done, Ben hobbled out to the stable and managed to bridle and saddle a horse. Jed came upon him as he tried to mount a skittish beast that eyed his stiff cast nervously. As Jed threw his saddle on a fresh horse, he bluntly rejected Ben's offer of assistance. Not that he had been wrong to, because a crippled man would slow him down or have to be left behind. Still, Ben didn't see it that way and proved to be as stubborn as Jed when he was told to keep out of his business. The last thing Ben remembered was Jed telling him that he'd be bringing me back to the ST no matter what. Then Jed sent a blow to Ben's jaw that succeeded in knocking him out long enough for Alice and Christina to drag him back to the house with strict orders not to let him near a horse.

Meanwhile, I was watching the horse and rider race against the pale edge of the horizon before they disappeared in a downward sweep, never dreaming that it might be Jed. The gentle curves of the valley bottom hid his breakneck speed and it wasn't until they swerved from the trail, fording a creek in a lunging leap, bypassing the the road for a more direct route, that my eyes widened in recognition at the faultless grace of the rider on the dun horse. He brought the lathered stud to a complete standstill just inches from where I stood, the foam from the horse's mouth spraying my clothing with a frothy moisture. He held the blowing animal steady as his eyes searched the clearing and the bordering fringe of trees before dropping them back to me.

"You're all right?"

"Yes, I'm fine."

"The baby?"

"She's inside, sleeping."

I watched the relief come to his strained features. I knew that he had pushed the dun hard from the ranch, but I could not know that his ride from Redmonton had been a duplication of the wild trip years back when he had learned of Julie's miscarriage and Travis's return at the same time.

Dismounting, he walked the heated stud, cooling him as he scanned the grounds for signs of Travis, avoiding the question he had to ask almost as if he were afraid of it. He turned to me roughly and stared, frightening me with the savageness I saw in his face. My skin prickled its awareness of him as I took in his eyes, red-rimmed from sleepless nights, and the lean cheeks caked with a layer of sweat-streaked dust. His clothing was damp with the horse's lather.

"What happened?" he demanded, his voice a throaty rasp, thick with trail dust.

I saw with my own eyes the direction his thoughts were taking as the emotions played across his face for me to see. But rather than say the words that would take him out of the past and bring him into the present, I held back, reacting instead with hostility to the doubt that preyed upon him. Jed did not trust me. He never would trust me. I could never change that and there would never be more than this for us. At the terrible question in his eyes, I ran from him in fear, afraid of the hurt he would inflict. I wanted to set us free from a lifetime of pain and mistrust.

"Nothing happened," I answered, straining for a lightness in my voice. "He came the night before last and was gone by morning."

His eyes sharpened as he stopped in his tracks, pulling me around to face him. "Did he hurt you?"

"No. You can see for yourself that I'm all right."

His concern turned dark with suspicion and his blazing eyes narrowed to slits as he considered my words. He sought evidence of the vengeance he knew Travis would have exacted from me. Disappointed, he looked away.

I had been right. He had again assumed the worst about me. He would rather have found me raped, beaten, bruised, or perhaps even dead, than know that I had let Travis have his way with me. He believed that I had gone to him willingly, like Julie. He couldn't very well go after a man for indulging himself in a woman who had welcomed his embrace. It was impossible for him to believe it had been as I said, that nothing had happened.

"Get the baby," he said in a voice that stung like a whip. "I'm taking you out of here."

He barely glanced at Jessica as I brought her from the cabin, but he helped lash the cradleboard to my back and brought Coalie to me for mounting. We departed the secluded valley in silence. I trained my eyes straight ahead between Coalie's dark ears, ignoring the pull of sadness as we climbed the wooded slope from the valley floor. Strapped to my back, Jessica looked out in fascination at the fringe of green and gold that marked our trail. The dun, recovered from his punishing run, picked his way alongside of us as Jed's detached features were lost in his private musings.

"How's Ben?" I asked, breaking the silence between us, my concern overriding the distaste for conversation. Suddenly I found myself longing for Ben's easygoing ways. I had not seen him since spring and Jessica was now seven weeks old.

Jed's reaction was swift. He gave an ugly laugh as his mocking eyes met mine. "You do beat all, Meg. You even find time to worry about Ben. Well, he's just fine. Of course, he was fixed on coming with me.

I had to persuade him that it wasn't in his best interests. I didn't want him interfering." And then Jed's voice lost the mocking note.

"Travis is mine," he said tightly. "It makes it awkward going after him now, you being so accommodating to him, but I'll pay him back before long."

I pulled up Coalie sharply, my fast-rising rage sending the words to my lips. "That's right, Jed," I cried. "You save Travis for yourself. What really bothers you about all of this is that now you don't have a good excuse to go after him, isn't that right? Did it ever occur to you that if something had happened to me it might be Ben's right to settle it with Travis? After all, you had all those years to pay him back for Julie. You don't really need me as a reason. You want Travis just as much as he wants you and it doesn't have anything at all to do with me."

"You don't know what you're talking about," he said fiercely.

"Oh, don't I? Maybe I understand more than you think I do. Travis did a lot of talking the other night."

As I urged Coalie forward, he grabbed the reins, halting him.

"He told you how it was and you let him—"

"Let him what, Jed? Why don't you say it?"

A low, bitter sound worked itself free from his throat. "Travis always was good at talking. He talked his way in and out of things so fast you'd hardly know he'd been there." He smiled at me with contempt. "Is that how it was with you, Meg?"

"No. I don't have to explain anything to you, Jed. You'll never change so it doesn't matter to me what you believe. But you are right about one thing. Travis is good with words. Much better, in fact, than you are. It only took me a few hours to figure him out. It would take more than a lifetime to do the same with you and I'm not even sure I'd understand you then."

He gave me an odd look, but his mind was still set on my betrayal. In anger, I struck the final blow.

"I know you'll always have your reasons for hating Travis, just as you have your reasons for hating me. But you can add another one to them if you want. You see, in spite of everything I heard about him, I rather liked Travis, Jed. At least he's honest. He doesn't lie to himself about anything he does. That's more than I can say for you."

With those words, I broke the slim thread of communication between us. Giving me a brutal look, Jed set his heels to the dun and left me behind to follow, as I would, the trail back to the main ranch.

Lifting her skirts high as she spotted us from the wide porch of the house, Alice flew down the steps and across the stableyard past the spot where Jed swung down from the dun. She crossed the short distance to where I brought up the rear of our small procession.

"Oh, Meg! I was so worried! When we found out what Christina had done...thank goodness you're all right!" Alice's words tripped lightly over one another, and then she turned to look at Jed. "You can't imagine what kind of bear Ben has been to take care of, Jed, after he came to..."

"Hello, Alice." Jed's greeting could not have been more reserved.

Confused, she looked back at me and, without further word, Jed led the dun away. She placed a hand on my arm, giving me a probing look, as I eased myself out of the saddle as Jessica slept on. Then the bruised, smiling face of Ben Trew was there, welcoming me back, and with a deep cry of gladness, I went into his arms. He put me from him almost at once, turning me around so that he could see Jessica for the first time. At the sudden activity she woke with a fretful wail. Ben grinned as he beheld her

face, and the pleasure that should have been Jed's
fell to him. He freed her from the cradleboard, and
as her wail became a screaming, hungry protest,
Alice rescued Ben from the confusion, shooing him
away as she promised him he could see us later after
we had rested and freshened up. Ben's eyes followed
us regretfully as we left him, but he did not try to
stop us. A baby took some getting used to, especially
a vocal one like Jessica.

The house was empty as we crossed the wide hall
and climbed the stairway to the bedroom on the second floor.

"I was hoping that Jed would bring you back before nightfall. I had this room readied for you," Alice
said. Softly she opened a door to a beautifully appointed bedchamber, different from the one I had
occupied during my first stay at the ranch house. As
Jessica quieted in my arms, I crossed the room and
stood at the window that overlooked the eastern rim
of Sam Tanner's valley. "This is a beautiful room,
Alice," I commented, turning back after a moment
to admire the elegant high-postered bed and the rich
furnishings that graced the walls. My eye fell to a
beautifully carved cradle on the far side of the bed.

"Jake, Jed's grandfather, made that for him before
he was born. I thought it would be nice if Jessica
could sleep in it, even if it were just for a little while,"
Alice commented, noting my face. "It'll be at least a
week before Doc Bennett comes back this way. I expect he'll tell Ben he can ride, then."

Then Alice's composure slipped. "Oh, Meg, I'm
sorry," she said almost tearfully. "I should have
known what Christina was up to. When I found out
that Travis had gone to the valley looking for you,
I could have killed her myself. To think she did it
on purpose! You know Sam almost sent her away,
after he found out what happened." She looked at

me. Her face clouded, and she continued with difficulty. "But I might as well tell you this now. Ben—
Ben asked him not to. He told Sam that Christina
couldn't have known what she was doing at the time.
In fact, that's exactly what she told Ben after she
returned to the ranch. Sam finally sent her to help
the cook out at the roundup site, but until then, she
spent most of her time with—Ben."

I sank down into a chair. It seemed Christina would
always be involved with the men closest to me. I
wondered if she had turned to Ben because she sensed
she had lost Jed. "Well, then," I said, forcing cheer-
fulness into my voice, "perhaps Ben will want to stay
on here, if he's formed an attachment for her."

Alice frowned at my words. "She's just playing
with him. I think she's doing it to get back at you."
She laughed at the sound of Jessica's milky bubble,
before a wistful expression came to her face. "I can't
bear the thought of not watching her grow up, Meg.
You know, I never gave up hoping that things would
work out between you and Jed. But I can see from
his mood that things haven't changed." At my dark
look, Alice sighed resignedly.

"I almost forgot, this came for you a while ago."
Alice dug her hand into her pocket and produced a
letter that was addressed to Jed. I looked at Doc's
familiar handwriting, but did not take it from her.
She handed it to me. "Jed said that it was really for
you after he read it. He told me to keep it until you
came through here. I guess he would have given it
to you himself if he had known he was going to see
you again."

I lay it atop the dresser to read later.

"Sam is expected back for supper. Will you join
us?" Alice asked evenly.

"Not tonight, Alice. I'm tired." I could not bear
the thought of facing Sam Tanner that night.

She gave me a close look. "You can't hide away

in this room until Ben is ready to leave, Meg. If you're worried about running into Jed, don't be. He's hardly ever around, and now that he has some of the boys delivering the horses for him, he'll be helping with the roundup. He intends to go on the drive after that. I guess he'll probably send one of the hands to keep an eye on things in the valley for him while he's away."

As usual, she knew me too well. But even Jed's absence could not induce me to share a meal with his father. What I had learned in the north valley about the stiff, self-righteous old man had only intensified my dislike for him. "Maybe tomorrow," I said to Alice, committing myself to no more than that as I put off the inevitable for another day.

Chapter Thirty-One

✍ MY RETURN TO THE RANCH HOUSE WAS
accepted by the entire Tanner family with little comment. Occupied with the fall roundup, they had little
time or thought to spare me. And no matter how the
Tanner servants regarded me, they did not hold Jessica's rather inauspicious beginnings against her.
Melting at the sight of Jessica lying sweetly in Jed's
old cradle, Sylvie never again complained about
bringing me my meals after my first night back at
the ranch, and she came to treat me in the same
manner in which any wayward member of the Tanner family was treated.

The letter from Doc was a comfort. He had written
Jed requesting information of my whereabouts. A
year had passed, he wrote, since the incident at Cross
Creek and, although he could not assure that my
reception in town would be without comment, he
would welcome me back if I had an interest in returning. But Doc did not know about Jessica, and

the gossip might be a bit stronger than he had anticipated. I hesitated to write him back until I was certain what my plans were, but I could no longer put off my meeting with Ben.

Apprehensively, I met with him outside the deserted bunkhouse and told him about Doc's letter. I found my eyes returning to his face. He had discarded the heavy growth of beard during the heat of summer and the weeks of inactivity had not paled the sun-browned skin. Although the jutting, clean-shaven jaw was strange to me, its strength matched the forcefulness in the depths of his blue eyes and it was impossible to look away from him. If I thought that Alice's hint about Ben's interest in Christina would make my task any easier, I was wrong. With a thrust of brutal honesty, he effortlessly ripped through the illusions I had allowed myself.

"So you're going back to Cross Creek," he commented, curiously undisturbed by my decision.

"I thought I might, at least for a little while, until I get my bearings."

"Is it because of Christina?" he asked pointedly.

I shook my head. "If there is something between you and Christina, Ben, it's my fault. I wouldn't blame you for turning to her." I stumbled awkwardly over my next words. "I'm over Jed, just like you said I would be," I said, acknowledging the emptiness that had come to replace the burning desire I once had for Jed. "But it's still no good, Ben. He'd always be between us, reminding us of how it was." I met his gaze as the tears welled in my eyes. "I do love you, Ben, but it's not enough. I loved him more and you'd always be wanting a part of me that I can't give you."

"I'm surprised at you, Meg," he said, "if you let yourself believe that's the reason you're turning me down."

I looked at him confused.

"You might say I expected this all along, at least since you've been here, on Tanner land." His blue eyes were candid. "It didn't take but one look at you and Jessica to know how things stand with you, Meg. If you can't have Jed, you'll give all your love to Jessica. You don't have room for anyone else in your life now that you have your baby. You've done more than just put Jed from your life, Meg. It's not just me that you don't want anymore. You won't let yourself want anyone again."

An unnatural quiet fell between us and I felt a sudden coldness in the air, as if the sun had already set behind the jagged mountain peaks.

"Oh, no, Ben," I said softly, devastated by his cold pronouncement. "You're wrong."

He met my mute appeal straightforwardly. "Am I, Meg?" I lowered my head, unable to face the plain-spoken love in his eyes and he picked up my hand, comforting me with his unvoiced loyalty. "I'll see you to Cross Creek, if that's the way you want it," he said finally. "As soon as Doc Bennett says I can travel."

"Thank you, Ben," I said. But when I left him, his haunting words stayed with me, and I wondered if he was right.

I grew restless waiting for Doc Bennett's arrival at the ST. Perceptively, Alice sought to keep me occupied as my restiveness passed itself on to Jessica. Against my better judgment, she talked me into accompanying her to the roundup site, making light of my misgivings. After my bitter exchange with Jed, I had no desire to meet up with him again.

We caught sight of the drifting curl of smoke that marked the roundup grounds long before the din of the cattle reached our ears and the gray blanket of rising dust clouded our eyes. Jessica slept soundly in her cradleboard, lulled to sleep by Coalie's even gait. Halting by a stand of trees that bordered the site, we looked on in fascination as the confusion sorted itself out into an assortment of smoothly co-ordinated activites.

"See those cattle over there?" Alice nodded with her head. I turned in the direction of the small cluster of red and white animals she indicated. "Those are Jed's. They're herefords. Ben picked them up for us this summer. They were at the '76 fair in Philadelphia. Jed's crossing them with Sam's shorthorns and plans on throwing a little longhorn into the mix, too. He thinks that they'll withstand the mountain climate and bring top dollar at market. He's pulling the bulls off the range for the winter," she advised me knowledgeably, proud of her membership in the cattle-dependent Tanner clan.

I turned away from the placid white-faced animals, afraid I might find Jed riding among them. Alice caught my pained look. "I'm sorry, Meg. I wasn't thinking..."

But there was no time to be lost in worrying of chance encounters. Amidst the several thousand head of cattle and bobbing heads of the ST riders, our attention was captured as a calf was singled out and roped with the utmost precision and then dragged unwillingly to the branding ground. A cowboy on foot broke from the group standing by the fire. Grabbing the calf, he expertly flipped him over on his side. Sitting on the animal's head, he positioned him for the other two hands standing by with a hot iron and knife for the branding, ear marking, and castrastion, all swiftly completed in a moment's time. As frantic as the pace was, the ST riders had an easier job than the hands on the other spreads. A wall of high mountains circled the valley, making it unlikely that strays would wander from or into Sam Tanner's domain. There was no need for the neighboring outfits to send their representatives to the ST roundup, and any strays Sam found were sold along with his own cattle. The brand was noted for later payment to the proper owner.

Sam Tanner spotted us almost immediately; but it was not Alice mounted on her cream-colored pony whom he noticed as he pointed his horse toward us, deftly dodging the men and animals in his path. Instead, his eyes fell to me, dressed in my buckskin breeches and a woolen jacket Alice had given to me to ward off the chill. Judging by its vintage and size, it had belonged to Caleb when he was a boy.

"Are you interested in cattle, Miss Logan?" he inquired over the sound of the bawling cattle, brushing a sleeve across a face stung by grit as the odor of burnt hair and dust from the milling herd thickened the air.

"I was thinking how fortunate it is that you aren't troubled by homesteaders, Mr. Tanner," I replied honestly.

Sam Tanner gave me a canny look. "That's right, I'd almost forgotten. You're Seth Elliot's girl. He raised you. It was you that was involved in that ruckus down in Cross Creek."

Stung by the unexpected attack, I tightened my fingers on Coalie's reins and he tossed his head nervously. But any retort that might have come to my lips remained unspoken as Sam's eyes went past me and then suddenly I found myself looking over my shoulder to see a pale rider on a dun horse in the haze of dust. As Sam voiced a welcome, I noted he watched me all the while.

"Looks like we've got some guests, son," he said as Jed drew up his horse beside us. "You think maybe you'd like to show them around? Randy's riding that little blue roan. The girls might enjoy watching a top cutting horse at work."

I barely heard Alice's reaction, for Jed's eyes had settled on my face and dropped to the jacket I was wearing, and suddenly I knew that it had been his, not Caleb's. He sat the dun casually, his long-limbed frame speaking his indifference.

"I hope you don't mind if I don't stay, Alice," I said in an even voice. Jed Tanner and I had nothing further to say to one another. "I think this dust is too much for Jessica." I saw her protest begin to form, but then, spying Cal, a wide smile broke upon her face and in the fleeting moment I was forgotten. Pulling Coalie's head about, I turned him in the direction of the ranch.

"Meg!" Once more I was face to face with Jed as he rode up beside me. "I'll ride back with you to the house, if you want," he offered coolly.

"No, it's not necessary, Jed. I can find my own way, but thank you," I said politely, looking into his unsmiling features. His lips tightened in a bitter line and then without a backward glance I set my heels to Coalie and put him in the direction of the crisp, clean air beyond the roundup site.

Doc Bennett's expected visit did not come and there was still no word of his arrival. There had been no other encounters with any of the Tanner men, and for this I was grateful, until the day Alice relayed Sam Tanner's summons to join his family that evening at supper. There was no reason for Sam to insist upon my attendence, so I dismissed Alice's invitation lightly, not counting on her troubled eyes to work on me the way Sam knew they would.

"I know how you feel about the rest of the family, Meg, but please, would you do it for me? Sam, well, he gets difficult when he's crossed. It's nothing I can't usually handle, but he seems out of sorts lately. He's hard to be around. He and Cal just returned and I think he feels like celebrating the end of the roundup. He made a special point of telling me to make sure you were there."

Seeing the dark look that came to my face, she drew back. Instead of pressing me further, she turned her attention to Jessica, who lay peacefully in my arms. She looked at the baby wistfully. I knew how much she longed for a child of her own.

"Her eyes are changing," Alice said softly. "They're almost gray, now." I stared down at Jessica and saw that she was right. They were just the color I would have imagined Jed's eyes to have been when he was a baby—a soft, serious gray before they had hardened to the color of storm clouds. I remembered Travis's reaction to Jessica and her likeness to Jed. Suddenly, a coldness settled upon me as I thought of Sam's dinner invitation. I looked at Alice sharply.

"Do you think Sam has any idea that Jessica is his grandaughter?"

She looked at me in surprise. "Of course not. Everyone assumes that Ben is the father. If he did," she said with a sigh, "I'm sure he would never let you leave here. Everyone knows how much he wants to continue the Tanner name. I know he's disappointed that I haven't already."

A nagging suspicion remained. Why had Sam insisted on my presence at supper that night? What if he did know? I tried to control my fear. There was little about me that should interest Sam Tanner. My possessions were few: a borrowed horse, some worn clothing, and a beloved child. Jed Tanner had taken everything from me that I had to give. Alice's words echoed in my mind. If his father knew about Jessica, would he try to take her from me? I regarded Alice intently. "Do you think that Christina might have told him?"

"Never," she stated positively. "Christina would be delighted if she could provide a grandchild for Sam. She'd never let on that you already have."

Alice's face clouded and she fell silent.

"I'm sorry, Alice," I said gently. "I shouldn't have brought it up. I know it's painful for you."

"You're being silly, Meg," she said with an unwavering look. "Christina wants Jed's baby so she can be part of the Tanner family. I already am. If Cal felt the way Sam does, it would bother me, but he doesn't. I want a baby for my own reasons. I don't care about heirs or the Tanner land. I've grown to love the ST, but I'd be happy with Cal no matter where we were. I'm not like Christina. I don't have to prove I belong here."

But Alice's distress still marked her face. Knowing how much I owed her, I forced out my next words. "Will Jed be there tonight, Alice?"

She gave me a knowing look. "He didn't come in with the others, Meg. Cal said he left early this morning to drive his strays back to the valley before the storm breaks." She cast a look through the window at the threatening sky.

"All right," I agreed reluctantly. "I'll be there, then. But I'm only doing it to make it easier for you, Alice. Not for Sam."

She gave me a warm hug. "Thank you," she said gratefully. She laughed at my expression, for I doubted very much that my presence would add to the occasion. "We dress for dinner, Meg. I have something that's perfect for you to wear," she said, wrinkling her nose at my breeches. "Sylvie will be happy to look after Jessica for you. She's the only thing that comes near to putting a smile on that woman's face."

She left me then, departing with a lighthearted step. Alice had a knack for arranging things. I had a feeling she would try to do the same to my life if I would only let her.

The sky darkened ominously that afternoon, permeating the house with gloom. Jessica's usually sunny nature for some reason reflected the gloom as if she sensed my unease. She arched her little back stiffly, defying my attempts to soothe her, until at last the dour-faced Sylvie came to me unbidden, giving me a reproachful look as Jessica quieted immediately in her arms. I uttered a strangled sound of thanks and fled from the oppressive house.

Ignoring the rising wind that blew across the valley and the words of warning from the stablehands, I headed Coalie toward the meadowland, giving him his head as Doc had so often loved to do. But the horse was nervous as if he, too, had sensed something in the air. My suspicions ran rampant. What if Sam did know about Jessica? Suppose, unbeknownst to Alice, he intended to take Jessica from me and give her to his beautiful daughter-in-law, who had shown no signs of producing an heir to carry on the Tanner name? Ashamed of myself for such a ridiculous, unfounded notion, I turned Coalie back toward the ranch.

Upon my return to the house I spied Alice, warned by my approaching footsteps down the long corridor, emerging from my bedroom. She flushed guiltily, coming up short before my disbelieving eyes.

"Alice!" I exclaimed coldly, as she fell victim to my overwrought imagination. "What on earth are you up to?"

She bit her lip under my reproachful stare. "Oh, Meg," she said, her rosy color giving her away and increasing my alarm that something was indeed amiss. In answer, she threw open the door, exposing the bed to my eyes. "I was afraid to give it to you myself because I thought you might not accept it. But I had it made.... I've had it ready for you ever since Jessica was born. I thought that maybe if you just found it like that, you'd wear it tonight without any questions, and afterward you wouldn't mind accepting it as a gift."

Across the white coverlet lay a dress of pale, dusty blue, the color of the sky just before it fades away to dusk. The neckline was a simple square cut edged in narrow bands of ivory lace that matched the trim on the long-sleeved cuff. The plain, unadorned skirt fell gracefully in soft folds from the fitted bodice. Breathtakingly beautiful, it was at the same time exquisitely simple.

"I thought it would suit you," I heard her say warmly before she rushed on. I was overwhelmed by her kindness and generosity. "It wouldn't be very hard to pack. It won't take up much room at all." Slowly, a smile came to my face that even the thought of Sam Tanner could not take away.

It was, I told myself later, a combination of the beautiful dress, Alice's efforts, and the last rays of sunset piercing the thinning clouds that made me look as I did that night. The dress flattered me in an unaccustomed way as it subtly exposed the fluid lines of my figure and revealed an expanse of flawlessly smooth skin at the neck and shoulders. At Alice's soft knock at the door, I turned from the mirror to greet her.

But Alice was nothing if not a perfectionist. Ignoring the beautiful gown, she gave a cry of chagrin. "You can't wear your hair like that!" she said, closing the door behind her. I turned back to my reflection in the cheval mirror, my hair looking much as it usually did, the newly washed tresses spilling down my back in an exuberant abundance. Without another word, Alice took the brush from my surprisingly unresisting hand. Magically twisting lengths here and there, she lifted them away from my face into an elegant chignon at the nape of my neck, securing it with hairpins suspiciously convenient in the waist of her pale mauve gown.

It was a stranger's face that stared back at me.

With the long sweep of hair pulled back and confined, I saw the fine-boned features as if for the first time. With the radiance of the sunset upon them, my eyes shone green and gold beneath the arched brows. The light gleamed softly across my sloping cheekbones, illuminating the few remaining freckles that danced across the top of the straight nose. My lips were parted slightly, as if surprised by what my eyes saw, and the pointed chin was poised challengingly at the image it faced. The features were more clearly drawn than I remembered them, as if a slightly blurred photograph had been brought into sharper focus. It was not a face where wistful dreams might find a home, and while there was no trace of vulnerability, neither was there hardness. I had endured all the difficulties of the journey westward, Cross Creek, and the north valley. I would survive, too, this evening with Sam Tanner.

Chapter Thirty-Two

✍ I DECIDED, AS WE PAUSED AT THE ENTRANCE to
the sitting room, that it was his years away at school
that had enabled Caleb Tanner to withstand his father's ways. He stood at the window, with his back to
Sam, as his father's disgruntled voice raised itself in
volume. Caleb listened wordlessly to the unbroken
tirade, seemingly not in the least bit intimidated by
the verbal upbraiding he was receiving. Wearing a
plain brown frock coat, it was obvious that he did
not have Alice's fondness for fashionable attire. He
possessed the same thick, solid strength of his father,
so different from Jed's tall, rangy build. But as evi-
denced by Alice's adoring look, there was little else
he shared in common with Sam Tanner. At Alice's
discreet cough, he turned, his mouth lifting upward
in a smile as he came forward to meet us.

Sam downed the contents of his whiskey glass, his
cold stare falling on me as Sylvie took Jessica from
my arms and Caleb escorted Alice and me to the

matching sea-green wing chairs positioned comfortably in front of the mantled hearth. Abruptly, he gave his attention back to his son.

"Can you tell me why in hell you pulled Grady and Joe off the herd? Where's your head, boy? Couldn't you have given 'em a few weeks, until those steers are at least trailwise? And for what? Hayin'? Suppose they stampede? Damn it, Cal, they'll be short two men!"

Caleb met his father head on. "Don't get your hackles raised, Pa. You know that every time Clete's predicted an early storm he's been right. He claims he feels one comin' on. It's his joints, he says. The other boys can manage without Grady and Joe for a few days. This way, if Clete's right, you won't get stuck with a herd of starving beef come winter. You know you can't count on Jed's range to winter all your stock."

Sam glowered at his son. "I'm telling you that Clete's been wrong before. That old buzzard's too old to be making predictions like that. Hell, I bet all his bones and joints ache. Mine would too if they'd been busted as many times as his!"

Cal gave a shout of laughter. "Hell, Pa, Clete's the same age as you and nobody's putting you out to pasture yet!"

Sam scowled at his son's humor. Then, his spleen vented, he turned his attention to me. His face tightened as he looked down upon me, his eye taking in every detail of my appearance.

"You're looking very lovely tonight, Meg," he said with a small smile that sent apprehension running through me. "I hope you don't mind me calling you that. In spite of Alice's influence, we still manage to be quite informal around here." He nodded assessingly at the elegant room and I noted the handsome secretary behind him as well as the rich sheen of the satin-backed occasional chairs that caught the gleam of light from a lamp sitting atop a Pembroke table.

"I don't mind, Mr. Tanner," I responded carefully, wary at this sudden show of rough charm. He would have been amused, I think, had he realized the fearful dimensions he had attained within my mind. "You've been very kind to us. I'm afraid that Ben and I have presumed upon your hospitality for too long."

"We were shorthanded this spring," he countered drily. "Ben Trew was a real help to us. Accidents like that can happen to anyone. Glad it wasn't any more serious than it was. Of course," he said, his eyebrows lifting sardonically, "I can't speak for Jed. I've never seen him worse tempered than since you've been around. Hell, he won't talk to anyone, 'cept maybe Alice here. But you can't say I didn't warn you about going to the north valley."

At Sam's discerning look, I bit back my retort. As if he wanted to test my mettle, he continued. "Now, I want you to understand that I don't feel that way myself. Me, and the rest of the family, too, well, we're only too happy to have you and your baby staying on with us. It's just what this big old house needs. Some young blood to amuse those of us that are just beginning to feel our age. Isn't that right, Alice?"

Alice stiffened under his indirect attack. But she quickly caught the angry set of Cal's face and sent him a warning look. In spite of Alice's almost fragile beauty, she was not afraid of her father-in-law. However, while she might have been willing to put up with his boorish ways, I was not. Of all of the things I had expected from Sam Tanner, I had not thought to be used as a means to hurt Alice. My anger unleashed a reckless impertinence.

"I'm afraid I don't agree with you, Mr. Tanner," I heard myself say in a steady voice that gave no indication of my inner turmoil. "You see, I don't believe that children are meant to be an amusement for their elders. Children are a responsibility and they should be loved and nurtured by their parents, so that when they grow up they are whole and strong and capable of loving in return."

Alice and Cal looked on in shocked silence as Sam's face became livid under his weathered tan. Not only had I struck a blow for Alice, but at the same time I had put the blame for the breach that existed between Sam, Jed and Travis squarely on Sam's shoulders. Meeting the old man's level gaze, I regarded him frankly. An inscrutable expression came to the craggy features and then he spoke to me calculatingly.

"I can see you're Seth's girl, all right. You may not be his blood kin, but you have his way about you. All those damned principles." I looked at him curiously, detecting a certain animosity at the mention of Doc's name.

"Doc ever tell you that he knew me?" he asked sharply.

"He said he was a friend of the family," I replied.

Sam grimaced. "That's not quite true. We were never friends. He and I never saw eye to eye. Seth courted Jed's mother briefly, the year before I married her. He asked her to marry him, but she didn't want to leave her father, Jake, alone in the north valley. He never did have the makings of a rancher," he added crustily.

"He's a fine doctor, Mr. Tanner," I said in an acid voice. Deeply resentful of this attack on Doc, I felt the last of my caution disintegrate.

Sam went on as if I had not spoken. "It must have been nigh on eleven years before he came back this way, asking about Rachel. The townspeople did some talking and he came here looking for her. Damned if he wasn't ready to take me on for what had happened to her all those years ago. If it hadn't been for

Jed, hell, I don't know what would have happened. He and the boy took to each other. He stayed on for a while, then he left. I'll be honest with you. I didn't much care for him. I didn't like the way he came in here and got on with my boy better than I did."

"And with his mother before that?"

It was a stroke that drew blood. Sam Tanner's eyes narrowed dangerously at my impudence as Cal jumped to my defense.

"Now, Pa, I'm sure Meg didn't mean any-thing—"

"Like hell she didn't! I bet she's never held her tongue in her life! Have you girl?"

"I probably haven't, Mr. Tanner," I said without remorse.

"Well, Meg, let's be blunt, then," he said shrewdly, "since that's the way you seem to like things." He paused, and in the weighty silence, I knew Sam had finally come to the purpose behind his summons to supper that evening. "You mind telling us exactly why you're here? Jed was never easy to get along with, but ever since he's come back to the ST and especially since you've been here, things are worse than they've ever been. Now, I think you have some-thing to do with that, and I want to know the reason for it."

"I'm sorry you feel I'm responsible for the way he is, Mr. Tanner," I replied evasively, determined he should not learn the truth about Jessica. "But I'm afraid that any problems you have with him are not my fault. I've only known Jed a short while."

Years of frustration and anger erupted in Sam Tanner. "Well, there's not a damned thing wrong with Cal!" he bellowed. "At least one of my sons isn't ashamed to call me Pa!"

"Leave her alone, Sam," a cool voice said. "It's a little late to be playing father to me. Like she says, this is none of her doing."

None of us had heard him come in. He stood at the threshold of the room, an aloof figure beyond the intimate circle of soft light. He looked much the way he did any night in the north valley, tall, dark, shadowy, never at the center of my life but always at the fringe, so that I could not claim him but neither could I forget him. He wore a dark blue wool shirt and carried his jacket casually over his shoulder. His weathered skin was reddened by the fierce bite of the wind and his eyes were deep pools of darkness as they traveled over me boldly with a knowing familiarity. For a moment it was as if the two of us were alone in that room. And then, afraid of the sensations his glance brought to me, willing up all of my strength, I looked away, promising myself I would never again submit to the passion that had so nearly destroyed me. I turned at the sound of Sam's voice and saw that he watched us closely.

"Glad you saw fit to join us, Jed. Seems mighty hard to pin you down these days."

He entered the room indifferently, his rough dress a sharp contrast to the quiet tasteful furnishings of the room, and halted before the fire that sizzled and crackled in the hearth, as the dripping sap teased the tongues of the flames higher. Hunkering down, he stretched his hands toward the heat, taking the chill from them.

"Evenin' Alice, Cal." He spoke over his shoulder in a slow, easy drawl. "Hope you don't mind me bargin' in like this."

Alice stared at him in a fascinated silence and Cal, too, regarded his brother quietly. Sam's face held a designing look.

"Your young friend here has been telling me a thing or two."

"Has she now?" For a moment I thought I caught veiled amusement in his voice, but his features remained blank.

Now all of Sam's attention was on his youngest son. "I've been meaning to talk to you, Jed, but you've been avoiding me. I didn't press it at the roundup because family business is just that. Belongs between these four walls. I'm sure Meg won't mind if we talk a spell, since she was there anyway. I want to know what happened between you and Travis."

Jed's stony voice never even faltered. "I never caught up with him, Sam. If you want to know about Travis, you'll have to ask Meg. Seems she managed to tame him all by herself."

His implication was clear. At the sound of the voice that carried not a shred of emotion, all eyes turned to me, but only Alice's held any sympathy. With Jed's eyes burning on my face, I took a deep breath and turned to Sam Tanner.

"I can't help what you or Jed assume took place, Mr. Tanner. Travis did come to the valley, as you know. We talked some and he left the next morning."

A short laugh broke from the direction of the fire and when Jed spoke, his mocking voice was dangerously smooth.

"How about that, Sam? She had Travis eating out of her hand."

Sam's eyes rested briefly on his son. "Is that a fact, Jed?" he asked sharply. And then Sam looked at me. "No matter what you may think, Meg, we aren't all as fast with our conclusions as Jed, here, is. I must apologize for him. He takes after me. It was some time before I learned from my mistakes. It seems that Jed is still making his."

Sam Tanner had sided with me against his son, but it was a hollow victory. I looked at Jed, whose wooden features hid the knowledge that his father had turned against him again and had chosen my lie over the truth—the truth as he believed it to be. Because Sam Tanner had set me free of Jed's damning censure, I had to free Jed of his own.

"It's not what you think," I said softly, my eyes finding his and aching at the hardness that lined his face. "It never was. Travis and I talked a lot that night, Jed. I told him that he must want to die an awful lot because if he harmed me, you would surely kill him for it."

I did not take my eyes from Jed and when I heard Sam's voice it seemed as if it came from a great distance away. "What else did you say to him, Meg?" Sam Tanner asked.

"Only that both he and Jed each blamed themselves for Julie's death. And that it should be over by now. Unless they meant to kill each other over her. And she's been dead too long for that."

The stillness that settled over the room was broken only by Sylvie's call to supper. Unexpectedly, I found Sam at my side. With a firm hand at my elbow, he escorted me to the dining table. The rich aroma of food dogged Sylvie's steps from the kitchen and filled the room, but I tasted very little of the fine meal that was served. The men, bypassing the fresh trout, boned and served in a delicate cream sauce, helped themselves to the huge platter of blood-rare beef on the sideboard. The elegant meal had not been prepared at the expense of a cattleman's appetite. Against the backdrop of the fine linen tablecloth and gleaming tableware, the crystal goblets sparkled brightly and I made a pretense of enjoying a meal I scarcely touched. The conversation passed around me and included me and I answered reasonably well to questions instantly forgotten.

I did not have to look directly at Jed that night to see him, so sharply etched was his image at the corner of my eye. The light that caught the gleam of Alice's smooth white shoulders and the shine of her yellow hair brought the glaring, rugged features and rough clothes into focus as if I stared at him, and when our eyes locked accidently, his pierced mine so deeply that I felt frozen in place. Jessica's soft, sleepy cry, sounding from the direction of the kitchen, was a welcome relief.

"I'll see to her, Sylvie," I said as she cleared our plates away, glad to have a reason to leave the table. Rising from my chair, I excused myself. Before anyone could deny my request, I made my way into the adjoining kitchen.

Paying no mind to the soft murmur of voices that followed my abrupt exit, I retrieved Jessica from her quiet corner of the room. But I was not fast enough and even though I moved quickly through the rear of the house and up the steep and narrow back stairway, I was forced to a halt as Jed mounted the final steps of the main staircase, cutting off access to my bedchamber beyond. Ignoring him and the rapid beating of my heart, I pushed past him. Coming to my door, I fumbled awkwardly as I attempted to open it without disturbing Jessica.

My averted face did not deter him. Forcefully, he gripped my shoulder and turned me toward him, resting a hand over mine as it tightly clutched the doorknob. He increased the pressure of his grip so that I could not move unless he willed it.

"Let go of me, Jed," I said angrily. "I don't know why you're here—or is it because of what Sam said?" I looked up at him then. "Don't expect me to be overjoyed that it took him to make you see the truth about what happened between me and Travis. I'm afraid that isn't good enough."

He looked away from me and back down the long passageway, as if carefully considering his words. "I want to see my daughter, Meg," he said finally, turning back to me, his voice raw with emotion.

"Why now, Jed? What made you change your mind?" I asked bitterly.

His eyes hardened at my hostility. Releasing my

hand, he pushed open the door to the darkened room
and guided me into the shadows. Closing the door
behind him, he came toward me. As I looked on wordlessly, he took Jessica from my arms. He lifted the
soft blanket away from her and I watched her disarm
him with her baby charm and saw his hard features
gentle at the sight of her. I steeled myself for what
I had to do. The sudden change in this coldhearted
man could not be allowed to make any difference. I
had worn myself out loving Jed Tanner.

"What do you want of me, Jed?" My words were
frosty.

He looked up from Jessica and his eyes bore
through me. "I want you, Meg, and I want my daughter."

I was determined that he should not see me waver.
"I know you want me, Jed. I've seen it in the way
you've looked at me sometimes, and I've also seen
the way you run from me when I've come too close.
It can't work. Once, it was all I hoped for from you.
I thought your wanting me would be enough because
I knew you could never love me. But not anymore.
It hurts too much. I can live without you. You've
made me strong, Jed, and all I want to do is take
Jessica away from here."

"You're leaving?" His voice rang out with a deadly
coldness in the dark, unheated room.

"That can't surprise you. It's what you've wanted
all along."

"What about Ben?"

"If Ben wants to come with me, we can take the
buckboard to Redmonton and a stage from there. If
we're lucky, maybe we'll cross paths with Doc Bennett then."

"And after that?"

"Your interest surprises me," I said churlishly,
angry with myself because my heart still raced at
the sight of his smoldering eyes. "I want to see Doc.

I read the letter he sent to you. I'm not sure where I'll go after that."

He gave a savage laugh. "And what will you do then? Will you pretend to be a grieving widow with a child to raise? I'm afraid people will see clear through you, Meg. It won't be easy for you to play that part."

"On the contrary, Jed. I think I might find it very easy."

"Is that fair to Jessica?"

"Leave her out of this! Your concern is a little belated, isn't it?" I snapped.

I turned my back on him and lit the lamp, adjusting the flame so that it cast the barest of illumination. Going to the wardrobe, I removed my bedroll from the bottom. Even with my saddlebags, it would hardly be adequate for our growing collection of clothing. With Jessica's belongings I would need to take one of Alice's valises. Jed spoke softly to his daughter and then, with relief, I heard him place her down in the cradle that had once been his.

I never expected his fury. All at once, I was whirled around and, seizing me in a brutal grip, he held my face to his, fiercely covering my mouth with his own. Surprise was his ally. Caught off-guard after all the long months of denied longing, I caught fire as I was held prisoner by the merciless strength of his arms. His mouth breathed life into my own, and then his lips scorched my neck, my throat, my shoulders where my dress bared them. I felt his hands on my back, as he molded me to him. I fought the traitorous urges of my body, willing them away in the strongest war I had yet waged against him. He would not hurt me again. This wanting, this softening was only because I had watched him hold Jessica for the first time. I knew all about him and his brief flashes of caring that set a person to needing him like an unfortunate patient to one of Doc's opiates. I could never have enough of him and never again would I subject myself to an all-consuming love, spawned in hope and destroyed by coldness. Never would he be allowed to do to Jessica what he had done to me.

He lifted his mouth from mine but did not relinquish the viselike grip on my face and his fingers tightened, forcing my eyes to open and see his stark features through a well of tears.

"Please, Jed. No more," I begged him.

He released me with a suddenness that sent me staggering backward.

"And I thought I was the fool," he said scathingly as he turned on his heels and left the room.

Chapter Thirty-Three

✍ "WHATEVER DID JED MEAN when he said you were leaving tomorrow? He told Sam—" Alice swept into the room without so much as a knock or a greeting.

"It's true?" Her wide-eyed gaze fell to the bedroll and I didn't wait for more of her questions.

"I have to tell Ben, Alice. Please watch Jessica for me." Taking up one of her shawls, I ran from the room, ignoring her distressed face.

The wind had died down and without the sharp, cutting edge, the night air was peaceful under a sky of swiftly scudding clouds. I made my way down the rise and toward the raucous laughter only slightly muffled by the bunkhouse walls. I did not hesitate but pounded loudly on the rough plank door, repeating the sound twice more before one of the ST hands appeared before me, clearly taken aback by the appearance of a woman dressed in silk.

Almost reluctantly, he gave me the information I

sought. Nodding my thanks, I turned in the direction
of the path that circled around the back of the ranch
house to Christina's cabin. A light shone cozily from
behind a brightly colored curtain and I rapped at the
door softly, remembering only too well the last time
I had seen Christina.

She came to the door immediately, almost as if
she had been expecting me, and threw it wide to
reveal Ben sitting at her table, his injured leg
stretched out before him, his hands familiarly cupping a mug of coffee as if he were quite used to being
there. A pie sat at the center of the red gingham
cloth, a large wedge of which had been removed.
With her lips stretching in a thin, arrogant smile,
Christina turned her catlike eyes upon me in a silent
question. I reminded myself that no matter what she
had done, she had had a change of heart; she had
gone to Ben and confessed her part in bringing Travis
to the north valley.

"I'd like to talk to Ben alone, Christina, if you
don't mind," I said to her.

She raised her head, affronted at my request.

"Go to the main house, Christina," Ben commanded her without questioning my purpose.

"I'm not supposed to be there," she replied petu-
lantly, throwing a hostile look in my direction. "Sam
ordered me to stay away until she leaves."

"I'm sure Sam won't mind, Christina," I said stiffly.
"I'll be going in the morning."

She could not keep the surprise from her face;
startled, she looked at Ben. But his eyes were on me.
With disgust clearly mirrored on her features, she
threw a wrap over her shoulders and left the cabin,
the jarring slam of the door ringing in her wake. It
was as if her subtle presence still remained; for a
moment, neither of us spoke. Then angrily, Ben set
himself upon me.

"What the hell's going on, Meg? You know Doc

Bennett will be here any day. What's the sudden rush?"

"Oh, Ben! He wants Jessica!" I cried softly, sinking into a chair by the table.

"I thought that was what you wanted, Meg."

"Not like this, Ben! You were right all along about him. You told me he'd bring me nothing but grief. I can't let him do that to Jessica, too. I'm afraid for her, Ben. I've got to get her away from here as soon as I can. I'm afraid of what will happen if I stay any longer."

Ben's bright eyes burned into mine. "Are you protecting Jessica or are you hiding behind her, Meg?" he asked me quietly. I drew back at his unexpected attack.

"How can you ask me that, Ben? You know what he's like!"

"I also know that you love him and nothing's ever going to change that. Is it so bad that he's finally admitted that Jessica is his and that he wants her? Isn't that a beginning?"

"Ben, please, let's not argue about this. Just say that you'll come with me. We can take a wagon to Redmonton. We'll catch up with Doc Bennett there."

He shook his head. "Afraid not, Meg. You'll have to see this one through by yourself."

"It's because of Christina, isn't it? You don't want to leave her," I accused him.

"Damn it! It has nothing to do with her. I'm doing it because I'm your friend."

"You won't stop me, Ben. I'll go myself. There's nothing you can say that will change my mind."

With a muffled curse, Ben pulled himself to his feet and came over to where I sat. He hauled me roughly to my feet. "You stubborn little fool. Sometimes I think you're just as bad off as he is! If Jed Tanner wants Jessica, he wants you too! Or are you the kind of woman who's afraid to love someone who cares for you in return? God knows I tried to get you to love me!"

I winced at Ben's accusation. He released me and dropped back. "I never had any luck changing your mind before. I don't know why I thought I could do it now. You're sure of this? Leaving tomorrow, I mean?"

I nodded. "I never should have come here, Ben."

Drawing my shawl more closely around me, I left him, wishing things could have been different.

He was waiting for me that night after I left Ben, detaching himself from the darkness to fall in step beside me. Patches of black sky showed through the skimming cloud cover and the night air was still. He tilted his head slightly as he studied me. "It's time you and I talked," he said. For a moment, the leaden quality of his voice reassured me.

"There's nothing to discuss, Jed," I said smoothly.

His hat cast a shadow of darkness across his eyes, but he was unmoved by my response. I turned to take the path to the house but he reached out and gripped my arm with iron fingers, pulling me around. His hand casually brushed against the silk of my dress, stunning me with sensation. "Are you running from me, Meg Logan?" he asked, in an unruffled voice.

"No!" I lied blatantly. "Jessica and I are leaving tomorrow. Nothing you can say will change that."

"You haven't stopped loving me, Meg," he said roughly. "You're lying to yourself if you believe that, and I don't think you really do. I've hurt you. More than any man has a right to hurt a woman who loves him. I know that. I'm not asking for forgiveness because I'll never forgive myself for that. What I'm asking for is a chance to try and make it up to you."

"No!" I said again, sharply. "Please let it end here. There's nothing for us together. It's not all your fault.

Even if you had loved me in return, it wouldn't have worked. I lost too much of myself in loving you, Jed. You were right to run from me. There's no need for apologies."

"I didn't come after you to apologize." He lay his hand lightly along the curve of my neck, his fingers curling slightly at the touch of my skin, and I thought I could smell the faintest whiff of the liniment he had used when he had bandaged my ankle that cold mountain night. "I love you, Meg," he said quietly.

I stared at him mutely, transfixed by his admission, and then my shoulders began to shake as quiet tears ran down my face. "It's too late for that, Jed," I said.

His mouth turned downward in a grim smile sensing my resolve. "You've made up you're mind, haven't you? Not a damned word I say to you will make any difference, is that what you're telling me?"

"Yes," I whispered.

"Then I'm going to make you listen to me."

Before I knew what he was about, he pulled me toward him and, abruptly turning me around, he thrust me foward in the direction of the tall, somber pines edging the upper meadow. Stumbling, I tore the hem of the silk dress and, at the damage done to Alice's beautiful gift, rage washed over me. "I despise you, Jed! Do you hear me!" In answer he turned me about and shoved me roughly against the scoring bark of a tree. And then, without warning, he released me, but although he did not touch me, his eyes held me prisoner just as surely as had his iron grip. His breath was ragged and his words came painfully.

"I'm going to teach you how to feel again, Meg." I felt his warm breath as it traveled the length of my neck.

"Damn you, Jed!" I jerked my head away from him, knowing only too well how much I craved his touch and how quickly he would break me this way. My display of open hostility only fired his will, and, his eyes hardening, he threw his hat to the ground. Aware only of the pounding of my heart, I stood frozen as he pulled me to him, his hands wandering to where my dress offered no protection against his stirring touch. At the closeness of his lean strength and the heat of his body, I began to struggle, fighting myself more than I did him.

He pinioned me against the tree with the hard press of his body. With his fingers, he released the pins from my hair, sinking his hands into the softness as he used the pressure of his mouth to force my lips open. He used his tongue lightly, grazing the inside of my mouth until I grew weak and my struggles subsided into a passive acceptance of his touch. But he was not content with that. Running callused hands down the sides of my body, he drew me even closer to his hard male strength, and suddenly I could no longer help myself and I leaned into him, wanting to be consumed. He held me close, aware that he had won, savoring his victory, the bittersweet lesson soon to be replaced by the willing passion we would joyfully bring one another. Our bed was of pine needles and I welcomed him with my body and the joining was as natural as two swift streams coursing together.

I lay quietly in his arms, my head cushioned against the soft blue wool of his shirt, my hair a streaming shawl between us. The passion was spent but not the need that had given rise to it. I turned my head and looked up at him, seeing his eyes darken as they met mine. His voice, when he spoke, was husky.

"I wanted you from the first time I saw you, standing there in the shadows of Doc's back porch. Did you know that?"

I smiled at the memory. "I thought Barton had hired you, Jed. I was afraid of you and drawn to you at the same time. I felt as if you could see right through me and were deciding my fate."

He gave a low laugh. "It was my own fate I was worried about. I was doing my damnedest to fight it." Then his voice turned grave. "You were the first woman I wanted that way since Julie. I don't mean those nights at a place like Rose's—they never meant anything. I'd leave there feeling as empty as before I went in. They didn't dull the pain, I guess I didn't want them to..." He tightened his grip on my shoulder. "You were right about me all along. I wanted to believe the worst about you. It made you seem more like Julie and I thought then it would be easier to forget you."

The wounds opened and bled, washing us each with the pain we had tried to put from us. When he spoke again his voice was slow and measured and he looked away from me out onto the pale sweep of moonlit meadow.

"After Julie, I thought I'd never care again. I never thought I'd even want to. I couldn't ever let myself believe that it would work between us, Meg. I had never forgiven myself for what I had done to her. I guess I was punishing myself. I told myself that what you and I had was no good. As hard as it was leaving you, I knew I couldn't stay."

"And then I showed up here," I said softly.

"And carrying my child." He chuckled, and I reveled in the sound. "It was a hell of a combination."

I looked at him in surprise. "You knew Jessica was yours all along?"

"I told myself she wasn't. And then I kept away from her after she was born. Otherwise, I knew I could never let you go. But I guess I knew it from the first. Admitting it took longer."

"Oh, Jed," I let my fingers drop away from the

hard line of his jaw. "But what about Christina? You—you flaunted her right under my nose!"

For the first time since I had known him, a look of abject apology crossed his face. "I'm real sorry about that, Meg. When you first showed up, well, I was angry. I thought I had put you behind me. I hadn't forgotten you, but at least you weren't here. I was afraid to trust myself around you. Later, when Christina came back out to the valley with Alice, I thought maybe she would help persuade you to keep away from me. I was still fighting you," he added quietly.

"She sent Travis to find me, Jed."

His face tightened at the name but he didn't speak. Travis had not harmed me but the bitterness between them would never pass. I removed my hand from his, trying to find the words I had to say.

"I'm afraid, Jed. How can we build on a past like we have? How could it ever work?"

Silently he rose to his feet. His lips were drawn in a thin line, and he reached down and pulled me to him so that our faces were just inches apart. He cupped my face in his hands.

"What do you want to do, Meg? Walk away from me? You came all this way to find me. Are you giving up now?" He saw the uncertainty in my eyes, for the pain of loving him had been so great, it seemed that I might die of it. He saw the doubt in my eyes and he gave my shoulders a gentle shake.

"Meg, after Julie, I stopped caring. And I almost succeeded in making you that way, too. It's no good if you take your love and bury it so deep you make yourself believe you don't care anymore. You poison yourself with it. It doesn't just stay a small and hidden part of your life. It colors everything you do. And then you begin to close off other feelings, too. What will happen if you give all your love to Jessica? What will that teach her? How will she ever learn to love and trust anyone else if you don't? I'm not saying it will be easy. I'll be damned if I know what made you love me in the first place. But if you still do, give us a chance. Don't become what I was, Meg. Give us both a chance."

A slight wind stirred the trees. The tears that streaked my face were not of happiness but of grief, the grief I had stored through a long winter and spring, the grief I had nourished through the summer and which I could now let go of.

"I guess Sam was right. He said the storm would pass over us," I said, gazing up at the blackness above, the barest twinkling of a star visible in the patched blanket of thinning clouds.

"Sam doesn't care that much about being right. He wanted Clete to be wrong," Jed said with a laugh.

"But how will he feel about me, Jed? I said some terrible things to him tonight."

"He knows about you and Jessica, Meg. I told him after you left the house tonight. There was no way I was going to let you leave here tomorrow. I told Sam that he wasn't to let you have a horse or anything else that was capable of taking you off the ranch."

He laughed at my incredulous expression. "I wasn't going to be fool enough to let you get away from me again. I realized how badly I'd messed things up between us, Meg. It was my own damn jealousy that put Travis between us like that. That's why I rode in tonight. But even with my good intentions, I still let it get away from me. Sam saw that right away. He hasn't lit into me like that in a long time. He's been afraid to, I guess."

"Then he doesn't mind about us?"

"Mind? No. You've caught his fancy. He likes the thought of a little unpredictability in his life these days. Gives him something to look forward to."

I took a sidelong look at the man standing so tall

beside me, all traces of the earlier vulnerability gone. His shoulders set squarely against the rugged skyline, he turned in the direction of the north valley. I didn't want to speak of Christina or Ben. There would be time enough for them tomorrow. Reaching for my hand, he held it tightly, drawing me to him. I had come home. Together, we made our way through the towering pines and into the peaceful calm of night, slowly walking across the wet meadow grass to the welcoming lights of the ranch house.

This is the special design logo that will call your attention to Avon authors who show exceptional promise in

THE AVON ROMANCE

the romance area. Each month a new novel will be featured.

CAPTURE THE DREAM Helene Lehr
On Sale in August   88476-3/$2.95
Set against the background of 19th century New England, this is the spellbinding story of a beautiful young woman threatened by a scheming husband after her dowry...and rescued by the passionate man who captures her heart.
Also by Helene Lehr—A GALLANT PASSION   86074-4/$2.95

ONYX FLAME Jan Moss
On Sale in September   87628-2/$2.95
The compelling story of a fiery young woman who finds herself torn between love and success when she lands a prestigious new job, and the heart of her handsome, dynamic boss...until in the splendor of old Japan, their smoldering desires turn to the fires of love.

BOUND BY THE HEART Marsha Canham
On Sale in October   88732-0/$2.95
Set in the Caribbean during the tempestuous days before the British-American War of 1812, this is the tumultuous story of a lovely blonde beauty, promised in marriage to a British Admiral, but bound by the heart to a daring American buccaneer.
Also by Marsha Canham—CHINA ROSE   85985-8/$2.95

THE DANCER'S LAND Elizabeth Kidd
On Sale in November   89219-7/$2.95
Amidst the turbulent background of Napoleon's conquest of Spain, a daring young lady is drawn into the conflicts of war, and into the arms of a handsome British Colonel who ignites her heart.

HEART SONGS Laurel Winslow	85375-5/$2.50
WILDSTAR Linda Ladd	87171-8/$2.75
NOW & AGAIN Joan Cassity	87353-2/$2.95
FLEUR DE LIS Dorothy E. Taylor	87619-1/$2.95

Look for THE AVON ROMANCE wherever paperbacks are sold, or order directly from the publisher. Include $1.00 per copy for postage and handling; allow 6-8 weeks for delivery. Avon Books, Dept BP Box 767, Rte 2, Dresden, TN 38225.

Avon Rom 10-84